Julia's Hope

Julia's Hope

LEISHA KELLY

Fleming H. Revell
A Division of Baker Book House Co
Grand Rapids, Michigan 49516

© 2002 by Leisha Kelly

Published by Fleming H. Revell
a division of Baker Book House Company
P.O. Box 6287, Grand Rapids, MI 49516-6287

Fifth printing, June 2003

Printed in the United States of America

Library of Congress Cataloging-in-Publication Data
Kelly, Leisha.
    Julia's hope / Leisha Kelly.
        p.   cm.
    ISBN 0-8007-5820-X (pbk.)
    1. Abandoned houses—Fiction. 2. Home ownership—Fiction. 3. Storms—Fiction. I. Title.
PS3611.E45 J85 2002
813′ .6—dc21   2002004759

Prologue
April 28, 1931

Samuel and Julia Wortham and their children left Harrisburg, Pennsylvania, with eight dollars and three cloth bags stuffed with their personal effects.

After the great market crash in 1929, all they had left was in those three bags. Everything else was gone. A good job lost, a house repossessed, and savings washed away as if in a moment. Hope lay miles away in a town called Mt. Vernon, Illinois, where Dewey Wortham, Samuel's cousin, was still earning a decent wage at a wheel plant. His letters said, *Come. I'll get you a job. Stay with Dewey till you get back on your feet.*

So the Worthams hitched their first ride at the pump station just four blocks from where they used to live. They sat facing backward in the bed of a '27 Ford, with Julia praying, Robert and little Sarah anxiously wondering about the adventures ahead, and Sam watching his dreams shrink away in the cloud of dust that swirled behind them.

ONE

Julia

The first ride was easy, and my heart pounded with anticipation. *Maybe this will work. We'll start over, maybe even find things better than before.* The children and I rode and sang and watched the miles pass all the way to Uniontown, Pennsylvania, where we were let out in front of a five-and-dime.

"What are we gonna ride in next, Mama?" five-year-old Sarah asked. "A real fancy car this time?"

I watched Sam staring down the street, looking thinner than I ever remembered him. He had our biggest bag over his shoulder, and he started walking backward, thumb in the air. My enthusiasm waned. *Lord, help us. This could be a hard trip.*

The road got much too quiet to suit us; only a few people were out driving. Some passed by us with a sorry wave, some without the slightest glance in our direction. Getting just seven miles to McClellandtown seemed to take forever, and we had to walk much of the way. It was enough to turn ten-year-old Robert sour on the whole idea.

We spent the night stretched on the floor of a church dining hall, and I thanked God for the deacon who let us in. We were all exhausted. I had worried about what we would do when night came, but the Lord was good to us and provided well that first night.

I lay awake awhile, listening to the quiet, trying to have faith in Sam and Dewey's plan. They were excited about living and working close together. But it was hard for me to trust. Maybe if I'd had a close cousin or a sibling, I'd have understood.

Sarah leaned against me in sleep, her soft brown locks trailing across my arm. She was a delicate thing, fine boned and fair, and people said she looked like me. Especially the bright green eyes. I wondered what she was thinking about this strange new move clear across the countryside into the unknown. She said so little, and it troubled me that she might be scared.

I knew what it was like to be scared when so young. My mother had died just three days past my fifth birthday. Father was rarely home, and when Mother died, I tearfully imagined long hours in our empty house, just me, alone. But those were unfounded fears. My days were soon filled with grand adventures with Grandma Pearl. And I could certainly hope there would be something grand for Sarah in this.

I snuggled beside her, willing myself to get some rest. There was no telling what tomorrow would hold. Robert lay on the other side of his sister, asleep, all curled in a ball the way he'd done since he was a baby. And Sam was just beyond him, on his back and, thankfully, not snoring.

I thought I was the only one awake, but then Sam rolled toward me slowly, his eyes open in the darkness. I don't know why, but I couldn't talk to him. I shut my eyes, and he didn't say a word. The last thing I remembered that night was the sound of his breathing.

In the morning we ate apples and the stale sandwiches that were left in my bag. The day was bright and clear and beautiful, and the birds' singing gave me a renewed hope. God had fed them; he would certainly provide for us too, somehow.

It took us quite awhile to get our first ride that morning, and Robert grumbled about all the walking we did.

"How else would you see all of this?" I asked him. "Some people live their whole lives never going twenty miles from where they were born."

"I'm going to go lots of places," he said. "But I'm not going to walk. First I'm going to get a bicycle, then a car. And then the biggest truck you ever saw."

"I want a real airplane," Sarah added. "I want to fly like a bird."

"How about a Model T?" Sam asked, and I turned my head. An old man with a generous mustache was slowing down behind us. He was kind and proved pleasant to talk to, but he took us only to Martin, where he said his sister lived. Buckeye trees seemed to thrive on every block there, and tulips were plentiful in the square. It was a nice enough town, but we walked almost an hour before getting a ride again.

Then we were let out on the east side of Fairmont, West Virginia, where the hills looked so pretty and the mountain laurel smelled so sweet that I was in no hurry to move on.

And that was for the best, since we ended up being there for awhile. We walked into town and bought the mulligan stew we saw advertised in a café window. It was cheap and good. Then when we started walking again, it began to rain, and we ran for the covered bandstand in the park. We couldn't have everything we owned dripping wet.

Julia's Hope

So we sat for a long time, waiting out the storm. I made Robert list nouns while Sarah danced with her rag doll. Sam became restless; when the sky finally cleared some, he was all set to go again. The sun came out as we walked, but it was lower and continued to dip until we were left along the roadside west of the town, watching the purple sunset. What would we do for the night?

I was worried, but I sat down and praised the glowing colors that God had painted across the sky, insisting that my children get a look at good things. But I knew Sam was worrying too. This was only the second of any number of nights that stretched out before us, all uncertain.

Eventually, a weary deputy found us alongside the highway and asked what we were doing walking after dark with the young ones still up.

Sam did his best at explaining, but the man just shook his head and looked at us as though we were the sorriest people he'd seen all day. But he did offer to let us stay overnight in the local jail back in Fairmont, saying the sheriff had done this before for stranded travelers. Robert and Sarah weren't too sure about the idea and I wasn't either, but I told them it would be quite an adventure just to see what a jail was like.

Being in the jail gave me an eerie feeling, even with the doors wide open. It was dark and cold and smelled like nothing I'd ever encountered before in my life. But the deputies were kind enough to move cots side by side for us, and I was glad to lie down. Sarah would only sleep with her head on my shoulder, and Robert lay on his back beside me, talking nonstop for hours as though silence might bring some sort of specter to this place that he didn't want to see.

Only Samuel seemed far away, though I could have touched him a thousand times if I'd tried. He scarcely said a word. I'm sure he must have thought I was still angry at him, since we would've at least had my inheritance to live upon if he hadn't invested it in Cooper stock without my knowledge. But it was done, and neither of us could change that.

The night was long, but we were blessed with a passable breakfast at the Fairmont jail, and I was sure the Lord would provide us with a quick trip the rest of the way across West Virginia and into Kentucky. But when night fell, we hadn't even reached Charleston. By then, all my misgivings about this move had returned. We had so little money left. What if something happened?

I tried not to think about this as we stood in front of a church in Big Chimney, hoping someone would let us in for the night. I played a guessing game with the kids, just to keep them occupied. Finally, a neighbor took pity on us and offered supper and the use of her porch.

It would have been a lovely night, were it not for the worrying. The air was warm, and the sugar maples in the yard swayed in a delicate breeze. So many stars were out that we lay there a long time, the children pointing while I tried my best to remember all the names I could.

The next day we got a ride into Morehead, Kentucky, and I was finally glad for the chance to see more of God's beautiful land. Everything was so green, everywhere we looked, except for the bluebells and field daisies dotting the roadside with color. I picked a yellow violet for each of the kids and then gave one to Sam, hoping he'd smile. He stuck the flower in his buttonhole but didn't say a word.

The good people who gave us our ride into Morehead made sure that we had lunch for Robert and Sarah. We sat in that town for an hour, drawing wary glances or being carefully ignored, before walking on. I sang every song I knew in Kentucky, several times, it seemed. Nobody took us more than ten miles at a stretch the rest of the day. Never had I talked so much about David and Goliath, Daniel and his lions, or the incomparable Doctor Doolittle. Sarah loved it all, from the stories, to the scenery, to the ride on her father's shoulders.

I almost concluded that I needn't worry for her over this trip. But when Sam put her down, she came straight to me and tugged at my hand. Her bright eyes were deep and suddenly uncertain.

"Mommy, today will we be home for bedtime?"

Usually I knew what to say. But this time? Home by bedtime? Oh, Lord, if we only *had* a home!

"Honey, we'll have us a good time camping somewhere tonight, and before long we'll be in Illinois."

"Are we gonna live there forever?"

I squatted to her level and gave her a hug. "The Lord'll provide us a home. We'll just believe that."

She chewed her bottom lip some, which she had a habit of doing, then looked over at her father. He was pulling our map out of his bag.

"I want our old house back," she said, the first she'd mentioned it in days.

And I couldn't help but sigh. "I do too, sometimes. But we'll have something we like just as much, maybe even better. Because God said all things work together for good for those that love him. And we love him. Right?"

She nodded but didn't say more. She just pulled her rag doll from the striped bag and plunked it across her shoulders the way Sam had carried her. "Going to Ill'nois, Bessie," she chanted. "Going to Ill'nois."

But Samuel and Robert were already reading the map with their eyes on our destination. Two days with such slow progress had made them testy, tense, and tired. We paid for rooms twice to avoid sleeping in a ditch, and I bought the cheapest food I could find. Despite all this, I tried my best to stay cheerful. But young Robert refused to stick his thumb out anymore and began walking three paces behind us.

Our situation was hardest for Samuel, though, knowing we'd had money, and especially that I'd had money, once. When we married, he promised me a house with curving chandeliers and plenty of roses. I didn't care about all that anymore, but he did. I could see it eating away at him as the miles passed behind us. Our lovely home in Harrisburg, the yard we'd filled with roses, were gone. And who could know what we would ever have to take their place?

I'd promised Sarah a home as good or better. I even tried to believe it myself. But the fear still lingered. Sometimes when you think things are going to improve a little, they just get worse.

By the time we reached Evansville, Indiana, on the second of May, Sam had woolly whiskers and a gaunt look I'd never seen before in him. He hurried us into the gray-looking town, determined to telephone Dewey in Illinois and tell him how close we were and how eager he was to work as soon as we got there. I tied on my rosy scarf in the growing breeze and sang "Blue Skies" for Robert and Sarah while Sam stood inside the *Evansville Daily* office, talking to his cousin.

Robert was finally excited again. What would Dewey's house be like? Were there neighbors? Was the school close by? Would we get a telephone again one day? And a radio to hear about Jack Sharkey in the boxing ring in New York City?

Sarah, bless her, had only two questions. Could she have pink covers on her new bed in Illinois? And would we find any theaters where we could go and watch Mickey the Mouse again?

I shared their anticipation, expecting Dewey's news to be as grand as it ever was, hoping he'd even consider climbing in his Model A and driving the distance to meet us.

But when Samuel stepped out of that office, looking like a stormy wind had dashed him against a wall of stone, the clouds descended over me and I turned away. I knew by his face. Dewey wouldn't be coming. Dewey couldn't carry all the hopes we'd pinned on him. We were alone.

TWO

Samuel

We joined the back of a soup line in Evansville, and I felt like a miserable father. Mine were the only kids I could see in line. I'd brought my wife and children across three states on the promise of a job that would never happen. I should have known. I should have realized that when Dewey couldn't send us money for traveling, his ideas were not all that secure.

The wheel plant was struggling now, laying off, about to close. No apologies from Dewey. He was so worried about his own livelihood that he had nothing to say about mine. And it hurt. We'd been like brothers since the third grade, when I helped him sneak off during one of his parents' drunken fights. We were both gone for two days, and I got a licking I'll never forget. But we were always in cahoots after that. And I could always trust that he was looking out for me as much as he was for himself. Until now.

I'd have turned back to Pennsylvania if we had anything to go back to. But there was nothing at the end of the line, or at its beginning. We were strung on a string and it didn't matter where we stopped.

Julia said nothing at all, and I thought this a mercy. She should have been weeping by now, but she hadn't cried once in a year and a half of struggle. First everything I'd invested was gone. Then the best job I'd ever had, tooling in Cooper's engineering plant. And then the house.

She didn't berate me for the way I'd let her down, but I knew how hurt she was. I knew she was bitterly disappointed. But she didn't even admit to being tired. She just picked up little Sarah and looked down the street.

"Remember Grandma Pearl?" she asked the children.

Robert nodded his assent, but Sarah shook her head. She'd been only two when Pearl died, far too young to remember.

"I lived with Grandma Pearl a long time," Julia told the children again. "After Papa died and I thought I had nothing left in this world. But she told me there's always a way. There's always good things just waiting for you to find them."

"Are we looking for good things?" Sarah asked.

"Every day," Julia answered.

I was surprised she could be so calm, but then I saw her eyes, just for a moment, before she turned away. I'd never seen such a jumble of emotion, as though all the hurt and uncertainty inside were finally welling up and spilling over. She couldn't bury the tears, so they just hung there like dew on the grass.

"I remember Grandma's garden best," Robert said. "She was funny, pulling weeds all morning and then eating some of them."

16

"She was a smart lady," Julia told him. "She knew how to use whatever God provides."

"He's providin' soup today," Sarah said as we approached the soup counter. "I hope they got vegible."

I turned my face away from my family. I didn't want them to see how it tore at me to introduce them to the stout lady behind the counter and tell her where we were from.

"I'll letcha eat tonight," she said with a frown. "But you need to be movin' on. This facility is for residents down on their luck. We don't entertain no vagabonds 'round here."

Vegetable soup was all they had, which of course pleased Sarah. One scant bowl and two soda crackers apiece. We ate in silence until Sarah suddenly asked, "What's a vagabond?"

Dear Julia, always trying to shelter the kids from our trouble, answered quickly before I got the chance. "It's someone who travels a lot, honey."

"Why don't they wanna ennertain 'em, then, Mama?" Sarah asked. "I think it'd be fun. They could tell about neat places. Like Affica, maybe."

Robert set his spoon down hard and grimaced at his sister. "Don't you know nothing?" he demanded. "She was calling *us* vagabonds! That means we're poor!"

Sarah looked at her mother with her round eyes full of question. I couldn't have said a word, even if I'd wanted to. The carrots and potatoes went down hard just then, like they were made of shoe leather. But Julia just looked over at Robert and told him to finish his soup. "Not all vagabonds are poor," she said. "Not of heart, at least."

A gray-headed old man told us about a church a few blocks down that had beds for the homeless. I thanked him, knowing we had no choice but to get what help we could. We walked to the church quickly when the soup was gone. And I was thinking the whole time that Julia

17

hadn't said one word to me and had scarcely even looked at me since I'd talked with Dewey.

She was bound to be angry, and I knew that one of these times she'd up and let me know how she really felt, but not in front of the kids. She'd wait till they were asleep, surely, and then tell me what a dismal failure I was. After all this time, I thought it would almost be a relief to hear her say the things I imagined she must be thinking about me: If I could have kept my job, or got another one, if I could have left Grandma Pearl's money in her shoebox instead of buying company shares, we might still have had our house.

The folks at the church were more pleasant than the soup lady, but they didn't seem to have a minute to spare for us. They gave us a room apart from the rest of the people who'd come to them, mostly men, and then left us on our own. The kids were soon asleep, and then Julia too. Still without a word.

But I couldn't even lay my head down. What would my family wake up to? What would I have to give them? We didn't even have Evansville's soup line to look forward to. We had nothing, and they would know it. I'd promised them Illinois, with prospering prairies and fields. I'd promised them Cousin Dewey, a happy welcome, a happy visit, and a future.

Dewey hadn't said to turn back. We were welcome to visit, since we'd come so far. But he held out no scrap of hope for me. There was not a chance of being hired.

I tried to pray, knowing Julia and the grandma she remembered so fondly would certainly think it best. But I found no light and certainly no arrows pointing me the way. By sunup, feeling raw inside, I decided that we would have to go on, if only to be doing something.

Julia accepted my decision immediately. She bought us day-old biscuits from a diner owner's nephew who was out peddling bargains from his Fleetwood wagon. He walked up and down the sidewalk in the business district, trying to sell what his uncle couldn't serve. And Julia praised him for his enterprise. The boy gave her a smile and two extra biscuits for being so nice.

Then when we got a ride, she chatted with the driver as though we hadn't a care in the world. Bolstered by their mother's calm exterior, Sarah scanned the fields for wildflowers and Robert sat quietly, without a single complaint about another day's travel.

Juli puts up such a good front, I kept thinking. I couldn't do that. But she had the children thinking our situation was no big deal, or at least no permanent problem. Just another day of doing what needed to be done.

My family would come out all right. They had the grace of God's angels and all the pluck Grandma Pearl had managed to grow in Julia. There'd be a way somehow. I could see them starting over, managing to make ends meet and finding a roof over their heads. But I could only see myself drowning, with every mile going deeper into the depths of my inability.

THREE

Julia

In the middle of the afternoon we stopped alongside a field somewhere near Dearing, Illinois. Sam didn't want to turn farther south again, which would take us away from Mt. Vernon. So the driver let us out. Not one vehicle passed our way after that, so I carried my tired little girl. After two hours of walking, angry clouds pitched over one another and the wind whipped Sarah's brown curls into my face.

I'd never felt so angry before. We were in the middle of nowhere and about to be stuck in the worst storm I'd seen all year. It was going to be bad, I could see that, though I couldn't say so for the sake of the children. We had to find shelter, and fast, before the storm's full fury broke over us.

Sam was the first to see a barn to the south of us, and I ran for it, trying my best to juggle my handbag and Sarah at the same time. Robert jogged alongside me, surely wondering what would become of us now. There'd been bad days before, plenty of them. But this one surely outdid them all.

I could hear the old barn creaking in the wind. What kind of a shelter was it going to be? I expected to see it give up and tumble to the ground before we even reached it.

"Hurry!" Sam yelled, but I wouldn't look his way. This whole journey had been his idea, to take our kids and hitchhike halfway across the country on the strength of Dewey's word. I didn't care what buddies Sam and Dewey had been. I didn't even care how badly Sam might be feeling. The only thing I could think of was his plans falling through again. We had nothing at all to show for our leaving Pennsylvania behind. We were stuck in a strange state, now with less than a dollar between us, and nowhere else to go.

The stubble from last season's corn made the unworked field a nightmare to cross. And it was getting darker. A sudden crash of thunder behind me sent Sarah's face into the folds of my coat. She clutched at me so tightly that my scarf slipped backward and my unbraided hair went flying in the wind.

"We'll make it, baby," I said to her. "We'll be inside before this storm hits."

Robert went sprinting ahead of me as fast as his lanky, ten-year-old legs could carry him. He reached the rickety old barn before his father did and pushed and pulled the floppy old door until Sam reached him and slid the thing open. I passed the two old trees that stood like sentries beside the barn and then ducked inside just as the downpour began.

Sam had already thrown his bags to the middle of the straw-strewn floor. What a stench this place had! Like a hundred years' worth of dirt and cattle and mice and wet, moldy hay. Robert crinkled his nose and stared at me.

But Sarah lifted her eyes for only a second. "I'm scared, Daddy!" she cried. The poor thing had always been scared of thunderstorms.

"It'll be okay, pumpkin." Sam tried his best to reassure her, pulling her from my arms to hug her close.

But I could see his eyes wandering over our shelter. The whole place seemed to rattle and shake with every thunderclap. There were holes in the roof and walls where the rain had begun pouring in. The west side of the old structure appeared to be solid, but the rest seemed to defy its own nature just to remain standing in that wind.

I knew I should be thankful for the shelter, poor though it was. In the right light, such an old barn would enchant me. But I was still too mad to find the good in this mess.

And Sam's tenderness with Sarah was suddenly tough to take. I found it hard to be angry when watching him kiss away her tears. I knew Sam loved us; I could never really doubt that. He hadn't meant for this to happen. He'd had no way of knowing the market would crash. Or that the Cooper plant would fold soon after. He thought he'd been doing me a favor by putting my inheritance into his doomed company. If only he'd just left it alone! The shoebox was good enough for Grandma, and it would've been better for us.

Robert set his gunnysack of belongings beside me and walked to the opposite side of the barn as Sarah leaned into her father's shoulder. Robert was braver than his sister when it came to things like thunder. But I was worried for him just the same, because I knew he worried with me, knowing as he did just how bad off we really were.

"Mom, look here," Robert called from the far door, which had been flopping in the wind until he took hold of it. I hurried to him, and he pointed to the southwest, past a rickety chicken coop to an old, two-story farmhouse. The back door was standing ajar, and we could see two broken windows.

"If somebody lived here, they'd shut the door, Mom," he said. "There's nothing in the yard but weeds."

He was right, of course. But it was not so much the condition of the place that told me it was empty. There was no dog, or it would have heard us and come to greet us by now. Ever since my first stay at Grandma and Grandpa's, I couldn't conceive of a farm without a dog.

There was no sign of anyone on these grounds. No cows. No chickens. No truck or wagon. Maybe the people were long gone, and their trusty dog with them.

And maybe the Lord had led us to an abandoned farm on purpose. The house stood there in front of my eyes, surely a better shelter for my children than this crooked barn. I looked up at the rain pouring in through the barn's holey roof. It didn't seem likely that even the dry corners of the straw-strewn floor would stay dry for long.

"Sam," I said. "This is no fit place to spend the night."

He didn't even turn around. "We'll make do, Julia."

I shook my head and looked out at the house again. I could tell it had been a nice one once, years ago. The dark windows and pillared porch drew me, and I had the irrational thought that God had placed it here, just this night, knowing how much we needed it.

"Can we go in?" Robert begged. "Please?"

Sam carried Sarah over beside us, took one look at the house, and shook his head. "We can't let ourselves into somebody's house," he insisted. "It's not right. We can wait out the storm here and move on."

"It's gonna get too cold out here for Sarah tonight," Robert reasoned. "Nobody lives here. Maybe there's even a fireplace."

Sarah perked up at that idea. The fireplace had been her favorite part of our house in Harrisburg. "Please, Daddy?" she joined in. "Can we go and see?"

"Somebody owns this place," my husband protested, looking down at the straw at his feet. He didn't like it, I knew that. But I also knew he would leave the decision up to me.

"I don't think anyone'd fault us one night, Sam," I said. "The storm may set in for awhile. We need a dry place to rest the night. And I'm not sure this rickety old barn will stand a good stiff wind."

He didn't say anything but just set Sarah down and picked up all the bags.

"Can we run for it?" Robert asked with the kind of excitement I loved to hear in him.

"We don't have much choice," I told him. "But wait a minute and see if the rain slows at all."

After five minutes, the rain had not let up. But when the wind sent a chunk of barn roof sailing in the air, we made a break for it across the wide yard anyway. With Sarah dangling from my arms, I burst through the open back door, right behind Robert. Sam stumbled in after me and dropped all our things in a heap on the kitchen floor.

It was already dark inside the house, but mostly dry. The kitchen smelled of must and had cobwebs generously spread in the corners. A sagging table, three chairs, and a dusty wood cookstove took up most of the room. I fumbled through my bag for a couple of candles and a match while Sam tried to get the door closed. It had a broken hinge and just wouldn't stay shut, so he propped one of the chairs against it to keep out the rain and wind.

I lit a candle and handed it to Sam. After I lit the second one, we all went together to the next room.

"Look, a fireplace!" Sarah exclaimed. "Can we have a fire? And popcorn?"

Just like Harrisburg, I thought. *That's all my kids really want. Their old life back.* "We don't have firewood, honey," I told her. "Or popcorn either. But we'll make do."

I put my candle on the mantle to light the room. The only furniture it held was a broken chair in one corner. I was glad to see that the windows were intact.

Sam went back to the kitchen and brought our bags. He pulled out our two thin blankets.

24

"Can we explore?" Robert asked.

"Let's eat now," I told him, trying to sound as pleased with our adventure as he seemed to be. But there were only two apples and a few old biscuits left in my bag. The Lord would have to provide tomorrow's breakfast.

I cut the apples in half and set a biscuit in front of each child. I started to offer Sam a biscuit, but he shook his head, so I gave him our old canteen instead. *There should be a prayer,* I thought, but I only whispered a rote blessing out loud. *Lord,* I prayed in my head, *help us make a life again. Give Sam a hope again. Help us be close like we used to be.*

It occurred to me then that I ought to pray for help in getting over the anger I felt toward Sam. But I didn't do it. I guess it was easier to think that I'd forgiven him already and was just entitled to my feelings beyond that.

I let the children have all the food. I couldn't have eaten anyway, with Sam refusing. I would find us more food in the morning. Even though it was only the first part of May, I could be confident of finding something edible among all the things growing outside. Grandma Pearl had walked me through the seasons on her farm, showing me what to look for. That was before Grandpa Charlie had died and we had to move to town. I could still remember how embarrassed Papa had always been by Mama's parents and their strange country ways. But I'd loved them dearly and had come to thank God for the things they had taught me.

Sam was sitting with his back against the wall, watching his youngsters finish off our last crumb. Once he looked up at me for a moment and then turned his head.

I should hug him, I thought. *I should tell him we'll be okay, that it's not his fault.* But I didn't move and couldn't seem to say anything.

Sarah leaned into me. "Sing 'Button Up Your Overcoat,' Mama," she whispered.

Sam looked at her with the barest hint of a smile, and I took heart. I did my best with the song, adding the hand

25

motions we'd made up as we hitchhiked across Kentucky. Then I jumped into my own silly rendition of "Bye, Bye, Blackbird."

And all the while as I sang, Sam watched me. What must he be thinking, me acting this way? I'd barely spoken to him for days. But I carried on for Sarah like this was some kind of picnic!

But whatever he thought, my antics for Sarah were genuine. No matter how worried I got or how mad Sam made me, I would still make light of our situation for my kids, just to see them smile. They were going to act like kids. They were going to play and laugh like kids, no matter how bad things got. And somehow, with the help of the good Lord, I'd find a way to fill their bellies, whether Sam found work again or not.

"Can we look around now?" Robert asked me eagerly as lightning crashed outside the window.

Sarah jumped onto my lap and wrapped her arms around my neck. "It's too dark, Mama," she whispered. "And too loud."

"Light a couple more candles," I told Robert. "It won't hurt to explore a bit, but only on the ground floor, do you hear? Don't try any old stairs."

Sam gave me a reproachful look but ended up helping Robert with the candles and walking through the rest of the downstairs rooms with him while I cuddled with Sarah and sang her another song.

"Are we going to live here forever?" she suddenly asked me. Her gentle whisper shocked me as much as if she'd shouted the words.

I should have told her no. But my mind turned to the house, the high ceilings, the dark woodwork I could see in carved detail with every flash of the lightning outside. There were two little shelves with empty kerosene lamps and a wide mantle with a huge mirror set above the fire-

26

place stone. Pale green drapes hung limp at the windows, still looking presentable despite their years.

It was a decent and sturdy house, despite the lack of care. And I was glad to be away from the road and strangers, glad we weren't hitchhiking through the night, trying to make it to Dewey's before morning. I didn't care if we ever got to Dewey's. Illinois had been Sam's promise. A job at the wheel plant. A place to stay. But there was nothing to that now. The plant would close just like Cooper's back home, and Sam had even said that Dewey was thinking to go south and ask for work in the mines.

I found myself hoping the storm would last for days on end, keeping us stranded here so we wouldn't have to face the decision of what to do next. We could use the rest. If only we had food, nothing else would matter.

Sam and Robert weren't gone long. They came back with three dusty blankets they'd found in the closet of a bedroom where one of the broken windows was. Sam apologized for the blankets but said they were better than the ground and warmer than a bare wood floor.

They'd found a pantry too, and the staircase going upstairs. That was it for the ground floor except for the kitchen and the sitting room we were in. Robert wanted to see the second floor, but Sam and I both told him no.

I shook out the old blankets one by one, wondering why anyone would leave them behind. Especially the quilt, with its diagonal rows of alternating dark and light. Someone had pieced together this now-tattered quilt, perhaps for a child or an aging parent. Somebody had loved this house once. Where were they now? The thought was hard in my stomach. People don't just walk away from a farm like this. They don't up and leave a home unless they have no choice.

I thought of our house in Harrisburg and wondered if there'd been a foreclosure at this house too, and another family, disheartened and humiliated, watching their possessions being auctioned away. But if that was the case, why was there no new owner? Why would a bank let such a house sit empty long enough for the spiders to lace webs in every doorway?

I stretched out two blankets on the floor, one for each child. They would be warm enough with a blanket of our own on top of them. Sam and I would huddle together under the quilt tonight, I decided. We would manage with nothing under us. And I was glad the kids wouldn't have to share a blanket like we'd done before. They would sleep warmer here. We owed a debt of gratitude to the owners of this place. Or the past owners. Whoever had left the blankets in the closet and the door wide open. Perhaps there would be a way to repay them someday.

The storm raged outside as I prayed with Robert and Sarah and settled them down for the night. They liked my singing, so I sang a couple of hymns. Sam was just watching me again. Then we both sat quietly until we knew the children were asleep.

"What are we gonna do, Julia?" Sam finally asked.

I got up and reached for a candle. "I'm going to take another look at that kitchen."

I didn't want him to follow me. But he did. I knew he would. I also knew it would plague him to know what I was thinking—that maybe it would still be storming tomorrow. And that I'd be glad of it, except for how it would complicate trying to find food outside. We'd have to use whatever we could now. We'd have to do whatever we could to make sure our children didn't suffer.

"What are you doing?" he asked me, sounding far away and bone weary.

"Praying for something we can use."

I was going straight for the kitchen cupboards when I nearly stepped on something small and dark that none of us had noticed before. A dead bird. Good thing Sarah hadn't seen it. She'd have mourned the poor thing sore. Sam picked it up off the floor and pitched it out the door for me. I stepped over the spot where it had been, pulled open a cupboard door, and held my candle inside. The cupboard held a bunch of old jars, most of them empty, but a few seemed to have something inside.

Sam had just come up behind me. "Honey, we can't—"

"I don't like this any more than you do," I blurted. "You know I don't like stealing. But we've got to do something. When Sarah and Robby wake up, they'll be hungry. God forgive me, but if there's anything usable here, I'm gonna use it."

With a prayer, I started pulling out jars, shining my candle on each one to get a look at the label. Parsley. Dill. Basil. Homegrown, but no telling how old. Something like that doesn't rot, of course, but it doesn't make much of a meal either. I pulled out more jars and suddenly felt like God had put these things here, just for me. A bit of sugar. Half a box of salt. Just a little baking powder, a box of soda, and three more matches.

The last jar was about a third full and rattled in my hand. It had no label, but it took me only a moment to realize what it was. Popcorn kernels. It was all I could do to keep from crying.

"Just what Sarah wanted," I whispered. "Sam, look. God's got a heart for the desires of a child."

"Will it even pop?"

"No telling. But as long as it's dry, it'll be okay. I hope it pops, but even if it doesn't, it can be parched—like the Indians used to do sometimes."

Sam looked away from me. "I'm sorry, Julia. That we have to do this."

I suddenly felt like dropping everything, just to hug him. I don't know why I couldn't. I guess a barrier had grown in me that was just too strong. But I took his hand, and he looked back at me. "The Lord will provide," I told him.

"I'll go foraging. You know me. And the season's good for some wild food."

I put the popcorn jar on the counter with the rest of the jars and started checking the other cupboards. I found a few dishes, an old skillet, and a dented saucepan with no lid.

"We'll be okay," I said as much for myself as for Sam. "We can't be too far from town. Maybe there's a grocery store. If the storm is over in the morning, maybe we can find the place."

"We couldn't buy much," Sam said. "Not to last us long. We've got maybe sixty cents, Julia."

I heard the gloom in his voice, and I didn't want any part of it from him right then. Things were bad. But they weren't going to be hopeless. I wouldn't have it so.

"Maybe there'll be a job for one of us," I suggested.

"How can you still say that?" he said fiercely. "We've been in plenty of towns. Nobody's hiring! Especially not a stranger. If I'd known the wheel plant was having trouble, we'd have never left Harrisburg!"

I shook my head. "What would we have there, Sammy? A line to stand in for bread? And another line to ask for a place to spend the night? It was no good there."

He looked at me, stunned. "You're not sorry we left?"

I'd been sorry, all right. And angry too. But I wasn't supposed to stay that way. Things happen for a reason. We were here for a reason. And I knew I'd have to make the most of it. "We had to do something, Sam," I answered him slowly. "Just like we've got to do something now."

He looked at me and nodded. "I don't blame you for being angry," he said in such a quiet voice that I could barely hear him. Then he put his arms around me.

I knew he loved me. He always had. And I still loved him. I'd just felt so let down, so unprotected. Maybe it was selfish of me. Sam tried, after all, to be a good husband. He always tried. I laid my head against his chest. "I'm

30

sorry," I told him. "I shouldn't have blamed you. Nobody saw the troubles coming. And we've made it this far. God will take care of us."

"I'm sorry," he whispered back.

"Shh. Let's get some rest."

The old quilt made me sneeze when first we snuggled under it. Our children were asleep beside us, one on each side, with smiles on their faces. *Never mind the dust,* I thought. *This is better than hitchhiking, better than Dewey's house, better than all the world to us tonight.*

Sam soon slept, tossing and turning as was usual for him now. But staring up at the high ceiling in that quiet old house, I couldn't even be tired.

Before long, I was up and pacing around the room, praying for my family. "We need a home, Lord," I said. "Please. Sometimes Sam scares me and sometimes he makes me mad. Like he's at the end of his rope, and I can't even help. I've been too angry to help him, and I just don't think he trusts in anything anymore, hard as he tries."

I stopped in front of the fireplace. It still had ashes and bits of wood sprinkled across the grate. Once the fireplace must have given this room such a cozy glow. And the warmth! There was nothing better on a chilly evening than to snuggle in front of the fire with your children. And put a pan of popcorn over the coals.

With a sigh, I relit the mantle candle and looked around again. It was dark, of course, but I could see that this had been a lovely place once, with the large bay windows on one side of the house and the striped wallpaper, just like pictures I'd seen in the *Saturday Post*. I picked up the candle and began to walk around.

The staircase looked solid and beautiful, at least in the dim light. The pantry was empty except for an abundance of shelves and a few more empty jars. The bedroom contained a dresser and a big metal-frame bed. What might the upstairs be like?

I stopped for a minute, well aware of how foolish I was being.

"Oh, Jesus, look at me. I'm hungry for a home too. This is the first one I've come upon for awhile, and now I kind of like it. Forgive me."

I turned to go back to the blankets, but somehow I couldn't. Nobody else was using the house. *Maybe if we could find the owner . . .*

The thought almost swept me away with it. Such a dream. A farm home. *Lord, forgive me. This place surely belongs to somebody, and I have no business having such thoughts about it.*

But I stood there for a moment and shook my head, unable to let the idea go. Maybe there was a chance. Someone around here would know who the owner was. And maybe the owner was a sympathetic soul who didn't want to leave the place to the elements. I walked back to the entryway and sat on the lowest step. "Lord God," I whispered, "only you could work out a thing like this."

In the morning I woke up humming, surprised by how good I felt. Sarah rolled over beside me and opened her eyes.

"Love you," I whispered in her ear, and she cuddled against my chest. The rain had stopped, and I could hear the birds singing. It was going to be a nice day, much to my disappointment. I couldn't bear the thought of taking this child out on the road again to hitchhike. Or Robert either. There must be another way.

We were quiet as mice getting up, and I helped Sarah put on her favorite pinafore and cotton stockings. She insisted on rolling the tops of the stockings down over her garters by herself, as usual, even though she never quite got the elastic straight. I had already pulled my hair back into a bun at the nape of my neck and was brushing Sarah's hair and humming when Sam woke up.

Just then, I noticed the returning pitter-patter of rain-drops, and I couldn't help but smile. Praise God! Sam wouldn't rush his kids out in the rain. We could stay put a little while longer.

"I'll pull on my scarf and take a walk," I told him, knowing he'd understand it was time I went looking for breakfast, rain or not.

Robert rolled over and asked to go with me, but I didn't want him fretting over our food. "It's enough if one of us gets wet, honey," I told him. "Stay in and read to your sister."

I finished the braid in Sarah's hair and pulled the children's books out of my bag for Robert. Sam didn't say a word as I pulled on my scarf and boots and went outside.

FOUR

Samuel

I watched Julia for awhile through the window. Her blue skirt swished about in the breeze as she circled through the yard and knelt for a minute beside the ramshackle shed. I couldn't picture what she'd find, but she'd find something. Just like her grandma, who used to say that a rich man was a fool if he didn't know how to be poor. God rest her. She'd given Julia peace and a way to provide.

It was more than I could do. Right now, I gave my family nothing. If I'd jumped off a bridge like Bill Harvey, my coworker, they'd be none the worse.

Behind me, Robert was reading. Sarah didn't make a sound. There was not a question out of either of them. They knew there'd be breakfast. Of course there'd be breakfast. Mother would take care of that.

I watched a minute longer, thinking of the flowered scarf she'd chosen out of her bag.

She had been wearing that same scarf when I met her years ago. Julia was thrifty, but it was a shame she hadn't bought a hundred more when we were able. Instead, she'd gotten things for the kids, never really caring if she ever got more for herself.

Her father had given her plenty when she was a little girl. Money had meant something to him, though she liked simple, reasonable things that didn't cost much. She'd never been in this kind of a spot before, that I knew. And it made me wonder why she never talked of leaving me.

I tried to push that thought away, and instead listen to Robert reading to Sarah. Robert was old enough to know the shape we were in. He knew his mother was out in the rain, looking for breakfast. I saw his sideways glance, as if he questioned what, if anything, I was able to do. I had the feeling he would have rather gone out and gotten wet than stay inside with me.

With a sigh I turned from the window and walked back into the kitchen, hating to be here, hating the need that had Julia rummaging for stale food in the cupboards last night. How could I expect my children to respect me? Especially Robert.

I walked to the pantry, which was just off the kitchen. I hadn't noticed it last night, but a handle stuck up from the board floor. A basement. If Julia was willing to pull jars out of a cupboard, maybe I should be willing to take a look in the basement.

The creak of the old door brought both children running to watch me. "You stay up here," I told them. "The stairs might not be sound."

Sarah stood obediently at the top, never one to volunteer herself into a dark place. But Robert ran for candles, handed me one with the matches, and promptly followed me down. I couldn't say anything to him. I suppose he felt that it was his responsibility to see that his father didn't miss something important.

There were at least two rooms in the basement. But I stopped in the first one, feeling sure I knew what Julia would say when she saw the stack of dry wood beneath one window. *The Lord led us.* The Lord was providing a fire over which to pop our ancient borrowed corn. She would smile. And Sarah would smile for sure. But I felt sick in the pit of my stomach, and I knew I wouldn't be eating any of it.

"Dad!"

Robert's yell was so sudden that I ran to him in the second room, fearing a snake or who knew what else.

"Dad! Look!" Robert was pulling on a piece of metal. It took me a minute to see that it was a bicycle. "Can we take it upstairs?" he asked. "Can I try it?"

"No! Robby, we can't just claim any old thing we find. Somebody owns this stuff."

I knew the inconsistency of my words was not lost on him as I pulled him into the first basement room to help me take the wood upstairs. "We need this," I told him. "To cook with."

"I hate living this way," he said. "When are we going to get a home again?"

I hurried up those sturdy old stairs with all the wood I could carry, thinking about Bill Harvey. He didn't have to listen to his boy's questions anymore and stand there with no answer. He didn't have to see his world falling apart.

Sarah was at the top of the stairs, waiting.

"Honey, we're going to have a fire," I told her.

She smiled like I knew she would. "I like this place, Daddy," she told me in a quiet singsong voice. "Can we stay?"

F I V E

Julia

What a place this was! What a place it could be! Someone had planted winter onions long ago, and they were still here, the trusty vegetable my dear grandma had loved. They would probably always be here, regardless of the season; that's what these onions were for. And strawberry plants! There were hundreds of them, competing with weeds in a big patch east of the house, just past the shed. There were no ripe berries yet, but I picked leaves, knowing that they would make a passable tea with a bit of the sugar we'd found.

It was dandelion and yellow dock that had me hopping about the yard, picking leaves. Robert wouldn't be thrilled with greens for breakfast, but it would be something to put before them, anyway.

I spun around for a moment, not minding the rain; going out picking always cleared my head. I admired the way someone had put a line of trees along the driveway, which stretched just north of the house and all the way back to the barn. What a sensible windbreak! No wonder we hadn't seen the house from across the field on that side.

I especially liked the walnut tree behind the house and the apple tree just across the drive from it, not far from the creaky old barn. What joy they would provide in the fall!

I could imagine some dear woman walking about with a basket, picking up drops, while one strapping boy climbed the apple tree to pick and another leaned over, gathering walnuts. What fine eating that must have been!

I should have laughed at myself for such dreaming. But the more I saw of the farm, the more I loved it. A well with a pump stood right behind the house, with more than a dozen jonquils clustered around it. I pumped at the handle and got enough water to rinse my bundle of greens. Fiddlehead ferns were just peeking their curly tops above the ground in a shady corner by the back porch steps. That might be lunch later. I glanced over at the stand of timber past the big backyard and prayed there might be mushrooms there. But my children were waiting. I knew I should go back in and give them my assurances.

"Mom, we've got wood!" Robert called as I came in. "Dad found it in the basement."

Thank you, Lord! I'd expected to step back out in a moment to try to make use of something wet to cook with.

"Thanks, Sam." I gave his shoulder a pat, but he didn't even seem to notice. "If you light the fire, I'll get the food ready."

Sarah bounced up to me, her braid bobbing. "Let's clean house, Mama. Are we gonna use the bed tonight?"

I couldn't answer her at first. She hadn't forgotten last night's whimsy, and now my thoughts mirrored hers. It seemed so natural that we should be here. So right. How could I get her to understand that we had to move on? How could I reconcile it for myself, even? I wanted to do exactly what she said. I'd woken up thinking about it. Clean this house. Make it a home.

But I knew Sam would never understand. And he would be right. You couldn't just walk in and claim a place. There was an owner somewhere. But, Lord, how wonderful it would be if he would drive right up and offer us the house, free and clear!

Sam used the charred scraps of wood in the fireplace and a page from a newspaper we'd found to light our fire. I put the greens and some onion in water in the skillet and boiled more water for the strawberry-leaf tea. How to pop the popcorn without a lid was a puzzle to me until I poured the tea water off into a bowl and decided to dry the saucepan, put the corn in there, and set the skillet on top of it, greens and all.

"This is a strange breakfast, Mom," Robert told me. "But kind of fun, I guess."

When the corn started popping, Sarah jumped for joy. It was easy to make that girl happy. A touch of the salt sprinkled over the warm corn would make her feel like she was feasting.

Then the sun suddenly shone through the dusty bay windows and bathed us in light.

"It stopped raining!" Robert cried.

I looked up at Sam, dismay hidden in my heart. He met my eyes but didn't say a word. I knew he would be ready to move on now that we had decent weather again. "We should stay on the road to Dearing," he'd say. "And then try to get a ride for Mt. Vernon, even though Dewey has nothing to offer us. We can't just stay here and trespass."

How could I tell Sam that I didn't want to go any farther? I didn't want to move one foot from this spot, unless it was to find somebody who could tell me who used to live here. There had to be a way. God doesn't make mistakes. Surely he'd led us all along. And surely it was him making me feel so at home.

God could make a way. He could lead us straight to someone who knew who had lived here and what happened. But it was a scary thing to think of facing a landowner and telling him I wanted this place, without money. Almost overwhelming. Sam would think me crazy. But we had nothing to lose by trying.

S I X

Samuel

Robert was by the apple tree and Sarah sat on the slanted old porch with her doll, Bess. Julia knelt by the well pump, rinsing the pots and dishes we'd used at breakfast. They all looked so comfortable that I hated to hurry them along. But the sun was edging higher, and I knew how hard it could be finding rides, especially out here away from anything. I wasn't anxious to spend another night in a strange place.

"I mean to check the timber," Julia told me suddenly. "Time's good for mushrooms, especially after a rain."

I shook my head, looking down the weedy drive toward the road. "Don't you think we ought to be getting on while the day's young?"

Julia set the skillet down and rose to her feet. "For what, Sammy?"

I looked at her in surprise, not expecting her to speak the futility that was in my heart. I didn't quite know how to take that. "I want to get to Dewey's by dark," I said.

"What would we accomplish going to Dewey's now?"

I reached out my hand and wasn't surprised that she didn't take it. "I'm sorry," I told her. "But we've got nowhere else. Not yet."

Her eyes suddenly blazed with an excitement that shocked me. "We've got *here,* Sam!" she exclaimed. "We've got *now!* And we can make the most of it! Look at the kids! First we moved in with Evie from the bank, then a city shelter, then we dragged them across the countryside, laying them to bed wherever we could find a place! Don't you think they could use a rest from all that?"

A weight, pressing on my chest, settled in deeper. "Of course they could. But we're so close to Dewey. They'll enjoy the visit. We can't stay here . . ."

Finally she took my hand and squeezed it, but what she said to me was no comfort. "Why not?" she argued. "We can't stay there either. Let's give it a day or two. I'm not ready to leave, and neither are they."

"You know we can't stay, Julia. We're breaking the law—"

"Sam, will you look at them?"

Her words were so quick and certain that I turned toward my children. Robert was up the tree now. And Sarah was meandering across the yard, picking violets.

"Sam, they don't want to go nowhere," Julia insisted. "They'd be happy on a farm just like this. Maybe we could find the owner—"

"You're talking crazy! We've got nothing! What are you going to tell an owner? That he should give us the place because our kids like it? The world doesn't work like that, Julia! He'd either laugh in your face or call the law on us."

"It's been sitting empty for awhile—"

"That doesn't matter! You can't just claim it! It's not right, not even to stay another day."

"It can't hurt to inquire," she persisted. "I know we've got no money. But we could offer to fix up the place. It'll just go downhill that much faster with no one here."

"Julia—"

"No, hear me out—"

"You're not talking sense. There's no way we could stay here!"

She looked up at me then and scarcely seemed to be the same woman who'd followed me across so many miles. "There's no way I'm leaving without giving this a chance."

Her words were like a slap in the face. She'd follow me no more. I'd failed her, and she wasn't having any more of it. No way she was leaving? Did that mean I could go or stay, and it wouldn't matter to her? That she'd rather have me gone than spend another day following me anywhere? I couldn't bear to think what her answer might be.

"What's wrong with askin' around a little, Sam?" she asked, taking my other hand. "How can it hurt just to ask the owner? Maybe he'd like somebody out here."

"Juli, honey, we've got no way of knowing where they are. And there wouldn't anybody just give away their land if we did find them. We've got nothing to offer them for rent, nothing to offer them at all. It seems like a nice idea, but it's useless. The longer we're here, the harder it'll be on the kids to leave."

She looked up at me, and her pretty green eyes were deep and stormy. "They need to rest. And you know Dewey's got problems of his own right now with his job gone. We've got nowhere else. Not a decent soul would blame us for staying a couple of days."

"And then what?" I couldn't believe that she wouldn't let the matter drop. "What good will it do sitting on this farm, getting hope up in these kids?"

She sighed. "Hope's all we've got. I'm not leaving, Sam, till I've had a chance to try."

I'd never known her to be so stubborn, and it made me furious. But more than that, it made me scared. Like she was already miles away, and I hadn't taken a single step. "Try what?" I countered. "Getting thrown off of here by the law, maybe? Seeing the hurt in Rob and Sarah when we're made to leave? You can't just have whatever you come upon! Lord knows it don't happen that way!"

She shook her head. "We won't harm anything. I'll clean up, leave things better than we found it. All we need is a chance to talk to the owner. They're not using it. Maybe we could find some terms."

She walked away from me.

"Julia."

She turned, only for a moment, with a look strong as stone about her. "I mean to go look for mushrooms now, Sam. You and the kids are welcome to join me. We'll take an extra bowl, in case the Lord would bless us with something else while we're over there. I don't want to have to go anywhere else today. We need a rest. We can find the town tomorrow if it doesn't rain."

I stood for a moment, just looking at her. Had poverty made her irrational, or my failure? She'd decided to make her own way; that was plain. She didn't trust me anymore. Had no use for me, more than likely.

"Robert John!" she hollered. "Sarah Jean!" She turned away from me to watch our daughter amble toward her, flowers in hand.

Robert descended effortlessly from his perch in the apple tree and came running. "Mom!" he yelled. "There's tiny apples in that tree. Lots of them. They'll grow, won't they?"

"Yes," Julia answered him quietly. "But it'll take months."

"I wish we could stay that long," he said wistfully. "It'd be fine, picking 'em. I could take a bucket up with me and lower it down to you with a rope."

He didn't seem to notice me standing there. Right then, none of them did.

"We'll have us an apple tree of our own one day," Julia told him. "Lots of space and a real big garden."

"Flowers too?" Sarah asked, holding up her haphazard bouquet.

"Sure enough. And those are lovely," Julia answered. "But right now, I'm going to take a walk in that timber over there and see if I can find some of those little morel mushrooms Grandma fried up for us once. Do you remember, Robert?"

"I think I do," he said hesitantly. "Are you sure we'll find some?"

"Well, no. But we can try. I need your help. The more eyes the better, okay?" She handed Robert the saucepan, and I stood in silence, watching them walk away.

But little Sarah suddenly turned around to me with her eyes sparkling. She held out her crumpled violets. "These are for you, Daddy," she said with a smile. "Aren't you coming with us?"

SEVEN

Julia

Walking out to the timber was a chore for me, knowing how I'd upset Sam. He didn't understand any better than I'd expected him to. He was thinking of the way things usually work, the way people do things when they've got options. But we had nothing but hope left, and hope doesn't work like anything else in this world. Even Papa would have admitted to that. Oh, but he'd scoff at me now, worse than Sam, even. Papa had to have his world in order. He wouldn't cotton to me taking up with a notion like this.

I kept my eyes on the ground around us, looking for the edible mushrooms. But I kept thinking of the things we could do here, even without money. I knew enough of doctoring herbs so that I could gather and sell some, if there was anyone in the town who would buy them. We could clean up the house and try to close off the broken windows as a courtesy. There was plenty of firewood to be had out here. We could replace what we'd used from the basement, even if we didn't stay another night.

I took a deep breath and looked into the trees stretching to the east in front of me. Shagbark hickory and sugar maples stood amongst the oak and cottonwood. The rain had left everything with a deliciously fresh smell, and I could imagine hickory nut pancakes with maple syrup. Grandma used to say that if a person had fertile land, they could provide for themselves everything they needed. "After you got a few chickens," she'd said, "you and the good Lord can grow all the rest."

As a child, I had dreamed of testing the idea, finding a place and living off what I could find and what I could produce. Papa had laughed at me, of course, telling me I should marry an upstanding city boy, one who knew how to make a company pay him what he was worth. I'd done it too. Or I'd thought I had. And things had been good for awhile. Papa would have liked the house we had, the neighborhood, and Sam's ambition for more. But that wasn't meant to be. And now my old dream was back, so strong that I tingled inside.

Robins and a woodthrush sang over our heads, and the spring beauties at our feet seemed to dance to their tune. I hadn't found a thing to put in my bowl, but the kids didn't care about that right now; they were too busy exploring. I told them just to stay within sight of me. And if they saw any mushrooms, ask to make sure they were the right ones, even before they touched them, since some kinds are poisonous.

Sam was only about three yards away from me, but we didn't speak. I'd really put a cloud between us this time, just when I'd thought I was ready to be closer again. We walked along in silence, searching the ground.

Ahead of us, Robert found the stream so suddenly he almost fell in. With pebbles on its bottom and moss along its banks, the stream was a pretty sight, just the sort of stream a homestead should have. The only thing missing was the blackberries I'd imagined as a girl, plump and purple and free for the picking. Instead, thistles and joe-pye trailed uphill on the other side of the water, with pickerel dotted here and there and a half dozen clumps of winter cress. I squatted down and began to break off leaves.

"Did you find a mushroom, Mama?" Sarah asked, running to my side.

"Not a one. But this is cress, honey. Pretty good stuff."

"Are we gonna eat leaves for supper too?" Her bright eyes revealed a hint of dismay at our menu.

But Robert was suddenly shouting, and I saw him pointing toward a fallen log. "Is that the right kind, Mom?" he yelled. "Is it a good one?"

With one hand over the leaves in my bowl and Sarah at my side, I ran to him and confirmed that he had indeed found our first morel among the rotting debris of an old oak. He was pretty proud. "Keep looking in this area," I told the children. "There's liable to be more where you find one."

I searched among muddy leaves and carpetweed to no avail. Robert circled me for awhile, and then we all walked downstream in our search, with Robert in the lead. He was soon shouting his complaint that he couldn't get where he wanted to go for the bramble bushes across his way.

I turned my eyes to where he stood and saw the band of thorny green and white stretched out to where the gurgling water made a sudden turn. I had to take a deep breath. So many bushes, dotting the woods to the south and east of us now. I could scarcely believe it. I took Sarah's hand and walked closer, wanting to be sure. Delicate white flowers were sprinkled over every branch like a promise. Some of the petals had dropped away to reveal tiny berries, still green as grass and hard as stone. Blackberries.

Sarah squeezed my hand, as if she could sense the impact the sight had on me. The sight of more blackberries than I could possibly count. Ripe in a couple of months or so. A treasure. A temptation. I wanted to throw down my bowl and run. It was too good here, and too stupid of me to think of staying. Someone else's land! We were stealing! I turned around in the direction of the farmhouse, not wanting Sarah to see the tears in my eyes.

"What's the matter, Juli?" Sam was behind me, his gray-blue eyes filled with cares.

I stopped dead in my tracks. I couldn't be upset, not when they were all looking at me and waiting for the good I was always talking about. And I knew I had to show them. I had to make them see that we would make it, whether here or somewhere else, and that everything around us was a gift from God, no matter where we were standing.

Sam just stared at me, waiting for me to answer, but I had nothing to say yet. Sarah broke our silence with an excited squeal and a tug on my arm.

"Look, Mom! Right by your foot! You almost stepped on it!"

Another beautiful morel mushroom, much bigger than the first. I leaned to pick it up, and Sam reached for my hand. "We could go into town today," he said. "Maybe there's a boardinghouse in town, if you just need to stop for awhile. I could ask for work—"

"Mama," Sarah interrupted. "Do these mushyrooms taste good as popcorn?"

I looked up at Sam and then tried my best to smile for Sarah. "*I* think so, sweetie. They're one of my favorites." As I spoke, I saw another spongy brown mushroom, as big as Sarah's hand, not ten feet away.

"There might be someone willing to take us in for a few nights without money," Sam continued, "if we do some work for them. It's worth asking about. We wouldn't be breaking any laws that way."

I turned away from him and picked our third mushroom, and two more beside it. But they looked pretty meager in the bottom of my bowl with the handful of cress leaves. Sam wasn't a hunter; he'd never been hunting in his life. And that was too bad, I found myself thinking. A rabbit would make a nice dinner for the kids, who were sure to be hungry even before noon today, considering our breakfast.

"Juli."

I glanced his way, at the same time noticing the sudden flutter of my apron. The wind was picking up.

"Did you hear what I said?"

"Look at the sky," I told him. "We're in for more rain."

Clouds were moving in like a great gray blanket covering up the blue. *Lord, don't let it rain yet,* I prayed. *Not till I have a decent meal in my bowl! Then it can pour till the cows come home.*

We searched for more mushrooms till the sprinkles hit our backs. We had just started back toward the house when I spotted a couple of little wild rose bushes, just like we had on Grandpa's farm. I had the kids help me strip off the old hips and some buds, being as careful as we could for thorns.

"This is fun," Sarah told me, not minding the rain at all.

"I wish we could live on a farm," Robert added. "We could run around outside all the time."

I looked into my bowl and sighed. They really didn't care that we'd found only two more mushrooms. Seven in all. They trusted me that much. I glanced at Sam, but he was looking at the sky again.

"It's pretty black in the west," he said. "Storm coming. I guess you'll get your way for tonight. We can go to town tomorrow."

We headed straight for the barn and picked through a pile of boards for something to cover over the broken windows. All the boards had square nails sticking out of them, which we pried up and used to tack the boards in place. One of the broken windows was upstairs in a bedroom, so we got our first look at the second floor.

There were just two rooms up there, one with nothing but an old bed frame and the other full of boxes and crates. I shooed the kids out of that room and shut the door. "We mustn't mess with anything unless it's a matter of necessity," I told them.

I rushed out into the rain and picked more dandelion, some lamb's-quarter, and winter onion to add to the cress for salad. It would have been nice to fry the mushrooms with cornmeal like I'd been taught, but without either corn or grease, I hadn't any choice but to try something new. I picked up a few sticks in the yard and had the kids roast the halved mushrooms in the fireplace. I then stewed the rosebuds and hips in water, sweetening the brew with sugar, hoping to come up with something palatable.

Nobody said much over a lunch like that, and the thunder started in earnest before we were through.

Sarah tagged behind me like a little shadow as I took a look in the basement, where Sam had found the wood. It pleased me to find a pile of rags and an old broom. And Sarah found a toad, which she thought the grandest thing she'd seen in her whole life.

"They eat bugs," I told her. "That's why they like basements and gardens. Lots of bugs."

"Do bugs taste good?" she asked, her eyes wide with question.

"Some of them might be all right," I told her, though at that moment I was wondering how a toad might taste. But Sarah would have none of that, I knew.

"Whatcha gonna do with those rags?" she asked as I bundled them up to take upstairs.

"We're gonna clean this place up," I announced. "It'll be our thanks for staying here."

51

"Can I help?" she asked. "I'm glad we're not in the thunnerstorm, Mama."

Sam had started knocking down cobwebs, knowing I didn't think much of having spiders dangling over my head. I swept the dust from the floors into a corner, scooped it up the best I could, and flung it all out the back door.

I had some paper with me in my bag, and I'd written out a page of sums for Robert, not wanting him to forget such things in the time it would take to get him settled into a school. He sat grumbling and ciphering as Sarah helped me wipe down the kitchen table and counters with water from the well and a couple of old rags.

"Why doesn't she have to do any figuring?" Robert asked.

"Because she's only five," I told him. "And hasn't had even a day of school yet."

"Well this ain't school," he continued. "Why can't I wait?"

"If you keep up, best as you can manage, you won't have to be left back for all the time you missed."

Robert looked out the window, and I let him daydream a minute. Finally, he turned his attention back to his paper but then looked up abruptly. "You think there's a school 'round here? I wouldn't mind figurin' so much, Mom, if it meant having some other boys around to play with."

I was glad Sam had gone to the basement for more wood. Both of my kids were as infected by hope here as I was. "When we have a place of our own to stay," I told Robert, "you'll make plenty of friends again. We'll look about the school first thing."

I hadn't been able to take a good look at the cookstove last night, but I could see now that it was a beauty. Maybe the finest wood-burning one I'd ever seen, once I had the dust washed off. The stove had cream-colored enamel and a warming shelf built right in. Not very old either. Someone had paid good money for it, that was for sure.

I opened the double doors of the big oven, wishing I had some flour. That'd be what I'd buy if we got into town and found a grocer. Flour. Beans. Maybe potatoes. But sixty cents wouldn't go far.

I scooped the ashes and what looked like an old mouse's nest out of the firebox just as Sam came upstairs with the wood. He stopped for a minute, seeing me at the cookstove.

"You're not wanting a fire in here tonight?"

I shook my head, knowing it wouldn't seem quite right yet. It would be like taking another step, thinking we belonged here, and even I wasn't ready for that. "I'm just cleaning, Sam," I told him. "As a kindness."

I dashed out in the rain again to cut the fiddlehead fern fronds for supper that night. We ate them roasted with salt, and the rest of the popcorn.

"Do other people eat stuff like this?" Robert asked me.

"It's been a bad year for a lot of folks," I replied. "When people can't get to a store, they eat whatever's around."

"They look like big curls," Sarah said. "Only green."

"Rolled up like a jelly roll," Robert fantasized. "Too bad we got no jelly."

"Or bread," Sarah added solemnly.

Sam looked from one to the other, his face ashen. "That's enough," he said. "Both of you." He got up and walked away from us, into the dark bedroom with the boarded window.

"Why's he so cross all the time?" Robert asked me. "He was nicer when he had a job."

I was stunned by my son's words. Everything had been nicer then; that was surely true. But I couldn't let him blame Sam for that.

"Honey, your father will always have a job. God made him your daddy, and the most important thing he'll ever do is love you the way he does. If he seems cross, it's because he'd like nothing better than to give us the best home we could ever imagine, plus all the jelly and bread we want. Lots of men have lost their jobs, through no fault of their own. He's thinking of you, wanting you to be happy."

I looked in the direction Sam had gone, hoping he'd come out and offer to tell the kids a story the way he used to when Robert was little. That would help. If he could just do that, it would be almost like old times between them again.

But something in Sam had changed. I knew it as well as Robert did. I wondered if there were any stories left in Sam to tell. The ache in him had swallowed all the stories, plus the spring in his step and the smile I loved so well.

I had filled my children with wild vegetables and a few cheerful songs, but I had done nothing to fill the void in my Samuel's heart.

E I G H T

Samuel

I sat on the floor, just listening to the thunder outside. It was too dark to see anything in that musty room, but I didn't care. I would have closed it off if I could have— sealed it like a tomb and stayed in there forever.

What would tomorrow hold? If it rained again, we were stuck here. And what else could Julia manage to scrounge up from that yard outside?

If it didn't rain, we could set out again, but even if I bought my children bread with the rest of our money, the knowledge that it wouldn't last crushed me into the ground. We could go on for awhile, eating whatever Juli found, sleeping wherever we could. But even if we managed the summer, come winter, we'd freeze or starve. It all came down to money. A job.

I heard Juli's footsteps and almost told her to leave me alone. I was angry, not at her, but at myself for not being more like her, not finding a way on my own.

"Sammy?" Her voice was timid, like she wasn't quite sure what I might say or what I might do.

"I don't want to talk right now."

She came closer, despite my unfriendly words. "That's okay," she whispered. "There's not much I can say, anyway."

She stood quiet for a moment, and then I felt her hand on my back, gentle and warm. "Robby's reading to Sarah again," she said. "Then they're going to lie down."

"Maybe you should be with them."

"They're fine." She leaned down and kissed my neck. "I miss you," she whispered. "I miss us."

I almost pushed her away. "I've got nothing for you, Julia," I told her. "You'd be better off without me."

But she kissed at my neck again like she hadn't heard a word I'd said.

"I'll ask after work tomorrow," I promised. "I'll even ask after this farm, if that's what you want, but you might as well know I don't expect nothing out of it. If the owners were to give someone this place, you know they'd pick somebody local. Maybe we'd have a better chance back in Pennsylvania."

She just leaned into me, ignoring what I'd said, easing me toward the floor.

"Juli—"

"Shhh." She kissed my lips for the first time in months.

"The kids are awake," I reminded her.

"They're fine."

"The floor's dirty."

"Not as bad as it was."

I sat there for a moment, wondering why she didn't hate me and how she could lay aside her feelings this way and act as though everything were fine.

"We can do this together," she said. "And that's the only way we can do it. I need you now more than I ever have."

I almost protested. But she kissed me again, and I couldn't hold myself back from her anymore. I put my arms around her and pulled her close. I hugged her tight and told her I would love her until the stars fell out of the sky. Juli, the light of my day, the gift that God gave me to share in my night. I would have fallen away if it weren't for her. I would have been like Bill Harvey, blind, alone, more dead than alive.

Morning had us up bright and early, packing our things back in our bags. The sun was shining and Julia was folding the blankets carefully and putting them back where we found them. I could think of little more than her apology to me in the night for being so distant and angry.

She sang as she made us strawberry-leaf tea again, even though there was nothing to eat with it. "We're on our way to town," she told the children. "We'll be eating when we get there."

"I don't want to go!" Sarah declared, folding her little arms across her chest. "Why can't we stay here?"

Juli seemed hesitant. "We have to find the grocery store, for one thing."

"Daddy and Robby can go! You and me can stay here and pick mushyrooms again!"

Juli knelt and put her arm around Sarah. "You have to make arrangements when it comes to things like a home," she explained gently. "We can't stay here any longer until we talk to someone, and it's far too soon to know what the answer might be. We might decide to go and visit Cousin Dewey for awhile. You'd like that, wouldn't you?"

"No," she said. "I wanna stay here."

"Well, we're all going into town and we're not about to leave you behind." Juli pulled a ribbon from her handbag and tied back Sarah's hair.

I stuffed Juli's Bible and a storybook into the top of the largest bag. Robert just stood beside me, listening to everything but not adding a word.

"Are we ever coming back?" Sarah asked quietly.

"I don't know, honey," Juli answered her. "God knows."

"I wish we had a car. Then we could go wherever we want."

"Well, maybe we'll get us a good quick ride." She stood up and took Sarah's hand.

"Does Dearing have a soda shop?"

Juli smiled at the sudden change of subject. "I have no idea. But we won't be visiting there, even if they do. Now if they have a library, that would be fine. We can take the time to read something new, if it's not too long."

Stopping at a library would never have occurred to me. But that was Julia. No matter what we had to accomplish or how little we had, she'd find a way to mix in something to make the kids feel special.

We started off while the morning was young. I looked back at the farmhouse and never expected to see it again, despite Julia's longing. But I thanked God for the house, because in it we'd mended the rift between us. I was still worried. I was still wondering about how to feed my children. But the world was not as heavy as it had been. I picked up Sarah and put her on my shoulders. It seemed like the birds were singing all around, and soon I spotted a wagon heading our way.

NINE

Julia

It was a gift of fortune, gaining a ride so quickly, even though it was a slow one. A bearded man and his teenage son driving a team of horses and a farm wagon sauntered up beside us and stopped with a friendly greeting.

"Say, there," said the man. "Out visitin' today?" He was looking us up and down real good, but smiling just the same.

"On the way to Dearing," Sam told him.

"We need to find out who owns the farm over the hill there," I added, figuring this was a neighbor who would probably know something about the farm.

The man glanced at Sam and then back at me and shook his head. "Ain't anxious to see it sell," he said. "Where're you all from?"

"Pennsylvania," Robert told him.

"Got family 'round here?" the man questioned with a frown.

"In Mt. Vernon," Sam offered. "We'd be much obliged for a ride in your wagon."

"Well, you can pile in, I guess," the man told us. "We's headed into Dearing, all right. But you ain't gonna find Mrs. Graham there. Last I knew, she was over to Belle Rive, but you can ask Hazel Sharpe. She'll know for sure."

My heart leaped up inside me. We had a name, a hope. Someone to talk to about the place!

"Don't know how you come to know about that old farm," the man was saying. "I'd buy it off Emma m'self if I had the money, but it ain't even for sale yet. We live just down the road. Graham field comes right up again' mine. Nice ground too."

Sam looked at me, and I knew what he was thinking. Just like he'd said, preference would be given to someone local if it came to that. And we didn't even have money.

"My name's George Hammond," the man told us. Then he gestured to his boy. "This here's Sam."

Sarah laughed. "That's my daddy's name!"

George chuckled. "It was my daddy's name too. What's yours?"

"Sarah."

"Wortham," Sam added and shook George Hammond's hand.

The wagon smelled of hogs and hay. We climbed up beside three wooden boxes, and George started the horses moving again before we'd sat down.

"Wilametta sent me with a list of things to get," he said. "That's my wife. I ain't gonna manage but about half of it, though, the way things are right now. Be careful with that box in the middle, young'uns. That's Wilametta's eggs. We'll be tradin' 'em for the dry goods, I expect."

"What's in the other two?" Robert asked.

"Robert!" I exclaimed, horrified that he would so casually ask a stranger's business. He knew better than that.

"It's all right, ma'am," Mr. Hammond assured me. "Got nothin' to hide, that's for sure. One on the right's full of feathers for Bonnie Gray. She's wantin' to make pillows and such for her daughter Juney's weddin'. But the other one . . ."

Young Sam Hammond snickered. "Take a look."

George Hammond hooted and turned to Robert with a smile. "Go ahead, if you want, son. Take a look. Might never see'd anything like it if you come from the city."

Robert reached for the box, then turned to look at me.

"Ah, go on," Mr. Hammond exclaimed. "It's all right, ma'am. It ain't gonna bite him."

The younger Hammond snickered again, and Robert lifted one corner of the old gray blanket that was stretched over the top of the box. He jumped back into my Samuel's lap, and both of the Hammonds guffawed in unison.

"Don't you worry, boy," George laughed. "It's deader'n a doornail!" He hooted some more, and I leaned forward to take a peek.

No wonder the wagon smelled like hog. In that box was a Yorky pig's head, the biggest one I'd ever seen.

"We saw the widow Hicks to church Sunday 'fore last," George was saying. "She told me she'd been hankerin' for some good headcheese, just like her mama used to make down in Tennessee. So when old Charlie there come up lame, I figured to put him to good use. She's givin' me a lamb. Gonna let the kids raise it up for me."

"You got other kids?" Robert asked, still looking a little green.

"Comin' out of the rafters, boy," George laughed again. "Nine of 'em. And one more on the way."

Robert leaned over to Sarah and nudged her. "There's a pig in the box," he whispered. "Wanna see?"

"Robert John," I scolded. "Just sit and be still."

"I don't wanna see no pig," Sarah told her brother. "Pigs is ugly."

"Pretty good eatin', though, little miss," Mr. Hammond said.

Dearing was about seven miles from the farmhouse, we discovered. It was quite a trip, with Mr. Hammond talking almost the whole time about his family, the economy, and a lot of people we'd never heard of before. He let us out on the main road, right in front of the grocer, saying he wanted to go on and get rid of old Charlie before he made his other stops. We thanked him for the ride, and he pointed to a tidy little house half a block down, its big yard separating Dearing's only bank from the rest of the businesses on the street.

"That's where you'll find Hazel Sharpe," he said. "She can tell you 'bout Emma Graham. Sure hope she ain't ailin'."

We thanked him again, and he shook his head. "My pleasure. Say hello to Emma if you speak to her, will you? We sure do miss havin' her 'round. Won't seem right, someone else being on the place—no offense, you understand."

He drove away, and we all just stood there for a moment, looking down the street. Compared to Harrisburg or Evansville, Dearing was hardly any town at all. You could easily see to the railroad tracks at the edge of town, and its little peak-roofed station.

There weren't many businesses in the town. A barber. A dry-goods store with room for only one dress in the window. A hatter, of all things, and across from the bank, the Seed and Feed. Over a rooftop I thought I could see a church tower, and it looked as if the church was the biggest building in town.

The grocery building was nice enough, although for some reason it was painted bright blue. But it was the smallest grocery I'd ever seen. Hardly bigger than our bedroom in our house in Harrisburg. Beside the grocery sat a much bigger building with a sign shaped like a chair. O'Toole's, the sign said. Kerosene lamps for sale, dirt cheap.

Robert and Sarah were already on the first of the grocery store's three steps.

"Pretty hungry by now?" I asked them.

"I could eat anything they got," Sarah said.

"Anything but pig," Robert added.

We bought a loaf of bread, a sack of flour, and a bag of beans. The proprietor took a look at our traveling bags and gave each of the kids a hard candy.

"Thank you, mister," Sarah said with the candy already in her mouth. "Now we're looking for the library."

Her words caught me by surprise. I'd forgotten that I'd promised them that. And here I was, anxious to meet Hazel Sharpe in the little house down the street.

"Can't say that she's open today," the grocer replied. "At least not till school's out. That's the way it usually works. You go two blocks west. Easy to see. Right next to the undertaker."

I thanked the grocer and herded the kids out of the store. We sat under a tree and ate most of the bread. It was a treat to me, plain as it was. And just as we were getting up, a short little woman, stooped over terribly, came out of the house down the street.

"Go on," Samuel told me. "If this is what you want."

I stood still for a moment, wondering why he wasn't moving. *Go on,* he'd said. He meant for me to talk to her alone.

I glanced in the old woman's direction. She'd stopped to close her front gate but then hurried on away from us, moving faster than I would have thought possible.

Sam gave me a nod but didn't take a step. *Fine then,* I thought. *It's my idea. I'll do it.* He kept the kids and the bags by the tree, and I went running down the street so fast I nearly lost a shoe. If I'd seen the woman standing still, I would have guessed her to walk with an uneasy shuffle. She looked like the wind could blow her over. But she moved like she was racing to beat the band.

"Mrs. Sharpe!" I called.

At first she didn't seem to hear me, but then she turned and gave me a stare like I'd never had before.

"I'm sure I don't know you," she said. "And just as sure you don't know me, neither."

"Well, yes, Mrs. Sharpe," I said. "But Mr. George Hammond said I ought to—"

"George oughta tell you straight, then!" she declared. "I ain't a missus! Never have been!"

"Oh, well, I beg your pardon, Miss, uh–"

"Miss Hazel is fine. And I'm going to the church. Can you imagine? Our new pastor's wife can't play the piano! At least she's willin' to take a lesson. I hope she's got the sense for it, you know what I mean?"

I cleared my throat, unsure of how to ask anything of this rather gruff lady. "Well, uh, yes," I stammered. "I hope so too."

"Who are you, anyway?" she demanded. "And what's George sending you to me for?"

"I . . . uh . . . I need to know where to find Mrs. Emma Graham."

Miss Hazel looked at me a long time, and for a moment I wondered if Emma Graham was unmarried too. But I was sure Hammond had said Mrs.

"I go up and see Emma when I get the chance," Miss Hazel said, her voice considerably softer. "What are you wantin' with her, anyway?"

I swallowed. "We want to ask her about her farm."

For the first time, Miss Hazel looked past me and saw my family waiting beneath the tree by the grocer.

"Her farm, eh? I see. You'll break her heart with that, you will. She true loves that old place."

I was taken aback; I certainly didn't want to break anyone's heart. "Do you think we shouldn't ask then? If she's wanting to—"

"Oh no, it isn't that. You might just as well. It'd be the best thing. She ain't never goin' home." Miss Hazel took another long look at Samuel and the kids. Then she stared down at my hands. "You hard workers, are you?"

"Yes, ma'am."

"And churchgoin', I hope."

"Well, yes. Once we get settled somewhere."

"She might not sell, mind you," Miss Hazel told me. "But you do all right by askin'. What you need is to go to Belle Rive to the boardinghouse. McPiery's place, got that? That's where she is." She took a deep breath, straightened her hat, and told me she couldn't be late for the pastor's wife's first lesson. Then she scurried away down the street.

The grocer told us Belle Rive was another four miles or so northwest. Closer still to Mt. Vernon. I knew if this fell through, we'd be going right on, into an uncertain future. And I had butterflies flying loops and swirls in my stomach.

"She's probably an old lady," Sam said as we stood on the side of the road just outside Dearing. "Probably widowed and can't keep up the farm by herself anymore."

Just like Grandma when Grandpa died, I thought. We'd moved to town, and it'd still been good. We'd had each other. I hoped Emma Graham had someone.

"Do you think we're doing the right thing, Sam?" I asked.

"That's up to you, honey," he told me. "We can still go to Dewey's and spend a couple of days deciding what to do next."

Julia's Hope

We walked along in silence, and I almost gave up the idea of the farm. How could I ask a stranger a favor such as this? Especially when it concerned something so dear to her heart. It was easy for me to see how she could love the place; I wouldn't want to part with it, if I were her. But, of course, she wouldn't have to. We couldn't buy it anyway. Maybe we could tenant for awhile, until she was ready to do something different. And by then, maybe we would've found something else, maybe something in the area.

We got a ride from an old couple who drove slower than Hammond's farm wagon and said scarcely two words to us the whole way to Belle Rive. But when we stopped beside an ancient-looking church on the edge of town, the woman turned in her seat and gave me a quarter. "Get the kids somethin', will you?" she said. And she and her husband drove away on the road toward Mt. Vernon. Sam would have liked to go on with them, I was sure.

I stood with the quarter in my hand and tears in my eyes, afraid of what I had come to the town to do.

"Are all the towns in Illinois this small?" Robert asked when the car was out of sight.

"Chicago's bigger than Harrisburg," Sam told him. "But I hear things are pretty hard up there."

"Things are hard around here too," Robert observed. "If people will eat a pig's head."

Little Sarah put her hand in my hand, her eyes on my tears. "Don't be scared, Mama," she whispered. "I bet there's something real good to find in this town."

I nodded to her but couldn't say a word. I wanted to buy them peaches with the quarter. Just because they loved them so well. I stood wondering about finding a grocer in this town when I saw a sign not even a block away from us. "BOARDERS WELCOME."

Sam had seen it too. "That's probably it," he said. "I'm not sure a town this size could have two boardinghouses."

66

Once again I considered giving up my idea. But Sarah expected me to muster my courage and find the good so that I could tell her about it. I looked hard at Sam.

"Are you coming with me?"

He only shook his head. I could see the love in his eyes, all stirred in with his sadness. I handed him my bag with a nod. *Might be better anyway,* I thought, *for a woman to be talking to a woman on this. At least, if that's the way Sam wants it, that's the way it'll be.*

T E N

Emma

I was sittin' by the window in my room at Rita's with an undone quilt bunched on my lap. Every day I tried to sew it a little more. Had to pull it up close to my face, though, to get the stitchin' halfway right. I was working at it when I heard the knock outside, but I didn't pay it no mind. There weren't many folks come to see me.

Before long, I tied off and cut my thread, then pulled back Rita's old lime curtains to get me a better look outside. An old willow tree not thirty feet from the glass took up 'bout all my view. We had one just like it out to the farm, till it come crashin' down in the big storm that hit in 1918.

God musta put this willow where it was on purpose, so I could look out and remember all the picnics me and Willard had under the droopy shade of the other one. I remember missing it something awful when it fell.

Would've planted another just like it, but Willard did the practical thing and put in an apple.

I sat there for a moment, dreamin' on whether the apple tree had bloomed and how well it might do for fruit this year without the prunin' it was sure to be needing. Didn't take much to get me homesick, I guess.

I thought of how the jonquils would be pretty 'gainst the white of the house that time of year. But the violas was likely choked awful by the grass, bein' along the garden's edge the way they was. And the violas was precious, since they came clear from m' grandmother's farm, to mama's, to mine. It made me sad to think there wasn't nobody but me to care.

I tied back the curtain and turned my head to business. *Oughta get this quilt done, just 'cause it's somethin' to do.* I cut a new length of thread but had my mind on all the green outside the window. Spring was the worst time for thinking on home and Willard and how much I missed 'em both ever' time I let myself. Just lookin' outside could start me off. You'd think I'd learn.

But there was a little fun in imaginin' Willard standing outside under that willow, watchin' and waitin' for us to be together again. I wondered if he was missin' me the same as I missed him. But maybe he'd be ready to give me the what for by now, for all this sittin' still so long.

He always said home was the place to live and die. And there I was, spendin' three good farmin' seasons in Belle Rive. There weren't no way 'round it. But what would he think? Willard wouldn't leave the farm when he was sick. Even when he took real bad, he wouldn't. But there I sat.

I was just leanin' into the window light, trying to thread my needle, when Rita tapped so sudden on the door, I jumped.

"Emma?"

"Might just as well come right in, Rita. You know you ain't gotta knock." I tried threadin' that needle again, but missed.

The door opened just a peek. "You've got comp'ny, Emma," Rita said. "Says she's from Pennsylvaney."

Now that were a surprise. I couldn't imagine what this'd be about. I pulled myself up in m' seat best I could, wondering who in the world had come.

"Don't recall that I know nobody out that way," I told her. "But send 'em in anyhow. Can't hurt to say hello."

The door opened up wide and Rita brung in a pretty young woman with squared shoulders and a real slow step. Even though I never seen her before, she acted like she was almost scared of me, all nervous an' wringin' her hands like she figured maybe she already done somethin' wrong.

"Just give me a holler if you all want tea or anything," Rita told us. Then she shut the door and left us alone.

The lady was young and fair for looking at, with a blue button-front dress, a flowery scarf, and the most amazin' green eyes. She was gazin' over the place and me. I must have been quite a sight in that old rocker, with my hair all down a mess, quilting scrunched so sloppy over my lap, and just one old shoe pokin' out from underneath.

What in the world might she have come for? I thought. *Albert up in Chicago, maybe? He knew lots of folks. Had something happened to him?* That kinda thinkin' give me an awful tight feeling in my throat, and I coughed to clear it away.

"You care for anythin', miss?"

"Uh, no, thank you."

She sounded so nervous. A whole lot more than I was, for sure, and I felt sorried for her. I pointed her to the wicker chair in the corner, the only other thing to sit on in the whole room, except for the bed.

"Set with me awhile," I told her. "Pull the chair up here, if you don't mind. An' tell me your name, why don't you, and what brings you here."

She said she was Julia Wortham. She had a pleasant voice. But she had an awful time fumblin' that awkward old chair closer. I kept trying to poke thread through my needle while she moved it, hopin' to sew while we was talking. I like keepin' m' hands busy that way. Keeps the mind from borrowin' worry.

But that old thread wasn't about to do. I wet it good with m' tongue, twirled it to a point, and thought I had it through that time. But when I gave it a pull, it weren't in.

"Can I help you?" the young lady asked.

"Can't see to find the eye no more, that's all! One of the worser things 'bout gettin' old." I gave over my needle and thread. It wouldn't hurt to let her help. I thought it might set her to ease some.

"I'd appreciate it," I told her. "Relax now. Nothin' 'bout me to be scared of. You know Albert?"

"Uh, no, ma'am. I was hoping you wouldn't mind me asking about your farm."

I watched her slide my thread through the needle on the first try, but I couldn't say nothing for a minute. The farm? I shoulda known to expect something like that. What else would anybody want with an old lady?

I took back the needle, knotted the thread, and swallowed down the tightness in m' throat. I didn't much care to talk about this. I weren't even ready to be thinking on somebody else wantin' the farm. It was my home, and there was too much of my life wrapped up in it. I didn't near want to turn it loose.

I could just see the old place come summer, prospering under the golden sun. And I could see m'self back there too, working in the strawberry patch or weavin' a little purple and yeller chain of violas to lay across Willard's gravestone. I had to take me a deep breath and think on the quiltin'. I wasn't ready to talk about the farm. Not yet.

"You sew, do ya, Mrs. Wortham?"

"Y—yes. A little. But I've never done a quilt. This is beautiful."

"Well, you ain't examined m' stitchin' to speak of, that's all. I can't see to put two together like I used to! Be a shame to hang it 'longside one a' Trudy Welty's!" I tried smoothin' the cloth a little. "Don't be lookin' too close at the underside, now! There prob'ly ain't a row a' stitches the same size."

Right away, she done the opposite of what I told her, turnin' up the edge of m' quilt and runnin' her fingers over all m' lines.

"Mrs. Graham," she said, "I think it's wonderful. I wish I could do something so well."

I stretched the quilt out a little more. "This un's a double weddin' ring pattern. First time I ever used so much paisley."

She kept on looking at the quilt, tracing over the interlocking circles. She sure was a nice young lady to be takin' such an interest when she plainly had something else on her mind. I knew I should let her get back to that, but I wasn't anxious to be no disappointment. I couldn't sell that farm no more than I could sell my grandmother. Or my own right elbow.

I took a deep breath. "It's a good enough quilt, I s'pose, but I'd be embarrassed for some a' m' friends to see it," I told her. "They'd be wantin' to rip stitches an' do it right."

Mrs. Wortham smiled. "I'd be proud of it, if I were you. It's one of the prettiest things I've ever seen."

I looked her in the eye for just a minute, but she dropped her gaze. "Mrs. Graham, about your farm . . ."

I swallowed. "Rita said you come all the way from Pennsylvaney. New married, is ya? Lookin' to buy 'round here?"

Mrs. Wortham dropped the quilt out of her hands and looked up like she was hurtin' over something. Then she spoke all in a rush. "Mrs. Graham, we've got no money to buy! My husband lost his job. We came to Illinois on the promise of another one, but the plant's closing. We have two children, and we were stranded along the road with a storm coming. We had nowhere else to go. If it weren't for your house, I don't know what we'd have done! Forgive us for staying, but we've got nothing right now, and I was hoping, I was just hoping—"

The stream of words come to a sudden stop.

"You been stayin' at m' farm?" My heart was pounding. "For how long?"

"Two nights." Mrs. Wortham looked down at her lap again, huggin' at the quilt edge with her skinny fingers. "I'm so sorry. But we covered the broken windows and got the door to close again as it should. I—I cleaned up a little for you while it was raining."

I started at a stitch again but could scarcely look at it. How was I s'posed to feel about this? It was likely true, just like she said. There *had* been some weather. But I couldn't be thinkin' on their trespass long, for wonderin' on the shape of the place. Nobody'd told me of it in such awhile.

"The house ain't gone down too bad, has it?"

"No, ma'am. Nothing that can't be fixed."

"What about the barn? And the chicken house?"

She was lookin' at me, pretty surprised by now. "Well, I guess everything needs work, but they're still usable, I think."

"They weren't none too good when I was out there last," I told her. "Been awhile since we could keep the place up, even before Willard died."

"I'm sorry."

I just gave her a nod. "How old is your children?"

"Ten and five."

"I had a boy once. He died in the war, some years ago now. That's his picture over there." I pointed over to Warren's handsome picture on m' bureau top.

She looked at it and then brung her eyes back to m' quilt. "George Hammond said to tell you hello."

"I was wonderin' how you knowed to look me up." I stared down at her tremblin' fingers, considerin' what it'd be like to have no home, like this woman claimed. For me, there'd always been the farm, since marryin' Willard with m' mama's consent at the age of fourteen. It made me feel bad, knowin' this woman was desperate and I was just keeping her waitin'.

"You say your husband's outa work?"

"Yes, ma'am," Mrs. Wortham answered real soft. "But he's a good worker when he gets the chance. We could fix for you, do whatever you want on the place—"

"You come askin' permission to stay?" I leaned back in m' rocker and eyed her good.

"Yes, uh . . . yes, ma'am. If it would be all right . . . at least until—"

"Till I sell it, you mean. Or till I die and it gets sold out from under ya."

"No, ma'am," Mrs. Wortham protested with a stricken look. "Just so long as you still felt all right about it, I mean, if it's all right at all. I was thinking you might want to go back there yourself."

I wasn't sure whether to laugh or cry on that. So I shook out the quilt an' reached for her hand. "Let me tell you somethin', child! I can't go home, much as I'd like to! I get spells with m' heart that put me to bed, and m' old leg won't hardly hold me no more, 'specially for stairs, even when I got m' two canes. I ain't no good without the other one."

She looked at me, all surprised. She didn't know the half of what I was talkin' about.

And without thinking no more on it, I lifted the quilt off my lap and showed her the cherry-colored afghan that was underneath. I seen her eyes notice my left shoe and that there weren't another one on the right side.

"That's the main thing that keeps me away," I told her. "If it weren't for that, I mighta been all right out to home awhile longer." Always such a pitiful sight to see, my one old leg stickin' out from my dress like that. In five years, there still weren't nobody could get used to it, least of all m'self.

"Had fever in it," I explained. "Got so sore infected, they thought I'd die. Had to take it off, right below the knee there. I ain't been good since, far as the farm goes, though I tried for awhile."

Mrs. Wortham was quiet, just looking at me.

"Oh, I know," I told her. "There ain't nothin' to be done nor said. But you can see why I can't manage the place. Can't hardly do nothin' no more."

"I'm so sorry, Mrs. Graham."

"Well, it ain't your fault, child. The good Lord, he has these things decided, you know. He'll tell me about it, one of these days."

"You're a very brave woman."

"Oh, now that ain't nothing more than just livin'. We all do 'bout the same as far as that goes. If I coulda kep' m' good leg up, I mighta been all right, but I fell in '27, and my hip's not been so good since then." I reached for the quilt and pulled it back to m' lap. "Be glad you're young. Be glad your kids is young too. They can take the hard times better'n us older folks sometimes."

Julia gave a little smile. "It's not been too easy for them. But they don't complain much."

"They're good youngsters, then. You musta taught 'em right." I looked at her a long time, and she turned her eyes away without saying nothin' more.

Julia's Hope

I took a look out to the old willow tree and thought of Willard's grave on the rise north of the pond. I'd been wantin' to go back there ever since comin' here, even though Rita was one of m' dearest friends. People had told me to sell, plenty of times, but I couldn't. I wouldn't even think on it for wantin' to go home again. But it wasn't gonna happen. And the good Lord well knew it was time I faced up to that. No matter what Willard mighta thought.

Looking at the quiet young mother sittin' in front of me, I knew I was gonna have to tell her something. They needed a home more'n I did. And I had no right under God's blue sky to be selfish. But a knot rose up in my stomach anyhow, so tight I could hardly breathe. It weren't easy to let go.

Mrs. Wortham was lookin' at me funny. "Are you all right, Mrs. Graham?"

"You got any family can help you?" I asked.

"I was an only child. My parents and grandparents are dead. Sam has his mother and brother in New York, but we can't go there. They can't help."

"Why's that?"

She bowed her head. "Edgar's in the penitentiary, Mrs. Graham. And Samuel's mother married a man who wouldn't have us coming around."

"Why not? What's wrong with ya?"

"Well, nothing as far as I can see," she answered without hesitation. "But it's been this way since we got married. I think because Sam's different now. He's—he's a Christian, like me."

"Well, there's hardly harm in that! But they won't help ya?"

"I don't think they could, even if they wanted to. They're not much better off than we are. We were on our way to Sam's cousin, but he lost his job too."

I lifted up m' needle, but set it right down again. I'd wanted to die still owning the farm, having that hope of going home again. I could feel m' tears tryin' to come, but I wasn't gonna let 'em, not in front of Julia Wortham's notice.

You don't need that farm no more, I told myself. *I'm fine where I'm at, and they got nothin'. What's a Christian to do?*

It took me one deep breath to decide. "I'll tell you what," I said to her. "A family's gotta have a home. You stay there and fix on it, like you said. I'll have some friends check about you now and then. We'll give it a year or so. An' if you do right by the place, you can have it."

Mrs. Wortham's mouth opened up slow, and then closed again. But then the tears come like somebody opened a gate for 'em.

"Mrs. Graham . . . oh, Mrs. Graham, are you sure?"

"Don't go tryin' to change m' mind, now!" I told her real stern. I had to be stern, or I'd start bawlin' m'self, and I sure didn't want that to happen.

"Mrs. Graham, I–I don't know what to say! I expected to tenant and pay you something when we could—"

"I'd like some apples off the tree, come fall."

She looked at me and then come bustin' forward with a hug. "Yes. Oh yes! But isn't there anything else?"

I couldn't hold it together no longer, even for the trying. "You can't have all the land," I said, struggling somethin' fierce with the words. "I'll need 'bout six feet of it. You have t' put me in the groun' next to m' husband." And then my tears come out too, and Mrs. Wortham hugged me tighter, tellin' me I didn't have to be so kind.

I had to push her away, had to get my sternness back. "I've made up m' mind, now! You do right by the place! I'll make sure and check! You let that George Hammond keep farmin' the field, if you ain't got the means. You do right by him too, you hear? He needs all he can gain from it to feed that family a' his."

"Yes, ma'am," Mrs. Wortham said, looking like she was in some kinda shock.

"Where's that husband a' yours? You're gonna hafta bring him so's I can meet him an' the kids if they're gonna be out to m' place."

Mrs. Wortham nodded, her tears still falling. "They're outside, Mrs. Graham. We were going to move on if you said no."

"Well, go get 'em, girl!" I scolded, tryin' m' best not to cry no more. "Get them youngsters in here!"

ELEVEN

Julia

I would never have expected the reaction I got from Sam. He sat right down by the side of the road and cried.

"I can't," he said. "We can't let her—"

"Sammy, come and meet her at least, or she'll be mad as the dickens about me not coming back in."

"I don't know a thing about farming! I didn't figure you had the chance of a butterfly in a snowstorm . . ."

The kids didn't know what to think of their dad, sitting in tears in the dirt. And they didn't know what to think of me either, running out the way I did, hollering for them.

"Mom, who is she?" Robert asked.

"A wonderful lady," I said. "C'mon, Sam."

Sam pulled himself to his feet and wiped his whole face with the handkerchief from his back pocket. "We can't let her do this," he said again. "Suppose there's family?"

"You can ask her about that," I assured him.

"I need to work and provide," he protested. "Not just be handed—"

"Sam," I said, taking hold of his arm, "you'll have to work, all right. She said she'd check to make sure we were fixing on the place. And she means some fixing, I'm sure."

"But—"

"We can do it! Really we can!"

He looked down at Sarah, who hadn't said a single word. "I can't believe this," he muttered. "God Almighty, this would never have happened in Harrisburg."

"It wouldn't happen anywhere without God's design," I said just as the front door of the boardinghouse opened.

Mrs. Rita McPiery, the owner, stood looking out at us. "Mrs. Wortham!" she called. "Emma told me to ask if your young'uns would want some buttermilk and a ginger cookie. She's a'waitin'!"

"Ooooh, can we?" Sarah said, looking at her father, not at me.

He nodded weakly, wiping at his face again. "Better at least meet her, I guess. Since she's wanting to meet us."

I took his hand and felt like I could float clear up to the sky. *God bless Emma Graham! Oh, Lord, bless that woman!*

"I knew we should live there," Robert said in a tone I'd never heard from him before. "It was just home, you know."

TWELVE

Samuel

Nothing seemed real, going back through Dearing that day. And back to the farm with Emma Graham's blessing. I tried to tell her no, but she wouldn't hear it. I tried to tell her George Hammond wanted the ground, but she said he had the use of it and that was good enough—he wouldn't keep the place up like she was hoping I would. She wanted the farm to be nice again, she said, the way Willard had it when they were young.

Mrs. McPiery sent us back with a sack of her cookies and three dry ears of table corn for seed. She took us aside as we were leaving and said to come back in a week with flowers for Mrs. Graham, and she'd give us seed for lettuce, turnips, and pumpkins too.

Julia was like a new colt, prancing around. "Oh, Sammy," she said. "We've got to get tools."

I just shook my head, thinking it would be good while it lasted, having a place to call home. But there was no way we could do the things Mrs. Graham wanted with no money. Paint the house? Fix that old barn? Put in a garden and see that there were flowers clear to the road? We were biting off far more than we could chew.

Mrs. Graham had only laughed at me, saying I'd make it just fine. Trust in the Lord, and I'd find a way. And then she said the thing that surprised me most. Everything on the place, even in that upstairs room in the house, was ours to use as we saw fit, so long as we didn't sell a piece of it till after she was dead.

Julia bought us a can of peaches in Dearing, and the first thing she did when we got through the door was start a fire in the oven. I'd never had cobbler like what she made that day, from nothing but flour and baking powder and peaches. Baked in the old iron skillet with the syrup from the can poured on top, the cobbler was fare for celebration.

And then we started looking around. Julia got out some of her paper and started writing down everything we had and everything we'd need. The sky was clouding up again, so we searched the barn and the shed first.

In the barn we found a rake and a pitchfork that was missing a tine. There was an old wagon with one wheel off, and a couple of milking pails. Julia was thrilled when we opened the shed.

"It's like Christmas!" she said. Two hoes, a post digger, a spade, and a double-sided axe. There also was a roll of chicken wire, a box of hand tools, plus more hanging on the wall, and a couple of metal things Juli said were wedges for splitting firewood. I just shook my head, feeling out of place. When she said we'd need a splitting maul to use with the wedges, I didn't even know what she was talking about.

I was used to coal. Oil. Even electricity. But we had none of that here. And Juli said this was no problem; there were probably plenty of neighbors that had never had those things and never would. But I was overwhelmed, picturing myself chopping wood all winter long and still trying to figure out how. And where would the food come from? Surely we couldn't grow enough corn and turnips from Mrs. McPiery's seed to last a whole year.

"Don't worry," Julia kept saying. "Don't worry. The Lord will show us how."

Emma had told us the dimensions of her land, and we walked over a lot of it, even going to Willard Graham's grave. Julia picked a bundle of spring beauties to leave there, and we prayed together, thanking the Lord for what he'd done.

There was a pond we hadn't seen before, just down the hill from the little stone marker. It had two boards sticking out to meet a post set in the water—the ricketiest dock I'd ever seen, but one it might be all right to fish from if you didn't wiggle too much.

The timber where we'd hunted mushrooms was Emma's too, though if we went on far enough past the stream, she had said, we'd come to the Hammonds' place. She always gave them equal claim to the blackberries and whatever else there was to find in the timber.

Maybe the Hammonds were mushroom hunting too, Robert suggested, and that was why we didn't find very many. I started to wonder if they would resent all the favor we'd been shown. Maybe they stood in need too. No doubt I'd have to visit George Hammond.

I was glad for the rain when it started. I was exhausted, but Julia was still bouncing around, talking about getting the ground ready for garden. I hadn't seen anything at all when we were at the farm before. But now, everywhere I looked, I saw something to do.

We went inside with a bowl of water, and Julia put in some of our beans to soak. Then we went upstairs and brought down one box. One box only, because it was almost dark and we had all of tomorrow ahead of us.

Coming back down those stairs, Robert took the steps by twos and Sarah hopped down them one at a time, singing a song she made up as she went along. They were so happy, and I had to admit it seemed right to stay now. But that didn't change the fact that I was scared beyond words. *What if I can't make this work? What if I fail again?* Juli and the kids and even Mrs. Graham were all on my shoulders, and I didn't want to let them down.

I set the box down on the sitting room floor and both kids took hold of the piece of twine wrapped around it.

"Now just a minute," Julia told them. "It's your father's job to open that box."

"How come?" Sarah asked, and I was wondering the same thing.

"Because he's not as excited as you are."

Robert looked up in surprise.

"These are Mrs. Graham's things," she continued. "And they're special to her. We have to treat each item with respect."

So it is with this whole farm, I thought. *God help me be equal to the task.*

THIRTEEN

Julia

It was late and the kids were asleep between blankets on the floor. Sam was sitting up, just as unable to sleep as I was. Around us lay the contents of one box. Just one little part of Emma Graham's life.

There were a set of lace doilies and at least a dozen embroidered dish towels. Candlesticks and linen napkins and a little book of pictures drawn by a child, almost surely Emma's son.

"Oh, Sammy," I whispered. "Maybe you were right. Maybe we can't really do this. This house has been her whole life."

I picked up a candle and reached for his hand. I wanted to see more. I had to know, before the kids were up again, if I could really handle such a total, and personal, gift. I hadn't thought through just what she was giving us. She knew of course. It wasn't just the house. It was every memory that went with it.

We went up the stairs slowly, each of us with a candle, feeling like we were entering something sacred. The first box I touched had a wedding picture on top with a folded quilt beneath it. Sam opened a box that held gardening gloves and a pair of trowels nestled into a straw hat.

I looked at him, knowing I wouldn't be able to stop the tears. "She kept all this, hoping she could come home. That's all she really wants. And she gave it up for us."

Sam closed his box before getting to the bottom. "It's not right, Juli," he told me. "I feel like we're stealing, even more than when she knew nothing about us."

"I know what you mean. What are we going to do?"

We walked down the stairs and sat down on the first landing, where the moonlight shone through the window. "If we could only give her something," he said. "I'd feel a lot better about it. But there's nothing half as good as what she's given us."

We sat in silence for a long time, and I thought of Emma downstairs, quilting by the fire, or out on the hill beside her husband's grave. "There is one thing," I ventured, barely daring to speak it. "The only thing she really wants."

"You mean—"

"We could bring her home, Sammy! She could have the lower bedroom so she wouldn't have to climb these stairs! We could take care of her, and she'd be right here where she could tell us just the way she wants things to be! I bet she knows how to do everything! And she knows the people around here too, in case we need help with anything."

Sam stood up, took about three steps down, and stopped. He turned and looked at me but still didn't say a word.

"It wouldn't be any trouble!" I pressed. "We have a lot to do, and I'd feel better about it if she were here to share in it! Sammy, I don't want to think about her sitting over there, homesick. It's too awful sad."

He ran his finger along the carved edge of the stair rail and shook his head. Then he went all the way down to the front door and shook his head again.

"It's not such a strange thing to do!" I declared. "I feel like I know her. And she's a Christian."

Finally he looked up at me again, and even in the dim light I could see the twinkle in his eye. "We can't go tomorrow for her," he announced. "We've got a lot to do, like you said. This place should look at least a little like home for her first."

I flew down those stairs and into Sam's arms, loving him so much at that minute that I could hardly stand it. "Thank you, Sam," I told him in the middle of my hug. "Thank you so much!"

The next day I washed the floors while Sam pulled weeds out of the drive and pounded a leg back on the sitting room chair. We dragged out the mattress from the downstairs bedroom to air in the sun and opened every window we could to get rid of the musty smell. Sam took out one of the upstairs windows and put it in the downstairs bedroom, so Emma would have sunlight to sew by. I was picking yellow woodsorrel to put in the beans, and Sam was trying to chop a fallen tree limb when George Hammond came riding up in his wagon.

"Say, there, you folks move pretty fast," he said, an uneasy frown working on his face. "Never heard of such a quick sale."

Sam set the axe aside and moved to greet our guest. "There wasn't any sale," he said. "We're fixing the place for Mrs. Graham to come home."

George Hammond was more than a little surprised. "She's not well, I understand. You folks plan to stay and do for her?"

"We will, if she'll have it so."

"If? You mean, you ain't settled it with her yet? What are you doin' here, then?"

"She told us to stay. But we'll feel better about it if she can come home."

"Well," Mr. Hammond said. "That's a thing for considerin'. Are you gonna plant the field, then?"

"She wants you to keep at it," Sam told him. "We got no way right now."

George took a good look around at the little farm, then turned his full attention on Sam. "Should've got you a horse, mister. You'll be needin' the work help, not to mention the transportation. Unless you got you one of those trucks."

"No, sir. Neither one."

George scratched his head and looked at me. "No cow, neither?"

"No."

"Chickens?"

"Not yet."

"You got no pigs. I'd have smelled 'em. You hunt right well, I take it?"

"Never been."

"Well, how're you figurin' to feed them little ones, then? I ain't never heard such a thing! You gotta have stock on a farm or you'll starve. Ain't nobody told you that? You thinkin' to get goats, maybe? Or sheep? We got pigs for sale."

"No money for any of it right now," Sam told him. "But I would welcome some advice."

George noticed for the first time that I was gathering plants, and he whistled real slow. "You folks is flat broke, ain't you?"

"The same as," Sam admitted. "Except for Emma Graham's generosity. I'd like to repay her, like I said, but you can see what I haven't figured out yet. We can't have the old woman home with nothing to feed her."

"You say you want advice?" George asked, suddenly spitting into the grass.

"Yes, sir."

"Start tellin' folks. Let us know when Emma'll be here, and the problem'll start takin' care of itself. I'd wager on that."

"Mrs. McPiery's expecting us next week," Sam said. "I'd like to bring her home then, if I had a way to drive her."

George grinned. "You can take my wagon, if you know how to drive the team."

"I don't."

"You're a city boy for sure, ain't you?" He shook his head. "That's a sorry thing. I'll send one of my boys with you. I'd promise to go m'self, but Wilametta wants me close to home now, on account of the baby. She thinks it'll be early, the way Harry was."

George turned and looked at me again. "Hard way for a woman with a man that don't know what he's doin'."

I stopped and stared at him. "Sam knows exactly what he's doing."

George Hammond just glanced over at the limb in the yard where the axe was still leaning. The limb barely had a notch in it. "I can see that he does." He grinned again. "I'll send William over here to cut that for you and maybe teach your boy to fish. Could use all the help you can get." He tipped his hat, and I felt like pitching a rock at him. He had no right insulting Samuel like that.

But Sam just stood there without saying a word until Hammond drove off.

"He's right, you know," he said. "I wouldn't know what to do with a horse if I had one. Or a pig, either."

"Never mind him," I said. "You'll learn."

But Sam left the axe where it lay and fixed the broken porch step instead. He was good enough with his hands. He always had been. I'd seen him do just about anything he was given half the chance at. He could fix a motor car or put together a radio. He could put electricity into a house, which I was sure George Hammond could not do.

Sam could do so many things that I'd been frustrated to no end when he couldn't find another job in Harrisburg. Everywhere he'd went there were lines, always with twenty or more men ahead of him. And it was the same way everywhere else we'd been. Maybe I was wrong, wanting him on this farm, where things were as foreign to him as hay to an alley cat. But he'd find his niche, surely. He'd even make George Hammond respect him.

After an hour or so, a boy about Robert's age came walking in from the timber. He didn't say much, just introduced himself and said he was here to chop a tree limb. Sam let him start the job while he watched, but then finished it himself and sent the boy to the pond for some fishing with Robert.

"I need to keep the blade sharp," Sam told me later. "And to watch my swing." He walked to the woods and pulled home several more fallen branches. We'd be needing more wood to cook with, even when it got hot. Not to mention a store ahead for the winter.

Robert and Sarah tore into my pot of beans, without complaining for the lack of ham to go with it. I rather lamented having no eggs or milk to bake with, but I made baking powder biscuits anyway. They weren't light nor pretty, but they were far better than having none. Both kids ate them crumbled up in the beans.

I felt rich watching them eat, just knowing that today they could get as filled up as they wanted to. This was the start of a new life for us, and they were as excited as I was.

"Can we open more boxes when we're done?" Robert asked. He was sitting on a chair we'd carried from upstairs, enjoying the last of Rita McPiery's cookies.

"First we clean up," I told him. "You can help your father outside while Sarah and I work in the house. Then we'll unpack more boxes."

"This is going to be real fine," he said, not seeming to mind the work. "Not only do we got a home, but there's neighbor kids! Willy Hammond said he's coming back tomorrow for some more fishing. I'm gonna make me a pole like his. If I catch a fish, you'll cook it, won't you, Mom?"

"Absolutely. But you can't be fishing all the time," I cautioned. "We've got plenty of other work to do. And we need to go talk to those neighbors and find out where the schooling's done around here. Doesn't seem like you should have to go all the way to Dearing."

Robert looked up at me in surprise. "Where else would we go?"

"Oh, honey, I'm hoping there's a country school lots closer. It would be small, but that can be real nice."

"Maybe they don't go to school. It's too early to break for summer. Ain't it Wednesday? Willy didn't say nothin' about school."

"Maybe they let out the day for some other reason," I suggested.

"Doesn't matter what the neighbors do," Sam said. "If we're settled here for awhile, it's time Robert was back in school. If there's none close enough, he can work on book education at home."

"Maybe we can find out tomorrow," I told them. "And we'll stop at the library next time we're in town. But for now, let's get some work done."

Earlier in the day I'd taken down all the old curtains, thinking to wash them and the windows. But we had only gotten the windows done so far, using nothing but well water. *Oh, how nice the place would smell if I just had soap!* I'd thought.

Sarah and I took rags and wiped down all the cobwebs from the walls and window corners. Then we washed the closet in Mrs. Graham's room and dusted the dresser inside and out. All the while, Sam and Robert worked over in the garden patch with the two old hoes we'd found in the shed. They came back in when they lost their daylight, and we all went upstairs, carrying candles.

"We should ask the Hammonds to save us feathers for a mattress," I told Sam after glancing at the old bed frame in one room.

"And what would we give in exchange?" he asked.

"Maybe I could offer to take her kids for a few hours once in awhile. She must be awfully tired with a new one almost here. She'll need help once it's born."

Sam shook his head. "We know that at least some of those kids are big enough to help. And they've probably got family around here anyway." He squeezed around the side of some boxes to get to the back corner of the storage room, where two more old chairs leaned against a washtub filled with clothing. He picked up the tub and carried it out to me.

We would put Mrs. Graham's clothes in her closet, because I would need the tub for my washing. We decided to unpack everything and put in place all that we could to get the house in order before Mrs. Graham saw it again. So we started opening boxes and sorting them according to the room we figured the stuff belonged in. It didn't take us long to accumulate quite a pile for the kitchen.

"I've got to wash out the cupboards and drawers, Sammy, so we can put these things away." I lifted up a serving spoon from a silverware set. "She has some nice things. A wonder she didn't take more of them with her."

92

Julia

The prize of the night was a box containing four delicate kerosene lamps and their glass chimneys, all packed
in newspaper. Two of the lamps still had a bit of kerosene
in the bottom. I carried them downstairs gingerly, the odor
tickling my nose. Sam followed with the washtub, Robert
with a box, and Sarah with her rag doll and a bundle of
towels.

Late as it was, we ate more beans. Then I washed our
dishes while Sam and the kids stretched out our blanket
beds. By the time I finished, I could hear Sam in the sitting room, talking about someone named Goompus in a
land far away.

It was the first story he'd told in such a long time. *Thank
you, thank you, God.*

F O U R T E E N

Samuel

In my dream we were still in Harrisburg, standing in some endless line. Bill Harvey was standing next to me, dripping wet from the river he'd thrown himself into. "Who do you think you're kidding?" he asked me. "Sam Wortham, in the sticks somewhere? You're more than a few bricks shy of a load, thinkin' you're gonna make that one fly!"

Sarah was yanking on my coat, struggling for my attention. "Daddy, Daddy! Will you please listen?"

I rolled over and opened my eyes. Sarah was cuddled beside me between two blankets, still sound asleep. The first light of dawn was just breaking through the windows. What an irony that Bill Harvey, who'd given up on life, would ridicule my efforts. "I'm listening," I whispered to Sarah. "Thanks for getting me up. I'd rather listen to you than old Harvey any day."

I pulled myself up, careful not to wake Julia. The dawn was so quiet. Nothing but a little bird made even the slightest sound. I went out and stood on the porch for quite awhile, looking over Emma's domain.

I couldn't feel for it what Julia did. I wasn't nearly as excited about the whole thing as the children were. Something about being here left me feeling empty and small. I'd worked so hard, tried so hard in Pennsylvania. But my efforts were worth nothing at all.

"I just want to earn my keep, Lord! I just want to provide for my family! Is that so terrible?"

I stepped off the porch, feeling ashamed and glad my mother didn't know anything about where we were. What would she say if she learned I was an old woman's charity case? I'd been a long time trying to prove I was worth something. What would she think now?

The bird started singing again, tittering away in the apple tree Robert loved so well. I sighed, remembering how grateful I'd felt and should still feel. *God bless Emma Graham. We'd be in Mt. Vernon already—with nothing—if it weren't for her.*

We'd be okay here for awhile, as long as we could get food. And maybe that was all that mattered. Even if we had to leave, life would go on. Somewhere. And maybe that's all life was: survival. Do what you have to until the Lord puts you someplace else.

With the sunshine bursting over the horizon toward me, I crossed the shaggy yard to the barn. I was supposed to fix the creaky old thing; it was one of the conditions of our being here. Get the barn, not just the house, in shape. As I looked up at the old rafters from inside, the task seemed impossible. No wonder Julia had been afraid to spend our first night in here. The roof was coming off. The walls were in sorry shape. I didn't know where to begin. I even wondered if it might be easier to tear the whole thing down and start over, but I didn't know how to do that either. I'd bitten off a lot more than I could chew.

In back of the barn, a fence stretched eastward. Some of it stood in fairly good condition, but the rest of it had fallen down and lay lost in the weeds. Maybe Emma Graham had cows once.

I turned around in time to see a mouse scurry across the old hay, and I almost laughed. *We do have animals here, Mr. Hammond. Mice and snakes and who knows what else. No wonder Julia thought there should be a dog.*

Looking out at the new sun, I could picture my mother laughing at me for standing here wondering what to do with myself. "Sam," she'd say, "why can't you just admit when you're being an idiot?"

Above me, a board was creaking in the gentle breeze. And behind me, I heard the sound of something moving, some little animal, but I didn't turn to look. More mice probably, figuring they owned the place.

"Lord, am I making a mistake?" I looked up into the dusty loft, and a piece of old hay fluttered down toward me. I wasn't sure what I wanted anymore. I wasn't sure what to do. Yesterday it had seemed like a good idea to bring the old lady home, but now I wasn't sure if I could handle any of it.

Just to have something to occupy my mind, I looked at the old wagon that sat in the west end of the barn. The wagon was small and probably well used once but wasn't much account now. The bottom had fallen out and two of the four wheels were beyond repair. It was a relic, not fit for anything anymore. But the thought that Emma Graham might feel the same way suddenly saddened me. *God bless her. At least she's giving me a chance, far better than I deserve.*

It gave me a certain resolve. Even if she couldn't live here, she should be able to visit, see the place, and go out by the pond where her husband's grave lay under the trees.

But it was such a long way to walk, with her not able to take a normal step. How would we get her to the grave site? There was just too much to think about. Too many problems I couldn't solve. Better to stop thinking and find some work to do.

I went to the shed for the axe and chopped at the branches I'd dragged up from the woods yesterday. At least we'd have a little wood, since the basement supply was gone now. I kept at the chopping until my shoulders hurt, and then I went inside again, carrying an armload of wood in case Julia needed more already. She was making some kind of muffins, and she turned to me with her prettiest smile.

"Oh, thanks, Sam. Just set it right by the stove."

She had her brown hair pulled back into a bun again, and wore one of Mrs. Graham's aprons. I had to smile; she looked so good to me. So at home. "You got the oven lit already?" I asked her, envying her ability to fit right in. She'd been raised for such a life by her grandma. But I'd been raised thinking that if I couldn't prove my worth by making a buck, then I wasn't worth anything.

"I set the fire in the oven right after you went out," she said. "It's about right now for the muffins."

I stood there for a moment, looking over at the box in the corner. Stuff we'd brought down from upstairs. And there was a lot more to carry down. I bowed my head. "This whole place, Juli. I'm not sure I can do this."

"I know. But we'll be fine."

I shook my head, feeling all jumbled up inside. "How do you fix a barn, Juli? The thing could fall on me, just like you said."

"We'll figure something out. Maybe it's not that essential."

I sat on a chair and put my elbow on the table. "I don't know what I'm doing," I told her. "Except chopping wood. And I don't do that well."

She smiled again. "Honey, I think you're wonderful. You've been doing all you can. You haven't said a sour word about what I've gotten us into. I know you wanted to see Dewey. And you're being a jewel to me, really."

There wasn't anything I could say to her. I didn't deserve her praise. She was the one feeding us. She was the one who knew what she was doing.

"Sammy, one of the wires is down on the clothesline pole outside. If you can find a way to put it up for me, I can hang things out to dry. I'll be washing our clothes with the curtains right after breakfast."

Without a word, I went outside, thinking it might be like this from now on. Me at a loss until Juli gave me bearings, telling me what I should do.

The clothesline wire hung down from one pole and stretched across the damp grass like a snake. I picked it up and pulled as hard as I could, but it wasn't long enough to reach the far pole. Never mind that. If Juli wanted it up, it would go up. I walked back to the barn for a piece of the baling wire that littered one corner and then went to the shed to check the toolbox for some pliers. It didn't take long to twist one piece of wire onto the other, stretch it the distance, and then tighten the thing as much as I could. We'd have wash hanging there soon enough. Just like regular folks.

Julia came outside, saying she'd seen spearmint along the front of the house yesterday. She went back in with a handful of leaves, and we had her strange tea with the muffins that morning. Then I kept fetching water, and she heated all she could, filled the tub, and washed out the kids' clothes first. I wondered how clean they'd turn out with no soap and no washboard, but Juli used an old potato masher, a scrub brush, and her bare hands. She did my clothes too, and hers, and then Emma's old curtains.

Samuel

I was outside, hammering a board back in place on the henhouse, when she came out to drape the laundry to dry.

"Chicken coop in pretty good shape?" she hollered.

"This I can fix, at least."

"That's good. We'll need chickens."

Yes, Julia, I thought. *You're believing for them too, aren't you? Any day now, someone's liable to come and hand us a chicken just as easy as we've been handed this place. That's what you think. That it will all just happen. Why can't I be like you?*

She hung up the clothes while I replaced the chicken wire that had pulled loose along one wall. When Juli went back in, I turned to the garden with a hoe, thinking that the better I whacked the dirt loose, the sooner Juli could plant Rita McPiery's seeds and have something decent to report.

By the time I went in with my arms full of broken sticks for kindling, Juli had scrubbed every cupboard in the kitchen, top to bottom. I piled my sticks in the corner behind the stove and then got Robert's help carrying down the rest of the kitchen boxes we'd separated last night.

Julia and Sarah spent quite awhile putting things away in cupboards and drawers, and the room started to look like a real kitchen. But it was messy the way my kindling just lay on the floor. I went back out to the barn with a handsaw, looking for decent boards and some nails I could pull loose from somewhere. With Robert at my side, I hammered together a passable wood box.

"You sure are good at stuff, Dad," Robert said.

"This isn't much."

"Mom's gonna like it."

I shook my head. "There's nothing for wood even by the fireplace in the living room. Surely the Grahams didn't go to the basement every time they needed a log. They'd have been up and down those dark stairs all day in the winter."

99

"You gonna make a box for in there too? Or a little rack thing like we had in Harrisburg?"

"The rack would look better."

Robert was quiet for a moment. "This is different than the city, ain't it, Dad? You don't have to have a job to work around here."

"I suppose there's always work to do on a farm," I told him. "But I'm going to be asking around town too. If I get a job, we've got some hope, with some money coming in."

"Mom says we won't need much money here. Once we get the garden in and some animals, we'll make it okay."

That was Julia. *No worries, kids. We're fine, broke as we are.* I shook my head again. "Everything takes money. There's a lot of things you can't get no other way."

"Like a milk cow?"

I smiled. "Yeah. Does your mother want a milk cow?"

"Yeah. And Sarah thinks it'd be keen too. Will it taste just the same as the delivery milk back home?"

"Not as cold without an icebox."

"Maybe we could get one."

"That takes money for sure."

Before we even got the wood box into the house, Willy Hammond came walking up through the yard, looking for Robert to go fishing again. I sent Robert on with my blessing. It would be good for him to have a friend, and good if we could manage some fish for dinner.

My box fit right behind the stove, and I piled it full with all the wood I'd cut. Sarah followed me back out to the garden, enjoying the feel of the turned-over dirt on her bare feet and asking a million questions.

"Daddy, will we stay here forever?"

"I don't know how long it'll be. I don't suppose anything lasts forever."

"'Cept God?"

"Yeah, except God."

"Can we grow tomatas?"

"If we get plants."

"And more flowers?"

"We'll have to. That's what Emma wants."

"Is Emma an angel, Daddy? Mama said she's an angel."

"Kind of. If your mama says so."

"I want to be an angel when I grow up. I want to fly around and give people stuff. Can Emma fly?"

"Not yet. Not in this world."

Julia came outside to dump the water she'd used scrubbing the woodwork and the stairs. She'd have the house looking fine before long. But it was hard to imagine it filled with furnishings, and harder still to think of the rooms upstairs with decent beds or the pantry loaded down with jars of food.

"We should plant the corn today," she told me. "The sooner we get the garden up, the better. I wish we had Mrs. McPiery's other seeds now too."

"I guess we have to earn them."

She gave me a look, got herself a hoe, and began whacking over the same piece of ground I'd already worked. "Kind of rough," she said. "But I've seen worse. Let's make some rows."

Dutifully, I raked my hoe through the dirt to create a shallow furrow, and Julia followed in my tracks, breaking up clods. "Corn does better in several short rows than one or two long ones," she said. "Pollinates better."

"No problem."

"What's pollynate?" Sarah asked us, and I left the question to Julia, not knowing the answer for sure myself.

"It's what bees do for flowers, honey," she said. "Taking pollen from one to another. I guess maybe the wind does it for corn stalks. They like to be close together so the pollen can blow back and forth. You get good ears that way. And more of them."

"Maybe with ears," Sarah suggested, "the corn can hear the wind coming." She giggled and then picked up a handful of dirt. "I'm gonna have a big garden when I grow up," she told us. "Big as the whole world. And I'm gonna have a truck too, like that one we rode in, and I'm gonna drive corn all over the place and give it to everybody for supper."

"That's a good idea," Julia told her. "You remember that. It would be a wonderful thing to do."

"You want to help, Mama?"

I could see Julia's smile, and it was almost infectious. "I'd love to. Maybe we can grow enough right here to share with the neighbors."

Dreamers, I thought. *Foolish dreamers. How I love you both! But don't you see where we are? Not one seed in the ground yet. We haven't enough for tomorrow, and all you can think of is giving it away.*

F I F T E E N

Julia

I was laying things out from boxes again when I heard the motor car coming up the drive. It surely wasn't Mr. Hammond, since he always seemed to go about with his team and wagon. Sarah ran to look out an open window just as I heard Sam shout hello.

The answer he received surprised me so much that I went to the window myself. "Where's the missus?" a female voice demanded. "You got her inside someplace?"

I knew the woman, but it took me a moment to recall her name. Miss Hazel Sharpe. The spinster from town. What in the world had she come out here for and why did she sound so angry? I nearly tripped over a kitchen chair on my way out the door to meet her. What would she think of the state the house was in or of the fact I had no tea and cookies to offer her? Had she come to inspect our progress? Surely Emma Graham had sent her.

Miss Hazel was on the porch, waiting for me to open the door. I marveled again at how fast she could move, as stooped over as she was.

"Well, there you are," she said. "What you done to Emma's house?"

Such words stopped me cold for a moment, and I could barely manage a hello. I noticed the young man leaning on the shiny black car. *Maybe Miss Hazel has money,* I thought, *or knows someone who does.* I hadn't seen such a car in a long while nor someone to come along just for driving it.

Taking a deep breath, I asked Miss Hazel inside as graciously as I could, hoping she wouldn't be distressed by my efforts at housekeeping so far. Sarah ran up to her, staring, and I shooed the girl outside to Sam, hoping to keep her away from the spice of Miss Hazel's tongue.

"Been cleanin'?" Miss Hazel asked immediately, eyeing me over the brim of her glasses.

"Yes, ma'am," I said. "There were so many cobwebs and—"

"For the life of me, I can't see how you can live with yourself!" the old lady suddenly proclaimed. "Movin' in here and actin' like it's yours, without payin' a dime! If I'd have known you wasn't talkin' of buyin', I'd have never sent you Emma's way! The old girl just doesn't have the sense to turn you out."

"Mrs. Graham wanted us to stay," I defended. "She talked my husband into it."

"You're a bold one, you are! As if it weren't your own idea to go beggin'! I know all about it! George Hammond thinks you're sufferin' in silence after your husband's notions, but Emma told me it was you come in with your sweet sob story and convinced her to give you the place!"

I stood for a moment, stunned. Was Mrs. Graham having second thoughts? Was she angry at us? "Miss Hazel,"

I dared ask, "is Mrs. Graham wanting us to leave her farm?"

"She ain't got the sense for that, girl! You've got her plum convinced you're decent folks needin' her handout! It's about the same as thievin', to my mind!"

I looked down at the floor. "She has blessed us," I said softly. "And we're grateful. Would you like a glass of water? Or a cup of spearmint tea?"

"You've got nothin' to give me that ain't Emma's," she snapped. "You're even using her dishes." She walked to the kitchen counter where I'd left plates and cups to air dry on a towel. "I remember when Willard bought her this set. Nothin' means much to you, does it?"

"You're wrong. You think you know us, but you don't."

"Well, I asked if you were Christian. Remains to be seen, I suppose, if you'll show your face in church."

"I would love to attend, Miss Hazel. But is there one closer to us than town? We haven't a car or a team."

"You tell George I said to bring you. Then you'll have no excuse."

She turned her back on me and headed for the living room. I hustled to follow her, but not wanting to rankle her further, I held my tongue. She was a difficult sort, one who was pleased to be displeased, as far as I could tell. She eyed the boxes we'd carried down the stairs and lifted a throw pillow from the top of one.

"I helped Emma pack these boxes," she said. "Of course, she didn't want to; just wanted to leave everything sittin' out, you know. But things is a lot safer from tramps out of sight this way." She set the pillow down and turned to me. "The worst thing 'bout what you're doin' is to get her hopes up like this. Rita McPiery's been her friend for as long as I have. She's better off there than bein' took care of by strangers! She ain't been good. What will you do when she comes down sick again?"

"I suppose we'd get the doctor."

"With no car and no horse? You're not even thinkin'! Or else you don't care. You just want the place, that's all, and come up with a way to get it."

Little needles jabbed about inside me, up and down. *What will we do if Mrs. Graham gets sick? Run for George Hammond and his wagon?*

"You know it don't make sense, her comin' out here," Miss Hazel continued. "It's cruel to lead her on about it. It's a good thing George come and told me or you might have got the thing done."

She started to walk away from me again, toward the bedroom, and my hands started shaking. She may have had a legitimate concern for Emma's well-being, but she was overstepping her bounds now.

What right did she have to decide we couldn't do this? What right did George Hammond have even bringing her in on it?

"Miss Sharpe, Mrs. Graham's of sound mind. We'll talk about this, and her health. It'll be her own decision if she—"

"You mean you think you can talk her into it, no matter what I say?"

"No. I mean she's no child. And we just want to help her be happy."

"You want this farm. That's what you've wanted from the start! It's thievin', no matter how pretty you paint it up to look! You make yourself an old lady's friend just long enough to get her name signed to papers. That's what you want, ain't it? If you had the deed, you wouldn't be talkin' to bring her here, now would you?"

"Yes. And we're not asking for a deed. It's enough that she's let us stay."

Miss Hazel stomped into the bedroom, muttering something under her breath. She looked in the closet, ran her finger along the top of the little dresser, and then turned her attention to the window. "This was Emma's room."

"It still is."

She wheeled around and gave me the most intimidating glare I'd ever encountered. *That poor pastor's wife,* I thought. *It must be terrifying to have this woman for a piano teacher.*

"You bet it still is," she hissed. "Not yours or no one else's until it gets sold, fair and square. I'll see to that, mind you. No matter what you say 'bout Emma and her decisions. She ain't seein' clear already, havin' you stay without so much as a red cent!"

"I was hoping you'd be of help," I said softly.

"Oh, I will be. But not to you."

"I meant to Emma," I pressed on, hoping to find a way to make friends. "Tell me about her illness. Or, if you would—"

"You've got frightful spunk about you! You should go back where you come from, if they'll have you!" She pushed her spectacles up on her nose and brushed past me in a huff. I followed her again, and we got to the kitchen just as Sam was opening the back door.

Oh no, Sammy, I thought. *Terrible timing. She's a wildcat liable to bite and scratch on her way out that door.*

He looked at me but didn't have time for words before Miss Hazel lashed out again.

"Mr. Wortham! What kind of a person are you? You should be supportin' your wife and young'uns, not letting her connive against an old woman like this! There ain't a thing wrong with decent work. A man ain't worth a plug nickel without it! You should be 'shamed of yourself, trying to steal a place instead of earning it!"

"I never stole a thing in my life," Samuel said solemnly. "And Juli doesn't connive. She does pray for folks, though." He surprised Miss Hazel and I both with a fine smile. "May I escort you to your car?"

Miss Hazel bristled. "Are you throwin' me off Emma's place when I've knowed her more years than you've been alive?"

"No, ma'am," Sam answered courteously. "It just looked as though you were leaving. But you're welcome to stay. Juli'd be glad to fix you some of her leaf tea, and you can have dinner with us if you would, though I can't promise what we'll have on the table."

The old woman just stared at him and then slowly turned her eyes back to me. "You're up to something," she said hesitantly. "I won't be a part of it." She took another step toward the door.

"You're welcome to visit anytime," Sam said, careful to step out of her way. "Forgive me for not greeting you in town the other day."

"Ashamed to face me, you were," she told him bitterly.

"Yes, ma'am. I suppose you're right. It's not easy being broke with a family. And you're right about work. If you hear of any jobs available, I'd thank you to give me word so I can apply."

"Pray for us," I added, feeling a warmth inside as I saw fresh color spread over Miss Hazel's face. "Pray for Mrs. Graham too. We're so grateful to her."

Without another word, Miss Hazel hustled outside, gave a quick glance to Sarah sitting on the porch, and then rushed across the yard. The young man by the car had to move quickly to open the door before she got to it. And they were gone as quick as they'd come, leaving a lingering cloud of dust in their wake.

Sam put his arm around me. "Herman said I should help you."

"Herman?"

"The driver. Her nephew. He said she talked all the way here about how she was going to set you straight. Are you all right?"

"I'm fine. And she can't do anything, Sam."

"We'll take what comes, whether she does or not. A lot of people may feel the way she does, that we're taking advantage."

I stepped away from his arms, my hands clenched, the heat inside me uncomfortable. "It's none of their business, Sam! We've done nothing wrong! It's only Emma Graham's business and ours! God has blessed us. He's going to bless her too, and nobody has a right to put their nose in!"

"That doesn't mean they won't."

I turned away. I almost snipped at him that Hazel Sharpe was only one person, and surely most people would have the decency to let Emma Graham make up her own mind about things.

But then I saw Robert making his way toward us through the trees, and I held my tongue. He was running, holding high three fish on a string like there was nothing that could make him more proud. I could see his smiling face, and I thought of all the good Miss Hazel was missing. *Why do some people insist on looking for the bad?* I thought. Oh, if she could have seen my son's delight, my daughter's contentment! If she could have seen Samuel's face the night he told me he'd welcome Mrs. Graham! She didn't know us. She didn't even try. And I could scarcely believe she really knew Mrs. Graham either.

Maybe it was Miss Hazel's snippetiness driving me, but I couldn't wait a week to go back to Belle Rive. I didn't want to ask George Hammond to take us to church, or to talk to anyone else until we'd had a chance to sit down with Mrs. Graham again. So the next day, with a bundle of field daisies and lavender lilacs from Mrs. Graham's front yard, we set out, getting a ride from Barrett Post, a nearby farmer.

I was just as nervous as the first time we went to see Mrs. Graham. Sam and I had agreed that before we made any further plans about Mrs. Graham coming out to the farm with us, we'd better make sure that's what she really wanted. Miss Hazel had a point about us being strangers.

I let Sarah hold the daisies, since she'd picked them for me. She was delighted to be seeing Mrs. Graham again. She'd drawn her a lovely picture of the apple tree with a smiling Robert sitting on one limb and waving.

But Robert wasn't smiling now. He didn't like going back before we were expected. He didn't like what his sister had told him about Miss Hazel. He thought we might be asked to move on, just when he'd begun to feel at home. He sat in the old truck with his shoulders humped and his eyes on his scuffed shoes.

"Boy oughta be in school," Mr. Post said in a deep baritone that revealed a hint of disapproval.

"We just came to the area," I explained. "He'll be starting as soon as we're settled. Where is the school from here?"

"'Bout a quarter mile south of Curtis Creek, over on Persimmon Ridge. Nice little old schoolhouse been there three generations."

Mr. Post was so stiff and unsmiling that I didn't tell him I wasn't sure of his directions. We'd be sending Robert to school with Will Hammond when the time came, I supposed, if the Hammond boy went to school. "We'd like to meet the teacher," I told him. "We've been doing what we can in the middle of travel, but it's high time Robert was in a classroom again."

My son turned to look at me. "Hope we'll be here long enough."

"Well," Post said, turning and looking at Robert with some understanding, "a boy needs to be planted, that's a sure thing. Gotta have your roots in good soil to.grow, that's what I say." He smiled for the first time and took a deep breath, like he was getting ready to unload something important. "You'll like the teacher, I reckon, son. But not too awful much. Elvira married my brother when

110

I was in the school m'self. She started her teachin' way back then. She's a fine'un, but she packs a lot of starch. I done m' best to lighten her up, bringin' snakes and craw-daddies in my lunch pail. Had me haulin' the water for three months at a time, she did. Don't take the tomfool-ery off nobody else, neither. She's a good'un for figures, though. And she counts it a true enough lesson if a boy's gotta miss a day to put in seed or bag a turkey for his fam'ly."

"Don't the girls go?" Sarah spoke up. "I wouldn't bring no snake."

Mr. Post laughed. "Sure, there's girls to go. But you're a mighty little thing. Better wait till fall, at the least."

We learned that Mrs. Elvira Post, wife of Clement Post, was a fine piano player and sang on occasion. She made the best blackberry jam and something called corn pre-serves, and she ended every school year with a program of songs and the reciting of poems. Church was once held on Sundays at the schoolhouse, but for twenty years now people had gone into Dearing, for lack of a second preacher.

Mr. Post was amiable the rest of the way, and Sarah seemed to like him. She showed him she could count to twenty-nine and spell her name out loud. Duly impressed, he invited us to his farm one evening to meet his family, including Clement and Elvira, who lived "'bout a stick's throw from the back fence." But he didn't say anything at all to Samuel until we got into Belle Rive and stopped in front of the boardinghouse. Then he gave Sammy a stern look and told him to do right by Emma Graham.

"She's mothered a whole lot of the countryside," he said. "It wouldn't set too well, her bein' taken 'vantage of."

Samuel shook the man's hand and thanked him for the ride. He turned to leave, but Mr. Post wasn't finished.

111

"Went to school with her boy. He was the finest soul you'd care to meet. I spent a lot of time over to Graham's place when we were growin' up." He shook his head. "I know the times are changin' and Emma won't be 'round much longer, but it don't feel right, somebody else out to her place. We'll get used to it, though. Long as it's done proper."

"I'll do right concerning her, Mr. Post," Sam promised solemnly. "You have my word."

"I'm hopin' you make good," the man replied. "For Emma and your young'uns. But you got at least one neighbor don't trust you for it. He come by yesterday, or I wouldn't even knowed you was out here."

Sam said nothing, but it made me boil inside to think of George Hammond traipsing around, telling everybody what he thought of us. He'd told us he had to stay home with his pregnant wife, so I wondered how good his word was. But more than that, I wondered how many people already knew about us and what kind of things they'd been told.

We soon stood outside Rita McPiery's door, waiting for someone to respond to the clank of the brass knocker. Rita had come so quickly when I had been there before that I worried she was not quite sure how to receive us. We knew Miss Hazel had been there. Who could tell what she might have said?

Finally the door opened, and Mrs. McPiery greeted us with a shy kind of smile. "You come on now and see Emma," she said. "I told her you were here."

I wanted to be a blessing so badly I could taste it. I wanted to make the dear old lady smile. But my feet wouldn't budge until Sarah put her little hand in mine. What if Mrs. Graham was angry? What if she thought we'd been trying to cheat her all along?

I put one foot in front of the other, but I was sure my knees were shaking as we went through the green and yellow living room liberally draped with crocheted doilies.

Mrs. Graham looked almost fragile when Mrs. McPiery opened her door, but she had a tiny smile.

"Mrs. Wortham, Mr. Wortham, come in."

Sarah let go of my hand and went running up to her like she'd known her forever, daisies flopping precariously from one hand. Thank the good Lord for an uninhibited child!

"Well, what's this?" Mrs. Graham asked, her smile for our daughter widening. "You got flowers for ol' Emma?"

Sarah dropped the daisies carefully in the woman's lap and went fishing in the oversized pocket of her gingham dress. "That's not all," she declared proudly. "I drew you a picture too!" She produced the work of art, which was folded twice and crumpled. With careful effort, she opened it up for Mrs. Graham to behold.

With steady fingers, Mrs. Graham held Sarah's drawing toward the window's light. I looked at the woman's hands, so wrinkled and spotted with brown. *She's held a pitchfork and spade as surely as her sewing needle,* I thought. *She's milked cows and shucked corn, raised a baby to manhood, and buried the ones dearest to her. How could my child's little picture ever compare to the booklet we'd found, so carefully saved, of handsome drawings by her own handsome son?*

Mrs. Graham was quiet for a long time. Finally Sarah could stand it no longer. "Do you like it? I sure hope you like it, 'cause I did the bestest I could."

Mrs. Graham lowered the picture slowly and patted Sarah's shoulder. "It's one of the finest things I ever did see," she said. "Did you mean me to keep it?"

"Yes, ma'am," Sarah answered with her eyes bright.

"I sure am glad of that. And thank you. It's been such awhile since I had somethin' new. Is this m' apple tree?"

"Yes, ma'am."

Julia's Hope

"Does it really look this pretty out there right now?"

"It's prettier than my picture," Sarah freely admitted. "I don't draw trees so good as Robert does, 'cause he's older."

"Likes to climb too, I see." She smiled and looked up at Robert, who ducked his head.

"Well, that's the best thing a tree's for," Mrs. Graham declared. "I'd go climb it m'self if I could." She looked up at me with a tender moistness in her eyes, and I knew she wanted me to talk, to tell her about why we'd come back so soon. I could see the questions in her.

"Mrs. Graham . . ." I looked up at Sam, and he took my hand. For a moment, I didn't know how to start, so I just held out the sweet-smelling lilacs to her and watched her take in their delicious fragrance with a long-lingering sniff.

"Oh, Mrs. Wortham, this is m' most favorite flower in the world! Unless it be the roses. They both smell so good! Here I been hopin' m' violas have done all right. I used to baby them so, but these are God's gift to spring, they are. Make you glad to be alive."

She called for Rita and asked her to put the flowers in water. After Rita had come and gone, Mrs. Graham looked up at me with some sadness. "I'm glad you come," she said. "I wasn't expectin' you back so soon."

I glanced at Sam again, and he squeezed my hand, somehow understanding how speechless I felt.

"Mrs. Graham," he said, "we're so glad for what you've done for us, it just didn't seem right. You lived there an awfully long time, and we know how much the place means to you. We've got a lot of work to do yet, but—"

"It's your house!" I burst in. "It's your farm! Oh, Mrs. Graham, if you want to come home, we'll help you! We'd be there every minute and make things nice as we can!"

"You know we've got no money," Sam added. "I've got no car either, to take you about. It might seem awful foolish, when you've got a nice enough place here, ma'am,

114

but it would be wearing at me. I'd feel guilty if we didn't offer and do all we can towards it, if that's what you want."

Mrs. Graham looked us both over, the wetness still clinging to her eyes. "Did Hazel come and see you? She told me she would."

"Yes, ma'am," I said. "I guess you know she doesn't think very much of us."

"Hazel's herself, child," Mrs. Graham said. "Ain't nobody else like her." She looked down at her lap and reached out for Sarah's hand. "You're not bound to do nothin' for me," she said in a soft voice. "All I said was to fix on the place."

"Yes, but—"

"No," she said firmly. "Don't let Hazel worry you none. We had an agreement, we did, before she ever come in the picture. If I want you on m' farm, that's my business. I offered it to you, and as long as you're willin' to work at it, I ain't takin' it back."

"But Mrs. Graham," I said, rather surprised at her words, "don't you want to go home?"

Mrs. Graham let go of Sarah's hand, laid down her picture, and turned to the window. I thought she was going to speak then, but she said nothing for several minutes.

"We understand you hardly know us," Sam finally told her. "It'd be awfully hard to put yourself in such a spot, I can see. But we don't want to just take what's yours, Mrs. Graham, and give you nothing. If you don't want to live out there with us around, I can understand, but let us find a way to do something for you. Come and visit, if you can. I would've never imagined a stranger being so generous with us, ma'am, and it bothers me not being able to return you a favor."

When Mrs. Graham turned around, a tear had traced one of the many deep, furrowed lines across her face. "Hazel had things turned 'round backwards, Mr. Wortham," she said. "I knew she did, but she don't listen to me. You're decent people. I knew that when I saw you."

"We have a lot to thank you for," he told her. "Even if we couldn't stay another day, it's been a relief to have a place for the kids to lay their heads."

"It can't be too nice out there, with so little furnishin'. And filthy too, I 'spect, if the door was left open."

"It's not filthy anymore. And it was better than another day begging rides, anyway. A lot better than having my children look at me, wondering if we'd be sleeping in a ditch someplace. It's been a godsend, and I know better than to think I deserve it."

Sarah put a hand on Mrs. Graham's shoulder. "Mama says you're an angel. I want to live at your house forever and ever, and I want to give people stuff like you do, when we get enough."

Mrs. Graham gave her a soft little smile and looked over at Robert. "You're a quiet one," she said. "What do you think about your folks tellin' me I could move out to m' farm again?"

Still staring down at his shoes, Robert took a deep breath. "I wish you would. We'd make it all right, and maybe everybody'd leave us be there for a real home. I never liked a place better in my whole life."

He glanced up for just a moment, but before Mrs. Graham could reply, he spoke again. "We don't eat real good, ma'am, but we always got somethin'. And we're willing to share, just like you."

Mrs. Graham turned her deep gray eyes to me, and I felt something shaking inside. "You've all talked about this, then?" she asked.

"A little. But we had to talk to you before we went any further."

"I told you, you got no obligation." Mrs. Graham lifted a hanky I hadn't noticed before and wiped her eyes. "I ain't a whit minded to ask you to leave, whether I ever see the farm again. I figure you're just what that old place needs. Some life again."

She suddenly reached her hands toward Sam and me, and we stepped forward, feeling equally uncertain. "You're good people," she said. "And I'm sorry you're strugglin' the way you are. If I had a pantry full of vittles, I'd send 'em with you today. But I want you to tell me now and tell me true. Not having to, not one bit, would you still want me out there with you? Would you?"

My hand was shaking in hers and tears filled my eyes. But it was Sam that spoke, clear and strong, and without a moment's hesitation. "Yes. I'd take you today if we had things fit."

I saw the shudder run through her and then the tears. She pulled herself forward in her seat to give Sam an enormous hug. "I used to do ever'thin'. Even help with the babies, you know. But I ain't no good no more," she said. "Not at nothin'."

"You could order me around," Sam offered. "I'm lost on a farm."

"Hazel'd be fit to be tied!" Mrs. Graham exclaimed. "She'd think I gone completely off m' rocker! She'd think I lost m' brains down a hole in the groun', leavin' Rita's when we ain't but two blocks from the doctor!"

That caught me up short. "That's a real concern," I said quickly. "I know a little about nursing the sick, but we want you to consider everything and do what's best."

"You know what Doc Howell does when we call him? He lays me to bed, if I ain't there already! There ain't nothin' else he can do. One of these days, I'll have a spell with m' heart and it'll be m' last, and there won't be nothin' he nor nobody else can do. The good Lord has his time for us to move on, and it don't scare me."

She turned toward Sam. "I'm gonna call Rita and have her fetch Daniel. He'll take us out there in his delivery wagon, I know he will."

Sam bowed his head. "I want you to come, I really do. But I need to get the place in better shape first—"

117

Julia's Hope

"Roof still on the house? Floor intact?"

"Yes, ma'am."

"Then don't you worry. I ain't a hothouse veg'table. There's nothin' out there can bother me! And don't tell me you got no food, 'cause I know that already from what your boy said. You were serious, weren't you? 'Bout me comin'?"

"As serious as I've ever been. It's your home and you belong there."

She gave us all a beautiful, sparsely toothed smile. "Then don't you worry. We'll help each other." After planting a quick kiss on Sarah's forehead, she reached for her cane and banged it on the floor. "Rita!" she called. "Rita, come and reach me m' bag! I'm goin' home!"

SIXTEEN

Samuel

I never dreamed we'd be taking her that day. But she was as excited as a child, insisting there couldn't be anything about the condition of the house to dismay her too badly. "We have plenty of time till winter," she said. "Plenty of time to make things fit."

She gave Robert and Sarah a book of pictures to look at while she ordered Juli and me around the room, picking up this thing or that. She was delighted, there was no question, and we soon learned that Hazel Sharpe had told her what we were thinking after she'd heard it from Mr. Hammond. And Mrs. Graham had been hoping it was so, believing in us all the while.

There was no doubt she meant to move home and meant to stay. There was also no doubt that she'd already talked it over with Mrs. McPiery, who seemed only mildly surprised and nearly as pleased as Emma.

Julia's Hope

Juli and I put clothes in one bag and sewing things in another, both of us wondering if we were really ready for this. But Mrs. Graham's enthusiasm was contagious, and we soon relaxed.

"We'll stop by Kelsey's for kerosene on the way out," she said. "Got to have me a lamp to see by. I sure hope the outhouse is still standing."

Juli giggled. "It is. And Sam cleaned it out already. It was just full of spiders."

She nodded knowingly. "It don't hurt to keep a few of those around. Less flies that way." She picked up her Bible from the table. "Put this in with m' clothes. It'll ride soft in there." She scanned the room, thinking. "Daniel won't have room for ever'thin' this trip," she informed us. "But we can take m' rocker. I gotta have that, you know."

Half an hour later, Mrs. McPiery's brother pulled up outside with his truck, and we loaded Emma's rocker and three bags of belongings out of her room. "We'll get the bed later," she told Julia, but immediately turned to the burly man who was to haul her things. "You'll get the bed and the rest of m' things, now won't you? Rita knows what's mine. You bring 'em out just as soon as you can."

Daniel Norse only smiled and scratched at his overgrown beard. "Where's the chickens?" he asked.

"There ain't but four I can claim," Mrs. Graham declared. "We enjoyed the others when the snow was flyin'." She turned around to Robert. "You want to go help Mr. Norse fetch m' chickens, son?"

Robert just stared for a moment, every bit as surprised as I was. "You got chickens?"

"I've always had chickens. I was keepin' chickens when I was the size of your sister. She can go and help you, if it's all right with your mama."

I was dumbstruck at this old woman who had her plan in action all around us. "You're bringing chickens with you?"

120

She gave me an odd look. "You got nothing against 'em, I hope. They're good layers."

"No." I glanced over at Julia, who was carefully folding Mrs. Graham's near-done quilt. She didn't look up at me, didn't say a word. But we both knew it was just what she'd wanted. Just what she'd trusted the Lord to provide. What kind of pull did my wife have with God, I wondered, that she should get her desires handed to her this way? Next thing it would be a milk cow.

I shook my head as Juli sent our children out back with Mr. Norse to watch him catch and pen Mrs. Graham's hens. Just then Mrs. McPiery strode up to us with two bundles.

"I got the seed I promised you," she said. "There's salsify too, and a bit of string bean."

Juli was glowing. "Thank you so much."

"Don't be strangers, now," the woman said with a tearful kind of smile. "You let me know if you get to needin' anything out there. Emma, I'll be comin' to see you time and again to make sure you're takin' care of yourself." She put both bundles in Julia's hands but turned and faced me. "I sure appreciate what you're doin'," she said quickly. "I never seen Emma so happy. There's not many folks would do what you're doin'."

I shook my head again. "It's nothing much—"

"She told me she same as gave you the place, Mr. Wortham," she said, taking my arm and giving me a scolding look. "You could've gone on your business with your fam'ly, enjoyin' your home, and thought nothin' more for Emma. But it's right Christian of you to consider her this way. You don't know how hard it's been for her, livin' here."

"That's enough now," Mrs. Graham cut in. "Would you mind gettin' me m' coat and m' sorry old boot? And bring me up two or three jars of them peaches we canned last year. The kids'd like 'em, I'll bet."

Rita smiled and gave her friend a hug. "I'm gonna miss you, Emma Jean."

It took a good while to leave Belle Rive. Emma Graham and Rita McPiery had a right to their good-bye, and they chose to say it proper over a cup of weak coffee and a slice of pumpkin bread. The chickens were clucking in their crates in the back of the truck, but I was in no hurry to go, even when the sky grew heavy with clouds. God was at work, and who was I to rush anything? I sat on the porch swing, praying that Mrs. Graham would be all right with her decision and that we weren't all being fools about the whole thing.

When the kids had finished the generous snack Mrs. McPiery had given them, they climbed up on the swing with me, one on each side. They were delighted with the old swing's sound effects and kept it going just to hear the creak with every push forward and the groan with every glide back.

"I'm going to be cooking for Emma," Julia suddenly said, as if the thought had just sunk in enough to worry her.

"I don't expect her to be particular," I said, trying to assure her. "She knows our situation."

"Yes. And she's bringing laying hens. Did you see Rita stick in that old rooster too?"

"I saw that."

"She's bringing peaches too, Mom," added Robert, who didn't miss a lick. "And she's got money, 'cause she's planning to buy kerosene."

Juli turned and gave him a stern look. "We'll never ask Mrs. Graham for money. Not for anything. Not ever. Do you understand?"

Robert frowned. "How come? She said we'd help each other."

"She's already helped us," Juli insisted. "She's given us enough."

"We'll have to work together out there," I told the kids. "There are a lot of things Emma can't do for herself, but she'll know what should be done. So you mind her good whenever she tells you anything, all right?"

Robert nodded briefly and turned his attention back to the swing. "You could make one of these, couldn't you, Dad?"

At first I was struck by his confidence in me, something I thought he'd long since lost. But then I took a good look at the swing and saw that he was right. I could make one, if I were to take the time. Or I could make a couple of chairs of similar design, which the sitting room really needed and which Juli could plump with cushions. Doing things for the house wouldn't be a real problem for any of us. It was the barn, the land, and the possibility of livestock that had me worried.

In a few minutes, Rita's brother carried Mrs. Graham out to his truck and set her in the front seat. She didn't look too heavy, but I wondered what it was going to be like tending after someone who couldn't get around on her own. I could see myself carrying her outside to sit in the sun. But then my thoughts turned to her husband's grave, which lay about a half mile from the house and across some rough ground. Sure, the place was a pretty spot, but I expected it would be an uncomfortable experience to be carried so far.

We all piled in the back of Mr. Norse's truck with Mrs. Graham's rocker and bags and the five protesting chickens in three separate crates. Then Rita came running out of the house with a box. The box looked awfully heavy, so I jumped down to take it from her arms and saw that it was filled with jars of home-canned peaches, beans, and such. I looked into the woman's face, feeling a mixture of gratitude and shame.

She must have known. "Before you say anything, now, Mr. Wortham, I gotta tell you that Emma helped me put all this stuff up. She's entitled to it, and you're entitled to it too, on account of you're gonna be keeping her place up and doin' for her now. Don't you be thinkin' poorly for it, you hear? We all need each other, and that's how the good Lord intended things to be."

How could I argue with the good Lord? At least out loud. But I still felt about eight inches tall, accepting her help. It had been awhile since I'd been the one feeding my kids, and it might be awhile longer.

I found myself thinking that maybe Mrs. Graham could spare me from her farm. Maybe there was some kind of job around there, even if I had to leave my family and go clear down to Marion to the mine. I'd do something. I had to. I couldn't live on Mrs. Graham's kindness and Juli's ingenuity forever.

"I'll tell my church of you, if you don't mind," Rita announced. "Sometimes they gives new folks a basket or some such, to help 'em get started." That was just what I needed. Another handout. I set the box of jars securely behind a chicken crate and thanked the woman, knowing I shouldn't be so bitter. She was only trying to help, and Lord knows we needed it.

I sat down in the open back end with Juli beside me. Sarah crawled into my lap. With a last series of waves, we left Mrs. McPiery and her boardinghouse behind. Julia started singing as we bounced across the countryside. And before long, we were passing through Dearing, where Mrs. Graham merrily waved at everyone she saw.

We were almost home. With an eighty-four-year-old woman and an impossible hope. My mother wouldn't be the only one to laugh me to scorn for this. The neighbors had already started. They would be looking out for Mrs. Graham, though. Looking real close.

SEVENTEEN

Julia

I loved watching Mrs. Graham enjoy herself so much. She seemed to know everybody we saw on the way and would pester Mr. Norse to honk his horn at near all of them. She even made him go past her church, just to show us where it was, and she beamed with pride when Sarah said it was pretty.

"M' husband, Willard," she said, "he helped put the steeple up."

I wondered if she'd be wanting all of us to ride to services with George Hammond. Lord, how we needed a car!

"I hear they got a new preacher," Mrs. Graham added. "Sure hope he's fiery. Ol' Hazel will give him the devil if he don't stand up and tell her what for now and again."

I couldn't help but smile. "Ol' Hazel" hadn't dampened Mrs. Graham's spirit, that was clear.

We stopped at Dearing's only service station, which we hadn't seen before because it was at the end of the street going west and past some houses. The station had kerosene around the back, and Mrs. Graham introduced us to the attendant, who affectionately called her "Grandma."

"Had him in Sunday school," she explained. "I was always Grandma to 'em if they needed one."

"Nice to meet you," the young man told us with just a smidgeon of distrust in his eyes. "Hope everything works out all right." He took Mrs. Graham's hand. "Good seein' you again. Will you be makin' it to church? Sure would be a blessing."

"We'll find us a way." Mrs. Graham smiled. "It ain't easy gettin' nowhere no more, but I gotta get back there, at least once, to meet the preacher."

Mrs. Graham's young friend looked at us for a minute and then looked at the hand-painted lettering on Daniel Norse's truck that announced him as a chimney sweep from Belle Rive.

"You need a ride on Sunday, Grandma?" he asked.

"My goodness, Charlie, you know George Hammond's an awful lot closer than you are!" She opened her purse and handed him a dollar.

"George Hammond has his wagon full already, and they may be away awhile, what with Wilametta fixin' to see the stork 'fore long." He looked down at the money in his hand and calmly passed it back to her. "I'll pay your bill 'cause it's so good to see you again. And I'll pick you up Sunday too. All of you, if it's all right. I got me a car, and it's got a backseat."

"Well, bless you, Charlie Hunter!" Mrs. Graham exclaimed. She turned to look at me. "Ain't he the nicest boy? Sure is gratifyin' to see 'em come up fine."

"That's very kind," I said to Charlie. "We would certainly appreciate the ride, if you're sure you have room."

Sam threw me a look of dismay, and I knew he wasn't anxious to set himself before people's faces, even in a church. What would Hazel Sharpe have to say? How would the other locals react to us? Certainly, it would be easier to keep to ourselves.

"We need to meet folks," I told Sam with a bit of uncertainty. It might be scary the first time, especially if it was the kind of church where people did more looking at you than talking to you.

But he nodded and hugged Sarah. "It's the thing to do. You like Sunday school, don't you, pumpkin?"

"'Specially when they talk about Daniel," Sarah declared. "And him being stuck in with lions!"

Mrs. Graham nodded her approval, and we thanked Charlie again for his generosity. Then we were on our way. We went past the library we'd never yet managed to visit, stopped and waited for a young man trying to pull his mule out of the road, and then were out of town.

Mrs. Graham turned to look a moment at Robert. "You like Sunday school too?"

"Only sometimes."

"Now, Robert—" I started.

"Don't be scoldin' a boy bein' honest," Mrs. Graham said. "There's been times I ain't liked it too well myself. Admittin' so ain't wrong, in the right company, at least."

"What's the right company?" Sarah asked innocently.

"Your folks mostly," Mrs. Graham answered. "And a few others you're especially close with. But don't be tellin' the preacher he's dull as old paint, and don't be tellin' the teacher you'd rather be fishin'. That don't wash. You understand?"

Both kids nodded and giggled at the same time. "Do you still teach Sunday school?" Robert asked.

"Lands, no. I've not been there in such a time. Guess it's Bonnie Gray for the youngsters now. It'd be a sight more than I could handle anymore, I expect."

Julia's Hope

"You haven't been to church?" Sarah asked in surprise.

"Oh, I've been. But not m' home church. And it just ain't the same. Rita goes to the Methydist in Belle Rive, and they's good enough folks. I just always look forward to m' own, you know. I come forward and asked to be baptized when I was about eight, and they took me out to Ollander's pond the very same day and dunked me. I reckon I've been happy ever since."

"Does it hurt?" Sarah asked.

"Does what hurt?"

"Gettin' dunked."

"Oh, Lordy, no! You just go down and then you comes back up, and everybody hugs on you like it was the greatest thing they ever saw happen! And I reckon it is too, when you think on it."

"I like swimming," Robert volunteered. "But it don't sound much like swimming."

"Oh, when they have 'em a baptism in summer, sometimes they make up a picnic, and the young'uns all go swimmin' after. There ain't nothin' to beat that for good fun, that's for sure. They used to dunk 'em out to our pond now and again, after Ollander's got sold. And I'd be busy then, makin' pies for all the folks."

We were quiet for a moment, letting Mrs. Graham reflect on the happy memories as we turned onto the country road where we'd nearly been stranded by the storm.

Mrs. Graham suddenly sat up straight. "I ain't even seen the place in such awhile! It's not gone down too bad, now has it?"

What would she think was too bad? "We've been working at it," I said. "But it takes awhile."

"Oh, I know it. Growed up in weeds, I bet, ain't it?"

We reached the end of her lane and none of us said a word. Mrs. Graham just looked and kept on looking after the truck had stopped as near to the house as it could go.

128

"You want I carry you inside?" Mr. Norse asked her.

"I'm in no hurry for that," she declared. "Just look, will you? Ain't it the best thing there is, now, a farm so good and peaceful? The house, it don't look too much different. Barn's a sight. But that's an old barn for you. They don't live forever. Maybe we can take down the east side and save this here end. You think so, Mr. Wortham?"

"It sounds reasonable, Mrs. Graham," he said. "But I haven't the slightest idea how to manage it."

She turned and looked at him. "Well, now. You're honest as your boy is. I like you both for it."

Mr. Norse had gotten out of the truck. "Where do you want your chickens?"

"Put 'em in the coop," Mrs. Graham declared and eyed Sam again. "Have you looked about the coop? Is it sound?"

"Yes, ma'am. I think so."

"Good," she declared. "Best shut 'em in it till they pick 'em a roost and get used to it. So they don't wander too far."

Mr. Norse took hold of a chicken crate and started for the henhouse. Sam jumped up and followed him with another crate, and then Robert jumped up too.

"Can I take the rooster?" he asked me.

"Sure," I told him. "But keep back at first if they let him out. He may peck."

I wondered about Samuel and the chickens. Would Mr. Norse expect him to turn them out of the crates? Samuel had never had chickens and had never touched one that wasn't dead. What would he and the kids do when the time came to butcher one?

That was one of many things they'd learn, I decided, but it was not for worrying on now. It would be awhile before we could butcher. We'd need more than four laying hens, that was certain. And thank God for Rita McPiery's rooster! We could have a brood before long.

129

When Mrs. Graham was finally ready to get out of the truck, the strawberry patch interested her most. With her two canes she hopped in that direction, with me beside her, wondering how in the world to help. Mr. Norse came out of the chicken house and ran toward her, giving me a frightful look.

"Mrs. Graham, now let me get you where you're going," he said quickly. "You don't have to do that!"

"Let me be!" she said, stopping him short. "I was managin' 'fore I ever met you, Daniel, and I ain't gonna be pinin' for them strong shoulders to haul me around once you're gone home! This is my farm, and I'm gonna get myself around all I can out here, even if it kills me!"

Samuel had followed Mr. Norse from the chicken coop and was looking at me gravely. I knew what he was thinking. *What if she overdoes herself or falls and gets hurt? What have we gotten ourselves into?* And I couldn't help thinking about what Hazel Sharpe had said about Mrs. Graham not having real sense. What if she was right, at least in some small way?

Mrs. Graham got as far as the shed, stopped to catch her breath, and dropped one of the canes. I tried to pick it up for her, and she waved me back, then dropped the other cane. Quick as anything, she slid down to her knees and looked up at me with a smile. "Now don't you worry. Ol' Emma's been exactly in this spot afore."

Moving slow and looking at the yard around her at the same time, Mrs. Graham began to crawl along steadily toward the strawberries. "They says you go back t' your youth when you're old," she said with a chuckle. "Ain't all bad either. I found me a viola already." She stopped and pulled a handful of grass from around the tiny flower I hadn't even noticed.

"We'll get us a trowel later and put this at the garden's edge," she told me. "It'll get cut here for sure."

Why the little thing was so important to her, I failed to understand, and I wasn't the only one. Behind me, Samuel and Mr. Norse were both watching her in silence.

"Whatcha still standin' around for?" she demanded of them suddenly. "You might just as well be takin' m' things inside, now don't you think?" She turned her eyes to me. "You be sure and draw Mr. Norse a drink before he goes. Nothing wrong with the well pump is there?"

"Oh no, ma'am," I answered nervously.

"Sure wish you'd call me Emma regular," she said. "Would sound nice comin' from you, and the young'uns too. Sarey, come here and help me look 'round for m' hop toad."

Sarah ran to her from where she'd stood in silence, holding my hand.

"Hop toad? You got one of your own?"

"I find me one every year," Emma said with a smile. "Put him smack in the middle of m' garden and there he stays, keeping back all the bugs he can eat."

"He's in the basement!" Sarah announced with excitement. "I seen him there!"

"Well, now. That's a fine place for one too. I'd leave him alone and hope for another out here. The more the merrier."

She glanced over to see that the men were unloading but still watching her. She sighed. "I must be an awful sight to behold. Ain't it so, Mrs. Wortham?"

"You just surprised us, being so determined. And please call me Julia."

"I told Rita I'd be back the day I seen m'self burdenin' you. I ain't gonna be carried all over. I ain't havin' it."

"You've got to let us help you."

"I will. When I need it."

She crawled on into the patch of strawberries. "Well. This ain't as bad as I expected. Could be a decent crop yet. Might have to beat off Wilametta Hammond with a stick."

She sat down among the plants and began pulling weeds like she could think of nothing better to do with her first few moments home.

Robert came up beside me with a long white feather in his hand. "What she needs is one of them chairs with wheels."

I put my arm around him and nodded slowly, not thinking she'd heard. But she had.

"Nobody around here's got one," she said. "Not even the doctor. And I ain't got the money to be orderin' such a contraption."

"How much is it?" Robert blurted out before I had a chance to stop him.

"I don't remember. Too much, that's all."

My son walked past us toward the porch. He said nothing more, but I could see how Emma's admission had shaken him. Somehow he'd expected her to be our cushion, with money to see us through, even though I had told him not to ask for any. I wished I could tell him not to worry so much.

"Don't you fret, now," Emma said, telling him for me. "The good Lord provides everythin' we can't do without, and a plenty more besides."

She turned to me when she got no response from Robert. "He's ahead of his years some, ain't he? Far as thinkin' ahead, I mean."

"Maybe so."

"Nothing to worry about. He'll be a fine fella one day. Maybe even a preacher. Leastways, somebody to want to help folks, I'll bet."

I saw Robert's sideways glance at me and the question in his eyes. Preacher? He wanted to make bicycles or maybe radios, if he could do it off by himself, without people looking on.

When Sam and Mr. Norse came out of the house to get the last couple of bags, she looked up at me again. "Would you mind getting Daniel a bite or two when he's finished, Julia? It'd be the kind thing to do, seein' as he brung us out here. Open up some peaches if you ain't got nothin' else cooked. And make sure he has himself a drink."

"I'm not sure he'll leave till he sees you into the house."

Emma shook her head. "I'll go in if it makes him happy. I'll be wantin' to take a look at it anyway. But I'll be comin' right back out, where folks belong on such a day as this. Ain't it the finest weather? Fetch me m' hat, will you, Sarey?"

Sarah's head popped up in surprise. She looked at me, and I told her where Sam had put the gardening hat we'd found. I didn't know of any other hat.

I felt a little funny, leaving her among the strawberries, but she assured me she was fine. And she'd given me a job to do. Feed Mr. Norse. And if I was going to do that, I ought to feed him more than Mrs. McPiery's home-canned peaches, at least for appearance's sake.

I ended up asking Mr. Norse to dinner, but he politely declined. All he ate were some peaches smothering a syrup-soaked biscuit, which he said was a fine treat.

Emma was sitting in her rocker in the sitting room when he left. She stared a long time at the big bare windows and then announced that she didn't want me to put her curtains back up.

"It'd be a shame to cover all that sunshine," she said, "and have anything at all in the way of m' view. Just got 'em years ago 'cause folks thought you ought to have 'em."

She was well satisfied with the way I had fixed her room, with the lace doilies and one of the kerosene lamps on the dresser. She propped Sarah's picture up on one of the doilies, but she didn't have a mind to unpack her bags or go through any of the things she'd left behind. True to her word, she wanted to get back outside.

Samuel helped her to the garden, where she inspected our work with a frown. "You done all right with what you

133

had," she said, "but the ground ought to be cultyvated better'n that if you want some fine eatin' out of it." She looked up at Samuel. "You're gonna hafta go over to George Hammond and get me back m' push plow."

I knew Sam didn't relish the idea of marching up to the neighbor and asking for anything, even if it was the return of Emma's property. But he took her simple directions with no argument and started off with Robert at his side. I busied myself by helping Emma with her renewed attack on the weeds in her strawberry patch, while Sarah went looking for toads beneath the newly spreading rhubarb leaves.

I had expected something different from Emma's first day home. Maybe that we would just sit on the porch and talk awhile or go through more of her boxes and put things away. Or that she'd want to inspect the buildings or find a way out to her husband's grave. I wasn't sure what to think of this down-to-business Emma who seemed to have nothing on her mind other than garden work. She was hardly even saying anything now, just pulling weeds here and there like she had nothing else to concern herself with.

I would have liked to talk while we worked. It would have made me feel better. But instead I just prayed awhile, hoping we were doing the right thing. And then I heard Emma sniff, and I looked up to see that she was crying.

"I never thought I'd get my hands in this good old dirt again," she said. "I could just kiss you. And the good Lord too."

E I G H T E E N

Samuel

I was halfway through the woods to the neighbor's house and wishing I could have gone the opposite direction. I was pretty sure George Hammond would give up the push plow for Emma's sake, but just as sure he wouldn't have much good to say for me.

Robert was excited, though, to meet some of the other Hammond children and see where they lived. He talked about fishing with Willy on that precarious board stretched over the pond and how good those fish had tasted.

Soon we were close enough to hear a child squealing, and a big black dog came bounding toward us with its mouth open.

"Boomer! Boomer!" a little voice called, and in no time, a girl no bigger than Sarah burst out of the bushes after the dog. She stood for a moment, staring, and I told her my name and asked where I could find her father.

"Pa's in the woodshed with Franky again," she announced with a bit of a giggle. "He tipped over a whole bucket of cream."

We followed her into the farmyard, where two boys smaller than her were playing tug-of-war with a muddy length of rope. One of them stopped when he saw us and ran his stubby little legs into the house, and the other one came right up to Robert and said hello.

"I'll get my pa," the little girl offered and took off toward the two rickety buildings behind the house, yelling all the way.

I was surprised by the looks of the place. Piles of boards and rusty old implements I could not identify were scattered about in the weeds. Three sheep were tethered in the front yard, to eat the lawn short, I supposed. And the whole place smelled like pig.

The house was no bigger than Emma's and in much sadder shape, though it'd been lived in all along. I couldn't be sure if it had ever been painted. The side door with its torn screen came creaking open slowly, and a tall girl poked her head out.

"Mama can't get up right now," she hollered. "But she sent me to see what you're needin'! Are you come from Emma Graham's place?"

"She asked me to see your father," I answered, feeling sorry for this girl, who probably had a lot on her shoulders.

It wasn't long before Mr. Hammond came hurrying from the hog lot, wearing knee boots and a big straw hat. "Sam, ain't it?" he yelled when he saw me and then didn't wait for my answer. "Harry," he said to the little boy now clinging to Robert's hand, "take your friend up to the barn. Willy and Kirk's in there."

Robert looked up at me. I waved him on, figuring it was harmless to let him have a few minutes' time with other boys.

136

"Whatcha need?" George asked.

"Emma sent me for her push plow. It's pretty important to her to have a good garden."

He straightened his hat and eyed me fiercely. "So you got 'er done, did ya? You got Emma back home?"

"Yes, sir. That's what she wanted."

"Fine arrangement you made fer yerself! Gonna milk her dry 'fore she leaves this world, ain't you?"

His accusation made me sick inside, but I refused to address it. "Can I get the plow?"

He smiled in an ugly, cold way that made me want to hit him. "You know what to do with it, do ya?"

"With a plow, you plow," I huffed, unwilling to admit that I'd never used one. "Where is it?"

"Ain't no hurry, now," he said. "Shoulda brought the wife, so's you could all meet the fam'ly."

"She'll come another time," I told him, calming myself. "I expect she would like to meet your wife."

"Ah, Wilametta's 'bout beside herself to think of a woman so close over there again. I figure Posts is close enough, or Muellers. But ya know how women is, wantin' another one close 'nough to walk to easy. If she wasn't 'bout to pop, she'd a' been over there already."

"I'll tell Julia how anxious she is to meet her."

"You do that. How's Emma?"

"Seems fine. Anxious to see the garden finished."

He looked me over again and shook his head. "All righty. Her plow's in the barn. Wasn't finished with it, but you can have it. Wouldn't want her sore at me."

He walked with me to a barn nearly as rickety as Emma's, and I could hear boys in the loft above us. The plow was a one-wheeled contraption with long handles. I'd seen one once in Harrisburg on the lot of a young family who grew tomatoes and cabbages to help make ends meet. But this plow was rusty and rough and looked like it could fall apart.

"Can she get around at all with them canes?" George asked me.

"Not very well," I told him. "I'll be doing the plowing."

He smiled and nudged at the plow bar with his foot. "Gotta get this part deep in the dirt," he said. "Or you ain't done nothin' but took a stroll."

"I know."

"Reckon you can pack 'er home?"

"Yes, sir."

"Whatcha plantin'?"

"Turnips and pumpkins. Lettuce. And beans." I didn't say anything about the salsify, because I wasn't sure what it was.

"Ain't puttin' in corn? I remember Emma bein' one to love some good roastin' ears."

"It's in the ground already."

"Plantin' corn afore lettuce," George mused. "Now there's somethin' new."

Julia might have understood the reason for his amusement, but I didn't care what he thought. I just wanted to leave his property so I didn't have to listen to him anymore. The plow wasn't any bigger than a bicycle, so I just picked it up with one hand and turned for the barn door. "Come on, Robert! We need to get back!"

"The boy kin stay awhile," George told me.

"He's needed at home."

"Well, I reckon he would be, at that."

There was laughter in Hammond's eyes. I knew it, and I had no patience for it. I wasn't so much of an idiot that I deserved his ridicule. I called for Robert one more time and started walking.

Robert climbed halfway down the loft ladder and then jumped the rest of the way, followed by Willy, little Harry, and two more skinny boys who must have been Franky and Kirk.

"Can we go fishin'?" one of the boys asked.

"Get yer chores done first," George told them. "Then get 'nough fer supper or it ain't worth you goin'."

"Can I meet them at the pond?" Robert asked me.

"Later," I told him. "We've got plenty of other things to do first."

We said good-bye and started into the woods, followed by the two littlest Hammond boys. Finally, I turned around and they hid behind a bush. "Go home," I commanded. "You're too young to be wandering out here on your own."

"No, we're not," Harry spoke up. "I'm five now, and Bert's almost three."

"Go hug your mama," I told them, shaking my head.

"Mama told us to play outside," Harry insisted. "We wanna come to yer house."

"Not today," I said as sternly as I could. "You get your father's permission some other time and one of your older brothers to bring you."

"All right." Disappointment was obvious in the voice of the little boy who fancied himself old enough to do as he pleased. They both stepped out of the bushes, and I could see that Bert had his thumb in his mouth.

"Go home," I told them again. And without another word, they turned and walked away.

"It'd be neat to have so many brothers," Robert said.

"Sometimes," I acknowledged.

"Can I go to school with Willy and Frank next week?"

"We'll talk to your mother, but I think she'll like that idea."

"They don't go all the time in the spring," Robert explained. "Not when they got anything else to do. And they don't go in the winter neither, when the weather gets bad, nor when their pa's harvesting, 'cause they help."

"Sounds like they don't get there much. That's not good, Robert."

"Once I know the way, I can go without 'em."

"I expect you'll have to."

We walked awhile in silence, and then Robert looked up at me with his eyes so serious I almost stopped walking.

"Emma needs one of them chairs with wheels. Remember Mr. Heddesy? He got one."

"Yes, I remember." I set the plow down and considered. "That would help Emma. A lot. But they probably cost a lot of money too." Mr. Heddesy had been the president of a large bank in Harrisburg. His whole family was rich and could get him whatever he needed. No problem. But we were in no such position.

"It wouldn't be too hard, would it?" he asked me. "I mean, to make something like that? You could do it, couldn't you, Dad?"

His question stunned me. "I don't know, son. That would take some figuring out."

"But you said you could make a porch swing. It'd just be smaller, with wheels underneath. And I'd help."

I saw the urgency in my son's eyes and was amazed at his trust in me and his hope for Emma. "Let me think on it awhile, all right?" I asked. "There's not much to work with out here."

"She really needs it, Dad. I wouldn't want to go crawlin' around outside."

I sighed. "I'll try, okay? I've never done anything like that before, so don't mention it to anyone yet. I'd hate to have her disappointed."

"Okay, Dad."

Satisfied, Robert started walking on, and I followed him with the plow in my arms and a new burden in my heart.

Julia was making dinner when we got back. Something smelled good, but I had no idea what it was.

Emma sat at the table, pulling pot holders and hand-dipped candles out of a box. Sarah was on the floor, cradling raggedy Bess in a dishcloth.

140

"Emma told me where to find poke in back of the barn," Julia said, as if that would mean something to me. I assumed she meant we would be eating the stuff, but I didn't care what it was or where she'd found it. I gave her a hug, glad she'd left the cookstove to greet me.

"Sit down," she admonished. "We'll be ready to eat in a minute. Long walk?"

"No." And I meant it. If I looked tired, it was because of the weight of George Hammond's scorn and the challenge of Robert's request. There were so many different ways to fail here.

"He give up the plow all right?" Emma asked.

"Yes, ma'am."

"Did he mention anything else?"

"Uh, no. Except that his wife is wanting to meet Julia."

"I'll bet she is. Loves to talk, that girl. And she loves m' strawberries too. Won't be long 'fore she sends one of her youngsters up, just to spy how near to ripe they've come."

Julia turned around. "They're starting to turn now. Is that a problem?"

"I don't suppose so. Reckon they need all they can get. She's been used to all of 'em, though, since I've been gone."

I glanced at Julia and squirmed in my seat, feeling even more uncomfortable with the neighbors than I had before. Let George Hammond farm the field, Emma had said— they needed it. No doubt. But still, that field was Emma's. And suddenly I was feeling very protective.

"Do they give you anything for the use of your land?"

Julia looked at me with horror, but Emma just laughed and set me straight. "My 'greement with Hammond is 'tween us," she said. "Don't reckon you need think on that business just yet."

I nodded, not wanting to say another word. But Emma wouldn't let me by so easily.

"They's right enough folks," she insisted. "Just got their ownselves on their mind. And they can't help it. They got to make a livin', same as you been tryin' to do."

Julia began setting dishes on the table, and I moved my elbow out of the way, wishing I could disappear. "Forgive me, Mrs. Graham."

Emma surprised me by reaching over and patting my hand. "Nothin' to worry about. I know George ain't tickled at me just now. He prob'ly thinks like Hazel, that I done somethin' stupid, comin' back here. Might be scared too, 'bout what I aim to do with him. But he'll come 'round, and you'll end up friends, just wait."

"Will Miss Hazel come around?" Julia asked timidly.

"She'll come 'round snoopin'." Emma smiled. "She'll be out here 'fore too long, tryin' to rescue me from somethin' or other. But she ain't nothin' to worry 'bout. All bark. And I always do whatever I please anyhow. Makes her madder'n a hornet."

I hadn't realized there was anything but green beans and peaches in those jars Rita McPiery sent, but Julia had boiled home-canned pork with some dumplings, and it was the best thing I'd had in weeks. We had poke shoots on the side and the rest of the jar of peaches Juli had opened for Daniel Norse. It was some real eating, but I was anxious to get done and get back to work.

"It's gettin' late," Emma told me. "Ain't you folks from the city? I didn't figger you'd be accustomed to workin' after supper."

Julia only smiled at such a thought, but I replied, "When there's work waiting, I'd rather get to it. I'd like to plow while it's still light, so we can plant first thing tomorrow."

Of course, Emma thought this a grand idea. And she wanted in on the work, even if she couldn't do the plowing herself. So I helped her outside, and Robert brought a chair. She just sat and happily watched me plod back and forth, pushing the plow through the heavy soil.

"We've had that plow a good long time," Emma told me. "An' I kep' it nice. But it looks like George left 'er in the rain a time or two. I'll not thank him for that."

I said nothing. I knew better than to stick my nose in again.

"You had a garden before?" she asked.

"Julia has. She planted a few things in our yard in Harrisburg."

"She's a fine lady. You been blessed to have her."

"Yes, ma'am."

I turned a corner and plodded on. Pushing the plow wasn't too bad, but it was harder than the tomato farmer back in Harrisburg had made it look.

The evening was hot, which didn't help matters. After awhile, I stopped to pull my handkerchief out and wipe away the irritating little band of sweat that had formed across the bridge of my nose.

Just then Emma took a deep breath and looked up at me. "She's been blessed as much, Samuel."

I stopped for a moment. It had been a long time since I'd dared to consider Julia blessed, about me at least. I gave Emma a halfhearted nod. "I'm sure Julia would have the decency to agree with you."

"Now you listen here, Sam Wortham."

I turned in surprise at the sudden touch of fire in her voice.

"Of course she's blessed! I can plain see it's just how she said! You've a mind to work when you get the chance, and the good Lord can't ask for better than that! You can't be blamin' yourself for the hard times! He'll bless the work of your hands, he will!"

I shook my head. "Then he'll be blessing your garden tonight."

"That's all right by me," she said. "An' it oughta be all right by you too." Her smile was timeless. She was one who knew what she was talking about. And I should listen. I should listen and learn. "One thing at a time," she continued. "You're faithful here, and he'll give you more. You just trust him."

"That's not easy sometimes," I admitted.

"Well, if it was, I don't reckon it would be worth much."

We were silent again, and I plowed on, stopping only to set a rock at the garden's edge. Of course she was trying to encourage me. I understood, but I wasn't sure it was helping me. Emma had blessed us, but I couldn't help but think that if we'd never met her, we'd probably be at Dewey's now, overstaying our welcome and trying to decide where else to go. That meant it was Emma's faithfulness, or possibly Julia's, that had us where we were. Certainly not mine.

Emma was pondering again, and when she finally spoke, it seemed to come clear out of the blue. "You got a brother in prison. What'd he do?"

That took me by surprise. Julia must have told her, though I couldn't imagine why. "He robbed a house while some people were gone away."

She was studying me now with real question in her eyes. "You ever steal things?"

I couldn't help but smile. I couldn't blame her for wanting to be sure about me. And she was entitled to an answer. "No, ma'am," I explained. "I guess I saw my big brother caught enough to be afraid it would happen to me. There wasn't anything else stopping me back then, though. Till I knew the Lord enough to care."

She sat there, nodding, and I suddenly felt like a child. "When is it you come to know him?" she asked.

"I was almost twenty. And I'd just met Julia. I wanted to marry her right away."

"Then you b'come Christian so she'd a'cept you?"

"So I'd accept myself, maybe. Thinking I could touch such a sweet little thing." Such an admission made me stop and shake my head. "I shouldn't talk like that. There was more to it. Julia wanted me to love the Lord, sure. But it came alive to me, you know what I mean? I'd heard about Jesus before, but it was just a story."

Emma was nodding and smiling, clearly enjoying at least this part of our conversation. "I know just what you mean. When I was a little girl, Mama would tell me stories all the time, and that's just what they was—nothin' but stories. Till old Herman Taft pointed his finger and said Jesus shed his blood for *me*. Oh, it just made me tingle inside, it come so real."

I smiled, wondering if Herman Taft had been the preacher. And that made me wonder what Emma's church would be like. And the people. They must be either very dedicated or else half crazy to let themselves get dunked in a muddy old farm pond. Emma was a sensible woman, and I couldn't quite picture her stepping down into a gooey mess like that. Did they wear their church clothes right into the muck?

"Are you comin' to church on Sund'y?" Emma asked, as if she knew my line of thinking. "They'll just love ya, I know it."

I wasn't at all anxious to go to church and meet Emma's friends. Not because they might be so different in their ways, but because of what they might think of me. I shook my head.

"They'll love the kids," I told her. "They'll like Julia fine too. But they won't take to me so well. There'll be some who'll say I'm worthless. And taking what's yours, besides."

"Oh, fooh! I'll set 'em straight if I hafta! And don't you sell 'em short 'fore you ever meet 'em! There ain't many that's as much to bicker and carry on as Hazel Sharpe is,

God love her! Most of 'em is the nicest folks you'd ever care to meet."

"Like the Hammonds?" I asked with one eyebrow raised.

"They's just themselves. Like Charlie Hunter. Now that's a fine boy."

I went back to my plowing, and before long helped Emma and her two canes back into the house. Julia had made what she called "root coffee" from some chicory she'd dug down by the road. Emma drank it up while I sat and watched the two of them talk like they'd been best friends for years. I finished my root coffee, told the kids a story, and then went back outside.

It was dark already, but with a shining full moon. I walked down to the barn, asking the Lord why I still felt so out of place. A hoot owl was calling somewhere nearby, and I thought I saw something small and quick run into the barn for safety. Not a mouse this time; it was at least three times that size. I followed the thing in, even though I didn't know what I'd do if I found it. *Do they have ground-hogs around here? Or skunks?*

With the moonlight pouring through the door, I could still see in the old barn, but I didn't see anything sitting there waiting for me. I could hear it somewhere, shuffling in the hay, but it wasn't showing itself. *Oh, well,* I thought. *There must be a thousand little critters running around the countryside that no one pays attention to. This one isn't hurting anything.*

I walked through the barn, wondering again how I'd ever approach the job of fixing it. Leave up the west side, Emma had said, and rebuild the rest. I went walking through that end and stopped in front of the old farm wagon. It wasn't near as big as George Hammond's wagon; the wheels only came up to the middle of my thigh. The wheels were metal, lightweight but sturdy as the dickens.

How two of them could have gotten broken, I'd never know.

I was just about to leave the barn when a thought hit me so sudden it gave me a tingling inside. I turned around slowly, almost afraid of what I was thinking. Robert was a good kid, but I'd expected to have to tell him there was just no practical way to do what he wanted. But there was a way. Staring me in the face.

I got down in the hay to take a look at the wheel axle, but, of course, I couldn't see it good, as dark as it was.

That got me thinking. I didn't want to work in the daytime on such a project. Better for the others not to know about it yet. At least not Emma. Or Robert, even though he wanted to help. Better to be sure I could do it before getting his hopes up.

I'd have to bring one of the kerosene lamps out sometime. I'd have to draw the whole thing out on paper first. And I might have to tell Julia. She'd be the one to follow me if I went to the barn night after night.

God help me, I began to pray. *Put the know-how in my head and steady my hands for the job.* A wheelchair. A way to bless Emma. A way to give something back. Thank God for Robert. Thank God for this old busted wagon. And thank God for Rita McPiery's porch swing or whatever got the thought started.

NINETEEN

Julia

Emma had said they were good laying hens, and she was right. There were two eggs first thing in the morning, and she said some mornings we could expect four. But we'd leave one hen setting for chicks soon enough. I could hardly wait for that. Eight or ten peeping chicks would be a decent start on plenty of eggs, and fryers later.

I gave the chickens some of the feed Rita had sent along and chatted at them fondly for a few minutes before I went back to the house. I'd have to ask Emma if she'd given them names. Seemed·like such important things ought to have names.

I carried our two eggs in like a prize and showed Emma. She'd been up with the sunlight, asking if I'd found any of Willard's old trousers. "I'm fixin' to work in m' garden again," she said, "and they'd be easier than m' dress to crawl 'round in."

She put on a pair of blue dungarees I'd brought from upstairs and then sat at the table, enjoying some more of my root coffee. She nodded with approval at the eggs.

"Let the kids have 'em," she told me. "Been awhile since they had good eggs, ain't it?"

I nodded to her.

"You know how to make a shortbread?"

"Yes, ma'am."

Emma smiled at me. "It'd be fine for breakfast under some more of Rita's peaches. You bring me the bowl, and I'll stir if you want. Won't be long, you know, 'fore we have fresh strawberries. Can't you just taste 'em?"

I turned to put a couple of chunks of wood in the cookstove. I thought of the many things I couldn't fix because we had no syrup, no grease, no milk, and very little of anything else. "Emma, doesn't it bother you at all?" I dared to ask. "Us having next to nothing?"

"You got nothin' to worry about, child. The good Lord'll provide, that's all. We'll be reapin' 'fore long. You'll see."

I reached for the flour and baking powder and a mixing bowl. "It'd be a good day to send Robert fishing."

"Not yet," she determined. "We gotta plant first. That's a job for the whole family, you know. Makes the garden belong to ever'body. Then he can go fishin'. I'd like to go m'self sometime."

I turned to look at her, thinking of the solitary grave out on the hill. "We can get you there today, Emma, if you want to go."

She quickly shook her head. "No. Not today. Got me aplenty a' things to do now, up here with you. Don't trouble yourself."

I was quiet, probably too much, getting back to cooking. Behind me Emma sighed.

"It's just I ain't ready yet to go see Willard out there," she said with sadness in her voice. "I wanna know you all a little better 'fore I start to bawl in front of ya again."

"Oh, Emma!" I spun around and took her hand. "Don't worry about that! It's the most natural thing in the world! We'll take you today!"

"No." She squared her shoulders and sat up straighter. "Not today. Got me the garden to think about. And plenty of other things, gettin' this place in order. Where's your husband?"

"He went out to the barn."

"Gotta have him look at that back fence for me. But first we'll have t' fix us a pen 'round the chicken coop today, so we can turn them hens out. I'd let 'em roam like I used to, but it's hard t' find the eggs thataway. You gotta put somethin' 'tween them and the foxes at night too."

I measured flour into a bowl and added a pinch of salt and a spoon of baking powder. *Sure would be nice to have some cooking grease,* I thought. *And a milk cow.*

"You know what we need 'round here?" Emma suddenly asked. "Milk for your youngsters, that's what. I'll have to have me a talkin' to that George Hammond! He plain knows we're here by now! He oughta have been right over yesterday, knowin' he's bound."

I looked over at her in surprise. "Bound? To give us some milk? Why would he think so?"

"He better more than think so, child! I give him m' guernseys when I left, though he couldn't pay a nickel for 'em. I told him we'd square up later and 'till then, they's still mine."

I set my spoon down, trying to remember if Hammond had said anything about having cows. "Maybe he sold them."

"He owes me cash money either way, now don't he?"

"Yes. I guess he does."

"Can't be too hard on the fella, though. He's got him a family to support."

"But if he told you he'd pay—"

150

"Then he oughta at least spare us some milk, if he's still got 'em," Emma concluded.

I turned back to my cooking without saying another word. That was between Emma and the Hammonds. But it sure seemed like George Hammond should have made some kind of effort to give Emma something before now, if only an explanation. Sam had said he wasn't too happy to give up the plow. Did he have more of Emma's things? Was that why he didn't like us around? Because he'd be called to account? Surely that was what Emma had meant yesterday when she said he might be scared.

I set the bowl in front of Emma and scooped some water out of the bucket to boil the eggs in. Emma stirred the shortbread and then dumped it into the baking pan.

"It'll stick like burrs on a dog's back, won't it?" she chuckled. "We can scrape it out today, but we gotta get us some lard. Maybe Samuel wouldn't mind fetchin' a few things from the store come Mond'y. I got a few more dollars."

"Oh, Emma. We owe you too much already."

"I never said you owed me nothin'. 'Sides, when you're cookin' for me, I'm fair obligated to keep 'round what I want, now ain't I?"

I turned toward her and shook my head. "You're too kind, doing such nice things for us. And letting Mr. Hammond by without paying you all this time. It's no wonder people think we're taking advantage. You'd give away your coat, wouldn't you?"

"Best get this in the oven," Emma said, handing me the pan. "Would you mind makin' up some more root coffee?"

An hour later, we were all outside. Sam and I each had a hoe and made furrows in the plowed ground. Emma and the kids put seeds in the rows, starting with the lettuce.

"Don't want them too deep now," she told us. "And when you come to the far end, that's where we'll put down the punkins. Don't need no rows for 'em, though. Just six

151

or seven good little hills." She looked up at Sarah and smiled. "It's the finest thing in the world, havin' all your help."

I watched her showing Sarah just how close she wanted the seeds spaced. Robert was moving ahead of them, anxious to get his seeds in the ground, but she called him to her side.

"Ain't no hurryin' these things," she admonished him. "What you're doin's worth doin' right. Come here, son."

Robert squatted down beside her. "Good Book says there's a time to ever'thin'," she told the kids. "A time to be born. A time to die. A time to plant. And a time to pluck up what's planted."

"When do you pluck up?" Sarah asked.

"I reckon that's talkin' 'bout weeds. Or else harvesttime, yes, when you clear the garden."

"What if you plant at the wrong time?" Robert asked. "Or sloppy and quick, like me?"

"Well, then the Lord can't bless the work a' your hands the way he would if ya done things in order. There's a season for ever'thin'. I like to think of that ever' time I'm plantin'. The good Lord has his ways of things, and the best we can do is work 'long with him. Like you all comin' out here, for instance."

She stopped to open up the bag of seed beans, and Samuel turned his head to hear her continue. "The way I see it is, you was plucked out of Pennsylvaney at the right time. And he brung ya clear 'cross them miles just to plant you here." She glanced up at me and then turned back and gave Sarah a little hug. "Your folks may not be seein' no daylight yet," she said. "But pretty soon they'll be settin' in some roots and pokin' their heads up a little. Just like the beans is gonna do."

Robert was frowning. "We planted corn some days ago, and it ain't even up yet. You suppose we done it wrong?"

152

"Takes time, that's all, child." She handed him a bunch of seeds and started him off in a new row.

"Are we really planted here?" Sarah asked her. "Like seeds?"

"Just as good as. And God done it too. Put you right where you belong so I could have your comp'ny 'fore I die."

"You're gonna die?" Sarah sounded worried at the sudden suggestion, and I had to stop and take a breath. Samuel was looking down into his dirt row.

"I'm fairly sure of it, child," she said. "But it ain't nothin' to be bothered about. I'll be plucked outa here and planted someplace better, that's all."

"When?" Sarah persisted, her eyes wide.

Emma was just starting to answer when we heard a rustling in the timber and the sound of voices. Emma perked up her head and looked at me. "Did you hear that?"

"Somebody's coming," I said, stating the obvious. "Probably some Hammond boys." They would be wanting Robert to go fishing with them. He'd been itching for it all morning.

"No, I don't mean that," Emma declared. "Them boys is comin' sure, but Lordy sakes, if George ain't sent us a cow 'long with 'em!"

Then I heard it, loud and clear through the trees. A low moo, almost a complaint, as if the beast were objecting to being dragged along.

Emma started to rise, but fell right back in the dirt. "I just knowed he'd do us right!" she exclaimed. "Praise be! Maybe it's ol' Rosey!"

We looked toward the trees where Willy Hammond and a big brother soon came out, leading a bony cow at the tail of a rope. Robert ran to meet them. Sarah jumped up in excitement. But Emma just sat there, staring at the animal. She shook her head. "Which one is it?"

Samuel looked at me and then back at the cow. I took his hand and waited for the Hammonds to come closer. As they did, I saw the disappointment in Emma's face. George Hammond had let her cow get scrawny.

"Bring her right over here!" she called to the boys. Then she turned to Samuel. "Help me up. Help me up."

Samuel lifted her while I retrieved her canes from the stone walk. She stood there in Willard's trousers with one leg rolled to the knee, the most dignified soul I'd seen in a lifetime of days. By the time the boys were close enough for her to see them, she was smiling.

"Lula Bell. What a blessing. This one was just a calf when I seen her last. But she's a lady now."

"Pa said to bring her to you to keep," Willy said. The bigger boy just looked at the ground.

"Well, tell your pa it's just too bad he couldn't come and bring her hisself this mornin'," Emma replied. "Would sure be fine to speak with him. And your mama too. But it'd take me to midnight gettin' through them woods."

"Mama can't be walkin' over, on account of her baby's due," the older boy spoke up.

"I know that, Joey," Emma answered. "But will you tell 'em for me, anyway?"

"Yes, ma'am."

But Willy was looking troubled. "Does that mean you won't be comin' over for the birthin' like you done for Rorey and Harry and Bert?"

Emma shook her head. "I been there for all of you, 'cept ol' Sam. But if your pa don't bring the wagon again, I'll be missin' this one, honey. I don't get 'round good no more. But don't you worry. Your mama, she'll be fine. Got a whale's share of experience, she does."

I looked at her in surprise. *She helps the neighbors with their babies too?*

"I'll fetch ya," Joey announced with conviction. "You oughts to be there."

"You make sure you ask your pa about it first," Emma admonished. "Then I'll be glad to come."

Joey Hammond leaned forward, took the cow's lead rope out of his brother's hand, and gave it to Emma. But he never acknowledged the rest of us standing there. "We best be goin'," he said, his voice low and solemn.

Emma patted the cow's nose. "She give you milk?"

Both Hammond boys nodded.

"You still got any of the rest of 'em?"

"Two more," Willy admitted. "They's all milkers, but Rosey's the best."

"Sold the others?" Emma asked again.

"To Jeth Mitchell couple a' years ago."

"Shut up, Will," said the older boy. "I tol' ya it's time to get home."

Emma looked up at Joey and nodded. "You go ahead. Tell your pa we sure do 'preciate him lettin' us have Lula Bell. And tell your mama hello."

"Yes, ma'am." The taller Hammond took hold of his brother's shoulder with a strong hand and turned him back toward the woods. Willy turned around enough to wave at Robert, and then they marched off together.

Samuel said nothing, but I couldn't be so easygoing. I took Emma's hand. "You can't let them get by with this."

"Now, child," she said. "He sent me a cow."

But I was hot inside. "*Your* cow, Emma! And he's got two more! And he sold some and never told you! You don't have to let him cheat you like this!"

Emma shook her head and smiled at me. "He's been feedin' 'em all this time. And he sure 'nough needs a good milker over there. He knowed he was obligated, seein' they's mine. But he's got to consider his own youngsters, you know."

"That doesn't excuse him never telling you. Never paying you a dime."

"Lula Bell's too close over here to m' strawberries. Samuel, will you take her over by the barn where the grass is thick and just tie her to that post? Lordy, we's got to check that fence over now."

Sam took the rope and stood studying the cow for a minute. Lula Bell was big even if she was thin, and I knew how awkward Sam must be feeling, being so close to her. But he gave a pull and they went together without much trouble to the barn. I watched Samuel tie her to the post and then jump when the cow came up close and stuck her nose in his shoulder.

"She ain't got milk till evenin'," Emma told me. "You oughta pull her some sweet clover and take it over there."

"You mean they already milked her this morning?"

"You can tell by the udders. But Julia, now, maybe they needed it."

I didn't say a word. Still steaming inside, I didn't want to blow my top over our selfish neighbor when it was Emma's business, not mine. But I hated that George Hammond was cheating her, using her, and claiming we were the ones doing so. I began to wonder about what Samuel had asked Emma before. Did they pay anything at all for the field? Or did she just let them by for that too, because there were so many Hammond mouths to feed?

It seemed crazy, me being so stirred by this. After all, she was giving to us too. But this was different somehow, and even Emma knew it.

I had a hard time putting thoughts of the Hammonds out of my mind. But we had to get back to planting.

"Lettuce goes 'bout quarter inch down, now," Emma reminded us. "Turnips just a little more. We don't wanna make them seedlin's work too hard findin' sun, you know."

"What's salsify?" Robert asked, reading the handwritten label on an envelope.

"Root 'bout as long as my hand. Real good for stew and such. Some folks say it tastes like oysters, but I wouldn't know 'bout that. Never did eat me no oysters."

Sarah had wandered over into the strawberry patch and was peeking around under leaves for a toad among the berries. "Mama, look!" she suddenly called. "A red one!"

"Don't pick it yet," I warned. "Let it get red clear to the tip."

Too late. She already had it in her hand. "It *is* red, Mama. Come see."

I went and found with pleasure that she had indeed discovered our first ripe strawberry. Looking around, I quickly found four more.

Emma was delighted. "Just a few days and we'll have to come out with a mixin' bowl! They'll be turnin' all over the patch. Oh, what eatin'!"

I handed her the berries I had picked. Sarah had already eaten hers. Emma handed one to Robert and ate the rest, obviously savoring the season's first taste.

"Don't none of you let no birds settle down over 'em now, or they'll be peckin' 'em up," she admonished us. "And you make sure and tell me if Wilametta sends any of them young'uns up here gawkin' at 'em. I'll give 'em a bowl or two, but they ain't pickin' the patch clean this year."

I felt myself steaming up again at the mention of Hammonds. *Lord, help me,* I prayed. *This is no way to live neighborly.*

"Sarah, come here." Robert was suddenly down on his knees in the dirt, looking toward the edge of the grass just a couple of feet away.

Sarah wasn't sure she wanted to trust him. "What for?"

"Just come here, will you? But not too fast. You'll scare him."

Sarah jumped toward him. "Who? Scare who? Show me!"

"Right there, silly. Right by them little yellow flowers. See him?"

Sarah ran straight for the sorrel flowers, and Emma laughed as a big toad and a little girl jumped at the same time, startled by each other.

"He's getting away!" Sarah cried in dismay.

"He won't go far," Emma assured her. "He knows where the garden is. He'll be sittin' under punkin leaves 'fore long, eatin' up them squash beetles. 'Least I hope he does that."

Emma stopped talking, suddenly staring into the green at Sarah's feet and looking as pleased as she could be. "Will you looky there! Julia, check where that toad was hoppin' and tell me if that ain't mustard coming up in the grass! Had me some go to seed years ago, but I figured they'd be done volunteerin' by now."

The plant truly was a mustard, as far as I could tell, and I marveled that a woman who couldn't see to thread a needle could pick it out among the weeds.

"Makes for good greens, you know," she told me. "Too bad there ain't scads of 'em all over the place. Dig her up, will you, and we'll plant her nice and easy at this end of the turnip row. Fetch me a bowl of water, Robert. They set so much better if you mud 'em in right."

Lula Bell let out a moo that made me jump. She just stood there, looking us over and busily chewing. I thought about the milking and wondered if Emma had ever used a stanchion. I didn't remember seeing one in the barn. Maybe she was on such good terms with her cows that they had always just stood still for her. I hoped that would work for me.

I went to get the trowel to move Emma's mustard plant, but I kept thinking about that cow. *Lord, give Lula Bell plenty of milk,* I prayed. *We need it, especially for Sarah.*

I glanced around the yard and finally spotted some clover, the red kind, though it hadn't bloomed yet. *I'd bet-*

ter do what Emma said and pull some for the cow, right after I plant the mustard in the garden.

There were two more little mustard plants coming up where the seeds must have dropped in the grass, and I set them all in a line at the end of the turnip row, like Emma had asked. Such a blessing, to have something up and growing already in that bare dirt. It made me wish for tomatoes and cabbage and peas. And potatoes. *Oh, to have lots of potatoes. Lord, we'd be all right then.*

Emma was down on her knees, tamping down the dirt over the turnips and lettuce. We put in the string beans and the salsify next, and then the pumpkin hills beside the rows where we'd planted corn. It made me feel so rich to look at that ground and know it was done. A garden was a promise from God, pure and simple. A little work and you reap the benefits. Just like it should be.

"Now, Robert and Sarey," Emma was saying. "It'll be your job to help me keep the weeds down come summer. Your folks is gonna have plenty 'nough to do."

I smiled at the looks on their faces. Sarah evidently thought it grand to be considered big enough for such an important task. Robert, on the other hand, made no effort to hide his distaste for the idea. But he knew better than to argue. He got up, brushed the dirt off his jeans, and frowned at me. "Can I go fishin' now?"

"After lunch."

Sam was putting sticks in the ground to mark our rows and the pumpkin hills. As I picked up our tools and the empty seed envelopes, the brown paper bag that had held the envelopes fluttered away in the breeze. I turned toward the barn after it just in time to see something small and gray scurry inside.

"Did you see that?" Robert asked.

"I surely did. And I think it was a cat."

"A cat?" Sarah piped up. "Where?"

"In the barn. Maybe. If that's what it was. But you stay away for now. If it claims the place, it'll get used to us after awhile. Probably half wild now, though, honey. It might scratch."

"Be a good thing if it is a cat," Emma added. "They keeps the mice down." She looked over at the cow lazily switching its tail. "We oughta send 'em somethin', you know, to thank 'em for bein' so generous."

I spun around, half expecting Emma to tell me she was joking. But she wasn't.

"I know you think he ain't been fair," she added. "But Lula Bell's a sight better'n nothin', you gotta admit, and he didn't hafta go that far. The good Lord'd have us to show kindness, even when it ain't the first thing on our minds."

"All right," I relented, still angry. "But what could we possibly give them?"

"I'll have to study on that. Not gonna be easy just yet to make a pot a' anythin' big enough to feed that crew." She rose to her knees with some effort and began brushing off Willard's trousers. Sam moved immediately to help her up.

"Get me to the porch," she told him. "Wish I still had me that swing."

"You had a porch swing?" Sarah asked, turning her attention from the barn to the house. In no time she spotted the hooks still in the porch ceiling. "We can get one," she announced. "And put it right there. Can't we, Daddy?"

Sam looked at me and then at Robert, who was suddenly smiling again. "It'll take awhile," he told the kids. "But I think I can make one. When we got time. All right?"

"Yeah!" Sarah squealed.

"You're turnin' out right handy, Samuel," Emma said. "If you can do that, I'll be braggin' all over Ham'ton County 'bout you."

160

We brought out a chair to the porch for Emma, then collected clover for the cow. Sam went past the cow and the barn toward the old fence, and I started walking over the yard, picking yellow dock and dandelion, then wood sorrel, flowers and all.

"Greens *again*, Mom?" Robert asked in dismay.

"We have to make do, Robert."

He scowled and plunked down on the porch step. "You know what I'd like? Chicken!"

"Robert John! We can't butcher till there's more of them! We'd be throwing away tomorrow to suit today!"

Emma nodded. "Your mama's got good sense. She does real good fixin', and we got no right to complain. Come here, boy."

Robert turned and looked at her with a frown. "I hate bein' poor," he said. "I wanta be able to buy store bread and jelly and a bunch of roast beef and stuff."

"Well, them days is comin'," she said. "Down the road a piece. Right now we can dream on it. Just think—we let one of them chickens set for a batch a' chicks, then another batch, and 'fore long, we got us a good flock. Plenty a' eggs ever' day. And come cold weather, we can be eatin' roast chicken to beat the band. This is the time for the green stuff now, though. You ain't gonna get much a' that in the winter."

"I'll be glad."

"Might get to missin' it when the snow's high, and wish your mama could get out and find you some wild lettuce."

I looked up at her. "You have wild lettuce around here?"

"Used to. Ain't seen none today." She smiled down at me. "You love it, don't ya, Juli, goin' out foragin'?"

"I would if it was just for fun."

"It is fun. Ain't no reason why we can't have fun 'round here. The good Lord sure ain't again' it. Robert, get you and your sister both a bowl. First one to fill it up with eatin' greens gets 'em a nickel."

161

"A real nickel?" Robert's eyes shone, and he jumped up and ran to the kitchen for the bowls.

"You needn't do such a thing," I told Emma. "They shouldn't be paid for helping."

"It's a game, that's all," she explained. "And I got me a nickel for both of 'em. We can send 'em to the store with Sam, and they can spend the nickels how they please, if you let 'em. It's good for kids not to worry, now. They ought not be thinkin' poor, even if they is."

I shook my head. "You can't be dishing out nickels every time they complain. I don't even want you taking your money—"

"Julia, honey. Do you see any other young'uns scattered over m' yard? Or anybody but your Samuel way over yonder?"

"No."

"I lost my only boy, but it ain't hard to dream that you're fam'ly. That I finally got me some grandkids. And a son and a daughter."

I could see her eyes fill with tears, and mine started too, just as Robert came bursting out the back door with the bowls in his hand.

"I ain't short a' nickels just yet," Emma went on. "I wish you'd just let me dream."

There was nothing I could think of to say to that. So I just gave her a nod and turned back to my picking. And soon Robert and Sarah were running over the yard, doing picking of their own. We had a big plate of greens that noon, and the kids ate them even better than they usually did.

I chose our Sunday clothes after lunch, one outfit apiece that was better than what we usually wore. Sarah's best dress needed some mending and mine was a sight for wrinkles. Both of Robert's pairs of pants were worn at the knee, but one not quite so bad; it would take a patch easily enough. And Samuel had one nice shirt, also in need of an iron.

I searched through some boxes till I found the iron Emma assured me was in there somewhere. Then I put the iron on the hot stove to heat while I finished up the dishes. Emma sat with her needle and thread and fixed Sarah's little dress while I spread out the other clothes on the cleared table to iron.

I had finished all of ours and started on a pale green dress of Emma's when we heard honking down the road.

I shook my head. "Somebody's leaning on the horn going past."

"They'll be turning in," Emma declared and laid aside her sewing to peer out the window.

Sure enough, a familiar-looking pickup truck drove up into the yard, and I saw a tall man step out of it. Barrett Post. With a covered pan in his hands.

Sarah was the first to greet him, and he sent her to the truck to retrieve something wrapped up in a dishcloth. I ran to the porch to ask him in.

"Louise figured you oughta have a housewarmin'," he said, looking past me. "Stars, you got Emma here a'ready."

"Barrett," Emma said with obvious pleasure, "come and sit, will you?"

I took the pot from his hands, and he pulled up a chair beside her. "Emma, it's good seein' ya. You're lookin' so good. You sure you're all right, bein' out here now?"

"Why wouldn't I be? Folks can only pine for home so long 'fore they gotta do something 'bout it or die."

I snuck a peek in the pot. A dressed chicken, ready to roast. Robert would be ecstatic.

Sarah ran up to me with her bundle. "Mama, I think it's corn bread!"

Mr. Post laughed. "Those is from Louise, now. You all enjoy 'em tonight. And no need returning the favor, seein's you're just gettin' settled and all." He turned back to Emma without the slightest hesitation. "They treatin' you good, are they?"

"The finest in the world," she declared. "You should just see how good they done puttin' in m' garden this mornin'."

I didn't want to intrude on old friends, so I ushered Sarah outside in time to meet Sam coming up from the barn.

"Who is it?"

"Mr. Post, remember, who took us into Belle Rive. But don't go in yet. I really think he'd appreciate having Emma's conversation alone for awhile."

"Not upset with us, is he?"

"He doesn't seem to be. Brought us a chicken and a pan of corn bread."

"It's a wonder," he said sarcastically.

"It's a blessing of God, Sammy," I insisted. "How's the fence look?"

"Pretty beat down. I'd better start this afternoon and do what I can with it, so that cow'll have some pasture. It'll take awhile, though. It's a good thing we've got a pile of lumber out there to work with."

He looked across the yard toward the henhouse and started walking to the shed. "Emma said to fix her chicken pen first. Do you know the way she wants it?"

"Pretty much."

He pulled the old roll of chicken wire out from the shed, and I was glad to see him so motivated to get things done. With Sarah trying valiantly to help, he carried the wire to the henhouse, where part of a fence still stood, going straight out from the back.

"We'll need at least one post over there to join to," I told him, "and then come back to the other henhouse corner." I heard a couple of squawks and the rooster's determined crowing. They were anxious to be out in the sunshine, I figured. Mr. Norse had set a rock against the wooden flap near the ground at the back of the coop. The flap would open into the fence soon enough, but if the chickens got out now, we might have a time rounding them up again.

Samuel had already tacked the wire on one side and was digging the posthole when Mr. Post came out of the house, looking for us. "Say, there! Most folks stop their work when they's got a visitor."

Sam looked up at him and nodded. "We figured you were Emma's visitor."

"She's fond of you. Ain't got no complaints. Speaks well in my book."

"Can I get you a drink, Mr. Post?" I said quickly, remembering I hadn't asked before.

"No. No, thank you, ma'am." He was still looking at Sam, and Sam was still digging. Sarah moved a little closer to me and then sat in the dirt, watching and listening.

"What you gonna do with that cow by the barn?" Mr. Post asked.

Sam took a glance in that direction. Lula Bell was still content, chewing her cud and watching us. "Emma said she's fine there, so long as she's got grass in her reach. I'll be moving her after awhile to the other side of the barn. It'll take some time to get the pasture fence in order. There's a good barn stall, though, to keep her in at night."

Mr. Post looked back toward the pasture. "Gonna be a fair 'mount of work," he agreed, "repairin' Willard's old fence."

"We were talking about that over lunch," Sam told him. "I'll be starting as soon as I get this done. Won't get very far today, though."

"Want some help?"

Sam stopped his digging and looked up in surprise.

"I got a guernsey heifer for Emma, if you let me and my boy come and work 'longside of you Mond'y mornin'."

Sammy sunk the posthole digger back into the dirt and then stood there, shaking his head. "Why?" he asked. "Why would you want to do that?"

"'Cause it needs to be done. Got to pasture your cows. You ever work fence before?"

"No."

"Sure will take you a long time alone, then. I'm wantin' to help Emma, and she's wantin' to see her place in order 'fore she passes on."

I shivered, to hear him speak of Emma passing. *Lord, no,* I prayed. *Not for many, many years. We need her alive and well and right here, telling us what for.*

"It's fine you helping Emma," Sam said. "But I'd be owing you for helping me at the same time. I ought to return the favor, but I'm not so sure I can. Especially when it comes to the cow."

Mr. Post seemed to understand that sort of thinking. "The cow's for Emma. As for you, I'll be needin' help on m' roof 'fore long. We can settle up then."

Sam smiled. "You'd trust me on your roof?"

"You done shingles before?"

"Yes, sir."

"Well, then that's a plus. I ain't gotta learn you." He stuck out his hand, and Sam took it. "You all come for Sunday dinner tomorrow, will you?" he asked us. "Want me to come for you?"

"Charlie Hunter's taking us to church."

He frowned. "Shoulda known Emma'd find herself a way to get up there." Mr. Post shook his head and looked us all over. "Have him drop you by after. Will you do that? My Louise'd be tickled to have you." He leaned down to pat Sarah on the head. "Don't you have a bigger fella 'round here someplace?"

Sam nodded. "Gone fishing."

"Good. He oughta go while he gots the chance. I was tellin' Elvira 'bout him. She'll be wantin' to look him over, for sure. He gonna start school next week?"

166

"We're planning on it," Sam said. "You may have to help us find the place. I'd send him with the Hammonds, but I'm not sure they'll be going."

"Can't say, that's true. They got their farmwork to do." Mr. Post gave Sarah another pat and went back to the house to talk with Emma a little more before going home.

Robert came back with two fish. We roasted them and the chicken, and the kids felt like royalty that night, eating so well. But Sam was quiet, even more quiet than usual. Overwhelmed, maybe, by a sudden friendship and an incredibly generous offer. Another cow for Emma. And fence work.

Emma beamed all through supper and hummed afterward as she tightened a button on her best sweater. It felt good to make her happy, to please her friends, and find the blessing of the Lord in it. Once Sam got used to the idea, I could see us prospering here. But I couldn't forget what Barrett Post had said about Emma passing on. The thought nagged at me, even while she was humming. *She wants to see the place in order. Before she goes. Before she leaves this world, and us, behind her. Lord have mercy.*

TWENTY

Samuel

Alone in the yard late that night, I thought of cows and chickens and fences and friends, and I very nearly cried. "It's too much, Lord," I said. "I don't know the first thing about cows. Or anything else around here."

Julia had tried her hand at milking Lula Bell and had gotten barely a quart. But that was better than nothing and more than enough to satisfy the kids. We were blessed, true enough.

But I had the future to face. And church tomorrow. Barrett Post didn't seem to care that I didn't know what I was doing, but there would be others who would more than care. They'd be outraged, like that busybody, Hazel Sharpe, and would do their best to drive some sense into all of us.

The thought of church in that little town made me so uncomfortable that I began to think of ways of getting myself out of it. *I could stay home to work on the pasture fence. Or check the roof on this house. It might need work too.*

But I knew that neither Emma nor Julia would think much of my excuses. Emma probably wouldn't like me working on Sunday at all, except to feed or water the animals.

Earlier I had carried in bucket after bucket of water for Julia to wash the kids. Then she'd helped Emma and cleaned herself up too. All in the big washtub, set right on the kitchen floor. Julia had expected me to wash in the water left in the tub and then haul it out to dump, but I couldn't bring myself to go in yet. The water was surely cold by now, but I didn't care. I didn't even care if I went to church dirty. It wouldn't make much difference to anybody.

Hazel Sharpe would be there, letting everybody know what a scoundrel I was. Taking Emma's milk and eggs for my own kids. Using Emma just to get help from her friends.

I was leaning against the apple tree, listening to the owl that was out again, when I heard the back door slowly open and close. In a moment, Julia was holding my hand, not saying a word but softly breathing beside me, her head resting on my shoulder.

"You think I'm a fool, Juli?"

She was quiet so long that I turned to look at her. Under the moonlight I could see the gleam of tears on her face. Finally she spoke. "No more than I am, Sammy, thinking this would be so perfect for us. What are we gonna do if something happens to Emma? Oh, Sammy, what if she dies?"

I took Julia in my arms, wondering what on earth could have upset her so. "Honey, she seems pretty lively. Up before us this morning and wanting to get right out to the garden."

"Oh, Sammy." I could barely hear her as she struggled to tell me what was on her mind. "Sammy, she looked so pale after her bath. I went and checked on her again after

I washed up, and she didn't want to tell me . . . but she was hurting. She was having pain in her chest. I helped her to bed, and she went to sleep. But it scares me."

She snuggled against me, and I held her, taking a deep breath of my own.

"What are we gonna do if one of these days she don't wake up, Sammy? She told me not to be thinking about running after a doctor. But it don't seem right, to do nothing. What do you think, Sammy? What should we do?"

"You think she's up to church tomorrow, or should we get Charlie Hunter to take her to Belle Rive to the doctor she knows? Would she go?"

"Wild horses couldn't keep her from going to church, that's what she says."

I couldn't help but shake my head. "That'd be beautiful, wouldn't it?" I exclaimed. "Us bringing her to church as sick as anything. They'll be hating us enough already."

"Oh, Sammy."

"I'm sorry. But we're making a mistake out here. We can't be responsible for a sick old lady with no car or anything. I should have known better. This is stupid."

Juli looked scared. "What are you going to do?"

"If she's got to go to church, fine. But then we'll take her back to Belle Rive, where she can get help. And we'll pack up and head for Mt. Vernon."

Julia shook her head.

"This was a nice break," I told her. "But it's not going to work with Emma sick out here. You know that."

"No," Julia protested. "She won't want to leave home again. She told us that when we brought her out here! She'd rather die."

"And she just might! And what would folks say then? Julia, this is not a sensible place to put ourselves in!"

"I don't care what's sensible! You promised Barrett Post you'd do right by Emma, and you're bound to that, Sam!

170

We've got to help her, not bring her back to Belle Rive again!"

"It looked like a pretty good place to me, Juli. Nothing wrong with it at all."

"But it's not what she wants. And not what we agreed to."

I turned away from her. Was I bound by my word to stay here, like she said, no matter how sick the woman got? Sure, she wanted to be home, but what kind of sense did that make?

I went in the house, grabbed the washtub, and wrestled it out the back door. It wouldn't matter now how dirty I got. Everybody'd be looking at Emma anyway. I sloshed the old water into the strawberry patch and then filled a bucket to take to the cow. Julia was still by the apple tree, wondering about me, surely, like I was wondering about her. How could she still be so impractical, thinking we should give Emma her way? She was the one who had come out of the house all upset over Emma's health. What did she want me to tell her?

When Juli finally went in, I couldn't manage to go with her. She'd be checking on Emma again first thing, and I didn't want to do that, not yet, to be sure I didn't end up saying something I shouldn't. I stayed in the barn quite awhile, but didn't even go and look at the wagon wheels or the pile of boards I could pick through and cut to make Emma's chair. What was the use?

Dreams can make you silly sometimes. They can make you stupid if you let them, blind to the truth of the simple way things are. You don't get something for nothing. Sometimes you don't get much of anything, even for all the hope in this world. And wishing can't change what's so.

TWENTY-ONE

Julia

Sam hardly got any sleep that night, and neither did I, hearing him go up and down so. Well before the rooster's crow, when I heard frogs off in the distance and a quail's call near our door, I rose up off the floor and slipped in to check on Emma.

To my surprise, she was sitting up with her frayed pink housecoat around her shoulders, looking out the window. She looked so gnarled and tiny and old. But happy. She turned her head and glanced my way.

"Some people near goes deaf when they get old," she said. "I'm so glad I still got m' good ears. It's a mercy the Lord give me, that's what it is."

"Emma, how are you feeling?"

"Near as e'cited as a child to be goin' to m' own church today! No place I'd rather be on a Sund'y mornin'." She eyed me critically for a moment and then shook her head.

"It's a beautiful mornin'. Gonna be one fine day, child! You wasn't thinkin' I'd waste it all lyin' in bed now, was you?"

I took a deep breath. "I was hoping not. But it worried me last night, you hurting so. I wasn't sure what to expect today."

She looked out the window again, toward the Douglas fir that stood at the timber's edge. "Them pains come and go," she said quietly and gave the bed beside her a pat. "Come and sit with me, will you? Is Samuel up?"

"Yes, but I'm not sure where he went. He was worried about you too." I sat beside her with some hesitation, knowing what Sam had told me last night. I knew it ought to be him in here talking to her. It would be easy for her to convince *me* we ought to stick things out. But Sam had the load of the world on his shoulders, and he didn't think things through in quite the same way as I did.

"Didn't mean to be scarin' you last night," Emma said quietly. "It don't scare me no more, I guess. I'm feelin' some better anyhow."

"Samuel doesn't like it, Emma, being so far from a doctor. He figures you'd be better off in Belle Rive again and us moving on."

Emma seemed to pale in front of me. "On account of the pains I had?"

"Yes, ma'am." I almost was sorry I'd said anything.

"Go get him. Find him, Julia. If I've come to be a burden already, I'll go back, but he's gonna know m' feelings on it first."

"Oh, Emma."

"Go on," she insisted. "Get him. Right this minute. Go on."

I knew of nothing I could say and nothing I could do but stand up with my heavy heart and go out and find him like she said. *Lord, move in this.*

Samuel wasn't in the house or on the porch. I could see the outhouse door standing open and there wasn't a sign of him in the yard, so I headed for the barn. It had almost become a refuge of sorts for him, strange as it seemed, since he never had much good to say about the old structure.

The frogs were singing a real chorus to us that morning, and somewhere from a tree I could hear a red-winged blackbird's sharp call.

"Sammy?" The barn doors were slid all the way open, and the dawn light had painted a patch of flaming gold on the old straw. *God, even a piece of nothing can look beautiful when you're in it!* I heard Lula Bell's soft moo, like she was calling to me from her stall. But I went past her, calling again for Sammy.

"Up here," he finally answered. "Don't make a lot of noise."

I couldn't imagine what could have drawn Samuel up to the one section of loft that looked strong enough to support his weight. But I eased myself up that old ladder, glad it was nailed right to the barn wall so it wouldn't shake.

"Samuel, what are you doing up here?"

"Ssh," he answered. "Look."

Nestled into the straw not three feet from him was a gray-striped cat giving suck to three tiny kittens. The mother lay with her head in the straw, looking a little uncomfortable with our nearness. She didn't seem big enough to be full grown. All three of the kittens were just as gray as she was.

"Wouldn't Sarah love this?" Samuel asked me, and I wondered what had come over him.

"Sammy, Emma wants to talk to you. She's sitting in her room, and she seems to be feeling better."

"I figured."

He didn't move.

"Sammy—"

174

"Pray with me, Julia," he said so softly that I could barely hear him. "I gotta make the right decision."

He took both my hands and kissed one of them so gently that I almost cried. I felt like telling him I didn't want to leave this place any more than Emma did. I'd just as soon live and die here, happy with the kind of life she'd had, the kids enjoying these kitties and everything else God sent our way.

But I said nothing, knowing it had to be his decision this time, like he'd said. We prayed together, and he rose out of the hay, brushed himself off, and started down the ladder.

"You coming back in, Julia?"

I hadn't thought to do otherwise, but now I shook my head. Maybe I shouldn't be there. Maybe I wouldn't be able to keep my two cents worth out of it. Sam knew how I felt. He didn't need to be hit in the face with it again.

"I better go ahead and get the milking done," I told him. "And check for eggs. Emma's just asking for you."

"Are you sure?"

I stepped off the ladder without turning to face him. "Of course I'm sure. Go on. She's waiting."

He went on without another word, and all I could hear was that quail again and the tender mew of a newborn in the straw above. Then Lula Bell started her lowing, and I wanted to sit down and cry. Just when everything looked so good. Just when things were coming around to fine, were we going to leave it all behind us? *Lord, does it have to be this way?*

TWENTY-TWO

Samuel

She was sitting on the bed, looking shrunken and gray. I stood in the doorway for a minute, trying to collect my thoughts and hoping she wasn't still in pain. I was about to ask, though I wasn't sure she'd want me to, when she spoke before I had the chance.

"Was you out to the barn again?"

"Yes, ma'am." I stepped forward but not too far.

"What you been doin' out there?"

I couldn't mention the wagon wheels or the plans for her chair. It didn't even seem right to say anything about a porch swing anymore. Frivolous. But what I did say seemed no less childish. "I found the animal we saw yesterday. It was a cat, all right. She's got kittens up in the loft."

"Well, ain't that a dandy!" Emma brightened. "Just the way it used to be! Had me a new batch of kittens near ever' spring. You'll make sure your youngsters get to see 'em 'fore she moves 'em, won't you?"

There was no way I could address that question yet. I didn't want them seeing. Didn't want them attached. "Emma—"

"Just come and sit down 'fore you say another word."

I looked at the chair over in the corner and took a step in that direction.

"Here on the bed. Right a'side me, now. I ain't gonna bite."

I sat beside her, wondering if she was feeling as heavy as I was. I stared down at my worn old shoes for a minute, waiting for her to say something. And finally she spoke.

"What you 'fraid of, Sam Wortham?"

"What?" I pulled my head up and looked at her. She was staring me over with something deep and serious in her eyes.

"What you 'fraid of? You're a good man. Purty strong. But ever'body's got something, now. What you 'fraid of?"

I hadn't expected that question, and I sat for a moment, fully knowing the answer but puzzling as to how to say it. "I guess I'm afraid for my family, ma'am. With no money coming in and the future to face, I wonder about tomorrow, let alone six months from now when winter comes."

"Julia said you was thinking to move on." Her voice was steady as a rock but there was pain in it as well.

"We'd see you to your friend safe and sound, Mrs. Graham. This is a good place you've got here, but you're just too far from a doctor—"

"I done told Julia all that doctor knows to do. Put me to bed. What good is that? Lula Bell could tell me that much!"

"But Emma, what if something happened out here and you got a lot worse?"

"Well, I know how I look at it, son. Of course I'll take worse eventu'ly. That's the way things is. But there's no reason not to enjoy ever' minute till then, is there?"

"I was thinking you might be worse already, after last night."

"Fooh. It was just m' heart pain. That's all. Can't hardly feel it now."

I stared down at my feet again, shaking my head. "It may not just fade away next time."

"I know that."

"But next time could be as soon as tomorrow. Or today."

"I know that too. You don't like the spot you's in, thinkin' to care for me, is that it?"

"No," I told her plainly. "I wouldn't mind caring for you, if I knew it was the best we could do. But it's not. I should have thought this through. We're no doctors. And I'm afraid for my family, what would happen next. That's why I'm thinking it'd be better to go now and figure something else out."

"Where would you go?"

"I don't know. Mt. Vernon. Though we can't expect to stay there long."

"You don't got to go nowhere, Samuel," she told me in earnest. "Nor worry 'bout what happens when I die. Just bury me and say g'bye and go right on livin' here. I'll sign you a paper on the place right now if you want it, so's nobody can dispute you stayin' on."

The breath caught in my throat, and I felt cold. *She'd sign a paper? To get me to stay?* "Emma, surely you've got family."

"None that cares a lick for this place, or they'd be here, wouldn't they? I done offered it to 'em once, when I moved afore. There's only a couple of nephews left anyhow, and my cousin Agnes's girl married to a preacher over to Farmington. None of 'em even comes around 'cept Albert, once in a blue moon. This farm's mine to do what

178

I want with. And I want you to have it. Even if you do think you got to put me back in Belle Rive."

"Emma, there's other people that would love—"

"Don't even say nothin' 'bout George Hammond," she said. "He might a' had all that's mine if he'd took care of what I put in his hands already. But you know how that is. Sometimes he don't care for nothin', whether it's mine or not."

"You don't know me all that well."

"I knows you enough to trust you. Don't be arguin' me. Just tell me if you'll take the deed. It'd set m' mind t' ease."

I sat there for a moment, my hands shaking. I didn't deserve to have this place handed to me; I'd barely started work on it. And people would say we'd swindled her for sure.

"Emma, I thank you. Truly I do. I never dreamed that you'd think so highly of me. But I can't take your farm. It ought to be yours, and I have no right to think otherwise."

"Well," she said slowly. "If it stays mine, I won't have nobody budge me from it again, not for nothin' but church, no matter how sick I get. I didn't come back here just to leave again."

"I guess I can understand that," I told her. "At least a little. I just wish you were closer to town."

"Don't bother me if I never see Doctor Howell no more. He ain't helped me none, far as I can see."

"Well, it bothers me a lot."

"Gettin' sick, gettin' old—them things is part a' life. I don't want you bein' scared of it none. Wouldn't make no difference where I was, that'd all go the same. But this is home, Sam. And I want you all here too. I'll pay you—"

"No, you won't pay me. That wouldn't be right."

She shook her head. "I was 'dreamin' yesterday 'bout your kids, that they was mine—grandkids, I mean. And I ain't never had a pleasanter thought. I'd like to claim 'em so, if I could. You're fine folks, good as family. Better, seems to me."

"You don't even know us that well," I protested.

"Well enough. Look at yourself, Samuel Wortham. You won't take m' house, bad as you need it, 'cause you just gotta do what's right. You're decent. And I'd be proud if you was m' own son."

The words shook me so deeply that I almost stood up, just to get away from her. *Proud? If I was her son? My own mother had never said anything like that.*

She took hold of my arm and gave it a gentle pat. "What's botherin' ya, Samuel? You just can't see clear to stay here with a sick old lady?"

"I can't see how I could have gained half the respect you're showing me, Mrs. Graham. I haven't earned it."

"You did. You love the Lord, don't you?"

"I try."

"If you won't take no paper while I'm livin', would you let me set it up that way for you once I'm gone?"

"I wish you wouldn't. Not yet. Not till you're good and sure. And you've talked to your family."

"You're a hard'un to bless sometimes, Samuel."

I shook my head. "You've done a fine enough job already, Emma."

"Will you stay?"

I felt like somebody had grabbed my stomach and squeezed it tight as a fist. I felt so inadequate, but what else could I do? Take us back to nothing? And let Emma down at the same time?

"I guess I'd better stay," I told her. "If you're real sure about this. But I don't know what I'm doing half the time. And it bothers me what people are going to say. Us keeping you out here away from your doctor and your friends. And using what's yours."

180

"You let 'em talk if they will. It ain't your job to handle 'em. But I sure will, if I catch wind a' any of that. You just watch if I don't."

She reached for her cane, and I looked at her in surprise. Seemed like she could whack somebody over the head without thinking twice.

"Best be gettin' them youngsters 'round," she admonished me. "We gotta be ready 'fore Charlie gets here. Can't have him thinkin' we don't care 'nough for church to have ourselves fixed up in time."

"Yes, ma'am." I stood up.

"Gonna be so good to be back there! You'll like it, you'll see." She smiled at me with the prettiest smile I'd seen out of her yet. I'd blessed her by being nothing more than willing to stay. And now I'd gone and promised her. What a way life can be sometimes.

Julia came in the house with the leaves from something she called borage to make up a tea for Emma. She poured the morning's milk over the rest of Louise Post's corn bread for our breakfast and made sure Emma drank all her tea, saying it would do her good. And Emma didn't argue, though she clearly didn't like it as well as the root coffee.

Soon Julia was washing out the pans, and before long she was singing. I guess I'd made her happy too, telling her we'd stay.

I took the time to fill a bucket and wash myself up good. I figured for Emma's sake I shouldn't smell too bad. Robert was moping and came up to me while I was buttoning my shirt.

"Dad, can't you and me stay home?"

"Nope. Not this time," I told him. "Everybody goes."

He sat in silence and watched me tie my tie. It was the only one we'd saved, and it was wrinkled again, despite Julia's ironing. "You might like Emma's church," I suggested. "She sure does."

"That's 'cause she's old. That's different."

"I think it's because it's been her church since she was a child."

"Well, see, Dad," Robert exclaimed. "That ain't the case with me."

"You could like it anyway."

"Will you?"

"Well, I'm going to give it an honest effort. And that's all I'm asking from you. Fair enough?"

"Will we have to go every Sunday?"

"I haven't decided."

Robert wiggled in his chair and scrunched up his face at me, so I told him to go comb his hair. As he left the room, Sarah came in, looking like a princess in her white stockings and big white hair bow. I wished I could manage to get her some nicer shoes. Hers were scuffed at the toes and soon to be too small.

In no time, Charlie Hunter rolled up the weedy drive in his Chevrolet. Emma started out the door without any help, and by the time I reached her, she was balanced on a porch step.

It was a fine ride to Dearing. Charlie Hunter drove faster than anybody else we'd ridden with. Julia put a scarf over her head and made a feeble attempt at holding Sarah's hair in place. Emma started singing hymns in a voice so rich that it was hard to picture her driven to bed last night by pain, or myself so close to leaving.

Not until we stopped in front of the church did I feel the tension rising up in me again. People were getting out of cars all around us, and more people were walking over from nearby houses. A farm wagon with a gray mare stood under a tree, and three little boys came sauntering up on the back of a mule. More boys were running around in the churchyard while three or four little girls about Robert's size huddled together in giggles beside a hawthorn bush. Some of the men were in overalls, some in suits, but all the women were dressed just as fine as they could manage. An old man with a long white beard was the first to recognize Emma, and when he called out her name, a half dozen of the ladies headed in our direction.

I began to look about nervously, expecting Hazel Sharpe to come puffing up to us at any moment. Emma immediately understood my worry.

"Miss Hazel'd be inside already," she told me. "She's always early."

When all the introductions and hugging were done, we proceeded toward the church steps. Charlie Hunter and I carried Emma up just as carefully as we could, and once she was inside she pointed a seat out to us.

"Same place," Charlie told me. "She always did want to sit in the same place."

"It was m' mama's seat," she explained. "The very place I was sittin' when the gospel come alive."

My family trailed into the pew beside her, and I noticed for the first time that all eyes were turned our way. Outside, the air had been full of friendly greetings for Emma, but now the scrutiny had begun. I wished that they'd commence with the service and then hurry it along so we could get home. But to my dismay, I realized that we were early.

Julia looked up at me and then reached over and squeezed my hand. I knew that meant she'd seen trouble coming. And sure enough, Hazel Sharpe was standing beneath a window, pointing us out to a grizzled old man and his prim-faced wife.

Emma had seen them too, and gave them a merry wave. At that moment I found a lot to respect in an old lady set on enjoying life, no matter what. And I remembered what she'd told me, that it was no concern of mine what people thought or what they said. So I turned my attention from the window to consider the simple cross at the front of the church and the nervous-looking young man who stood beneath it.

I could hear Miss Sharpe's snipping voice coming closer, but the nervous man was coming closer too, walking in our direction with his eyes on Emma. The two got to us right at the same time, and Hazel held her tongue just long enough for the man to introduce himself as Paxton Jones, the new pastor.

"Well," Miss Hazel said to us then, "I'm glad you could manage to come out this morning. Honestly, I wasn't expectin' you."

"Wouldn't miss it for the world," Emma beamed.

The pastor spoke up. "It's so nice to meet you—"

"Emma, land sakes, we coulda brung you to church from Belle Rive if you'd have just said something," Hazel interrupted. "You didn't have to endanger yourself—"

"Posh," Emma said, shaking the pastor's hand. "I've been lookin' forward to hearin' you, Pastor Jones. Been itchin' for it for days."

"I certainly hope I don't disappoint," the pastor replied timidly, with a sideways glance in Hazel's direction.

Hazel spoke up again. "I'm gonna have to have a word—"

"Joy of the Lord is your strength," Emma exhorted the pastor. "You let his fire wrap 'round your bones and don't let nothin' nor nobody stand in your way." She turned her eyes to Hazel and took the woman's hand. "Ain't it grand how we're all just a family for blessin' one another! Why don't you bless me, Hazel, dear, by fetchin' me a glass a' water?"

"You could send that lad there side you," Hazel snapped. "I ain't done—"

"You know he ain't never been here afore," Emma insisted. "Ya don't put a guest to errands, even if he knows where the water's kep', which he don't."

184

"Well, I declare if you ain't become just the same as rude, Emma Graham," Hazel huffed. "And you knowin' I had somethin' to say."

"I'll be glad to speak with you right after the service," Emma assured her, but Hazel had already tromped away.

"You'll hafta forgive me," Emma told the pastor. "I'm old and I ain't got the time for no tongue-wallerin' ways. God love her, though, and I surely mean that."

The pastor smiled shyly. "I heard you were a blessed lady, Mrs. Graham," he said in a quiet voice. "You've blessed me already."

After awhile, a teenage girl in yellow ruffles brought Emma's water, and I could see Hazel over by the wall, talking to somebody else. Her frown was so big I couldn't help but wonder if anyone else noticed the picture of the smiling Jesus behind her. *Strange place for her to park herself,* I thought. *Like an angry sentinel, standing in the way.*

But I knew I shouldn't think such thoughts. Emma had said "God love her," and Julia didn't seem bothered by her either. My wife had engaged herself in pleasant conversation with a poofy-haired woman who sat in the pew in front of us. Before long, Julia would be making friends. She'd probably already decided she liked this church.

I looked around at the people again. Some looked friendly enough, though others I wouldn't have dared to approach any more than I would Hazel. Most of the people eventually got around to greeting us, whether friendly or frowning. And I found I could tell the difference by a handshake too, between those distrusting and those willing to give me the benefit of the doubt.

Emma was clearly enjoying all the attention, and Julia was having a good enough time too. The kids were sitting up proper enough to make me proud, saying hello when it was required of them and patiently waiting for something else to happen.

But I was ready to get out. I was embarrassed to answer the same old questions. To Emma they'd all say, "You mean, you're back *home?* And they're *staying* with you?" Then they'd turn to me and ask if I worked. Finding a dirt hole to slide into would have been a mercy.

Sarah and Robert were soon ushered into a Sunday school class, and all the adults sat in their seats and listened to Hazel's prim-faced friend drone on about holiness. I was sure I wasn't the only one relieved when Sunday school concluded with the sound of a bell.

Then Hazel tromped up to the piano. I wanted to hate her playing, but it sounded pretty good, even though I'd never heard the hymn before. We were all expected to sing anyway, three hymns in all, from the books that had been left on the pews.

The church was hot by the time the preacher started, and I felt sorry for the poor man, sweating and nervous as he was. But he did a passable job and had a pretty way of praying, and the service turned out to be fairly good, all in all.

Mrs. Jones invited us to dinner, but we had to turn her down since we were already committed to be at the Posts. She and Julia talked a long time and were soon laughing away. *It's started already,* I thought. *She's gone and got herself a friend here. Now no matter what happens, even if Emma dies, she won't be wanting to leave. God, what a peculiar way you work things sometimes.*

Since Emma and Julia were still talking and looked like they could be at it awhile, I let Robert and Sarah play outside with some of the kids they'd met. They liked it here too. I was the only stick-in-the-mud, thinking I'd just as soon be back in Harrisburg.

Lord, what's the matter with me anyway? I see my family happy, know what all you've done for us, but I still stand here thinking thoughts about going backward. Or forward. Harrisburg. Or Mt. Vernon. When really, right here hasn't been so ter-

rible. Maybe you planted us, like Emma said. So why am I wiggling around, resisting setting in roots? Why can't I be more like Julia or the kids, and set myself to enjoying life, money in my pockets or not?

We were all outside again when the grizzle-faced man that Hazel'd been talking to came up to me and stood with his hands in his pockets, looking me over before he said a word.

"How do you do?" I offered, trying to begin the conversation on a pleasant note.

"Come from Pennsylvania, huh?"

"Yes, sir." I sighed, pretty sure I could guess what was coming.

"We–ll," he said, "we don't know how y' come to figure this was the place for you, but we'll be watching, you can count on that. Sister Emma, she's dear to us, and I sure wouldn't lift no finger to be hurtin' her feelin's, you know, but that don't mean we can just look t' other way 'bout you crowdin' in, takin' her place—"

"I haven't—"

"Now you just let me talk!" The old man straightened his posture, and his mustache quivered when he spoke. "They don't teach you no manners where you come from, do they? Pity them kids a' yours, if they don't grow up no better!"

I looked for Robert and Sarah instantly, and several heads turned with mine to see them under the trees, well out of earshot.

"I'll be tellin' the preacher all I know," the old man continued. "He needs to hear it, what you're doin'. Maybe he can talk some sense into Emma yet. She always would listen to a preacher, better'n her own friends." He looked over at Miss Hazel, who was heading our direction.

"I've knowed Sister Emma since she weren't tall enough to look over a grasshopper's back," he declared. "But she ain't never listened to me. Shoulda sold that place long ago. There'd be some local boys to crave it, I can tell you. Then she wouldn't have no problems with outa towners wantin' to bleed her dry. But she wouldn't listen to me. No, sir."

I just stood there with my back against Charlie Hunter's car, knowing there was no use trying to get away. Four or five more of the frowning type had crowded in, and Hazel Sharpe had gotten herself into the middle of them.

Emma looked up from the front seat, where she'd been sitting and talking to a clear-eyed woman and the girl with the yellow ruffles. She saw my plight and turned her sights on the man in front of me. "Eldon Henley, don't you go stickin' yer nose in where it don't belong!"

"Now, Emma," Hazel spoke up, her face tense.

"Don't even try to shush me," Emma said immediately. "You got no right gettin' yourselves in Samuel's face! He's a good man, and m' guest to boot. You all just leave him alone, or he'll be thinkin' I got me a church full a' heathens."

"We got every right bein' concerned for one a' our own!" Miss Hazel insisted. "We can't just be lettin' folks come in and hornswoggle you outa—"

"Just a minute!" Emma said, stopping her cold. "You don't know nothin' 'bout m' business at all! These is fine folks that ain't took nary a cent! They're m' friends, and they been better to me already than you ever been."

Hazel stepped back as if she'd been slapped. "I—I just don't know how you can say such a thing. You've knowed me so long—and you know Eldon was meanin' well too. We all love ya s' much—"

"You got a funny way a' showin' it, Hazel Sharpe," Emma declared. "Tellin' tales on m' friends without even waitin' long enough to see if you got matters straight, which you don't, a' course." She took a look around at the crowd. "Go home to Sund'y dinner, all a' you. You never thought much on me while I was up to Belle Rive, so it hadn't ought to bother you much nows I'm home."

188

"Never thought on you?" Hazel exclaimed. "I can't picture how you could say such a thing! When we been like sisters!"

I looked from one to the other, surprised by the sharpness of Emma's words, even though she'd promised to defend me.

"Hazel," Emma sighed, "a blue moon brung you up to see me. And then you done nothin' but complain. And it was the same way with some of the rest of you. Delores Pratt and Bonnie Gray, now they was good to come regular 'nough with a smile on their face, but they've gone home a' ready to feed their grandbabies. And I'm goin' over to Louise Post's now. I'll be seein' you all, Lord willin', come next Sund'y. I love every one of ya, but I'd thank ya to see the matter straight with me 'fore you run your mouth. These is good folks, and that's all there is to it! Now, where's Charlie?"

One of the frowners broke into a smile, shook Emma's hand, and wished her a good day. Charlie left a pretty young lady standing by an evergreen bush to come in our direction, and I called for Robert and Sarah.

Eldon Henley quietly said good day to Emma and started to turn away, but Miss Hazel wouldn't let the matter rest. Turning to Julia and me, she said, "You ain't gonna get by with this, turnin' her agin' her own friends thataway! Worst case a' hoodwinked I ever seen! But it ain't gonna be! I'll have you found out and run off her place yet! You just wait!"

She stormed off, and everyone near us just stood for a minute, struck by the woman's furious outburst.

"Never mind her, now," Emma said. "Shoot, you all be praying for her. That's Hazel. But she'll come 'round."

Emma went right on talking to yet another friend while the kids climbed in the car behind her. But I watched Miss Sharpe's stooped shoulders getting farther and farther down the dusty street. And my stomach twisted into a knot.

Emma had once said that the woman was all bark. But somehow I knew she'd made no idle threat. She was convinced of our guilt, though I wasn't quite sure why. And she had a plan to save Emma from herself and get rid of us. I was sure of this, but there was no way to prove it. We'd just have to wait, like she'd said. Wait and see.

TWENTY-THREE

Julia

Oh, what a lovely day it was! I was so relieved that Emma felt better; it almost seemed as if last night had never happened, she was so full of pep. Hers was a beautiful church, so homey and quaint, with some very sweet people to talk to. Of course, a few folks were a bit sour, but you get that anywhere. And it was mostly Miss Hazel's doing. That's Hazel, like Emma said.

I felt like I'd known Juanita Jones, the pastor's wife, for years. We talked and laughed like old friends, and I was already anxious for next week, when we could accept her invitation to dinner. Her husband's sermon about the Good Samaritan was good too. I heard Emma afterward telling the couple behind us that Sam was rather like the foreigner in that story—good-hearted whether he was trusted or not.

Pretty soon Charlie was driving us along in the sunshine. Emma must have been feeling as good as I was, because she started singing hymns again. And, oh, I was feeling blessed. I saw some more borage not far from the road and thought I ought to do my best to find some more at home. Vervain too. "Good for what ails you," Grandma had once said. At least it wouldn't do Emma any harm.

I knew Samuel had come to terms with Emma, even the idea of her getting sick. And we were going to stay. Praise the living Lord for that! We'd been planted, just like Emma had said.

It hardly seemed like any time had passed at all when we approached the Posts' farm. I was hoping the school-teacher and her husband would be there, and I wasn't disappointed. Mr. Post was standing outside when we pulled in, and the first thing he told us was that his brother and Elvira were there for dinner too.

The Posts had a pretty place, white and cheerful with a rosebush out front to greet us. Everything was in order and looked freshly painted or brand new. Charlie helped Sam get Emma inside, but he couldn't be persuaded to stay. "Have a dinner date of my own back in town," he said and then winked.

Almost right away, we heard barking from the backyard.

"A dog!" Sarah proclaimed. "Mommy, they got a dog! Oh, can we see?"

"That's just the thing to do," Barrett Post said with a gleam in his eye. "I got me somethin' better 'n candy back there."

He looked to Sam, who gave a reluctant nod, and our children followed Mr. Post toward the sound.

Louise, who had come out to the porch to meet us with a towel in her hands, shook her head at her husband and then took my hand. "You'll have to forgive him. He loves

192

Princess well enough, but there's just no way we can keep her eight puppies. Trying to pawn some off on you, that's what he's doing. But you don't have to feel obligated, if you got no way to feed 'em. Your youngsters are welcome to visit 'em here."

She asked us in, where Emma was already in lively conversation with Elvira. So I went in to meet the teacher while Sam followed the others around the back to see the puppies that were sure to warm Sarah's heart. She loved anything with fur and a great many things without it.

Louise Post had a lovely sitting room with oak furniture and yellow seat cushions. But I felt strange in there talking while she worked in the kitchen, so after awhile I excused myself to see if she could use some help. Before long, I was peeling boiled potatoes for the potato salad.

"Don't like to buy no potatoes," Louise told me. "But we'll have to, till the crop comes in. Got a box of 'em the size of a hog wagon down in the root cellar, but every one of 'em's gone to sprouts as long as your arm." She spooned mayonnaise and a dollop of mustard into the bottom of a bowl. "Cut your pieces right in on top," she said. "That's the way I do it."

I smiled at her upside down way of doing things and asked if they grew their own potatoes every year.

"'Cept the year Howard was born," Louise answered with a far-off look. "Barrett broke his arm. And me with a newborn, we didn't get much garden in. How 'bout you? You planting much?"

"Not as much as I'd like. We have a little corn and beans, lettuce and such."

"Potatoes?"

"No, not yet," I admitted and saw the smile spread quickly across her face.

"How would you like some of the mess I've got? They're good for nothing 'cept to plant, and we don't have the room for all of 'em. We could send you home with a box or two. Emma'd probably laugh me to scorn, though, seein' sprouts so long."

An answered prayer, sure as I was standing there. "Thank you so much, Mrs. Post, but I doubt Emma would laugh. She just might kiss you, as much as she loves a garden."

"She does that. You're right."

I rose to the counter to get a serving spoon just in time to see my children out the kitchen window. Rolling in the grass, both of them, with puppies all over the place. And Samuel, sensible as he usually was, stood there with a pup in his arms, staring it in the face. "They are surely going to have to wash up now." I sighed, thinking how the children would beg to take a puppy home when it came time to leave.

"You'll be lucky not to go home with a dog in your lap," Louise said with a laugh. "'Course, if you think on it, they're good to have around. Keeps the coons out of the corn. And fox away from the chickens too. You got chickens?"

"Yes, ma'am. Emma has."

"Emma's such a sweet thing, letting you stay with her. And it's good of you too. Barrett told me all about it, and it's a decent arrangement. A little different, but what's that? These days, folks need to work together."

"Thank you. Not everybody sees it that way."

Louise shook her head. "I expect not. We heard some things. But I just tell folks to mind their own business. Or go and talk to Emma, like Barrett did."

We set the table and called everyone to a dinner fit for royalty. Louise Post could certainly cook, even if she did things upside down or backward, like putting forks on the right and gravy underneath the meat on her plate. And it was a real treat to have fresh-churned butter with her homemade bread. And a cherry pie.

Elvira Post did most of the talking during dinner. She asked Robert all kinds of questions, and then would think of some more for Samuel or me. Pretty soon, she knew more about us than most people find out, or care to, in weeks.

"Helps me teach," she claimed. "To know how my students live and think things through. Believe me, you ain't the only ones."

"That's sure true," her husband, Clement, confirmed. "Can't go no place without her pesterin' folks right and left over stuff that wouldn't interest me in the least."

"You oughta be interested," Elvira told him. "Nothing in this world's more interesting than the people around you."

"Wish you'd take more notice of church, then," Emma gently admonished. "How better to know all them folks that goes, Elvira? Especially them that's your kids. They oughta see the schoolteacher in church more than Christmas, you know, if it weren't for nothin' but the example. And that goes for all a' you."

The table was silent for a moment as the Posts turned to their food. Finally, Elvira managed to speak.

"You're right, Emma. I know it. I oughta go more. For an example, like you said. Tell you the truth, I been lucky not to have parents complainin' at me over it. Teacher before me was there every Sund'y. But church was right at the school then, and she only lived 'bout two skips away."

"Dearing ain't so far," Emma maintained. "Not for somethin' so good as church. It'd do you good too, Barrett."

Mr. Post set his fork down with some emotion. "You know I ain't been since my pappy died, and I ain't goin'. We all respect you 'round here, Emma, but you're gonna hafta leave me 'lone about that."

After another moment of silence, Louise started talking about what a year it was going to be for berry picking and wasn't the rhubarb coming up nice. Elvira invited our family out to the schoolhouse to see what it was like, and Clement said that if we hurried we could catch Sparky and

Tubs on the radio after dinner. Robert cleaned his plate real fast after that. Pretty soon, we were all in a half circle around the blue, table-type metal radio that stood in the corner of the room Louise called her parlor.

I enjoyed hearing the radio again, even though the volume was too loud. Mr. Post had broken one of the knobs off, and it sat on top of the radio, next to a vase of grape hyacinths.

One program was just not enough. Sparky and Tubs ran for a half hour, and Robert and Sarah couldn't have been pried off that floor with crowbars until they found out what came on next. I'd never heard KMOX out of St. Louis before, but it had the same jingle for Wheaties cereal that I remembered hearing in Harrisburg. "Won't you try Wheaties? Wheat is the best food of man . . ."

Emma sat back with her eyes closed, a big smile on her face. I wondered if she'd been here many times before, listening with the Posts to one radio show or another.

To Robert's delight, a Western came on next, one with wild galloping noises and a blaze of gunshots. He would have liked more, but Mrs. Post ushered us outside as soon as the show was over, in order to show off her garden. But she promised the kids she'd have us over sometime on a weeknight to listen to Jack Armstrong and Little Orphan Annie.

Her asparagus was fat and enticing, and she had parsley, basil, and apple mint clustered along the east side of the well. They had a beautiful yard and a garden worthy of envy. I began to imagine what Emma's might have looked like once, and what it could be again. What wonders could be done with a little land!

I envisioned grapes growing on an arbor fence, and dill, sage, and a hundred other herbs surrounding the house. We could stretch the daylilies from the front ditch clear to the other edge of the property and plant tulips to lighten the place come spring.

I could have gone on and on with such a fancy, but Sammy put his arm around me and asked if I didn't want to be leaving. Emma was looking tired.

Emma was ready to go home, but she was far from admitting to being tired. "We have to make sure old Lula Bell has water," she said. "And milk her besides."

Of course, the kids were not nearly so anxious to leave a place with a radio *and* puppies. They'd found their way to the woodshed again, where Princess kept her litter. I could see the longing on their faces as they reluctantly set down the pups they'd been cradling and watched them tumble over one another on their way back to their mother.

But they didn't say a word. Robert went and sat by Mr. Post's truck, and Sarah took hold of my hand, her eyes checking to see if I'd noticed what precious little creatures the puppies were. They were good dogs, all of them looking like their golden labrador mother, but I didn't say anything either.

It was Samuel who finally took pity on the kids and asked Emma if she wouldn't mind bringing home a dog one of these days. I felt glad inside when she said she'd be tickled. A farm ought to have a dog, after all. But it worried me, just a little, to think of feeding it. We had a couple of weeks to consider that, though, before any of them were ready to leave their mother.

On the way home I wondered what had come over Samuel, favoring a puppy like he had, when just last night he was ready to pick up and leave. But I didn't have to ask him. In the back of Mr. Post's pickup, he slid his arm around me and whispered that he was going to try to live the life God gave us and not stew and fret for something else.

"Maybe we're supposed to do this," he whispered to me. "Maybe God looked down on Emma and sent us to her on purpose."

197

I nodded, looking through the back window glass at the coiled gray braid resting just above Emma's lacy collar. "She needs her farm, Sammy. And she's claiming us like family."

"But she's got family already," he said. "Some, at least. And they've got rights when she's gone. That's the way it needs to be. She offered me the deed this morning, but I can't take it, honey. We'll just be blessed doing what she wants as long as she's living." He kissed my cheek and was quiet several minutes.

Knowing what he was saying, I hoped Emma would live forever, but I couldn't help but think of that solitary grave on the hill. Willard Graham. Waiting.

In my heart I knew that Emma wouldn't do a thing to put off her date with heaven, that she'd come home to die as much as to live. Such an understanding made me feel all jumbled up inside, sad and happy all at the same time.

"I hope she's with us a long while," Sam finally said. "But when God calls her home, we'll find a way someplace else. Just as good. I promise."

I sat there with my head on his shoulder, thinking of Mr. Henley outside the church, and Hazel Sharpe, and anyone else who could think my husband capable of swindling an old lady. Understanding the choice Sam had made put a new fire in me. *How dare anyone think for one minute that Sam Wortham has an ounce of cheat in him! Let them say such a thing again, and I might have to set them down a notch or two myself!*

TWENTY-FOUR

Samuel

Julia had asked to see the school, so Mr. Post drove us past there before taking us home. The school was set back on a side road and almost hidden by trees, so it would have been hard to find on our own. The old building looked more like a church than a school, and it even had a steeple tower where the morning bell hung ready to ring. There was an outhouse on each side of the building and two separate wells, each with a bucket and a tin cup hanging from a post.

I could imagine boys playing ball on the patchy lawn, but there was nothing else in the schoolyard but a hitching bar. Apparently some of the students came to school on the back of a horse or mule. Robert seemed to like the looks of the place, and I was glad about that. He'd be anxious to start in the morning. But Sarah liked it too, especially the paper flowers in the windows. She whined a little that Elvira had said she couldn't come till fall.

"Don't let it trouble ya none, little missy," Mr. Post told her. "They ain't got even a month left a' this year, anyhow. And your mama'll need you at home that long."

Sarah brightened up to think that she might have an important job ahead of her. But I wondered about books and things, and asked Juli what Robert would be needing.

"Mrs. Post said he could share till this year is out," she said immediately, but didn't tell me what we'd have to have by fall. Pencils and paper tablets for both kids, at the very least. We'd have to have money.

I felt unsettled, letting myself think about what was coming and all the things we'd need. New shoes for both kids, but especially Sarah, who pulled hers off every chance she got because they were starting to pinch her toes. And coats, good heavy ones, to keep the kids warm on the walk to school. We'd had coats for them last winter, but had left them behind, not having room to carry something that had come to be too small anyway.

Julia had told me when we left Harrisburg that we had the whole summer to watch God provide for us before fall. At the time, I thought she was just trying to brighten me up a little. But she'd really believed it, and we'd seen a lot provided, there was no doubt about that. But there comes a time when God expects a man to find his way, set his hands to some work, and make an honest buck.

I had to look for a job. Had to, no matter how much needed to be done on Emma's farm. But I knew it might take a miracle to find a job. Two men from Emma's church had been south of here somewhere working in a mine, but they'd lost their jobs. Everybody was laying off, and nobody was hiring.

I was still thinking such thoughts when we got home. I was anxious to get to work again on that fence, thinking that the sooner it was finished, the sooner I could hunt for something with pay involved. But Emma didn't favor working on the Sabbath, just like I'd figured, and it seemed best to respect that, at least as far as she could see me.

So I took the kids to the barn to see the kittens I'd discovered that morning. And despite my worries, I was glad we were here and glad I was a father, when I saw my kids' smiling faces down in the hay, getting so completely involved in the wonder of life. I'd thought the mother might not like us hanging around so close, but she didn't seem to mind the kids at all. She just lay there, receiving a nursing kitten and Sarah's gently petting hand equally well.

While they were still in the loft, I set to work on Emma's chair. I'd drawn out what I wanted to do, but I hadn't figured out how I'd manage the problem of mounting the chair over the wheel axle and have it stable without being clumsy as an old cart. I decided I'd get to that after I had the chair part made.

I was using a design of simple slats, like Rita McPiery's porch swing, only smaller. I found some boards I thought I could use once they were cut to size. But I didn't want to do any cutting right now. The kids would hear that and come to see what I was up to, and I wasn't ready for explanations yet. So I went hunting for nails of a size to do the job right. It wasn't easy to find any less than eight penny, but when I did, I pulled them carefully out of the boards and stored them in an old chipped cup I'd found in the straw.

Mrs. Post had sent us home with leftovers, and Julia wanted to return the favor and have the Posts over sometime. I pulled nails, thinking how that might seem to them, to come over here and eat yard greens and whatever else we might have around. They'd given us coffee, good and black, and it had tasted better than candy to me. What would they think of us, digging up the blue-flowered chicory for Julia to grind and roast and pour into their cups?

Maybe the Hammonds would understand such things. Maybe they did it themselves. But Posts and Hammonds seemed a world apart. One appearing to be well off and the other maybe as poor as we were. Considering that, I didn't feel so bad toward George Hammond. I even said a prayer for him before going back up to the house that night.

Mr. Post and his grown son, Martin, came just after breakfast the next morning, ready to help me with the fence. They acted as if it were nothing at all for them to be so willing to help.

"That's the way people do things around here," Barrett said. "At least they used to. And they still should. If folks'll help raise a barn, they oughta be willin' to help with anything else when there's a need. And Emma gettin' her cows back is worth it to me."

That comment took me by surprise. Did everybody know that Hammond still had some of her cows? And that she'd never been paid for any of them?

"Got me some good cattle off the bull Emma give me," Post explained. "Figured I owed her one brung home. The one I promised is third generation. Come from real good stock. She'll be good for you, no lie."

Maybe Post didn't know about Hammond. His was generosity repaying generosity. I could picture Emma giving away a bull; it was just the kind of thing she'd do.

Post gave me an inquiring look and then nodded his head, as if he'd decided on something important. "For an hour or two of labor," he suddenly said. "I'd be willing to stick her in with old Beau and get her bred, if that's what you want."

"Bred?" How would we manage it? A cow giving birth! Julia would be thrilled, but I felt weak in the knees. "For a couple of hours labor?" I had to ask, still stunned by the man's offer.

202

"I could use me some help in the field," he told me. "Fact is, I'll need a lot a' help all season. Wayne Horne moved all the way to Missouri, and my boy here's done got him another plot a' ground, plus a pair a' twins to keep him busy. I hired me a couple a' boys that used to work the Scranton mine, but I'm needin' another hand."

I just stood there, surely looking dumb, trying to keep from falling over or bawling in front of the man. Another answered prayer, that a job would just walk up to me this way, without me even having to hunt for it. Why would God do such a thing? Why would he care?

"You mean you're offering me work, just like that?"

Barrett gave me a nod. "I'll swap you fencin' for roofin'. Then you give me a hand awhile, and I'll see you get yer cow and calf. After that, if I like the way you work, I'll call on you time and again, for cash."

I reached my hand to Mr. Post. "Thank you," I managed to say. "You'll like my work. I'll make sure you do."

He smiled a wide and toothy smile. "That's what I figured. We ready to get started?"

The Posts worked fast. And Barrett talked the whole time.

"I hear they're gonna close Lake Creek 4," he told me. "Won't be no workin' mines in the whole state 'fore long! Dad blum shame! Used to set records, we did, for coal 'round here. My cousin Edmund at the New Orient says Illinois's got more coal than all the rest of the world put together. Don't know 'bout that, you know, but one sure thing is the world ain't buyin' much of it right now."

I wondered about Dewey, who'd said he was considering applying for work at the Paulton mine. What would he do now?

"They say there's a bank closin' down in Marion," Post went on. "I been keepin' my eye on ours. Can't trust it to be there forever. You get any money, hang onto it. Pays to keep your cash hid in days like these."

He stopped and looked at me, silent for several moments for emphasis. "Don't know how things was where you come from," he said. "I hear some places is fine. But 'round here, a lot of folks is sinkin' on account of the mines. Affects ever'body one way or another."

I looked to the yard, where I could see Juli planting potatoes. She seemed to be hopping about, rejoicing in things just the way we had them. Did she really understand how bad things were? Barrett said the whole area was affected. Bad times were everywhere.

The worrying made me so tense that I forgot how happy I'd been just moments before when offered a job. *How can Post afford to be hiring men? He must be even better off than he looks. But will it last?*

"Take a look next time you're in there at that Dearing store," Post went on, not realizing the effect he was having on me. "Prices is gone way up. And they say I might not get thirty-five cents a bushel for my wheat this year. Could be some kinda winter."

I set an old post down hard in my fresh-dug hole and wiped the sweat off my forehead. "Get much snow around here?"

"Oh, Lordy!" Post proclaimed. "Snow! I seen it to my belt and more. 'Course, that ain't every year. Now's the time to think on them things, though. Got wood cut?"

"Not much."

"There's time. You can always do that when you ain't got nothin' else to do. Emma still got that nice little kerosene heater in the sittin' room?"

"No. I haven't seen a kerosene heater."

"Prob'ly gave it away when she moved. That's Emma for you. Heart a' gold."

I'd thought plenty about wood for the cookstove and the fireplace, but it hadn't occurred to me that we might need more heat than that.

"You're gonna need that outhouse shored up," Post said, changing the subject. "It's leanin'."

"I'll get to that after the fencing."

"Always somethin' to do, ain't there?" He laughed and looked over at his son, who'd been working the whole time without saying a word. "Martin's got to fix his brand-new porch! Brother-in-law come and hit smack into the corner of it with his Chevrolet coupe! Ain't that the richest! And him thinkin' he's a dandy one too!"

Martin didn't look too pleased with the mention of it. I told him I'd help him if he needed it, since he was helping me. He nodded his appreciation before walking to his father's truck for a barrel of nails.

"That's a good boy," Barrett told me.

"I can tell."

"Hang it all if his wife ain't got him goin' to church, though."

Julia had sent Robert to school that morning with his lunch wrapped in newspaper, so I was a little surprised to see him walking home before noon.

"Teacher sent us home," he told me after climbing up on our board fence. "Said she had a toothache." He watched us for awhile, apparently waiting for the Posts to get out of earshot.

"She's an odd teacher, Dad," he confided. "Made us all sing in our chairs first thing. And she made me recite the alphabet like a little kid, just to see if I had decent teachin' where I come from. We didn't even say the pledge till right before we left."

"Everybody has their way of doing things," I told him. "It doesn't sound all that bad."

"There isn't but seventeen of us in the whole school! Five of 'em are boys about my age. I like that, but Mrs. Post said it's a terror having so many boys. Only four girls,

Dad, in the whole school. They don't like it neither, I can tell, getting picked on."

"Maybe you'll have to look out for them. Make sure the other boys don't give them such a hard time."

"Then they'd be giving *me* a hard time, Dad. Orville Mueller already said I was a shrimp. I sure don't want him callin' me no sissy."

"You have to do what's right, Robert."

"Aw, Dad. It's bad enough just being new."

"Think about it. Think how you'd feel if one of those girls was your sister. And she'll be there next fall. Maybe things can improve a bit before then."

"Maybe Orville Mueller won't be back. He's big enough to get a job, Dad. Maybe this is his last year."

"Still, think of what I'm saying. Most of the boys *will* be back. Sometimes it takes just one to teach the others a better way of doing things."

Robert was quiet awhile, thinking. "Mrs. Gray said something like that in Sunday school. That we can change things just by doing what we should."

"A pretty sound lesson."

"But Dad, Teacher stops 'em whenever she sees it. The other times, I can't do nothing. It's before school or after, mostly. And the worst of 'em are the ones bigger than me."

He was in a dilemma, and I knew it. I didn't want to condone anyone getting tormented. But I didn't want him coming home with black eyes either. "Do your best is all I can say right now. We'll pray on it."

"Does God want me to fight, Dad?" he asked. "On account of the girls?"

"That's not the best way. Not usually."

"Willy said the only way to stop Orville Mueller is to offer a fight. But there isn't anybody willing to do that."

"He's big, then?"

"Yeah. And mean. He pulled Esther Cohen's hair and knocked her books in the ditch."

"There's not much brave or tough about a bully."

"Maybe not. But there's plenty of fearsome."

I gave his shoulder a pat, not sure what else to tell him. After a long pause, he looked into my face like he was trying to judge the sort of reaction he'd get from what he was about to say.

"I almost went up to the front in Sunday school, Dad," he said. "When Mrs. Gray asked who wanted to give over their heart to God. She said we could come up and announce to the world that we was gonna be used for good works, not bad."

"Why didn't you go?"

"Nobody else went, except Mrs. Gray's daughter. And some of the boys were snickering and carrying on. I couldn't, Dad, not being so new, or I'd never get any friends."

"You'll have to consider what kind of friends you want."

Robert just looked at me for a moment, then hopped down from the fence without another word and started for the house. I glanced over at the Posts, who were working about twenty yards away. I thought that maybe I should have said more, that maybe Robert needed to hear what a good boy I thought he was.

No, I decided. He needed to walk off, thinking. And then decide for himself where he stands.

I would have prayed on it right then and there, but Barrett Post had dug another hole, and I had to hustle to drag the post up from where it fell in the weeds.

George Hammond got himself busy in the field next to us that day with his horse-drawn plow, preparing the ground to plant before Emma could change her mind about it. His boys Willy and Kirk came to take Robert fishing after supper. And some folks I'd never met came up the road in a green-painted wagon, offering us a spice cake and asking to see Emma. Covey and Alberta Mueller, they said. And they stayed into the night with Emma, talking up a storm. They seemed nice enough, and Julia was pleased to have their company. But I couldn't help thinking about a big boy named Orville Mueller. The bully. Was he their son? What might he be doing while his folks were away?

I got so restless that I finally took Sarah off to the pond, where the boys were still fishing. They'd caught seven and were trying to decide how to split them three ways.

"Just take the extra," I told the Hammond boys. "You got a bigger family."

When the Hammonds left, Sarah started dancing around me in the moonlight. "Tell a story, Daddy," she begged. "Right out here in the wide open."

I sighed. I was so full of thoughts about neighbors and bullies and the coming winter snow, but I sat on an old log and gathered my girl on my lap. Robert plunked his fish into an old bucket and sat beside me.

"There was a certain polliwog named Alice," I began. "And Alice lived in the mud at the bottom of a little bitty pond."

Sarah laid her head against my chest, and Robert stared out over the pond in front of us. "Are you making this one up, Dad?" he asked.

"Yeah, this one."

"Hush, Robby," Sarah scolded. "Daddy, go on."

"Alice the polliwog lived way down deep in the mud. She only had two problems. Winter and a bullfrog named Ogelvie." I took a deep breath, wondering how they tolerated my dumb little tales. After all, it wasn't hard to tell them. I just said whatever came to mind.

"Alice had made a nice house with mud walls and a mud floor and had everything just how she wanted it. But when winter came she was much too cold. And when Ogelvie the bullfrog came, he always leaned on one of her walls and knocked it right over. Then she'd have to work

208

as fast as she could to fix it back up again. And Ogelvie never helped."

Robert picked up a stick. Sarah closed her eyes.

"One time, the winter was so cold that the pond froze all the way to the bottom. The mud was thick and hard to move in. Alice stayed home, huddled under seventeen blankets just to stay warm. But Ogelvie was tough and strong, and he hopped right out in that cold, hard mud all the way to Alice's house and asked her for tea. And when he was drinking it, he leaned back on her wall and knocked it right over. Alice was mad. Really mad. But the bullfrog just laughed and went away."

Robert glanced up at me, then pulled out his pocketknife and commenced to whittle. I kept expecting him to outgrow my storytelling and leave it for Sarah alone to hear. But this hadn't happened yet.

"Poor Alice had to get out from under her blankets and into that deep, cold mud. She had to fix her wall before the cold froze up her whole house. She worked real hard, and all the while she thought how good it would be to have a nice friend. Not like Ogelvie, who always broke down her walls. Not like the fish either, who just swam away or else tried to eat her for dinner. She thought and thought about that and almost had her wall finished when she heard a little cry coming from the path outside. She didn't want to stop, but she did anyway, even though her house was getting colder and colder. Somebody was crying, and she had to know who, to help them if she could."

I shifted Sarah onto my shoulder and she snuggled against me.

"Alice found a little polliwog even smaller than herself," I went on. "He was crying because a big bullfrog had leaned on his house and broke it all to pieces. There was no way he could fix it. 'You can stay in my house,' Alice told him. And the little polliwog was so happy that he helped Alice fix her wall. Then they went inside and snuggled under the blankets and found they were much warmer together than they were alone. They didn't even mind Ogelvie as much anymore, because now when he broke a wall, there was someone to help fix it. It's more fun that way, everyone knows."

I stopped. Robert was looking at me strangely. "Is that the end?" he asked.

"Yes."

"Some story."

"Thanks." I stood up, lifting Sarah with me. She opened her eyes, but closed them again immediately. "Bedtime," I told her. "Let's get back to the house."

Just then we heard the rustling of brush and the obvious crunch of footsteps on the twig-strewn path.

"Willy Hammond, are you listenin' in?" Robert called. But there was no answer. Only the sound of feet, and not very big ones, running away.

TWENTY-FIVE

Julia

For Tuesday breakfast, Emma and I cut the sprouts off some potatoes we'd kept back from the planting box. Louise Post had sent us home with some of her leftover pork, and I used the fat we'd saved from it to fry up our hash browns. Oh, they were good, with just enough salt left in the box to make them right.

"Got to go to the store today," Emma reminded me. She'd made sure yesterday to ask Barrett Post to take us. And he'd said Louise would be just delighted to visit with Emma so that we could all go together. Sam wasn't a bit anxious to go, but I told him Post was expecting him and it wouldn't be seemly to stay at home with Emma and Louise. He mumbled something about working in the barn, but changed his mind when Barrett came to pick us up and asked him to sit up front so they could talk about what they'd need to fix his roof.

Elvira Post had called off school so she could see a dentist, and Robert was excited to be able to go with us and spend his nickel. Sarah had hers too, held tight in her clenched fist until I suggested she stuff it in the pocket of her skirt for safekeeping.

I didn't make a list, but Emma did, and she insisted we take it along with the money she pulled out of her box-shaped purse. Her generosity was awfully hard on Samuel, and he kept apologizing to her about having to use her money.

"Nonsense," was all she'd say. "I'm a'wantin' all this, so I oughta pay for it."

"I'll pay her back," Sam told me. "When I first get paid cash. I'll pay for everything after that."

I kissed him and we were soon rambling down the road in Barrett's old pickup again, the breeze flopping Sarah's scarf in every direction. She was having trouble keeping it on and it almost blew away once. I must have tied it for her a dozen times, but she kept fiddling with the ends. Still, we laughed about it, and Robert exclaimed what a time she'd have keeping her things in order on the way to school next fall.

"I don't want to go," she declared. "I like it home with Emma. Can she be my grandma, Mama? Please?"

Sam heard that, even up front. So did Mr. Post, and he answered in a voice loud enough for all of us to hear. "Why not? Might as well be. Warren would have liked you all. I'm fairly sure of that."

Driving down the road with his arm hanging out one window, he went on, telling us that Emma's son, Warren, had been one of his best friends.

"We used to call him Wig, after his initials," he said. "Warren Immanuel Graham. A real shame to lose him. He was a lot like his mama. Nothing to complain about. I think he'd be glad you're with her. She wanted more kids around. She always did. Always welcomed anybody, just to have 'em around."

Julia

He chuckled a moment as he turned a corner. "I remember one year her bein' so good to an old tramp that my mother got plum riled at her. Said we'd be invaded by tramps 'fore long, once the others caught wind of it. Don't seem like we get too many more, though, seein's we ain't next to the tracks. Them that is, they're the ones that have gotta watch."

We were in Dearing almost before we knew it. Mr. Post said he'd be next door looking for a lamp while we got our groceries. But he hadn't even gotten out of the truck before I saw Miss Hazel hurrying in our direction from her house down the street.

She had a cherry-colored hat on her head that bobbed while she walked. She clutched her purse in both hands and rushed at Mr. Post just as he was slamming his door shut.

She didn't even wait for him to turn around. "You oughta be ashamed of yourself, Barrett Post! Haulin' these people into town to spend Emma's money! Ain't you got a lick a' conscience about you no more?"

I could see Samuel looking like he'd been hit in the face. I sent the kids into the store ahead of us so they wouldn't hear any more.

"What makes you think they's here to spend money?" Barrett asked her.

"I got eyes, ain't I? They're goin' in the store."

"They's here for groceries, true enough. But you don't know what kinda arrangements they got, Hazel. You sure don't got no way a' knowin' if it's Emma's money or not."

"I'd bet the roof off my house it is."

"Well, I could use one right now, Miss Hazel, but I still don't see how it's any a' your business. Go on home and leave these folks alone."

"I come for some lard, and you ain't sendin' me home till I get it!" she huffed at Mr. Post as she started for the door of the grocer. Sam was already beside it and pulled it open for her, but she didn't even look at him.

213

I hurried inside after her, wanting to be sure she didn't snip at my children, but Sam stayed outside. I caught a glimpse of him over by the pickup again with Mr. Post, leaning into the rusty side. Post was talking, and Samuel, looking beaten, just stood and nodded his head.

Mr. Hastings, the owner, greeted me immediately. I said hello but hurried to the cabinet where Miss Hazel was standing right next to my Sarah.

"Move enough that I can reach in for my lard," Hazel commanded her. "There ain't nothin' in that case pertains to you anyhow, little girl."

Sarah moved over but said, "Yes, there is. I want some cheese. And I got me a whole nickel."

"Well!" Hazel huffed. "Let's hope you got it honest!"

I couldn't help myself. She had no business speaking like that to any child. "Miss Sharpe, I beg your pardon. But you hadn't ought to be so hateful to a little girl—"

"Hateful?" She looked stunned, as though it were perfectly normal to question openly someone's honesty. "She was the one rude enough to talk back to an elder," she snapped at me. "The poor thing needs manners, just like her parents. Excuse me, now, so I can pay Hiram for the lard."

She pushed past me and walked to the cash box. Then Sarah looked up with a big sigh and declared, "Boy, is she cranky."

I knew we were in for it then, and I tried to apologize to Miss Hazel before she even got started, but there was no stopping her. She turned around, slow and steady like she was working her words around in her mind. "Mrs. Wortham," she said coolly, "if you or your child ever decide to insult me again, I shall call for William Turrey, the deputy, to instruct you in the sort of conduct we approve of in this town."

Instead of scaring me, as she probably intended, her threat only rankled me further. "What do you think he'd

214

say to *you*, Miss Hazel, if he heard you talking to a child the way you did?"

For a minute I thought I heard a chuckle, but Mr. Hastings ducked into the back room so quickly that I couldn't be sure.

"Hiram!" Hazel called. "I'm waitin' up here!" She was looking at me differently, as if she thought I might hurt her somehow. "You all should leave town," she said. "Before you get yourselves in such trouble that folks won't let you leave."

"We have nothing to hide. And no reason to fear anyone. We wouldn't hurt you or Emma or anybody else."

Mr. Hastings had come up behind the counter. "That'll be ten cents, Hazel."

But she didn't seem to hear him. "You don't consider it hurtin' to be tryin' to take an old woman's land? And actin' like you're her friends just to get what you want? You don't think that hurts her none?"

"We're not trying to take anything. Ask Emma."

"She's all twisted 'round by your sweet talk! I seen that. Have you got the deed a'ready? Prob'ly not, or you'd have her clean off a' there."

Robert walked up behind Hazel and set a jar of jelly on the counter. He paid his nickel without a word and walked outside. Sarah came and stood beside me, cradling a chunk of cheese in one arm. I was boiling inside, but at the same time felt sorry for this hardheaded woman. I didn't want an enemy, but I sure didn't want harassment every time we came to Dearing either.

"My husband refused the deed," I told her, my voice as even as I could make it. "Emma offered, but Samuel wouldn't take it. We're going to stay for awhile, that's all. So long as Emma needs us." I thought maybe she'd listen and understand just the way it was. But she wouldn't hear me at all.

"I know what you're up to! Don't you think I don't! You're lyin' through your teeth! And you're in for a time of it once Emma's kin gets here! That's a sure thing! I'll make sure they know just what you're doin'! And before you can shake a stick, they'll be down here to throw you clear off a' there! I'd go if I was you. I'd go now, so's you don't have to face 'em. Ain't gonna be no good in it for you, I can tell you that! Everybody loves Emma, and you're gonna be in a piece a' trouble!"

She slapped a dime on the counter, turned around, and walked out.

Sarah squeezed my hand. "If I buy the cheese, Mommy, can I eat some of it now?"

I leaned down and kissed her.

Hiram Hastings sliced off Sarah's nickel's worth of cheese and gave her an extra taste. We started in gathering the items from Emma's list then, and Sarah stayed as close as she could to my side. I felt like crying. I didn't want to fight with Hazel Sharpe. And I worried how all those words had affected the children. I'd tried to keep them out of it and ended up with them right in the middle.

"We're gonna have a lot of food, huh, Mommy?" Sarah asked me. "I love corn bread. I sure am glad Emma wanted you to make some corn bread."

I reached for a box of salt and a little can of baking powder, sensing that Mr. Hastings was watching us, though not unkindly.

"Mommy, what's a piece of trouble? Is that as much as a heap?"

I scrunched down to Sarah's level and took her in my arms. "Honey, don't worry over what that lady said. She doesn't understand us, that's all. She doesn't understand what Emma wants. It'll all be fine. There won't be any trouble. Not a piece or a heap. 'Cause we haven't done anything wrong."

"She said somebody was gonna throw us off."

"We'll tell Emma. If she's got relatives coming, she'll be happy to know about it."

216

I kissed her forehead and rose to take our goods to be tallied up. We had a lot, that was sure. Bacon and sugar, sweet potatoes and butter and cream. More flour, plus cornmeal, oatmeal, and lard. Rinso soap and lots more besides. I would have felt warm about it all if not for Hazel Sharpe's speech.

We bought a chunk of ice, wrapped it in a clean blanket, and set it down in a box with the food that had to stay cold. The kids found it exciting to have ice of our own again, and Sam let Robert chip off a piece for each of them.

I would have figured we'd have gone on home, then, to save as much of our ice as possible. But Mr. Post wanted to go to Reed's Hardware for his roofing supplies. He took Sam with him and dropped us off at Dearing's little library.

"Won't have time for readin' your books here," he said. "Ask Betty to let you take 'em home. We won't be gone long."

The library was tiny, just one small room with three bookshelves against one wall. But it was enchanting just the same. I went looking for Emily Dickinson, while Sarah pulled *Peter Rabbit* and *The Tale of Tommy Tiptoes* off the shelf. I didn't see what Robert had until we went to the lady at the desk. He tried to cover the title. *Illustrated Bible Stories.*

"You'll have to have a card," the lady said. "You live around here?"

"Yes, ma'am."

That was good enough for her. The only other thing she wanted was my name. Then she filled out a card and presented it to me, and we were ready to go home with our books, feeling like we'd had a trip to town indeed.

Emma was asleep when we got home, which worried me since it was only lunchtime. But Louise said they'd eaten early and Emma had just wanted a nap. They'd been working together on Emma's quilt, I could see that. It was almost finished and prettier than ever, spread out over the table the way it was.

I wondered what Louise could have come up with for their lunch but was too ashamed to ask. And she was too polite to mention how little food we'd left in the house. She seemed delighted to help me stock the cupboards, but she didn't know of the cool pit Emma had told me about.

Willard had dug her a pit in a corner of the basement one year, lined it with bricks, and covered it with a slab of cement. None of us had even noticed it when we were down there the first time. Willard's pit kept things just as cool as putting them down a well. Even cooler, Emma had said, if you threw in a block of ice, which we were about to do.

I was glad I wouldn't have to move a basket out of the way every time I went to the well for water. The cool pit was a fine arrangement. Not as nice as one of those electric refrigerators, but fine just the same. The only time we'd need to put anything down the well was if the cool pit got full. And that wasn't likely to happen any time soon, or maybe ever. By butchering time it would be cold enough to leave things hanging on the porch.

We set what was left of the ice in first, on a tray with ropes tied to the handles so we could pull it up when we needed to. Then we covered the ice with blankets to keep it longer. All the cold food went into a basket, which was lowered in on top. I wasn't sure how long the ice would last—a whole week if we were lucky, but we'd use the cool pit just the same when the ice was gone. Good thing it wasn't a floody basement. The bricked floor had only been a little damp when we first were down here, even after that big storm.

I imagined a kindhearted man, as Emma's husband must have been, down here with a lamp and maybe a friend or two, working to lay all these bricks down. He'd done a fine job; the bricks were smooth and even, the seams barely noticeable under my feet.

"Oh, goodness," Louise suddenly proclaimed. "Emma's bicycle is down here! I would have thought she'd a' thrown it away!"

"Emma rode the bicycle? I thought it must have been Warren's."

"Oh, it was Emma's. And she was something, she was. You should have seen it. She come out to our house one time with a pie in the basket! Don't know how she done it! You couldn't get me on one of them things."

The thought of Emma on a bicycle was a marvel to think about, all right. But I had to turn my thoughts to lunch. I fed everybody corn bread and bacon and beans. Sam and Barrett went back to fix the rest of the fence, with Robert helping them this time. Louise stayed and pulled weeds awhile with me; then we moved some of the wild lilies into the yard where Emma wanted them. I was anxious for Emma to wake up, so it wasn't long before I was ready to go in and make everybody some store-bought tea.

It was kind of fun lifting the ice back out, even though we'd just put it in. Sarah wanted to lick it, so I whacked her off a chunk big enough to fill a teacup. She didn't want any tea. She just sat with her cup, licking away.

Emma woke when she heard us talking. I thought she was looking pale, but she wouldn't admit to feeling poorly with Louise there. I wanted to tell her what Hazel had said about relatives, but thought I'd better wait before bringing up Miss Sharpe.

The rest of the time the Posts were there, Emma and Louise worked together on the quilt, getting it nearly finished before nightfall. I didn't want to leave the house, so Sarah and I worked upstairs, washing the walls and floors. We set some boxes on their sides, one on top of another, to make shelves for our things, and then straightened all our bedding out on the floor.

Then, as though the Lord had sent him, Daniel Norse came over with Emma's bed and the rest of her things from Rita McPiery's. He carried everything in for us and then brought in a little basket of goodies from Rita's church. There was canned milk, a jar of honey, a little sack of red beans. And surely for Emma's benefit, a package of flower seeds.

"Oh, tell them thank you, Mr. Norse," I exclaimed. "You've all been so kind."

He just nodded and said he had to be going. So Louise and I took apart the old bed and set it at the foot of the stairs for the men to haul up to our room. We set up the new bed downstairs for Emma and smoothed the covers on for her. I'd be glad not to sleep in the sitting room anymore. But I was a little nervous that all of us would be so far from Emma at night. We'd have to see that she always had one of her little bells by her bedside.

So now we had one bed upstairs. I decided we'd slide the mattress onto the floor for the kids, since it wouldn't set in the other old frame by itself until we had cut some slats. Sam and I would sleep on the box springs with a quilt or something underneath us. It made for passable bedrooms—there were far worse conditions to be in. And I was confident that our days would be full enough so that we'd sleep well, regardless of what we were lying on.

Emma seemed rather excited to open up one box and pull out her beautiful Seth Thomas clock. She had me put it up on the mantle, with a candle on each side.

"There now," she said. "That's just how Willard liked it." She had me pull her basket-weave chair to the middle of the room and spread out a braided rug that had been on her floor at Rita's. "Ain't it lookin' like home?" she asked.

Louise was glad to help us unpack the rest of the things, but kept saying that before long she and Barrett would have to be going. Sarah and I hurried to make oatmeal cookies to send home with them, since they'd refused my offer of supper. They were expecting Sam the following afternoon, they said, but we were all welcome to come. I decided that if Emma wanted to go to the Posts' again, then I'd go too. But she didn't want to go.

She was real quiet that night, and I finally asked her if she was feeling all right. "Oh, well enough," she told me. "You know how it is."

"Your chest hurting again?"

She barely nodded, not wanting to admit it. "I think I do too much," she reasoned. "Like the day we put in garden. That's what it is."

"Then you'll have to let me do more for you."

"I'd ruther you never even tol' Samuel or the children 'bout this, now," she told me. "No sense a'worryin' 'em. That Sam might want to run us to a doctor tonight, but I don't need it. I'm fine as lamb's wool. You'll see."

"I don't keep things from Sam," I told her. "But I would from the children, if that's what you want."

"'Course it is," she said sternly. "No sense worryin'. I'm feelin' better, anyhow."

And she truly did seem to be. She ate heartily that night and sat in happy attention as I read *Peter Rabbit,* a couple of Bible stories, and a lovely poem before putting the kids to bed.

When I came back downstairs to clean up the kitchen, she asked me to read her more of the poetry.

"You like Dickinson?" I asked.

"I surely do. She's got such a purty way a' sayin' things, you know?"

"I never would have expected us to be so much alike."

"God arranged it, he did. Knowin' I always wanted a daughter." She spoke with certainty. "I couldn't have no more, you know, after Warren. Don't know why. We lost three in the tryin'. Don't know for sure what was wrong with me."

"I'm so sorry, Emma."

"It weren't your fault. God had his plan, that's all, knowin' we'd find each other one day. You don't mind if I like to think of ya as mine, do you now?"

"No, I'm honored."

She turned toward the window. "What's your Samuel doin' in the barn again tonight?"

I looked out the window to where a faint glow was barely visible through the cracks of one barn wall. "He didn't say. But I think he may be working on that porch swing for us."

TWENTY-SIX

Samuel

It felt good to be pounding on something. With some smaller nails I'd gotten from Barrett Post, I hammered together the whole frame of Emma's chair. There'd be no pulling those nails out. I whacked every one of them till there was nothing sticking up enough to hit.

I'd talked to Dewey that day over the telephone stuck in a corner at the lumberyard. I hadn't told Julia about it yet, but Dewey had told me he was trying to sell his house—if he couldn't get work in the mines around West Frankfort, he'd be heading east. We had family back there, he said, and ought to be closer to them.

Thoughts of my mother and stepfather, Dewey's mother, and our cousins Louis and Baynes, were enough to sour my stomach. Not one of them would turn a tap for me. I'd wished Dewey luck, and he'd done me the same, and that was the end of it. Go to my family back east? I couldn't imagine it. Going back to my mother would be like volunteering to step down into a mire pit.

I could still picture Miss Hazel charging at us in Dearing, and right then memories of my mother and Dewey's mother, June, were not that different. They'd snipped and snarled at every turn, nothing ever good enough for them. But they didn't hide their crotchetiness under a churchy coat. They'd cuss you like a sailor to your face. It made my head hurt.

But I'd come to Illinois thinking of family, mine and Dewey's. Sure, I'd let myself get stopped here at the farm, but I still wanted to see him, and I didn't like the notion of him going so far. I'd suggested we get together, that he come and see us, but he wouldn't promise me anything. He even said he thought I shouldn't have come to Illinois.

I guess nobody thought much of us being out here except Emma, and maybe the Posts or Rita McPiery. They'd been good to us, but the weight of everybody else was a little hard to bear. Hazel Sharpe had beaten herself into my brain, and yet Julia and Emma and even Robert were anxious to get back to church next Sunday. I would be happier being isolated, to just dig in my heels and never leave this farm, except to work for Post.

But this farm was a big part of my worry. I knew we'd have to do better to make a decent time of it for winter. And how would my kids react when the day came for Emma to be leaving us? I wasn't fool enough not to notice how pale she looked. And she wasn't moving around much either. Sometimes people in that condition don't make it through till spring. That would make the winter even more difficult for me, wondering if we'd be burying Emma in the cold, hard ground.

Such thoughts weren't good for anything, I well knew. But still I couldn't shake them. What would we do when Emma died? Where would we go? How would my kids handle the grieving? What if one of them was the first to find her gone?

I pulled a wheel axle down loose from the old wagon and sat for a minute, thinking about the hard task of shortening it. I finally decided that the wagon axle was too heavy to put on a chair, and that gave me the problem of how to mount the wheels without it.

I walked to the shed, thinking that Willard Graham must have been a pretty handy man. He had stuffed lots of different tools in his old shed, plus wire and some various metal scraps. But nothing ideal for a purpose like this. *Lord, help me figure this out.*

From nails on the wall hung Mr. Graham's handsaws, three of them. And the newest-looking one, the hacksaw, would cut metal. I took it from its place and went back to the barn, studied that axle for a minute, and then started to cut. I didn't need an axle, long or short. All I needed was the ends that the wheels fit to, somehow mounted one on each side of the underside of the chair.

Now I knew I could finish this thing. And maybe that's what Emma was waiting on. She hadn't been to the grave yet, didn't even seem to want to go, though we'd asked her a couple of times. She surely knew the distance was too far to hobble with those canes and didn't want to ask to be carried. I'd have to make sure this chair could handle the tough terrain. I'd push her. I'd make sure she got there. With a lap full of flowers and the sweetest of memories sweeping over her heart. She'd smile, she'd cry, and it would be worth all this effort.

TWENTY-SEVEN

Julia

Before old Jack the rooster crowed the next morning, I heard Emma moving around downstairs. The kids were still asleep, and I thought Sam was too, but as I started to sit up he reached his hand to mine and sighed. "You suppose she's making root coffee already?"

"I don't know. I'm going to find out and see if I can help."

"Sick yesterday, wasn't she?"

"Yes. She was sick, but I don't think it was too bad."

"What if she has one of those naps sometime, Juli, and Sarah runs in to see her and finds her dead?"

"It's not going to help anyone to think of things like that."

"It could happen."

"No. The kids know to leave her alone when she's napping. But she's strong, Sam. She could live a lot of years."

He sat up, his eyes looking dark and pained in the new dawn light. "I hope she does. I like her as much as you do. I'd just as soon she live forever, but she's past eighty with a bad heart, Juli. She could die tomorrow."

I wanted to get downstairs and see if Emma was all right. More than that, I wanted to end this kind of talk because I didn't want it swirling around in my mind. "If she goes, she'll be with her Willard. I think that will suit her fine. And we can't be worrying about it."

"What's it going to be like, though, honey? Having to tell neighbors and church people? Are we really going to be able to handle everything that'll come, us staying here?"

"What would Emma do if we don't? We've got her started now! To hear her tell it, she has all she wants. It'd be plain cruel to back away now. Don't you think?"

He sighed again, plopped down on his back, and stared at the ceiling. "We've been through this before, haven't we?"

I got up and started buttoning my old work dress. "Yes. And I don't blame you, but we can't be changing our minds every time she gets sick. Hazel said she might have relatives coming. If we're leaving, that would be the time to go, once she's in their hands. If we're staying, we ought to be resolved to it, no matter what, for Emma's sake. We can't just abandon her when we had an agreement."

"You're right."

He was quiet for a moment, and the sounds from downstairs stopped. I leaned and touched his shoulder. "I'm going to go check on her."

"Okay," he whispered and leaned and kissed my hand. "I want to stay," he said. "But it's an awful thought, saying good-bye to her, even if it's years away."

"It'll happen with all of us."

"Maybe so. But I'd rather not think about it." He stood up and reached for his shirt. "I love you. I could hold you all day, but you better go on."

I gave him a quick kiss and went to the stairs, tying my hair with a scarf as I went down. I could hear her again, and this time it was the shuffle of her canes against the hardwood floor. By the time I got to the bottom of the stairs, I could see her on her way to the kitchen, dressed in a pair of Willard's old overalls.

"Good morning, Emma."

She turned her head. "Oh, did I wake you?"

"It's time to be up. I ought to be milking Lula Bell before long."

"Thought I'd do that m'self this morning." She turned around and went back to making strenuous progress toward the kitchen.

Lula Bell would be lowing before long, no doubt ready for the milking, and we were ready for the milk. But I could not picture Emma heading out there on her own, handling the bucket, the stool, the cow, and her canes, all at once.

"Emma—"

"She knows me. She ain't gonna give me no trouble."

"But when you do too much, remember? I can do it, and it's no trouble at all."

"It's a trouble to me, thinking of you doing all the work around here, and me sittin' in one place so long and never gettin' out with the stock. I always did love 'em, you know. 'Specially m' milk cows."

I wasn't sure what to say. Who was I to tell her no? But I didn't want her overdoing it and ending up in bed again either. "Sit with me a minute," I finally said. "Let's have some tea."

"I want flapjacks for breakfast. How 'bout you?"

"Sounds wonderful." She let me help her the rest of the way to the table, and I poked at the coals in the cookstove, threw in a couple of dry cobs, and soon had the fire started.

"You think I'm just bein' foolish, to think a' doin' some milkin' m'self?" she suddenly asked, almost daring me to disagree.

I set a pot of water on the stove and turned toward her. "Not foolish," I said carefully. "It's perfectly understandable. A little hasty maybe, after being sick yesterday. I wish you wouldn't work yourself too hard. Rest today."

"I didn't do nothin' yesterday. And I don't like sittin'. You get sick of that after awhile. I used to do ever'thin' and go wherever I pleased."

She was suddenly quiet, perhaps thinking of those times. And I didn't know what to say. What would I be like if I'd lost one leg and someone younger tried to tell me not to do so much? I probably wouldn't handle it well, not with half the grace that Emma had.

"You know," she said, "I got me a bike in the cellar. At least, I reckon it's still there. That's where Albert put it last time he come down. I didn't want to get rid of it, but that just goes to show you my ol' hard head. It's plain to a blind man that I ain't gonna be usin' it no more. Oughta have Sam pull it outside for Robert. He could be ridin' a bike to school."

Emma had a nice idea, generous as always, but it struck me as terribly sad. She was closing another book she didn't really want closed.

"He's fine walking, Emma," I assured her. "That's what the neighbor boys do."

"Ain't no use that bicycle just sittin' around doin' nobody a bit of good! If he wants to walk with the Hammonds, that's fine, but I sure s'pose he'd like ridin' sometime, don't you?"

"Yes, I suppose he would."

"Fine. You let me bless the boy, then. Closest thing to a grandson I'll ever have."

Her words pained me, but I couldn't put a finger on why. I almost felt like crying as I measured the cut tea leaves into Emma's cup strainer. I ended up spilling some of it on the counter, so I brushed it off into my hand and added the spilled stuff to my cup, not wanting to waste.

I brought Emma the sugar, and she spooned some into her cup. I realized that I hadn't told her what Hazel Sharpe had said yesterday at the grocer's. Last night I'd been so concerned over her not feeling well that I didn't want to burden her with the unpleasant encounter.

"Emma," I said quietly. "I'll go do the milking if you'll let me, but first I need to tell you I saw Miss Hazel at the store yesterday. She said you might have relatives come to visit."

Emma straightened herself in her chair. "Did she? Well, ain't that funny, them tellin' her and not even writin' to let me know!"

I took a deep breath and sat beside her. "She's upset with us, Emma. She still thinks we have your thinking all turned around. She said she asked them to come and run us out of here."

She was quiet for a moment, and I didn't know what to expect. But then she laughed. Actually laughed, while I was sitting there worrying that such news might upset her. Obviously, she was looking at the situation from a different direction than I was.

"Well, now," she began when she was able. "She's got a surprise comin', don't you s'pose? It'll be just fine seein' some a' m' folks again. Wonder who it is comin'? Prob'ly Albert. She knows him the best, and he'd be willin' to come down from Chicago for a real 'mergency. Always said he would be, anyhow."

"Emma, don't you think it'll upset him, finding us here?"

She nodded and gave me a kind smile. "He'll be upset a'ready, if Hazel's been talking at him. Folks that don't know her good sometimes listen too much." She leaned over and started rolling up her one flopping overall leg.

230

"Emma, doesn't it bother you at all?"

She glanced up at me. "Not a whit. And don't you let it bother you neither. It'll be just fine, seein' him again! An' I'll be tickled to introduce you. He'll like you fine. I'll make plain sure of that." She took hold of one of her canes. "Cup a tea's a fine thing, but chores is waitin'. If you want to tend to Lula Bell, then I'll make breakfast. I ain't dead yet, and I ain't gonna act like I am."

That pretty well settled it. I put everything that Emma might need in easy reach, and then she shooed me outside, saying she could handle flapjacks by herself.

Lula Bell was already lowing from the barn by the time I got outside. I took the time to rinse the milking pail at the well and then hurried on.

Emma was like Grandma Pearl in a lot of ways. So independent and practical. Grandma had loved milking, not for the work but for the fresh milk and what a person could do with it. She used to churn fresh butter on Tuesdays and Fridays, and even sold a bit of it to the doctor's family in town. I would be glad when we had milk enough to make me want to churn. Maybe we'd have butter to spare too, one day.

I sat on the old three-legged stool and stroked Lula Bell's side. She turned her head to look at me as I wrapped my fingers around an udder. I remembered the first time I'd ever done this, back in Grandma's barn, with Grandma standing there, giving me pointers. "You can't just squeeze," she'd say. "You've got to work it a little to make the milk come."

Sam came in the barn, gave me a kiss, and told me he was going to shore up the outhouse after breakfast. I could hear him tinkering in the west end of the barn, and then there was silence except for the mew of a cat and the happy splash of milk against the pail. We would have more than what Sarah and Robert could drink with breakfast this morning. Maybe we'd be lowering some into the cool pit for the first time.

I was turning the cow out to graze when I heard voices from the timber. As I walked around the side of the barn with my milk pail, I saw two girls slip into the yard and head straight for the strawberry patch. Hammonds, almost surely.

One girl was nearly as big as me, and the other was Sarah's size. They bent down, looking for ripe berries, somehow not managing to notice me.

"Good morning," I called, and they both jumped.

"Ma sent us," the biggest girl hurriedly explained. "She's got an awful cravin'."

"For strawberries," the little one added, looking just a bit fearful of my reaction. They told me their names were Lizbeth and Rorey Hammond. And I told them what Emma had said, that they could have a couple of bowls full this year, but they wouldn't be able to have them all.

"Tell you what," I offered. "Your mama's timing is excellent. They're coming on beautifully. I was going to pick some more today. But I'll help you pick. You can have whatever we find. Then in two or three days, I'll help you pick the patch again. But the rest is up to Emma to decide."

I got down on my knees, hunting the ripest berries with the girls, when I should have been taking the milk in or getting the eggs. And the gesture didn't go unnoticed.

"We didn't 'spect you'd be nice," Rorey remarked. "Ma said you might run us off."

"Neighbors are supposed to be neighborly," I told them. "And do for each other when they get the chance."

I got to thinking about that and about these two girls, neither of them clean, in clothes worn out worse than mine. The Hammonds had needs—that was always Emma's reason for being so lenient with them. And whether she had the wisest approach or not, she knew what she was talking about. Maybe I'd been too hard. Not for George's sake, but for his children's.

"Does your mother need anything other than strawberries?" I asked timidly, not sure how they'd react to the inquiry.

"Sassafras tea," said the little one. "With honey in it."

"Hush, Rorey," her sister told her. "I'm gonna see to that."

"Well, if you go hunting sassafras anytime soon," I said, "I'd like to come. There's enough in these woods for two families, don't you think?"

Lizbeth seemed a little uncomfortable with the idea of me tagging along. "I guess. It's Ma usually goes."

I nodded to the girl, who looked somehow old and young at the same time. "When is her baby due?"

"Any day. We'll be fetchin' Mrs. Mueller this time, Ma said. But I'd kinda like to come after Emma too, long as she's willin'. Or you. It don't hurt to have help enough. You got experience, ain't you? A little anyhow, with two children."

I was a bit shaken by their approach to this child's birth. Just gather up the neighbors, whether you know them or not. "Wouldn't your mother like a doctor?" I asked.

Both girls shook their heads. "Takes too long. Costs too much too."

"I don't know that I could do much," I told them. "And Emma would have a hard time getting over there quickly."

"That's what wagons is for, ma'am," Lizbeth said with a look I might have gotten had I told her I'd been born in a cave.

"Is your mother doing all right, then?" I asked timidly.

"Well enough, in her shape."

"If you need anything, come say so," I heard myself saying. Maybe these Hammonds took what they wanted sometimes, but maybe they still needed us to care about them, just like Emma insisted on doing. "You're welcome anytime. Tell your folks. Okay?"

"Yes, ma'am," Lizbeth said, clearly surprised at what I had said. "You can come over too. Ma ain't mad at you. Not none. She even tol' me she'd like to meet ya, an' I know she means it. You'll come, won't ya? How 'bout today?"

"Today?" I could hardly picture myself suddenly showing up in front of Wilametta Hammond, a total stranger. But why not do it? I could bring her a shortbread to go with her strawberries. Emma had wanted to give them something, and maybe that would do nicely. Maybe we'd even end up friends.

When the girls had left with their bowl of berries, I took the milk in and found Emma frying her flapjacks.

"I seen 'em out the window," she said. "Hope you told 'em they can't do that every day."

"I did."

"They's good kids, though. I like havin' 'em around once in awhile. Oughta get Sarey together with that Rorey 'fore long. Wouldn't they just hit it off?"

"They invited me to come see their mother."

"You oughta go. And take Sarey. It'd be just the thing. Wilametta'll talk your ear off, but you'll like meetin' her. And Sarey's liable to 'come best of friends with Rorey and her little brothers, them bein' neighbors and all."

When Sarah came downstairs about two minutes later, she was mightily disappointed to have missed meeting the neighbor girls. But she quickly got excited with the idea of visiting them. She skipped along behind me all the way to the henhouse and was just as pleased as I was that three of the four hens had eggs that morning. I decided to let one of them just set. Emma was happy with that. She said the hen'd be glad to lay more, and with God's blessing we'd have chicks running around in less than a month.

While we'd been outside, Emma had boiled sugar in a little water for syrup. We finished off every flapjack she made, and the rest of the bacon from the Dearing store.

"Great breakfast," Robert said, and went off to school with a smile on his face.

Right away, I mixed up a shortbread and got it in the oven. I didn't want to leave Emma alone, so I knew I'd have to get to the neighbors' and back by lunchtime, when Sam had to leave to work on Mr. Post's roof. Sam was a little apprehensive about my visit to the Hammonds', but then told me to greet George for him.

Before long, the kitchen was clean and the baking was done. I laid a clean towel over the batch of muffins meant for us and wrapped the hot shortbread in another towel. Emma gave me simple directions to the Hammonds' farm and then set to work, sorting through a lidded basket we'd found at the bottom of one of her boxes. With the shortbread cradled in my arm, I set off walking through the timber to the Hammond house. Sarah, with a handful of daisies, skipped merrily along at my side.

The walk was lovely. The blackberries had already lost nearly all of their flower petals, and I made the delightful discovery of a mulberry tree not fifty feet from the creek. Oh, that would make some fine jam!

As we walked near the pond, it occurred to me that the cattails along one end would be dry and woolly come fall. I thought I might be able to pull off enough fluff to stuff a pillow or two. If it didn't smell funny. I couldn't remember if dry cattails had a smell.

We arrived at the Hammonds' in less time than I'd thought we would. Sam had described the place to me, but still I was surprised. It was worse than I'd expected. Like nothing had been bought, painted, or fixed in half my lifetime. Rorey and two poorly dressed little boys crawled out from under a porch that looked as if it could fall on them. They were dirty as little piglets when they ran up to greet us, and squealing just as loud. I hesitated to turn Sarah loose to play with such a bunch.

"Stay with me," I told her. "Till we meet Mrs. Hammond and you give her your daisies."

George was nowhere around, nor were any of the bigger boys. Lizbeth was in the side yard, hanging clothes on a line that leaned so far she had to bunch things up to keep them off the ground. She looked tired and was paying very little attention to her younger siblings. But when she saw me she looked surprised. So much so that I thought I'd scared her. Then she saw the pan under my arm and smiled.

"For us, Mrs. Wortham?"

"Yes. A shortbread to go along with those strawberries."

"Oh, that's what Mama wanted. And I ain't had time to get to it yet. That sure is nice."

She took the shortbread quickly in her hands, as if she feared I might change my mind. Then she ushered us up the porch steps, each of which seemed to slope at its own separate angle, and led us through the dusty, cluttered house to her mother's bedroom.

Wilametta Hammond was an extremely large woman who would have been large even if she weren't so immensely pregnant. The wood-frame bed she was propped up in didn't look like it could hold her. The floor all around was cluttered with all manner of things. An old shirt. A filthy sock. A dented teapot. A broom handle. As if someone had merrily tossed things about and then let them lay.

I could hear Mrs. Hammond's coarse breathing from the doorway, though she wasn't asleep. Her chubby pink fingers gingerly held a cloth to her forehead. She looked exhausted just laying there, the sweat forming little streams down her face, though the room was cool.

She hardly moved when Lizbeth ushered me in, but managed to show her excitement just the same.

"Lordy, you're the neighbor, now, ain't' ya? Ain't ya? And me lookin' so frightful! Oh, come in anyway! I was a'prayin' you'd want to visit sometime!"

"Mrs. Hammond—"

"Oh, please call me Wilametta."

"Wilametta—"

"Looky there what a precious doll you got!" She gestured toward Sarah, not giving me a chance to string three words together. "C'mere, you sweet thing!" she cooed. "Let me look at you."

Sarah looked up at me with her eyes wide. I nodded to her and gave her arm a little pat, and she bravely went just close enough to the bed to drop her daisies on Mrs. Hammond's very round middle.

"What's this?" Wilametta exclaimed, her blue eyes round and wide.

"For you," Sarah whispered. "I picked 'em."

Wilametta scooped up the greater part of the bouquet and took a long hard sniff. "Oh, these is nice. And ain't it the sweetest thing you ever did see, her bringin' 'em to me? You thought of it all by yourself too, didn't you, child?"

"Yes, ma'am," Sarah answered timidly, reaching backward to take my hand.

"Such an angel." Wilametta's smile was pretty and friendly, but then she shocked us both with a sudden bellow.

"Rorey! Rorey, child!"

The poor little girl had followed us in and was standing almost right behind me, though her mother hadn't seen her. She jumped and was at her mother's side before I could have shaken a stick.

But Wilametta had turned her attention to Sarah again. "Did you ever see a baby goat where you come from?"

Sarah shook her head.

"We got you a treat, then. What'd you say your name was?"

"Sarah."

"Ah, that's a beautiful name. It's Bible too. Did you know that? And I knowed a Sarey once that could sew the finest dresses you ever hoped to see. They looked like they come from some New York factory, and it was all by hand."

Finally she turned her head and acknowledged her young daughter, who stood waiting patiently. "Rorey, be nice now and take little Sarey to see Shuck and Billy, will you?" She smiled up at me. "That's twin goats we got out back. Sure hope they's the only twins we ever have 'round here." She laughed and gave Rorey a nudge in Sarah's direction.

Rorey didn't need any more prompting. She grabbed one of Sarah's hands and gave her a little pull. "C'mon," she whispered. "You'll like Shuck and Billy. They got head bumps where the horns is fixin' to grow."

Sarah looked up at me again, still uncertain. I told her she could go, but just to see the goats. She seemed relieved at that, but the instruction was as much for me as it was for her. Hard to tell what sort of things children could encounter around here unsupervised.

"You ain't gonna let her play?" Wilametta questioned. "She don't have to come right back in! We needs a chance to sit and talk. Long as they leave the pigs alone, there ain't nothin' dangerous out there."

"She's not used to a farm just yet," I explained, hoping Wilametta wouldn't realize that I didn't feel right giving Sarah the same liberty on this farm that I gave her on Emma's.

"She brung shortbread," Lizbeth piped up. "I set it in the window. You want I bring you some?"

"No," Wilametta said, suddenly more quiet. "No, not yet." She watched Sarah go out the door with Rorey, then

238

turned her attention to me. "I jus' don't understand it," she said. "You let us at the berries. Now you come bringin' shortbread. But George said your husband weren't no friendlier than a polecat in the cornfield. You sure he don't mind you off here with us?"

"No. He doesn't mind. He said to tell George hello," I said, a bit surprised that anyone would think Sam unfriendly.

"George'll be surprised," she told me. "He took it in his head that your husband don't like him none. Sure is nice of him to send a greetin'." She looked at me a minute in silence. "I thought we was in for a feud," she finally said. "You bein' here's relieved my mind some over that. Lizbeth, get the woman a chair."

I watched the older girl scurry to the next room and drag back a chair that looked homemade, with a woven back and spindly legs. She scooted it right up beside the bed, and I sat in it reluctantly, somehow not wanting to be within reach of Wilametta's big pink arms.

"Hard to understand Emma these days," she said. "We always been the ones takin' care a' things for her. We always put in field for her and kept the 'quipment up, you know. We even offered her to stay here, long time ago, 'fore you come on the scene."

What was I to say? I could see why Emma wouldn't want to stay with the Hammonds. She liked an orderly, pretty farm and would have a hard time with people who didn't even seem to notice what frightful shape their place was in.

"No offense, you understand," Wilametta continued. "But we'd a' done just anything for her! Don't really know why she's picked you up. She's so good-hearted, though. Wouldn't never turn out a stray or nothin'."

I still said nothing, and she laughed nervously. "Not that you're strays, now! I didn't mean that. But her giving you her place, it don't figure as ordinary, you know that. Seems by rights—"

She stopped suddenly, perhaps realizing that this line of talk was not such a good idea. I'd certainly heard more than I wanted to.

"She hasn't given us her place, Mrs. Hammond—"

"Well," she said slowly, with obvious relief. "Ain't that a welcome thing to hear! But I don't understand what you're doin' there, then. We didn't move in till we had us a good agreement—"

She stopped again, her face turning from pink to red. "Maybe it's time for some shortbread."

But I'd noticed what she'd said. And I wouldn't let her change the subject so easily. "Did you get your property from Emma, then?"

Wilametta's eyes turned cold, and I immediately regretted my question.

"We signed papers good and legal with Willard," she puffed. "More'n twenty years ago! And we was entitled too, seein's George's pappy worked this land 'fore him! But you, comin' all the way from God knows where! What you got for these parts is beyond me!"

"I'm sorry, Mrs. Hammond. I didn't mean to offend you."

"Maybe it's city ways, I dunno. But you ain't especially easy to be neighborly to. That's what George told me."

We were both quiet for a moment, and I tried to figure out what I could say without making matters worse. Even to excuse myself and go home might be considered rude now.

As I sat there, I noticed one of Sarah's daisies slide off Wilametta's large dress and fall to the floor. Without a thought, I leaned forward and picked it up. The others were still in her lap, and I saw that there would be room enough on the bedside table, which already held a worn Bible, a dishcloth, and a candle, for a vase of flowers.

"Would you like them in water?" I asked. "They'd look so cheery there on the table beside you."

240

She stared at me as though I'd spoken in Greek, but then her face began to soften. "You surely don't need to do that," she said. "Lizbeth! Come an' put these flowers in some water!"

Lizbeth rushed in from wherever she'd been, gathered the flowers, and went back out again. Mrs. Hammond certainly had obedient daughters. She might have had a husband who was rude and a home that seemed to be falling apart around her, but the conduct of her daughters spoke well for her.

Lizbeth was back in no time with Sarah's daisies in a quart jar dripping with water. She set it on her mother's end table without wiping the bottom or setting anything beneath it. I thought of the ring the water would make on the old oak, but I didn't say a word.

"I do 'preciate your thoughtfulness," Wilametta told me. "Bringin' a cake and all. I s'pose you're tryin' to be all right in the ways you know, and that's kind of you."

"I was thinking I might offer to keep some of the children sometimes," I said quickly. "So you can rest once the baby's born. We're needing feathers for another mattress, if you expect you'll have any to spare, and I've no other way to pay you for them."

"It'll be some time 'fore we have enough again to stuff a mattress," she said. "We do fine too, with the children. They can see to themselves, for the most part. Every one of 'em knows what they ain't s'posed to be about. And they mind too."

"That's wonderful, Mrs. Hammond," I told her sincerely. "A lot of children don't mind."

"Mine do. They fetch the belt if they don't. But you got you a pretty nice little girl too."

"Thank you. How old is your Rorey?"

"All of six. And ready to help me with the newborn, she is. I do hope it's another girl. I got me seven boys a'ready. That's enough for one woman."

I couldn't help but smile and acknowledge that it was. I found it hard to imagine what life would be like if I had nine or ten children running around instead of two. *What a lot of food they must need in this house!*

"Rorey's so small, though," I said. "And Lizbeth surely has her hands full too. Isn't there something you could use some extra help with?"

"I'm just hopin' you let us at the berries, that's all. Emma always let us have all the berries we want. Blackberries too. Dewberries. And hickory nuts in the fall."

"We can surely share."

"Good hearin' you say that. You can be jus' completely sure I won't forget."

"I won't forget either."

"George says you'll run us out our home, just as soon as Emma dies. We meant to pay all along, you know, but the crops ain't been so good, year after year."

There was a twinge of fear in her eyes, and I realized that the Hammonds owed Emma for more than the cows and the use of one field. She must have carried them patiently, or maybe forgiven them entirely, over and over for years now.

What would they do, really, if Emma died tomorrow and a bank or a lawyer or an unsympathetic relative stepped in and took a look? The Hammonds had reason to fear.

"We should be friends," I suddenly said.

"We might could be that, I suppose," Wilametta said cautiously. "Don't know 'bout our men, though. They can be more hardheaded."

"Sam's really nice," I told her. "He'd never cause you any trouble."

She frowned. "But you need more'n feathers, don't ya? He ain't got you fixed up very well, George says. What're you eatin' over there?"

"We're managing all right. And Sam's been working hard."

"I know one thing. Even if we ain't got cash, George always makes sure we got plenty enough to fill our bellies. We ain't never short of good meat and butter, that's for sure. You want to stay for lunch?"

"Thank you, but I can't. I need to go back and cook for Sam and Emma before Sam leaves."

She sat up in surprise. "Leaves? Where's he goin'?"

"To help Mr. Post on his roof. In exchange for the fence work he did for us."

I didn't say anything more about Sam working for the Posts, figuring it might create hard feelings somehow. It *was* unusual that Mr. Post hadn't gotten himself another local man that he'd known a lot longer.

Wilametta was looking ready to say something else when we heard a crash and a scream and a whole garbled series of yells outside. I jumped from my chair, thinking I'd heard Sarah's voice among the jumble.

"Merciful heavens!" Wilametta shrieked. "Lizbeth, run and see what's happened!"

I stared at the woman for a minute as she took up a square of heavy paperboard from the side of her bed and started fanning herself. "Those kids," she muttered. "You never know."

I didn't wait, not for Wilametta to raise her head or Lizbeth to come back with a report. I ran from the room without another word and found my way to the outside door.

"Sarah!"

"Mama!" I heard Sarah yell in reply.

A little goat with two-inch horns came trotting around the side of the house and almost ran into me. Behind the first one came two more, running just as fast. Then another, much bigger, followed by Willy and a smaller boy, both shouting.

"You ain't gonna catch goats thataway, stupids!" Lizbeth yelled. "Shut up and coax 'em with some grain!"

Julia's Hope

I could hear my Sarah crying, so I followed the sound and eventually found her, lying on the ground in a tangle of wire and boards. Parts of a leaning fence stretched beyond her in both directions, and I could see what had happened. A little thing like Sarah had managed to collapse the fence.

"I didn't mean to," she sobbed. "It just broke."

Rorey looked up at me anxiously. "I hope you ain't mad," she said. "It weren't Sarah's fault. All she done was climb over the fence. We always do that. Guess we knows the right places for it, maybe."

I took Sarah into my arms. She wasn't hurt badly, just banged up a bit on the elbows, one knee, and her chin. She was more scared than anything else. But she was already becoming calm.

Only Rorey had stayed with Sarah; the other children were still chasing goats. "Pa'll fix the fence," Rorey assured Sarah. "Don't you worry. He won't be too mad."

I looked up at the girl, wondering just what sort of reaction George Hammond would have. *Mad? I should hope not. He ought to be mortified, having a neighbor girl hurt on his property because of something he should have fixed.*

"Mama, can we go home?" Sarah asked me as I wiped her chin with my scarf.

"We will," I promised. "First we have to go in and tell Mrs. Hammond what happened."

"Do we have to?" she asked, almost crying again. "I didn't mean to let the goats out."

"I know. And she'll understand." I lifted her up, and she bravely hobbled along beside me, clinging to my arm with both hands. "Are you all right, sweetie?" I asked, feeling bad for her, even though she had bucked up so well.

"My leg hurts."

"Do you need me to carry you awhile?"

She smiled a little and wiped away a tiny tear with the back of her hand. "You don't haves to, Mommy," she said. "It wasn't your fault."

I stopped and swooped her into my arms. I knew Sarah could be a tough little trooper, but she didn't have to be *that* tough. "C'mon, sugar," I told her. "Let's say bye to Rorey's mom."

Rorey tagged along behind us, almost on my heels. "You're strong, Mrs. Wortham. Mama never picks me up. She can't, 'cause I'm too big. You sure are strong. Could you pick *me* up?"

"Honey, mothers who are about due for a little one aren't supposed to be lifting such big girls," I told her. "I'm sure your mother's plenty strong when she's not expecting."

"Don't know," she answered. "She ain't even picked up Berty in hunderds of years, and he's littler than me! She ain't never picked me up. Honest!"

I turned and looked at her for a moment, wondering if there was any reason at all for such a whopper. She surely had no concept of what a hundred years was. Maybe she was just hoping to get me to carry her sometime too, just for the fun.

I stepped onto the wide porch, carefully avoiding a place where half of a board had fallen in. I didn't knock. Lizbeth was still herding goats, and I knew Wilametta wouldn't get up just to open the door. I walked in, shifted Sarah's weight in my arms, and headed back to the bedroom.

"Oh, heavens," Wilametta exclaimed, looking very red. "Is the little angel all right? What happened? Rorey, don't stand there. Get Mrs. Wortham a wet cloth. Hurry on, now."

I told her what had happened and said we were headed home, though Sarah wasn't hurt bad.

"You ain't gonna hate me now, are ya?" she questioned. "You ain't gonna be tellin' Emma bad on us?"

"She might ask what happened," I answered calmly. "But I won't tell her anything but the truth."

"Oh," she frowned, suddenly shaking her head. "It was just one of them things. You know. We got good fencin'

245

all over. Them boys must a' loosened somethin'. It'd be better not to tell her nothin'. Don't you think? She don't need be troubled over such a little thing. Don't you agree it's a little thing?"

I didn't know what to say. If the Hammonds were so worried about what Emma thought, then why hadn't they been more careful all this time? Did Wilametta really think a broken fence would matter more to Emma than being lied to and left unpaid?

Suddenly she scrunched up her face and looked at the ceiling. "Oh, dear," she said. "Oh, dear." She looked pale, and for a minute there, scared.

I set Sarah down in the old woven chair and stepped a little closer, my stomach turning a flip-flop. "What is it?"

Rorey came in with a dripping rag, and Wilametta told her to go out and get Lizbeth, whether the goats were in or not. The girl shoved the wet cloth at my hand and disappeared. Wilametta watched me dab at Sarah's scraped knee, but I watched her.

"Are you all right?" I asked. "Do you need help?"

"I will 'fore long. There'll be news for the church folks on Sunday, I can just tell. I sure do hope for a girl. Wanta name her Grace. Don't you think that's a pretty name?"

"Yes. Beautiful. But can I do anything? Are you all right?"

"Oh, it was quite a kick, that's all. I just feel so tight I could bust. Gonna have Lizbeth fix me a footbath and get George from the field." There was a strange sort of look in her eyes. I couldn't tell for sure what it was. Pain, maybe, but she wasn't wanting to let on.

"Do you want me to wait?"

"Oh no. Get your little one on home. I'm fine. Just so sorry, so sorry she come up hurt. You okay now, sweetie?" She turned her eyes to Sarah, but I could see she was sweating even more than before.

"I'm okay," Sarah answered bravely, reaching for my hand.

"Mrs. Hammond, maybe I should stay till your husband gets here."

"No. I wouldn't keep you. We got it figgered out. He'll be fetchin' me Mrs. Mueller when the time comes, but that ain't just yet, don't you worry."

I wasn't convinced. Something had changed about her whole demeanor. "Mrs. Hammond, I could—"

"Means a lot," she said softly, looking away. "Means a lot that you said you was willin' to be friends. I sure hope that ain't changed. I sure hope Emma ain't gonna be mad. You tell her we do just as best as we can."

There were tears in her eyes. She was a true mystery to me. Boisterous and brash, then solemn and emotional. Of course, being pregnant could account for all that.

"Mrs. Hammond, Emma seems happy to have you here—"

"Won't you call me Wilametta? Oh, dear soul, I never did ask your first name."

"Julia."

"Julia. That's pretty. Fits you. Sorry 'bout your little one. Do run on and fix some vittles for that man a' yours." She took a deep breath. "Tell Emma it'd be the dearest blessing to see her again! And it ain't that I wouldn't have her. I'm just callin' for Mrs. Mueller this time 'cause I don't want to be no trouble. You know she ain't been well." She breathed out heavily and scrunched her face again.

"I felt so bad last time," she went on, the strain apparent in her voice. "My boys fetched her, and she was a god-send to me and Berty when he come. But she was so sick, Julia. Just so sick I thought she'd die. I been scared ever since that she was gonna die. And then where would we be? You just don't understand. And George, he ain't one to say. Ain't nobody would understand but maybe Emma herself! We ain't got nothin' but here!"

"It's not helping you to worry over such things right now," I said gently. "Can I get you something?"

"Oh, Lizbeth, where are you?"

As if on cue, Lizbeth came running into the house, all hot and sweaty, and stopped in the doorway, almost breathless. "Big Bill's the only one out now, Ma, an' you know how stubborn he can be."

"Oh, child, forget the goat! Get me some salts for m' sore feet, will you?"

"Mama?"

"Don't fret," Wilametta commanded. "Just do as I say."

Lizbeth turned and walked out of the room, suddenly looking two shades paler herself.

"Well, Julia. It's been fine."

I heard the sound of the front door again. Lizbeth had gone back outside, and I heard voices but couldn't make out what they were saying.

"Do you need me to do anything?" I asked again, not sure I was bold enough to ask if the labor had begun.

"No. No, you ask Lizbeth to get one of the boys to take you home in the wagon. Little one won't have to walk so far that way."

"If you need anything—"

"Now, don't say that. I reckon you know how beholden I am already to Emma! Ain't gonna be tangling myself up owin' you too. Wouldn't never get clear."

I took her plump hand in mine, and she looked at me in surprise. "There's no owing anybody involved," I told her. "This is neighborly, and sisterly. If you need anything, you just tell us."

"All right," she said finally, almost in a whisper. "You're kind to say so. I'm gonna nap a bit 'fore lunch, if you don't mind. Just soak m' feet and rest awhile."

There was nothing more to be said. We'd been dismissed, and I had to trust that the Hammond family knew what they were doing. I carried Sarah out, and she hugged against my neck.

One of the boys had already hitched the wagon and was on his way to the road. But we didn't call after him. It wasn't so hard to walk. I carried Sarah about half way, and then she said she was feeling better and walked the rest. As soon as we got back to the yard, Sarah ran for Sam, but I went straight for the house.

Emma had her quilting out again, stretched over the kitchen table. It didn't look like there could possibly be much left to finish. I stepped toward her, almost breathless.

"Emma, I think the Hammonds' baby will be here soon. Wilametta didn't want to say so, but it's not hard to tell how uncomfortable she is."

She looked up at me and smiled. "I daresay if she was hollerin', you'd know for sure. There ain't nobody hollers like Wilametta. If she's talkin' to you, she's likely got some hours yet. They gonna come for us?"

"I don't think so. They're going to get Mrs. Mueller, she said. Right now she's going to soak her feet and rest."

"Oh, boy."

"What?"

"She does that, child. When she's hurtin', she does that. You best do what you can to keep Samuel here 'case they have to come for us. Unless, a' course, you want Sarah comin' with us."

"No, ma'am."

"I oughta give her this quilt, big as it is," she said. "I ain't got another thing prepared for no baby. Don't know where my mind's been, not to think of that before."

"Emma, I don't know if she'd want you to do that. Seems to bother her how much they owe you already."

"Baby comin's a whole other matter. Wouldn't be right not to give her somethin'. What do you think? We could cut up a sheet for some diapers. An' it don't take half an hour to make a couple a' bibs. Shame I didn't think to buy 'em no powder."

I just stood there for a minute as Emma sat and thought. Maybe it was endless with her, this wanting to give.

"I got a purty yellow towel," she told me. "Big enough 'least for two bibs. Yellow's good for boy or girl. What's she favorin' this time?"

"Girl."

Emma grabbed for her canes and pulled herself up. "Too bad I ain't got booties. Nor yarn for 'em."

It was all too much for me, thinking of Emma still itching to make up a baby present. Lula Bell was recovering from poor treatment, and a score of other cattle had never been paid for. But Emma held no hard feelings at all. The Hammonds ate her berries, left her plow in the rain, and went for years without paying her what was due. Still, here she was, fumbling toward her bedroom to look for a yellow towel.

"Emma—"

"I'm makin' it just fine."

Tears welled up inside me. "I know you are," I managed to tell her. "I'm just not so sure about me."

She stopped in her tracks and turned to look at me. "Juli Wortham," she said slowly. "Whatever is troublin' you?"

My words came rushing out without me taking time to think about them. "I thought I was good! Do you know what I mean, Emma? I managed to be the way I thought I should be for my kids no matter how hard things got, and I managed to forgive my husband, even though I blamed him for the longest time. I thought I was good, the way I could handle anything that came my way without letting it beat me down too bad. But Emma, you're half angel or more, the way you give like it's all you're about! You've been so good to us, even trying to give us this place! And what you've done for the Hammonds— oh, Emma, she told me they haven't paid you for the property—"

"I'm right surprised she'd mention that."

"I was too. But Emma, you just keep on. You don't even seem to realize how unusual you are! Do you know anyone else that would've let George Hammond farm that field so long for nothing?"

"Now, Juli—"

"No, Emma. You could have thrown them off long ago! You could have laughed at me when I came and told you I didn't have any money. You didn't have to let us stay, any more than you've had to put up with the Hammonds all these years!"

"Well, I guess I didn't wanta laugh at ya. Nor put 'em out, neither."

"But I would have. I was already pretty fired up at George Hammond, and here I am on your property, the same as they are! I thought I was good, not so bitter and hateful as this! Next to you, that's what I am. Sour and cold and hardheaded—"

"You ain't never seemed to me to be so sour."

"Emma, you know exactly what I'm talking about! You know what you've done for us! And Sam said you gave Barrett Post a bull once. I bet you—"

"Oh, Juli, I've had lots a' years for them things."

"But people don't usually use their years like that. Emma, don't you know how special you are? How can you keep on like this?"

One of her canes wobbled a bit. "Help me to m' room, now. Ain't no use to talk. We still got work to do. I wanta cut them bibs while you're cookin'."

"Oh, Emma."

"Hush, now, and help me."

We spread her basket of sewing scraps and rickrack all over the bed. I got her the towel, and she found just the right pieces to make a decorative edge and tie ribbon. The bibs would be lovely, and Wilametta would love them, whether she had a boy or a girl.

"Juli, don't you know Paul kep' makin' tents, even while he was preachin'?"

Her words were so sudden that they took me by surprise. "He did? You mean Paul in the Bible?"

"Sure 'nough. He made tents. Bible says so. Kep' workin' so's the people wouldn't have to take care a' him. You know what that means to me?"

"No, I don't."

"Well, folks should work. You know that. You do your best, that's all you can do. But he wouldn't a' had to. He was makin' roofs over their heads, that's what he was doin'. Not for hisself. He was makin' roofs for other folks and preachin' at the same time. And I figure he was 'bout the greatest man ever was, 'cept the Lord hisself. You understand, Juli?"

"No, I'm not sure I do."

"He done things for people. So did the Lord. You know that. We ain't bein' what we should if we're just thinkin' on ourselves. It don't matter what I give you, nor the Hammonds neither. I can't use it, 'specially not now." She set down her ribbon and gave out a sigh. "If they'd paid me ever' cent all this time, child, I wouldn't be no better off. I never did need but so much. Might as well let other folks use the rest. Plain to see that I'd a' been selfish otherwise."

"Emma, other people don't see it that way."

"You think when that boy come bringin' the Lord bread and fish, that the Lord shoulda just sat an' ate it all his own self?"

"Well, no, he couldn't. He fed the five thousand."

"That's right," she said with a smile. "Didn't look like it, but God's got plenty for ever'body. So it don't hurt me none to share."

We barely had lunch done when Barrett and Louise Post came to get Samuel. Louise may have had it in mind to stay and visit, but when Emma told her that Wilametta

Hammond was about to have her baby, she offered to take Sarah home with her so I could help if we were called on.

"You know how I am, Emma," she said. "I never was no help for birthin'. Might as well keep the little one for you. You want us to bring you by there now and save some time?"

"She said she wouldn't need us," I protested. "They're getting Mrs. Mueller."

Louise frowned. "They surely don't know Alberta's gone down to her sister's in Marion. She ain't gonna be back till tomorrow. I'd go over there myself, but I always end up on the floor. Even when it was my own boys comin', I fainted dead away."

"You better take us then," Emma said matter-of-factly. "They'll be hunting the countryside for the Muellers. Be better to get there 'fore the worst of it."

Her own health and mobility didn't seem to occur to Emma, or to Louise either. But my hands were shaking just thinking about it. My memories of childbirth were patchy, cut in splinters by the joy and pain. I couldn't imagine being there for Wilametta's baby.

"Don't you worry," Louise assured me. "Emma's the finest midwife there ever was. She'll tell you just everythin' you need to do."

Midwife. No wonder everybody thought it was perfectly normal to call on Emma. I could picture her somehow, bringing child after child into the world. Why had no one told us before that she was a midwife?

"You're looking pale, Julia," Emma said with a twinkle in her eye.

"I'm feeling pale."

"You do what needs done, honey. That's the best call a' God there ever was." She gave my arm a little squeeze. "We ain't got nothin' if we don't do for each other. That's the way folks is s'posed to be."

Emma must have loved the very idea of a birth—she was glowing with anticipation. "Put my sewing things in a bag, will you? And a couple a' sheets an' extra towels? Oh, Juli, what a time!"

Paul the tent maker. Emma the midwife. They were far beyond me, both of them, and I felt small and bare.

Samuel accepted the whole situation far better than I did, pulling Sarah into his lap and explaining that she would be going to play with Mr. Post's puppies so I could help Rorey's little brother or sister be born. He kissed me as we climbed together into the back of the Posts' pickup. I threw down Emma's sewing bag, my hands still shaking. How would the Hammonds react to us showing up over there? They hadn't asked us to come. Wilametta had meant for me to leave and could scarcely have been more plain about it.

Yet Emma was actually whistling a jolly sort of tune. She knew her part, knew her call, and was confident that Wilametta Hammond would receive her like she was water to quench a thirst.

Sarah sat next to me, smiling, her bumps and scrapes forgotten. "Say hello to Grace when you see her, Mommy," she said proudly. "Give her a little kiss from me and God."

TWENTY-EIGHT

Samuel

George wasn't home when we got to the Hammonds'. He was out looking for the Muellers like Emma had said he would be. Poor Julia was looking worried, especially when their oldest girl came running out of house. The harried-looking teenager was so glad to see Emma that she burst into tears.

"Joey and Frank've been wantin' to fetch you," she said, "But Pa's got the wagon."

"She pretty uncomfortable, then?" Emma asked her.

"Yes, ma'am. She ain't hollerin', but she say somethin' feels differ'nt this time."

Julia was as white as I'd ever seen her. I squeezed her hand, and she grabbed for Emma's things.

"Samuel, you're gonna hafta carry me right to Wila's side now," Emma commanded. "Lizbeth, you get the little ones to help you make sure there's plenty a' clean washin' water drawed, then keep 'em far enough that they don't hear nothin'."

"Yes, ma'am." Lizbeth wiped her hands on her droopy pink apron and took off running.

I'd picked up Emma before, but this time she seemed as light as a child. "Now don't stew," she told me. "We'll make out just fine."

Julia climbed down from the truck behind me. She didn't say a word except to tell Sarah to stay put and that I'd be right back out to her.

I felt funny leaving them, with Mrs. Hammond looking red and sick and Julia in the kitchen, trying to get the stove lit. Emma told the rest of us to go on, which I thought was crazy. Didn't any of them think to get a doctor? Wasn't that where Barrett and I should be heading, instead of over to his place to patch his roof? I even said so, but Emma assured me that Wilametta wouldn't have a doctor set foot in her house.

And Barrett was in a hurry to get going. He even honked his horn for me, but I wouldn't leave without hugging my wife and gaining some assurance from her that it was all right for me to go. She told me it was, that women did fine with midwives most of the time and that she'd be okay just as soon as she got done shaking in her shoes.

"I'm sorry I got us into this," she said.

"How do you figure *you* did it?" I asked.

She looked like she was about to cry. "This was all my idea. There's just so much I didn't know we'd have to think about."

I held her tight until Emma called her name.

"They'll thank you for doing your best," I said.

"Please just be praying," she said, and then went to see whatever it was that Emma needed. I reluctantly went back outside to the waiting truck.

"C'mon!" Barrett called. "It's bad luck for the menfolks to be staying about at a time like this!"

"Does that include doctors?"

"No. But a lot of women prefers it just women, and I reckon I understand that. Ain't that so, Louise? You gonna stay and help out?"

"It's so, but I don't aim to stay. I get weak-kneed if there's any blood and such."

I could hear some kid crying not far off, and it made my stomach burn. "Don't you think it makes sense for all of us to stay?" I asked them. "At least till George gets back? That biggest girl might need help with the kids or want to be with her mother."

"You're right about that," Barrett agreed. "Louise, if you went walking with the youngest ones, or some such, you might not even hear no yellin' from the house. Be good if you'd do it. Most of the women 'round here'd do it, if they found theirself here like this."

Louise didn't look happy about that suggestion. Being on the Hammond property at all seemed to be distasteful to her, but she reluctantly agreed, and Barrett smiled.

"Gonna have to leave Sarah too," she said. "You men can't watch her up on no roof."

"We need to be here," I told the Posts. "In case something happens and they need the truck to get more help. It's not right, us just leaving them here without George and his wagon."

Barrett gave me a frown. "It's bad luck. I ain't goin' in that house."

"You don't have to. We can stay out here."

Barrett was quiet as Sarah and Louise got out of the truck to go find Lizbeth.

"Tell you what," he finally said. "I can understand you feelin' thataway with your wife bein' so new at this. You set out here and wait, if that's what you want. I'll go on and see if I can't find George and tell him what's goin' on."

It wasn't what I had in mind, him leaving with the truck. But it was better than nothing. "Thank you," I said. "If you can't find him, come back and tell me."

He nodded, got in the truck, and drove off. Sarah came running back to me. "Please," she wailed. "Can I stay with you?"

Louise looked in our direction for a second, then headed back toward the barn, where the noise of children was the loudest. Pretty soon Lizbeth came flying past us to go back in the house, and I heard what sounded like singing coming from the hayloft. That was hard to picture, Mrs. Post in there singing with the Hammond kids, but it made my heart glad.

That's when I remembered Robert. How would he know what was happening if we weren't home by the time school was out? Maybe there was a Hammond at school with him, and maybe they'd stop here first. But not being sure of that, I decided I'd better walk out and meet him when the time came, if we were still here. And we probably would be, since these things took time.

"Let's pray for Mrs. Hammond," I told Sarah, and she took my hand.

"She's havin' a baby, Daddy. She's gonna call it Grace. She told me so."

"Fine name. I couldn't think of a better one."

I bundled up my daughter in my arms, and we prayed a brief prayer for the mother and her baby, and Emma and Julia too.

"They've got goats, Daddy. I broke the goat fence."

She showed me the broken fence. It was no wonder the thing fell. Wasn't much of a fence, held up by wire and a nail or two. The goats were now all crowded in a little pen on the far side, waiting for somebody to repair the damage and give them more space. I wondered what George would say if he came back and found me at the job. I could tell him I had to, since it was my daughter that broke it down. I couldn't just sit there, doing nothing, that was sure. I needed something to keep my hands busy, or my brain would churn too much. It was as simple as that.

TWENTY-NINE

Julia

I'd never seen a breech birth, never dreamed I'd have to. But we were there less than an hour when Emma said it wasn't the head coming first. What scared me most was that Wilametta had passed out limp on the bed.

"Sam could go after a doctor," I whispered.

"Ten mile without no horse or truck," Emma reminded me. "And she's this far 'long. Baby'd be gone 'fore he got halfway here."

Lizbeth was shaking like a leaf, poor girl. I would've had her out the door, but she'd begged to stay. She'd bathed her mother's feet and her face, and now was squeezing her hand and muttering a prayer.

I had water to wash the baby and to wash Emma, but I ended up splashing some of it on the floor. These walls, these floors, everything needed scrubbing down, but I couldn't do it now, no matter how much I wished to turn my mind to something mundane.

Emma had said she wanted me right by her side so I could hear every instruction she gave me. I heard, all right, and I did my best, but I was walking on jelly, my clumsy hands just going through the motions. I'd never felt so totally inadequate in all my life. Wilametta looked for all the world to be unconscious, her baby was breech, and I was not as strong as I'd thought myself to be.

"I done this once before," Emma assured us. "Tricky thing, but you can be sure the good Lord's got it all in hand."

That set me to crying, and I didn't know why. I could just imagine Emma suddenly keeling over, and then where would we be? God help us.

I passed Lizbeth another wet cloth to bathe her mother's forehead and spread a fresh sheet at the foot of the bed to receive the baby.

"If George gets back, or Mr. Post, can we send them for the doctor?" I asked Emma hopefully.

"You can try," she told me. "Barrett might go. But George wouldn't. Not to save his hide, he wouldn't. He don't believe in it."

Emma was up on the lumpy old mattress, balanced next to Wilametta's knees, looking every bit of her eighty-four years and then some. "C'mon, now, Wila. Push," she said. She looked worried, and I turned my eyes away. But somehow Emma knew that Wila was hearing her.

"Can't," Mrs. Hammond muttered, and I was mighty glad just to hear her voice.

"You're gonna hafta, girl!" Emma scolded. "You want her out here with ya now, don't ya?"

Wila didn't answer, just gave out a terrible moan. I wondered why in the world she hadn't told me before that she was having trouble. Maybe she hadn't really known yet and didn't think I could have done much anyway.

"C'mon, now, Wila."

The poor woman suddenly screamed, and Lizbeth clenched her teeth and started to cry silently. She squeezed her mama's hand again and kissed her cheek. Wila finally pushed like Emma had told her to, while I prayed. In the kitchen, the kettle was whistling, but not one of us paid it a bit of attention.

"Here come them legs," Emma said. "Juli, honey, get yourself up here."

That command made my hands shake, but there was nothing to do but obey. I got myself just as close as I could as Wila started pushing again.

"You be ready," Emma told me. "If the head don't come easy, you'll have to give her a push."

I didn't know what she meant by that. And I couldn't understand how Emma could look so tired but strong as the hills at the same time.

Wila gave out a yell that surely could have been heard all the way to the pond. "Can't do this, Emma!" she shrieked. "Can't do this!"

"You ain't got no choice now, honey! Oughta see what I got here too. You got you a girl! Can't stop now."

"Grace," Wila whispered and tried to lift her head. Strands of sweat-soaked hair flopped against her cheek.

"Don't you be movin'!" Emma warned. "Not yet, Wila. You'll be holdin' her soon enough, now." She braced herself as Wila fell back against the pillows, yelled, and pushed again.

I could see most of the baby laying across Emma's arm and prayed we were finished. But Wila was still pushing and getting no farther.

"Right here!" Emma commanded me. "You feel that? Push now! Gotta get her head free so's she can draw breath!"

I put my hands just where she showed me and could feel a hard little lump in Wila's abdomen.

"You watch! When Wila gives her a good hard push, you push too, now!"

She reached for Grace's head with her free hand, and I felt like my stomach had been flipped over sideways. *Did you have this in mind, Lord? Did you know what I was getting myself into, wanting to stay here?*

"'Bout got her, I think. Come on, now, baby." Emma had a strange gleam in her eye, a passion I could not fathom. God help me, I wanted to run. I would have run, clear out of the room, if there'd been anyone else to take my place. But Emma wanted to be here and would stay even if a wagon full of doctors rolled in. She would stay just to take Mrs. Hammond's hand. And I thought I finally understood her. Hammonds were family too.

"Wila, honey, I think I got her," Emma announced. "Lord willin', I do! Push now. Come on and push."

Wila barely had any strength left. She moaned and strained and then fell back against the pillows again.

"It's all right, Mama," Lizbeth coaxed. "We's almost done. Emma, ain't we almost done?"

"Almost. Don't you go passin' out on me again, now, Wilametta, hear? Push. You're gonna have this baby t' the breast 'fore you can say jumpin' Jehoshaphat! Come on!"

I looked up at Emma and saw the sweat dripping down from her wrinkled old nose. She looked worried, but just about mad too, she was so determined to see this through. I thought I heard boys' voices outside for just a minute, and then Sam's, but I wasn't sure. Wila was pushing again, and I pushed too, and suddenly the hard little lump was gone.

"Looky there!" Emma exclaimed. "Oh, praise the Lord! Ain't that the prettiest thing you ever seen?"

Wila gave out a moan and then sank away in a faint. It wasn't till then I realized Emma was crying. I grabbed a towel to wipe the sweat and tears from her face, thinking that she had to be able to see. It was more than a marvel, her doing this when she couldn't manage to get her own needle threaded. But she grabbed the towel away and wiped off the baby, blowing on the little face at the same time.

Little Grace Hammond hadn't made a sound or moved a muscle. Emma wiped around her nose and mouth and gave her little feet a swat. "Get me some water," she ordered. "Not too hot. Let's get her good and mad."

I brought the bowl and dipped a clean cloth in it. Emma bathed the tiny child's face and neck, and the baby finally wiggled one arm and made a little noise, like the bleat of a sheep. Emma took a clean towel and patted her dry.

"Did you hold them scissors in the fire?"

"Yes, ma'am."

"Get 'em. Got to cut this cord, honey, so we can wrap her up and keep her warm."

I lifted the scissors, but I was scared to do the cutting. What if I did something wrong?

Emma tied the cord in two places with bias tape she'd brought in her sewing basket. She looked up at me and must have seen the terror in my eyes, because she took the scissors and did the one quick cut herself.

"Get me the little blanket Lizbeth brought in."

I handed her the pretty thing that really may have been Lizbeth's, it looked so old. But it was clean. Trimmed with lace and bands of yellow, it was one of the nicer things I'd seen in the Hammond house. Emma wrapped the baby and handed her to me.

"You take her, Juli," Emma said. "I gotta see to Wila, get that bleedin' stopped. Lizbeth, rub her good, will you? See if you can get her stirred back 'round."

I felt so dumb and helpless, just standing there, holding the baby. I was scared Wila would die, scared Lizbeth would give up and get hysterical, scared Emma would fall over from exhaustion. I prayed hard, wishing I could run outside and scream for the whole world to pray with me.

Tears coursed down my cheeks before I could stop them, and then little Grace Hammond finally let out a holler.

"God bless my mama," Lizbeth cried as she clung to Wilametta's hand.

"She's breathin'. Now don't you worry," Emma told her.

Wilametta moaned and opened her eyes a little bit.

"Get that baby over here," Emma called, and I rushed forward.

"It's a girl, honey," Emma said, and I could see Wilametta smile.

"My Grace! Oh, is she pretty, Mrs. Wortham? God bless you! Lizbeth, is she pretty?"

"Very pretty, Mama."

I laid little Grace between Lizbeth and her mother. Wila didn't look to have the strength to hold her, but Lizbeth scooted her up to her mother's chest.

"Oughta known after nine babies that this'un wouldn't be long at comin'," Emma scolded. "You shoulda sent George after me first thing."

"No, no," Wila said, looking pale. "You rest, Emma. Lizbeth, make her rest."

But Emma would have none of that. She got me started cleaning up but she wouldn't leave me to do it alone. I was surprised at the stamina she had shown that day, hovering over Wila and refusing to rest her own weary bones. You learn more about a person when you live things right beside them, and I imagined I'd learned Emma pretty well after all this, though I'd known her so short a time.

George came in about a half hour after the birth and didn't say anything at all. He just gave Wila's hand a squeeze and touched little Grace's cheek, and then went back out. I'd never seen him look that way, like a boy almost, humbled by something bigger than himself. I felt the same. I expect we all did.

THIRTY

Samuel

I knew the birthing was done. I'd heard as much. I'd sent Sarah farther off into the barn to sing with Mrs. Post and was still piecing together fence when George came out the back door of the house. He didn't see me at first and almost walked right past me. When I asked how they were inside, he jumped.

"Kinda hopin' there won't be no more'n ten," he said. "Wilametta looks so blame tired, I don't know what we'll do."

I wasn't sure how to respond to that.

"Got a girl," he told me. "I 'spect that ain't no more'n right." He took a hard look at the fence and at his pliers, which were still in my hand. "What are you doing here, anyway?"

He didn't sound angry, just surprised to find me on his property, let alone with my hands working on anything.

"I . . . uh . . . wanted to help. I heard that my Sarah broke your fence."

"She done this?"

"Yes, sir, but not for trying to."

"S'pose it coulda been the old billy just as easy, or one a' my little ol' wild injuns runnin' around."

"Maybe."

"Your wife's inside," he said, as if he'd just woken up to who I was.

"I know."

"I got me another girl."

"You told me."

"Wilametta's already callin' her Grace, but I been thinkin' we oughta call this'un Emma. Stands t' reason, don't it? Emma Grace. How's that sound?"

I couldn't help but smile, seeing a side of George Hammond I hadn't seen before. "It sounds fitting."

"I didn't think she'd come," he said solemnly, turning his face toward the distant field. "Bein' sick, you know, and havin' you to turn her again' me."

"That wouldn't gain me anything. Emma cares about all of you."

"I reckon she cares 'bout ever'body." He was quiet, just studying the horizon. "You know Miss Hazel means to have you 'way from here, don't you?"

"I know."

"What're you gonna do about it?"

I tried to think of what to say, but the first words out of my mouth weren't at all what I'd had in mind. "I'm going to build Emma a wheelchair."

"What?"

"I've got to get it done," I explained. "No matter what else happens. She needs it, and she's always doing for everybody else."

George cocked his head. "You know how t' do somethin' like that?"

"Almost have it figured out. I need some bolts, though, and a couple of smaller wheels for balance in the back. I saw a picture of one once that a fellow made for his granddaughter after she had polio."

"Well . . ."

He let that one word hang in the air a long time. "I got plenty a' hardware in a couple a' buckets in the barn," he finally said. "Can't say it'd be what you need for bolt size, but you can use what you want. I'd have to study me on them wheels, though. How big you need?"

"Not less than six inches, I don't think. Or much bigger than a foot. It's got to handle the rough ground but not be too big and heavy."

George looked down at his scuffed gray boots. "Wilametta and the baby don't appear too strong, but they'll come out fine. Did I tell you they'd come out fine?"

"I understood you to mean that."

"Need help on that chair?"

His offer took me by surprise. The last time I talked to this man, he'd been as hard as a stump. *Nothing like a birth to soften things,* I decided. *And having us here right in the middle of it too.*

"I might need help," I admitted. "Getting the chair on the wheels so they can still turn, but not bounce her clear out of there. I need a metal piece under each side of the seat for some give. You know what I mean?"

"Like buggy springs."

"Yeah. Something like that."

"When you workin' on this?"

"At night. So she won't know."

"Why is that?"

"I guess because I'm not real sure I can get it done."

"You'll get it done. By God, you will. Workin' on it tonight?"

"I don't know."

"I'll be there past sundown. We'll get 'er done, boy."

"Won't your wife need you tonight?"

268

"Lizbeth tends a whole lot better than I ever could. I won't be gone long. An' one of the boys can run over if they need anythin'." He took the pliers out of my hand and tightened down a wire that hadn't even come loose.

"I aim to give Emma a chicken for her help, or another a' her cows, even, but I'd like to be a part a' this, if you'll let me. She's done a lot more for me over the years than I managed doin' for her. Guess maybe she tol' you I ain't got no claim on nothin' no more. Got so far behind on payin', I ain't got a leg to stand on. I figure when Emma dies, we'll be throwed out on our ears. You might be the ones doin' it too. But Emma needs a chair, like you said. It ain't no more'n right."

"Bring the buckets and a light," I told him. "It'll be easier finding what we need with everything there together."

He smiled and extended his hand. "You ever do much butcherin'?"

I shook his hand. "No, sir."

"Might have you help me when it gets cold enough. For a side a' pork. What d'ya say?"

"I never did anything with hogs before. You'd probably laugh at me."

"I never teached it to no city boy, neither. But you'll learn. If you think you can put together a wheelchair, I s'pose you'd do for figurin' out a lick a' other stuff, don't you reckon?"

I didn't have time to answer. Lizbeth had run past us to tell the others the news, and now George's kids and mine were coming up from the barn. Robert and Kirk had been in school when Mr. Post stopped by to tell Elvira that the baby was coming. She had dismissed the two right away, saying they couldn't possibly think with that on their minds. Now Kirk was in front of the others on his way to the house.

"You go to the well and wash 'fore you set one foot inside," George told them. "Lizbeth, you go and see if your mama's ready for any a' these hooligans."

269

THIRTY-ONE

$\mathcal{J}ulia$

I finally got Emma to sit down in a chair in the kitchen, where I was stewing shepherd's purse for Wilametta. She and her baby were both asleep and seemed to be doing well. I'd taken the liberty of making some coffee too, and was trying to coax Emma to have a bit to refresh herself with.

"I'll tell you, Juli, I hope to never see another breech! God have mercy, it scares me to pieces."

I was still shaking myself, but I tried not to show it. "You didn't look scared. Most of the time, anyway. You ought to eat something. There's some bread here—"

"I couldn't eat a bite. Not a' nothin'. I'm so glad that's over." She plunked her arms on the table and sighed. "That Lizbeth'll think twice 'bout havin' any babies now. Might not even want to get married after today."

I couldn't deny that. I'd thought it was too much for the girl, but she wouldn't leave, and her mother hadn't wanted her to. Thinking back on it all made me queasy, and I had to sit down.

"Emma, did you really have a breech baby before?"

"Sure enough, I did. At least fourteen years ago. But I lost 'er then." She was quiet a minute. "The only time I ever did lose any, Juli. Didn't want to tell 'em that, though. It'd been the finish of 'em today, just expectin' the worst."

"How many babies have you helped along? A lot?"

"Near fifty, I guess. I used to write 'em down, but I lost m' book in the rain one night when the wagon tipped on the way home. That was the first time I hurt m' leg. There wasn't no doctor when I started. Lot a' folks still'd rather not call on one. Folks has got them automobiles now, though. They can get to one most times, if they need to."

"Should we get Wilametta to go, do you think? She's so weak."

"I got nothin' again' it, but the worst is past. She won't be wantin' to go, and George ain't gonna favor takin' her. It ain't their way. I just thank the good Lord for pullin' 'em through. I wouldn't want their last mem'ry of me bein' over such a loss."

"Oh, Emma." It scared me for her to say such a thing. And she looked so awfully tired. "Emma, can I help you lie down?"

"Not here. Once we get home, maybe. We'll be needin' the rest, you an' me. But I gotta stay awhile longer, till Wila's up and ready to take some a' that broth or somethin'. You done good. You oughta be proud."

I could hear the sounds of children just outside. Emma heard them too, and shook her head before I could say anything. "They can't come in," she said. "Not 'less they tiptoe for a peek, one at a time. Can't be wakin' 'em. Not yet. This ain't no time for shenanigans."

THIRTY-TWO

Samuel

We stayed at the Hammonds' till well after dark. Mrs. Post helped the oldest girl fix us some supper. Once Emma was satisfied that Mrs. Hammond was gaining strength and the baby could suck, we all piled in George's wagon, and the oldest boy took us home.

Mrs. Post was a little distressed at her husband for not coming back, but I told her he might be just as distressed at me for not doing any roofing.

"He can just stay on that roof!" she snapped. "If he's gonna leave me somewhere, he oughta have the decency to come back for me."

We took her home first, and Barrett's truck was there, but he didn't come out. "Don't you worry about the work, now," she told me. "He'll be by tomorrow. I'll see to that. It ain't your fault such circumstances come up. You did the right thing, makin' me stay. Hate to say it, but I rather 'joyed myself with them fool kids."

"She'd be a good Sunday school teacher," I told Julia when we'd left their farm. "If Emma ever convinces them to go to church."

I was in the barn a couple of hours later when George Hammond came in with his kerosene lantern and buckets of nails, screws, and bolts. I hadn't expected him at that hour. He should have been asleep, the same as me.

He studied my drawings by the lantern light and then took a look at the frame chair I'd made. "Looks like it could work," he said. "You got them wheel mounts. Was you fixin' to set 'em in place tonight?"

"There's a three-inch strip of metal brace along the bottom edge of that old wagon," I told him. "I was taking that off. If we could cut two pieces to size and bend them to a crescent, I'd like to rest the chair on that, bolt the metal to a frame of two-bys, and mount the wheels from the bottom frame. We could end up with a basket right under the seat for carrying along a bag or something."

"You got your thing worked out, ain't you? What about them little wheels you ain't got yet?"

"I'll have to jut them out from the frame in back. I won't know for sure how to do that till I know what kind of wheel I'm working with."

"You ever make a car?"

I looked up in surprise at what sounded like a true measure of respect in his voice. "Not by myself," I told him. "My cousin and I and a couple of friends came up with a pretty good Tin Lizzie from wrecks. I used to love that kind of work. But it was really play, I guess."

"So if you had somethin' to work with, you could make a car?"

"I suppose. If I had the parts."

"Well. Seems to me like you could've got a city job."

273

"Had a good one for awhile. There's a lot of guys like me right now, though. Not enough work to go around."

"Yep. I been hearin' that. Pays to keep livestock, like I told you. Least you know you're gonna eat."

"Can't do that without land, though."

"Yep. That's what scares me."

He looked at me, deep and solemn, his face a mix of strange shadows in the kerosene light.

"It ain't that I ain't wanted to pay Emma, you understand," he said. "I jus' do a better job makin' food than cash. Then I trades me food for the stuff we need and end up never seein' a dime. Ain't had enough left over to bring her nothin' decent. She's got good land, that ain't the problem. We ain't had the weather for it recent years. 'Sides that, I can't work it the way I oughta without another horse or two. Bird and Teddy is gettin' too old to put in a full day. That slows ever'thin' down. I'd give 'em pasture if I had another way of it. Hate to hitch 'em at all anymore."

He sighed at the telling of his troubles. "'Course, nobody'll trade for 'em. Can't get a loan neither. Willard had him a tractor, a 1920 Fordson. Made me feel like a king, 'cause there ain't many got them 'round here. But she quit on me 'bout four years ago. Been all downhill since."

Such information was enough to set my blood pumping. "Tell you what. I can't help you get a horse, but when I get done with this, I'll take a look at Willard's tractor. I've never laid hands on one before, but I doubt you could have killed an engine like that entirely. I might be able to get it running."

"Lordy, you could turn out a respectable neighbor after all."

He was serious, from the look on his face. And there was nothing to say but a simple thank-you.

We worked for about an hour, making the chair's base frame and mounting the old wagon wheels. I pulled the rest of the metal strip off the wagon and was going to do my best punching holes through it with a quarter bit and Willard's old hand drill.

"Be easier hot," George told me. "Easier gettin' the bend right too."

"I know. But I don't have a forge."

"Frank Cafey does. I'll take you over there tomorrow."

That decided, we parted ways to get some sleep. But I lay awake for a long time, considering what a miracle had been done. The man I could have almost called an enemy had been turned around for a friend. It was easy to see that, separately, George and I probably would always be struggling here. But together, we just might make things work.

Robert wanted to take Emma's old bicycle to school for the first time the next morning. I pulled it out for him and looked at the wheels on it with some longing, but decided they were too big anyway. It was a Red Rider, kind of old, but in pretty good shape, with a basket to hold his books and the biscuits Julia wrapped up for his lunch. I sent him off early so he'd have time to stop at the Hammonds' and tell George I might be at the Posts' till suppertime.

Barrett was over before we'd even finished breakfast, ready to get me on his roof and get that job done. I had an obligation, so I gladly went, even though my mind was still on Emma's chair. All I lacked was a set of small wheels and a few more hours' work, and the thing would be usable.

I hammered shingles down almost that whole day, new ones that were long and thin. I thought Barrett must be doing pretty well to be able to afford that. Back in Harrisburg, I knew people who nailed the old ones back in, or tin, or whatever they could find.

Barrett didn't say much while we were working, and Louise said he was sore at her for scolding him the night before. He said his truck wouldn't start, but she didn't believe him, especially since it had run fine when he went to pick me up that morning. But when it came time to take me home, the truck wouldn't start again, and Barrett whooped and hollered for Louise to come and witness the fact.

I took a look at the truck and eventually got the thing running, while Barrett talked almost constantly about the turn-crank model he used to have.

"I liked it," he said. "Weren't too easy to reckon with of a winter morning, though."

We were just about to leave when I spotted George Hammond's wagon coming up the road.

"Better wait for my neighbor," I told Barrett. "He's taking me to see Frank Cafey."

"Now there's a stubborn old man, that Frank," Barrett said. "Gonna starve, he will. Ain't much call for a smithy no more. I told him to get hisself another job, but he ain't never been one to listen to me."

He looked down the road and watched George get closer and closer. "Now Hammond here, he comes in a wagon still! Don't know if he ever did drive a car, do you? Most folks ain't like that. He still goes to Frank for his horseshoes, but there ain't too many doin' that no more. Everybody that matters for much got 'em a car back in the twenties. And them that ain't got one is doin' some itchin' for it now. You're one of 'em. You're progress-minded, I can see it."

He turned his hat slightly to better block the sun. "You ain't gonna be happy at Emma's for long," he declared. "She ain't even got a pitcher pump in the kitchen over there! You'll up and leave one of these days for a city job again, once there's jobs to be had. I can see it in you. You got to have good things."

276

I glanced his way, wondering how he'd managed to draw his conclusions. Maybe we wouldn't have to leave to have good things. We might get a car one day. A pitcher-pump kitchen sink with a line to the well, or even complete indoor plumbing, could eventually be installed. And Julia would be happy even if it never was.

As George turned down the lane, Barrett just shook his head. "What're you doin', goin' with him over to Frank's? You ain't got no horse."

I wasn't sure why, but I didn't want to tell him about Emma's chair. So I just said I had a couple of metal pieces to bend and left it at that.

George was hollering in a minute, and Barrett hollered right back. "Shut up, you old fool! We know you're there!" But he softened as George stopped in front us, and asked how his wife and baby were doing.

"Both cryin' today. Ever' time I come in the house. But that's the way it was ever' time with Wilametta, so I guess they're fine enough. She fawns over them little ones, she does. Counts their fingers and toes 'least six or seven times an hour."

"This'un got the right number?" Barrett inquired with a grin.

"Far as I can see. Can't get too close without her startin' to squall."

"You ain't even picked her up yet?"

"Well, yeah. Once. But I'm gonna wait awhile 'fore I do much a' that. I like 'em sturdy, you know, so's I can bounce 'em on m' knee without catchin' the devil from Wilametta." He looked over at me with a smile. "My boys brung your wife and Emma back over today, just to see 'em. I know Emma's one to wanna do that. She ain't lookin' good, though, neighbor."

"Too much e'citement," Barrett declared. "Next time, you Hammonds hatch 'em yourself."

George shook his head. "Ain't no wonder you only had two. Mean old cuss." He motioned me toward the wagon. "Come on. Quicker we go, quicker we can get home."

"Ain't nothin' quick about you an' your old wagon," Barrett jested. "I could watch my hair grow, waitin' on ya." He took his hat off and whacked it against his thigh, as if he had dust to knock off. "Give my best to that wife a' yours," he told George, and then turned to me, looking sober. "Do what you can to keep that Emma restin', will you? I ain't anxious to hear no kinda bad news."

When I climbed in the wagon, I could see that George had already been by our barn for the metal pieces we needed to bend. But he waited till we were down the road a quarter mile before he told me to take a look in the old wooden box he seemed to always have riding in the back of his wagon. He looked so jolly all of a sudden that I asked him if he was hiding another pig's head.

"Somethin' better. Take a look."

I turned in my seat and did what he told me. "Had a baby buggy when Lizbeth was little," he said. "Them boys've tore the thing apart. Rorey thought we oughta use it for Emma Grace, but there weren't no way for that. The basket's pulled clean apart. 'Bout what you need, though, ain't it?"

Two six-inch metal wheels with a swivel to them. Mounted from the top. I could have kissed Lizbeth, Rorey, and all the rest. It was just what I needed. Thank the good Lord and George Hammond.

THIRTY-THREE

Julia

I was glad to get home from the Hammonds' for the second time. Though it was wonderful seeing Wila and the baby doing so well, Emma had me worried. She wouldn't let on that she was feeling poorly, but she let George Hammond take her straight to her bed when we got back. I saw him head for the barn before he left, but I didn't even care what he was doing. I was too busy thinking about what might help Emma feel better.

I got Emma some tea and the tin of crackers she'd asked us to get her from the store. She thanked me and asked if I had any paper. So I sent Sarah upstairs for the paper in my bag and pulled a chair up close beside her bed.

"I need to set down my intentions, Juli, dear," she said in a quiet voice.

"What do you mean, Emma?"

"To ever'thin' there's a season. A time for ever' purpose under heaven."

She was staring up at the ceiling, and my chest started feeling so cold and tight that I could hardly breathe.

"Emma—"

"A time to be born, an' a time to die. A time to plant, an' a time to pluck up what was planted—"

"Emma."

I had to stop her, had to get her thoughts turned away from the awful direction they must have taken. She couldn't be deciding to die. It *wasn't* time.

Sarah ran in with my paper and pencil. I took them from her, but she just stood there, looking from one to the other of us, and I knew she shouldn't stay. "Sarah, please go outside a little while and play with Robert."

Emma gave the girl a smile. "Go on up t' the loft an' see if them kittens is still there. If you can find 'em, pick out the prettiest little bundle and name 'er Gracie. Will you do that for me?"

"Yes, ma'am." Sarah went out, clearly pleased to have such a special duty to set her attention to.

"Always did want to name a kitty that," Emma told me. "Seems just the right time. That Hammond child, she's a miracle, comin' through thataway. God's grace, that's what it is on us." She looked at the paper in my hand and reached out for it. "I'd have you do the writin', but I want it real clear that I done it myself. It'll be Albert to see to things. He's the only one ever does come."

"Emma," I suggested, "maybe it would be better if you just sleep awhile. I'll make supper, and—"

"Now, Juli, I need to do this. It's been such a week! I never did hope to see such times no more! But a body can't live forever, an' I want to make it plain what I want with what's mine when I'm gone. Albert'll honor it, when he sees I done it myself."

280

"He could be here any day," I protested. "Miss Hazel said so. You can just tell him yourself."

She looked at me a long time, and I was praying she wouldn't tell me she wouldn't be here that long. Finally she smiled. "I ain't meanin' to scare you, child. You jus' never know, that's all. I hope t' put it in his hand. It'll be real fine to see him again. An' I ain't plannin' on bein' took to m' grave 'fore I've had a chance to get out to Willard's one more time."

"Oh, Emma. Hearing that, I won't be so anxious to take you."

"Well, there's more than that to consider! Don't fret now! Who's gonna help you get this old place ready for winter? I don't aim to go no place, leavin' you unprepared! But we can't tell it ahead, honey. I want m' intentions put down, just in case. I brung in m' last baby yesterd'y. That I know." She took my hand, and I could feel the tears welling in me.

"You been planted out here," she said. "An' I'm gonna be plucked away to a better place. It was Emma Grace's time t' be born. An' it'll be my time to die one of these days. Ain't nothin' sad about it. Just pays to be ready."

I reluctantly gave her the paper and pencil and a book to lean them on. It was a struggle for her to see something up close like that, and she worked real slow. She didn't tell me what she wrote, except to ask me for the spelling of some words.

In a little while, I heard a motor on the road and thought it was surely Mr. Post bringing Sam home. But when I heard the honk of a horn in the driveway, I ran to the window, knowing very well it wasn't them.

I'd seen plenty of cars like this one, a hand-crank model with no top. But Juanita Jones was sitting there on the passenger side, with her hair all tied up in a checkered scarf. Pastor Jones was just stepping out on his side, wearing a derby hat and a Sunday suit. I couldn't imagine what brought them out, but it was a delight to see them.

"Emma, it's the pastor and his wife."

She sat up in the bed, her eyes shining. "Oh, get 'em some tea! Bless their souls! A shame I ain't up!"

Pastor and Juanita told us that Elvira Post had sent her husband into town to tell them Mrs. Hammond had her baby. I thought that was pretty nice, and they did too, considering that the Posts didn't even go to church.

They'd come out to see Wilametta and the baby and arrived there not ten minutes after we'd left, but they didn't stay long, since both were looking ready for a nap.

"I was so glad we brought powder and soap and such things, along with the diapers," Juanita told me. "Mrs. Hammond said they almost never have store-bought around."

They carried in a pan of dumplings that I would have thought they would leave with the neighbors, but they assured me they'd given the Hammonds a pan full too. I'd loved the pastor and his wife on Sunday, but them coming out to see us made me love them all the more, just for taking the time. Pastor Jones went in and sat with Emma, and they got to talking about the history of the church. Thinking Samuel would be home any minute, I asked Juanita if they wouldn't stay for dinner. I sure was glad we had something decent in the pantry.

Our visit was wonderful, and Juanita pitched in while I fixed food and got the table ready. I just couldn't understand what was keeping Sam so long and began to think that one of these days it might be nice for telephones to be available out here in the countryside.

When Sam finally did come, it was with Mr. Hammond instead of Barrett Post, and both of them went out to the barn, even though they must have seen the car sitting in the drive. Finally, I sent Robert to call them in.

I invited Mr. Hammond to stay, but he only came in long enough to greet the pastor and then say he had to get back home. I saw the look he gave Samuel when he left, and I wondered what in the world they'd been up to. How it happened that those two were conspiring together I just didn't know. But I did know they had something up their sleeve.

Samuel didn't make the slightest attempt to explain, and we had a pleasant meal with the Joneses. Emma came to the table but went right back to bed afterward. I told the pastor that I thought she was feeling more poorly than she let on, so he prayed for her. Then he said they had to be going, that they needed to be in Mt. Vernon the next day to see another minister and his family.

I thought the mention of that town might get Samuel thinking about Dewey and revive the wish of going to see him. But he said nothing about it, just grabbed the one leftover dumpling, downed it in a hurry, and then excused himself just as politely as he could and went back to the barn.

I told Pastor and Juanita that Sam was a little shy with people he hadn't known long, and they didn't mind. They said they could admire the work he was putting in. Of course, I didn't tell them I didn't know what he was working on out there.

Robert and Sarah and I walked them to their car, and I promised we'd do our best to get to church on Sunday. After they left, Robert snuck in the barn and then came right back out with a smile and took Sarah inside to read a story. I went in the house to check on Emma, but she was already asleep. I had Sarah and Robert to bed soon too.

"Dad didn't want Sarah comin' in the barn," Robert whispered to me as I leaned to tuck him in. "Didn't want her to spoil the surprise." He had such a look of delight that I had to ask if it was something I could know about. "I ain't tellin," was all he'd say.

So when I knew they were all asleep, and when the kitchen was clean and Sam still wasn't in, I went out to see what he was doing.

I could hear a tap-tap as I entered the barn with a lantern. But then it stopped. I went toward the west room, where a glow of lamplight was shining under the wood-slat door.

"Sammy," I called out. "What in the world have you been doing in there all this time?"

Sam didn't say a word. He just opened the door and gave me a smile, and I could see for myself. The only wheelchair I'd ever seen, looking big and beautiful and amazing. I knew he could make things, but I couldn't picture how he'd accomplished something like this.

"George helped me bolt the chair over the frame," he said right away. "Now I've just got to finish getting the back wheels on."

I was speechless, looking at the wonder in front of me. I'd assumed he had been working on a porch swing or maybe on the barn itself, but here this sat, worlds better. "Oh, Sam, it looks finished already."

"I've just barely got them set on, though, Juli," he explained about the small wheels. "I had to figure out how to mount them to the frame first. Now I've got to find the right size bolts, or something that will work. They'll fall right off left like this."

"I didn't know you were doing this! It's amazing. To put this together so fast."

"It would have taken a lot longer if I hadn't gotten George's help."

"How did you manage that?"

"I didn't. I guess it was providence."

"Just think of what Emma will say," I gushed, thinking ahead. "She's going to love you, Sam, more than she does already for working so hard on this."

He smiled. "I thought I'd ask in the morning if she's ready to go out to Willard's grave. Then I'll show her the chair. I can take her over there with this, even through the grass and everything. I know I can. Sarah can help her pick some flowers. She'll love that. She needs to go, Juli. It's just something she needs to do."

He was right, and I was thrilled with what he'd done. It was beautiful. It was perfect. And I was so proud that he had such a glorious heart about him. But all the things Emma had said to me earlier that day went churning around in my mind and stuck there. I couldn't help it. I burst into tears.

"Julia, what's wrong?"

"It's good, Sam. It's real good." I couldn't tell him more. I couldn't manage to say that the very idea of Emma going off to the grave site frightened me now. I knew it was silly. She'd said herself that there was more to accomplish than that. Of course she should go. And she'd be happy. She'd ride along with a smile and a fistful of flowers. She'd probably have a good cry by the pond and come back feeling blessed.

I gave Sam a giant hug and told him we ought to get some sleep, because tomorrow would hold quite a bit for us. He didn't want to come in, though, till he had those wheels fastened on. So I stayed, talking to him about Lula Bell and church and a thousand other things while we dug through a mound of screws and nails, trying to find what he needed.

When we finally went back to the house, I was startled to find Emma awake, sitting up in her room with a candle lit. Sam went on to bed, maybe thinking he'd let his secret out if he even stopped to talk to her for two minutes. But I had to stop.

"Are you all right, Emma?"

"Oh, sure. Birthin' a baby's good for the soul, child. I was just sittin' up a bit, reflectin' on it. You had a chance to do that?"

"Tell you the truth, I'm not sure I want to."

"Well, it ain't somethin' you'd want to do ever' day, that's for sure."

She motioned for me to come closer, and I did, tired as I was.

"You all sure must like night air," she said. "Especially that Samuel. Don't he ever turn in before midnight?"

"Oh yes. Sometimes."

She gave me a funny look. Of course, she must know he was doing something special out there all this time. But she didn't ask. "Sure was good of the pastor to come out," she said casually.

"It sure was."

"Be nice to know if Miss Chuckles has another egg under her in the morning."

"Yes, I just believe she will." I smiled at her mention of the chicken's name. That one made a funny sort of clucking noise, different from the others.

"You know, we oughta have Posts to dinner. Maybe even Hammonds, but, Lordy, what a lot of food we'd need for that bunch!"

"Yes. Kind of makes me wonder how in the world they manage."

"They get by. George don't know no better than to do things the way he does 'em. It was Willard told me we oughta give 'em a chance with that old place, since he done some growin' up down there. But I wasn't sure if George had half the sense God give a goose, you know. I wanted to sell it to Arty Cumberland and see if they could find any coal."

"Really?"

"Yes. Shamed to admit it, but I was in'erested in bein' rich back then, child. Willard havin' land was fine, but I figured it'd be that much finer if we could dandy up and go throw 'way five dollars or more ever' night, just havin' fun. 'Course, we never done that. Never could. But I thought I'd like it."

"My father used to think like that," I told her with a nod. "I'm sure he actually did it a time or two, though. Grandma thought he was the silliest thing, buying me such expensive clothes when I already had things to wear."

Emma laughed, and her eyes were like dark wells in the room's flickering shadows. "Oh, I'll bet he dolled you up, now didn't he, bein' his only child?"

"Sometimes," I admitted. "But I liked Grandma's home-made dresses far better. He hated that. Said I looked like an urchin he'd seen once in the mountains."

"But you was comfortable, wasn't you?"

"Much more so than in anything fancy. I still feel that way."

"So's all a' life, Juli. The plainer you live, the more comfortable you're gonna be. Pays to not gather up too much, you know, lest it get ya feelin' all stiff and pinched on. I ain't never met rich folks that could relax same as me. I never met nobody happy, neither, that didn't give 'way more than they oughta. An' let folks take 'vantage of 'em now and again too. You leave it all in God's hands and you come out far better. I learned that a long time ago."

"It's hard to imagine you ever having trouble with that idea, Emma."

"Oh, we all change. You gotta let things be sometimes."

I stood for a moment, just watching the candle dance in a breeze I couldn't feel. Moonlight from the window shone on the worn, woven rug at the foot of Emma's bed, and I thought how truly right she was. I couldn't imagine her happier in a mansion full of carpet and chandeliers of gold. But it seemed an odd time for her to be talking to me like this. Maybe she had her reasons; maybe there was something I was supposed to hear.

"Emma, I don't have trouble with the simple things."

"Oh, I know, child. You love a mess a' string beans and a good ol' rooster just the same as me. But next time you see the Hammonds, you'll be thinkin' again 'bout them cows and the money you reckon they owe me. I know you already. I can tell. But I want it let alone. That's what I'm gonna give George Hammond, honey. All a' what he's got. I aim to tell Albert the same thing once he gets here."

"People will say he doesn't deserve it, Emma. He could've at least come and talked to you. To explain the way things were."

"He won't admit it, maybe, but he's ashamed. I know him too. And I ain't wantin' his young'uns growin' up nowhere else. They b'long right where they is, deservin' pappy or not."

I shook my head. "I doubt I'll ever see it quite like you do. But I can accept that. It's not up to me, anyway."

"That's right. An' it ain't up to Albert. He might be thinkin' he'll have to fix things for me. He's a good'un, he is. He'd sell his right shoe fer me. But he ain't gotta do nothin'."

"What did you tell him about the Hammonds last time he was here?"

"That it weren't his business. If he gets here this time, though, I'll have to speak m' mind on it. I ain't seen him since I moved over to Rita's. I offered him to stay out here then, but he wouldn't. Kinda takes to city life. I ain't sure why."

"Some people like being so close to everything."

"It'd make me crazy, thinkin' that if I dropped a spoon, they'd 'bout feel the rattle next door."

I laughed. "It's not so bad."

"Sure 'nough. That's why you love it here so well." She looked up at me and nodded her head good and slow. "You got dirt and weeds and berry patch in your blood, Juli Wortham. You wasn't meant for no city! Now blow out the candle and get to bed. Tomorrow won't be waitin' on nothin'."

Too tired to argue, I waited till she was lying down again with her pretty old patch quilt up to her elbows. Then I leaned over and blew out the candle. There was still enough light from the window that I could see the smoke curling like a wisp of cloud toward heaven.

"Good night, Emma."

"Good night. Can you make a good milk gravy?"

I stopped by the doorway. "I think I can try."

"Well, that's what I want tomorrow, even if I ain't got sausage. We still got some canned pork?"

"Yes, ma'am."

"That'll do. Pipin' hot on some biscuits, it'll be fine as anything. 'Cept strawberries, a' course. Ain't no beatin' them."

There was no need for a reply. I went to the bucket of water in the kitchen for a drink and thought I heard her slow breath of sleep before I got past her room again to go upstairs. Bone weary, I made my way in the dark to our hard box-spring bed and I laid myself down. I doubt even two minutes passed before I went to sleep.

Old Jack the rooster woke me up the next morning before I was ready to hear him. First thing I thought of was that tiny baby over at the neighbor's place, and nine more youngsters, all sizes, every one of them dirty and needing their next meal. But George always put food on the table. Wilametta had assured me of that. And I'd best get to thinking about my own business.

The sun was just coming up. I needed to milk Lula Bell and start on Emma's biscuits and gravy. Sam was up too, and went straight out to the barn to check the chair over completely before Emma began stirring.

Robert woke early and was nearly beside himself, being privy to such a surprise. But Emma slept later than usual, and he could hardly contain his impatience.

"Do I have to go to school today, Mom?" he asked, his eyes gleaming.

"I think you should. There's no real reason not to."

"I want to see Emma get a look at that chair! If she's not up, can I wait?"

"I think she'll be up. Take the bucket, Robby, and get me some fresh water."

Lula Bell was doing her best, but there wasn't milk enough to give both children the morning glassful I wanted them to have and still have plenty for the gravy. So I opened some of the canned milk that came from Rita McPiery's church to make up the difference.

Robert came back in with the dripping bucket and immediately downed half his milk. Pretty soon Sarah was up and asking for milk too, the way she did every morning now that we had a cow. I was feeling rich just thinking on what Sam had done for Emma. Being angry at him had been so foolish. We were blessed. And, like Robert, I could scarcely wait to pass it on.

The biscuits were almost done, and the gravy was waiting by the time Emma got up, but she wasn't even hungry. She made her way to the sitting room to read her Bible by the big window. Robert ran outside to get Sam.

"You don't have to wait breakfast for me," Emma said. "Takes awhile sometimes to get up an appetite. You go ahead."

Just then Sam walked into the house, positively beaming. "Emma, it's a beautiful day. I'd like to take you for a walk."

She looked up real slow, like she was wondering if he'd lost his mind. "I believe I'll just stay here, if you don't mind. I ain't no flower to be flittin' around with."

Of course, Sam wasn't deterred in the slightest. "I thought you might want to get out to your husband's grave, ma'am, since you haven't been in all this time."

She looked from him to me and then to Robert, and must have thought it an odd thing to be smiling over. "What in the world are you all so anxious about it for? You got somethin' hid in the sugar bowl, that's what it is! Out with it, one of ya!"

Sarah looked at me in surprise, but Robert looked at his father. "Don't tell her," he said. "You gotta show her."

"We made you something," Sam said with a voice so quiet and low that it seemed to be coming from far away. Before Emma could say another word, he laid her Bible aside, picked her up, and carried her toward the door.

"There ain't no fixin' that wagon," she proclaimed, trying to figure us out. "Willard told me so. You'd have to replace two a' them wheels an' one whole axle. And you ain't gone an' done that."

"No, ma'am, I haven't."

Robert and Sarah and I followed on Sam's heels as he took Emma to the porch. And they didn't have to go a step farther. She saw it the second we were out the door. Sam had pulled the wheelchair out of the barn and set it on the stone path in front of the garden. Nobody spoke.

Sarah was the first to move, suddenly jumping off the porch and running for the chair. Before anyone could stop her, she was up on it, leaned back in the seat.

"I like this, Daddy. Will it go really fast?"

"It's not for you, pumpkin," Sam said. "It's for Emma."

He set Emma down on the porch steps and went to wheel it closer. Sarah got down to help him push. Emma didn't say a word. I couldn't think of a thing to say either. Emma just looked at me, and then at the chair again. For a moment, I couldn't tell if she was happy or not. She had a look almost like hurt about her, and I thought perhaps it was a hard thing to be reminded of your limitations.

But when I saw the tears filling her eyes and just hanging there like a mist, I put my arm around her. Sam wheeled the chair right in front of her and turned it around so she could see the wheels in back.

"Julia, dear," she said finally. "Ain't you got biscuits cooked? I do s'pose we're gonna need full bellies 'fore we go on an outing."

The tears were now streaming down her face. Sam and I didn't quite know how to respond.

But Robert stepped down, very gently took Emma's hand, and patted it in the tenderest gesture I'd ever seen from him. "Do you like it, Emma? We care an awful lot for you, ma'am. I'm glad you like us like family. Dad worked real hard on this. I just knew he could do it, and he did."

Emma pulled him toward her so quickly that Robert was startled in the midst of her hug. "He did indeed," she said. "An' you're better'n family."

When Emma finally let Robert go, she looked up at Samuel, and my eyes blurred with tears before either of them spoke.

"You even look just a touch like Warren," she said, slow and solemn. "Kinda tall an' brown like him."

"I would have liked to meet him," Sam said. "I've heard he was a fine man."

Emma smiled. "He'd like this, he would. Just the sort of thing he'd do. He pulled a dog 'round here one time in a little wagon after it got its leg broke. Crazy thing went chasin' after an automobile. Wish I could show you that wagon, but I ain't got it no more. Gave it to Philip Cameron's boy."

Sam nodded. "He sounds like a wonderful person."

"He was." She laughed a little and then wiped her eyes with one sleeve. "You know, he kep' a chick in his room once for three days after a cat got after it! Buried it real decent too. You never seen the like. I was plain sure he was gonna be a preacher one day."

292

She looked down at her hands and then at Sarah and Robert. "Listen to me," she said, wiping at her tears again. "Don't I sound jus' like an ol' woman, talkin' about them times? We got the whole day ahead! Robert, son, I wouldn't be no more surprised to find you a preacher one day than to see the sun risin' tomorrow mornin'! You got such a good heart, and that's what it takes. We'll go out and see Willard, all right. But you'd best go to school, 'cause you're gonna need that ejication."

"Yes, ma'am." He looked at me with a measure of disappointment but didn't begin to argue.

"What about me?" Sarah asked immediately. "Can I go when you go for a ride?"

"Well. I s'pose I'll leave that up to your mama."

We all ate biscuits with gravy, except Sarah, who wanted butter and cinnamon on hers. But it was clear that Emma was not impressed with my gravy that morning.

"Don't you worry, Juli," she told me gently. "Most of what you've cooked's been right passable so far. I'll learn you the gravy one of these days."

I took a chunk of the pork, put it on a biscuit, and wrapped it in paper for Robert's lunch. He tied it with string himself. "What would you think," he asked me, "if I brought a chick in the house sometime like Emma's son did?"

Emma looked like she couldn't make up her mind whether to laugh or cry. "Willard done that once too, when we was kids!" she said. "Had his chick right in here by the stove. His mama like to throwed a fit! But he done it for me, 'cause I was so upset 'bout it fallin' in a fresh-dug posthole. I reckon I loved him clear back then, 'cause he fished it up for me with a stick and a string. We wasn't but 'bout seven years old."

"I think he'd like you rememberin' stuff like that," Robert told her.

"I reckon he would." She patted his arm, and he gave her another hug before leaving for school.

I let Sarah run outside to pick some flowers, and before she got back, Emma had asked me to let Sarah go along to the grave. "Are you comin', Juli?" she asked me then, and I didn't know how to answer. I'd talked to Emma a lot more than Sam had, but it seemed that there was something special going on between them today. Maybe it would do them good to share this adventure with no one but a five-year-old flower carrier.

Emma understood that better than I expected her to. She asked me to get her hat and canes. She'd walk to the chair, she said, and let Sam do the work from there.

"I never seen such a contraption. But if he's handy enough to make it, I can sit in it."

She looked so beautiful, sitting in the chair, wearing her big straw hat and a smile on her face. She gave Sammy's hand a kiss and told him she'd never heard of anyone doing such a thing for someone before.

It was hard pushing once they got off the stones, I could tell that, but I knew Sam would never let on. They moved up the little hill toward the timber and turned back and waved.

Emma looked so happy. But the worries surfaced in me again. She'd told me just yesterday that after she saw the grave she could die. And she'd already made a will and told me where it was.

No, I told myself. *She'll be just fine. She wants to see Albert.* It was easy to wish that he'd be long years in coming, if he ever came at all.

I saw them go into the trees and out of sight, with Sarah dancing around them like a fairy. How would she react, I wondered, to the grief that was bound to come over Emma when she reached the grave? Maybe it was too much for a five-year-old to see. Perhaps I should have gone. Or kept

Sarah with me. But Emma had accepted things just this way, as if they were no more than right.

I went back inside to clean up the kitchen, and then busied myself in the strawberry patch, pulling up henbit and picking some more ripe berries.

I was just about done when I heard a motorcar off in the distance. Before I could think anything about it, the big old rooster went tearing across the garden patch and out to the barn.

"What's got into you?" I called. I set the strawberries down by the well and went to take a look. There was nothing I could see by the chicken coop, no reason for him to run away like that when inside were all his ladies and all he could want.

"Crazy chicken," I called out. "I suppose you'll want me to help you back in again soon!"

Jack gave a squawk, and I realized that the car sound was much closer. I turned just in time to see a shiny coupe at the base of Emma's lane. Driving in.

A wave of anxiety dashed over me. *What if it's Albert? What if he's mad as a hatter over Miss Hazel's bitter words? What can I possibly say?*

I forgot all about the rooster and the strawberries and just watched the black car come up slowly and park beneath a leaning sweet gum tree. Only one man sat inside. All I could tell was that he was wearing a short derby and seemed to be studying me before he even got out of the car.

I could've kicked myself for not going with Sam and Emma. They were traipsing over the timber, by now surely at the side of the grave. I wiped my hands on my apron and wondered if my hair was an awful mess. There was nothing more I could do but pray I wouldn't say something stupid.

Finally the man stepped out of his car, still looking at me. Whoever he was, he was tall and dressed fancier than most of the people I'd seen around Dearing. He hesitated at first, looking around, and then quickly moved toward me.

"I'm looking for Emma Graham," he called out rather gruffly.

"She'll be back in a little while," I told him, trying to sound friendly. "Can I get you a cup of tea while you wait?"

He looked angered at my suggestion. "Where's she gone?"

"Out to her husband's grave, sir. She hasn't been in quite a while. They shouldn't be gone long."

He glanced toward the house and then back at me with a frown, this time looking me over from head to foot. "Mrs. Wortham, isn't it?"

His tone was harsh; there was no doubt that he was angry. Whoever he was, he looked big and fierce and mad enough to be dangerous.

"Yes, sir," I replied, the words almost stuck in my throat.

"Your husband took her clear out in the woods, then. In her condition."

He was so abrupt it set my knees to shaking. "Yes, but—"

"If you've hurt her in any way, I'll have the sheriff out here so fast it'll make your head spin! You'll be sorry you ever set foot on this farm!"

THIRTY-FOUR

Samuel

Emma sat a long time, gazing down at the flowers we'd placed among the weeds in front of Willard's grave.

Sarah looked up at me, waiting for one of us to say something, but we didn't.

When she was finally ready to move on, Emma leaned down and arranged the flowers just so, taking up a handful of them to lay on top of the stone.

"He was a fine husband," she said. "Never did carry on the way some do. Never drunk nothin' he couldn't feel free to share with the preacher."

"That was a real blessing," I told her, thinking of my father coming home so drunk that he'd fall on the floor before making it to bed. And after him came a stepfather who wasn't much better. Liquor bottles lined the dresser in their room, and I hated it, knowing even as a small child that it shouldn't have to be that way.

"I know you ain't Warren, Samuel," Emma said in a quiet voice. "I don't want nobody thinkin' I've lost track a' m' senses. But you're what the Lord's brung me, do you understand? I want you to be same as a son, you hear?"

I just nodded my head, thinking it was no time to argue with however she chose to think of me, or whatever she wanted to call me. I could serve her needs and be happy doing it. And she was probably right about the Lord sending us—he certainly hadn't led us anywhere else.

"We should be gettin' back," she suggested. "I'm gettin' mighty tired. You done a fine job on this chair. But the ground sure is rough."

"I'm sorry about that, Emma." I wished there was something I could do about that, but, of course, there wasn't. Pushing the chair was much harder than I'd anticipated, especially over grass and rocks and hills. But she'd hung on and didn't say a word of complaint.

"Thank you," she said, her voice even quieter. "I've really wanted t' come out here all along."

"I thought so."

We wheeled on over crevices and channels I hadn't noticed when I was out here with just Juli and the kids. We had to stop every few seconds just to get one of the wheels loose to roll again.

"It'll be easier in town," she assured me. "Won't that be somethin', ever'body gawkin' at me in this here thing! You couldn't get me up the stairs of the church, though, I don't s'pose."

"I'll carry you, like we did before. And then carry this in too. If you want it in."

"We'll have t' bring it 'least once," she determined. "So they can see what you made me. After that, it won't matter. Don't need no wheels to sit in church."

As we headed back toward the house, Sarah stopped to pick some of every wildflower she could find. It wasn't hard for her to keep up, though, as slow as we were going. She would slip a few yards behind, then come running back with a handful of blooms to deposit carefully in Emma's lap.

Each time Sarah brought more flowers, Emma thanked her and gathered them all in a little heap in the apron she'd brought along. Before long, she was singing a hymn I couldn't remember the name of. All the bumps and jostles of that chair moving over the uneven ground made the song a challenge, and several times Emma's voice fell off awhile as we bumped our way over something in particular. But she always started back up again, and she kept up the song the rest of the way home.

By the time we reached the cleared area along the fence line, I was sweating down to my toes. This business was harder work than anything I'd done in a long time, but I wouldn't stop, not for a minute. And if she'd said she wanted to go back to the grave, I would have turned right around.

THIRTY-FIVE

Julia

He finally told me his name was Albert Graham and that he was absolutely furious to find us here. I wished for Sam and Emma to get back, but at the same time was almost glad they weren't here. Mr. Graham wouldn't listen to a word I said. He told me I could make any excuse I wanted or try to paint things up as pretty as could be. Words didn't change things.

"A cheat's a cheat," he snapped. "You're here, using what's hers, while she wastes away." He turned toward the timber and looked as if he were thinking of running out there.

Not a bad idea, I thought. "How long since you've seen your uncle's grave? Do you know the way?"

"Of course I know the way!" he snapped and stomped away from me. But in the sudden silence, I heard them. And I knew he'd heard them too. He stopped in his tracks.

It wasn't half a minute till we saw them, coming through the weeds, with Emma singing, Sam pushing with all his might, and Sarah dancing around them with flowers in her hand.

I just stood there, knowing what an impact the sight of them must be making on Albert Graham. Strange that they didn't seem to pay us the slightest attention.

It was Sarah who noticed us first. Then the singing and the wheelchair stopped. For a split second nothing could be heard but the rustle of breeze and a lark across the field.

Emma broke the silence, as only Emma could, with her excited yell. "Albert Tucker Graham! Oh, praise the Lord! If it ain't the finest thing to see you! Come here, boy!"

He stood for a moment, seeming surprised at the welcoming joy in Emma's voice; maybe he'd expected us to turn her against him. Then he walked in her direction, taking a good look at Sarah as she ran past him on her way to me. Samuel still stood there, his hands on the old hammer handles he'd fastened to the back of the chair. I took Sarah in my arms and stepped closer, not sure what to expect.

"Albert, meet Samuel and Julia Wortham," Emma said, but Albert didn't reply. He leaned over to give his aunt a hug and then stood again, just looking at Sam.

"Where'd you get the chair?"

Sam took a step to the side, as if giving Albert room. "It was made for her."

I looked at Sam and shook my head. *Why doesn't he just say he made it himself? It might matter.*

Albert went around behind the chair, looking it over. "You all right, Aunt Emma?"

"I am. I been to see Willard. Can't believe how long it's been. Oh, Albert, you oughta go. He loved you so."

"There's not even anything to hold you in on this thing."

Emma turned and looked at him with just a touch of indignation. "Well, I wouldn't want to be tied to no chair, would I? That's what these here arm things is for, to hold on. I ain't feeble, Albert! No more'n I was the last time you was here."

"That's not what I heard."

"You can't believe ever'thin'. Oughta know that by now."

Albert glanced at each of us for a moment, then turned his attention back to his aunt. "Hold on then, Aunt Emma. I'm taking you to the house."

It was with a great deal of difficulty that he got the wheelchair moving through the tall grass. Pushing it across the wide farmyard was an obvious strain, but he wasn't about to accept Samuel's help.

"Aunt Emma, it must have been a pitiful trip with this thing through the woods."

"A few bumps is nothin', to get where you want to go!" Emma countered. "I've heard there's folks in the mountains that'll walk more'n a hunderd mile over rocks, just to hear a preacher. This ain't nothin' like that."

"I doubt those stories are true."

"Well, you ain't never been there to know."

Albert cracked his first hint of a smile. "You're well enough to argue, at least."

When he finally got Emma wheeled up to the porch, he stopped a minute to look over the chair again before he turned to Sam. "You did this yourself. Those are my grandfather's wagon wheels. Still got the G he always marked on the inside there."

Samuel didn't say anything, and no wonder. It was impossible to tell if Albert was expressing appreciation for the work done or disapproval for the use of those wheels.

"I came to talk to you, Aunt Emma," Albert said. "And I mean only you. I'm taking you in the house, and I want you to tell everybody to stay outside."

"Ain't no need bein' rude to m' friends," Emma scolded. "I reckon they heard you. C'mere, Sarey, honey." She reached her hands to my daughter, and I let Sarah down to go and hold Emma's hand.

"You ain't been proper introduced," Emma told her nephew. "This here's Sarah Jean. Sweetest thing that ever did run 'round out here. A shame none a' the Grahams ever had 'em no daughters."

She gestured toward me. "That's Julia. I seen you met her first. Hope you wasn't too terrible rude. There's a boy, Robert. He's off t' school. And that'un's Samuel. He built this, all right. Surprised me with it this mornin'. Should a' known that's what he was up to so late."

"It's not a very pretty contraption."

"Got the job done," she argued. "Think a' me tryin' to get back there any other way! You borrowed Lowell Jacoby's horse cart, Albert, an' nearly lost me in the crick! This is a sight better'n that."

"Will you let me take you inside?"

"I will. You want I get Juli to put us on some tea?"

Albert shook his head. "I don't want anything but time to talk things out. I've heard some bad things that need to be set straight."

"Well, I can do that. We'll have us the tea after."

Albert picked her up easily, but her apron fell open, showering the chair and the porch steps with wildflowers. Albert stopped and stared a minute, taken by surprise.

"Don't worry," little Sarah offered sweetly. "I'll pick 'em up for you. Me and Emma, we like flowers."

"I can see that." He looked a minute at the colorful mess and the little girl's bright smile. Then he turned back to the house.

"You all excuse us," Emma said. "We'll be a minute or two."

They went inside, and Albert shut the door.

"Is he gonna live here?" Sarah asked us.

"I think he's got a home in Chicago," I explained.

"Then maybe we'll all go there."

"No, honey."

Sarah started piling flowers on the top step, and I sat next to them and looked over at Albert's nice car.

"Emma's our family now, Mama," Sarah declared, her eyes serious. "And he's Emma's family too. Don't that mean he'll stay?"

THIRTY-SIX

Emma

Albert eased me inta my rocker real careful, like I was somebody's baby doll. 'Fore I could say anything, he dragged up a kitchen chair and sat in front of me, all serious.

"Aunt Emma, why do you want to be out here with these people?"

It made me smile, knowing how concerned he was, and him treatin' me like a child. What might that Hazel've told him, anyhow? "Truth is, I'd wanna be out here whether they was or not," I told him. "Couldn't get it done afore, though."

"But why *are* they here?"

"'Cause I told 'em to stay. They ain't got no home to go to, Albert. They ain't got much a' nothin'."

"But why is it your responsibility? You hardly know them."

"I know 'em plenty by now. And they's the most decent folks you could care to meet. You oughta visit a bit with that Samuel. You'd like him."

"Emma, he's living off of you! And not turning a tap to care for his own family!"

"Hogwash! You oughta see him work 'round here! He don't sit idle, that's for sure! You got no right to talk, none at all, when you ain't got the least notion how it is!"

"Did he even try to find a job?"

"He's got him one with Mr. Post, part time. Bothers him plenty that he ain't found nothin' better. But it ain't his fault."

Albert wasn't convinced, though. "I know a lot of people are out of work. That doesn't excuse him trying to take what's yours."

I scrunched back in my seat. Albert and me always did disagree a lot, seemed like, but we always come 'round to agreein' in the end. "Albert Graham, what d'ya think? That he's talked me inta givin' him this place?"

"Has he?"

I just rocked forward and laughed. "I tried! I tried givin' it to him, Albert, an' he wouldn't let me! Ain't it the most a' somethin', you comin' accusin' him of stealin', when he won't so much as take a gift! You been list'nin' to the wrong breeze blowin'!"

He shook his head. "Miss Hazel told me—"

"There's your problem. Right there. You know her, how she'd skin the cat for comin' in sideways! She don't like nobody. She don't know nothin'."

"She cares about you, Aunt Emma," Albert was careful to say. "I know she's coarse and all that, but she's just concerned. She says the Worthams are just fooling you, to get the land."

I could almost laugh again at such a notion. "Well, then, they're foolin' theirselves too, to turn it down when it's offered! They didn't have to help me none, neither. Coulda left me at Rita's. I tol' 'em they could stay anyhow."

He was quiet. Had to take a minute to consider that. "You really tried to give them the farm?"

"Yep."

"Why?"

"'Cause they'd value it. They's good people. And they need it. But Samuel didn't think it was right."

Albert crossed his arms. "Why not?"

"I reckon he don't figger he's earned it, and that there might be some kin a' mine in'erested. Like maybe you."

I don't think he was expectin' that. Him and me'd talked about this farm before, but he wouldn't of thought Samuel to care. Took him awhile to answer. And then he reached over and took my hand.

"Aunt Emma, I know you love this place. But you haven't known them very long. I guess I can understand if you wanted to tenant it out to them. But wouldn't you be better off over there with Rita?"

"It was fine enough, all right," I admitted. "But it ain't like bein' home."

"Then do you want to come to Chicago?"

"What for?" I asked him, all puzzled.

"To stay with me and Stell, of course. We've got room."

Couldn't help smiling at that. Albert was always a good boy. "It's real nice of ya," I said. "But that wouldn't be like home, neither. An' I heared you was comin' to run *them* off, not me."

He took a deep breath and reached for my other hand. "My main concern here is you, Aunt Em. Eventually this place'll have to sell, anyway—"

"I ain't sellin' it! I'm leavin' it to somebody!"

"Fine. But you need to look out for yourself in the meantime."

I guess it rankled me that he didn't think I was. "I'm right where I wanna be, Albert. And these folks is good as fam'ly. You'll see, if you give 'em a chance. The good Lord knowed what I needed, and he sent 'em. I true believe it. And I wanna die right here one of these days, just like Willard did. I don't wanna be no place else, and that's possible now, 'cause of the Worthams. They don't much like me talkin' thisaway. But we got facts to face, Albert. You up to that?"

He wasn't happy, that was plain. I was worryin' him good. But he nodded his head. "I think I'm up to it. If that's what you need."

It was. I had to say this to somebody, an' it sure couldn't be Samuel. "I'll tell you straight out, Albert. I ain't gonna see another summer after this'un. I knows it in my heart, you understand? This here's m' last chance to be out here, and that's what I want. I'm gonna be leavin' this place to somebody 'fore long. You want it to be you?"

He frowned but squeezed both of my hands. "If that's what *you* want."

"Would you come here if it was so? Would you care 'bout it?"

"I'd come. I'd see about things." He sighed. "But I'd have to sell it, Aunt Emma. I can't live down here, not with all I've got up north. I hope you understand. I wish I could tell you something else, but that's the truth."

"I know it. You always been that way. But I'd leave it to ya anyhow if you tell me it's right. You're the closest family I got."

He was lookin' pained by all this. "I can't decide that for you."

"Well, if not you, Albert, I'll be leavin' it t' Sam Wortham. That's m' mind on it, but I don't want you sore at me."

"I don't understand it. I don't know why you want them around."

"I tol' you. They's good people. An' it's the only way I had a' comin' home. I'm happy with things the way they is. Real blessed."

"I guess I can see that."

"I don't want 'em put out. You wouldn't try, would you, Albert?"

He was quiet a minute. "You sure you know what you're doing, Aunt Em?"

"I'm havin' the time a' my life! It's sweet, seein' all the activity 'round here again. You oughta stay awhile, Albert, an' see what I mean."

He looked down at the floor. "What about the Hammonds? You still plan to give that bonehead his plot of ground too?"

That weren't right, and I let him know it. "He ain't as bad as that! An' it oughta be his! Willard didn't have to be s' hard all them years ago, makin' George's pappy sign it over! When he was still laid up in the bed with his back broke too! Coulda give him time to gain strength an' see if he could turn things aroun'. He mighta paid us what he owed!"

"The way I heard it, George's father was never good at paying anything, any better than George is."

"I'm tellin' you, Albert, Grahams ain't always been a merciful lot! Your grandpappy came by *this* place less than kind too. Buyin' it for next to nothin' from folks that was too busy grievin' to know better! I can't be the same way!"

"You're not. You never were."

"Oh yes, I was. Me an' Willard was both selfish as the dickens when we was younger, but you learn a thing or two over time, thank God! I'm glad as can be that Willard decided to give George a chance. He was thrown off once as a child, an' I ain't gonna be the one to do it again!"

Albert sighed. "So you let him keep his place without money, Aunt Emma? For mercy's sake? You just give it back, when neither he nor his father could make good? That's not our fault! You've got nothing to be ashamed of! You don't have to do it. And you don't have to give your home to strangers, either."

"It ain't have to. I *want* to. But you got a right to contest it, Albert. Just tell me now. I'm givin' ya the chance."

He got out of his chair and walked to the window. He turned and looked at me, then turned right back to the window again. It was a long time 'fore he said anything. And when he did, he said it real slow.

"Aunt Emma, you know me. You know I've got enough. I could tell you it was my grandfather and Uncle Willard, and I've got a right to step in. But you'd go to your grave thinking me the stingiest beast you ever laid eyes on."

"Now, Albert—"

"Let me finish! Nothing's changed with you. I can see you're not going to be swindled, unless it's by choice! And I should have understood when Miss Hazel called me that it was just you up to your own ways again. I ought to be able to talk sense into you, but the truth is, you won't ever change. You got it about you that you're supposed to be some kind of saint! Maybe we can give away our shirts and be blessed for it. Maybe you're right. I don't know. But I can't argue with you. It's your land."

"They need it, Albert. Hammonds and Worthams. They got nothin'."

"You think they'd have anything more? Really? Would it change them? Or would they lose it in a few months or years, anyhow?"

"They'd 'least have a chance. I like to give 'em that, if you don't mind."

He didn't say nothin'.

"They been good to me, Albert."

"Maybe so, Emma. I'm willing to see things your way. But if I ever find out different, I'll pin them to a wall someplace."

"Don't be angry at 'em, now. Wasn't none a' them asked me to do this."

"Emma, it doesn't hurt to look out for yourself sometimes."

310

"It surely can. I knows what I was like, Albert, and it ain't a happy feelin'. But it was Lizbeth changed me. She was real sick her first winter, an' I come to care that she make it through. Changed the whole way I look at that family ever since."

"I certainly hope they're grateful."

"All them babies is mine."

"So are a lot more in these parts, looking at it that way. Including me."

"An' I'd do all I can for any one of ya, if you was needin' as much. But you ain't, Albert. You ain't. But they is. We gotta care for 'em. God give us that."

"There's no talking you out of anything."

I wasn't sure if he was angry with me or not. "Lord love ya, Albert. I sure hope you can stay awhile."

"I can't. Not long." He was quiet, lookin' out the window again with his shoulders kinda sagged.

"You oughta go an' see Willard while you're here."

He turned and looked at me. "What do you think he'd say about all this?"

"I don't pertend to know. But he was a good man most a' the time, 'specially when he was older. An' when he weren't good, he was sorry on it later. You'll un'erstand me better, Albert, in your time. You got the same kinda good in you."

THIRTY-SEVEN

Samuel

Emma and Albert were quite awhile in the house alone. I went and chopped wood while Juli and Sarah took to pulling weeds.

It was hard for me to think of anything except this nephew who'd come charging down clear from Chicago to help his aunt. Whether she needed it or not, he'd thought she did, and he cared about her or he wouldn't have come. He was the one that had rights here. Including the right to make decisions about Emma, should it come to that. When you got down to brass tacks, I was the one who didn't belong.

Emma would speak her mind, I knew that. And he would probably listen. He might even let her have her way, but that didn't mean he had to like it.

I whacked at a chunk of hickory with all the strength I had in my tired arms and tried to put myself in the place of Albert Graham. What would I feel like if it were me called to see about a relative who couldn't manage too well on her own?

That was a hard thought, and I had to consider my mother. What if it were her, sick and needing someone with her? I'd go. I'd have to. But right now, she didn't even know where I was, unless Dewey had told her. I couldn't imagine her welcoming me the way Emma had welcomed Albert.

But I knew I should write. I should let the relatives back east know how we were doing and how to get in touch with us. They were kin, after all. I could admire Albert Graham for his sense of that.

When Albert finally came outside, the first thing he did was ask Julia to fix Emma's tea. Then he went walking into the timber without another word to any of us.

He was gone for at least three hours, longer than we had been, even with the unwieldy chair to maneuver. Juli had made lunch, fed us, and kept back some warm food for him. Eventually he came back with his jacket off, his sleeves rolled up, and his nice shoes as dusty as an old book. He sat with Emma again, ate his lunch, and then found me in the side yard, cutting wood.

"Aunt Emma's got her mind made up," he said with a shake of his head. "She wants to be all the way out here, miles from a doctor."

"That concerns me too," I admitted. "Doesn't seem to bother her, though."

"She's ready to die. She even says so right out. Maybe I would be too, at eighty-four, but I wanted her seen to by someone I knew. I like Rita McPiery. She'd do anything for you. Anything at all."

I didn't know why he was talking to me. I couldn't even tell just how he was feeling about things, or why he'd come out here. "I believe that," was all I could say. Rita McPiery was a decent lady, there was no doubt of that, and Emma had been in good hands with her.

"She won't come to Chicago with me," he said. "Too far. She's just as planted out here as if she were a tree with roots. I guess it'd be like chopping her down, expecting her to live anywhere else."

He took the axe out of my hands and gave the nearest log a vicious whack. I stepped back a couple of paces.

"I guess you know what she thinks of you," he said. "I guess you know she wants to give you this whole place. You and George Hammond, the ignorant freeloader."

"I told her no."

"That's what she said. But you're still here."

I sighed. "Truth is, I don't know where else to go. We didn't plan this. And now if we move on, I'm not sure what'd come of her."

Albert let the axe head drop to the ground and leaned onto the handle. "She doesn't want you going anywhere. She wants you to see about things for her till she joins Willard on the hill over there." He looked off into the clouds. "I don't like thinking about it. I guess if I could, I'd keep things the way they've always been, with Aunt Em and this place to come to. I don't want her gone, you know? I know I don't get down here much, but I'll miss her. I'll miss the whole thing."

There was nothing for me to say, and I wondered why he was talking like she might be gone tomorrow.

"She wants you to have the farm, free and clear," he said. "She wrote it all down, and she wants *me* to help her make it a legal will."

He seemed almost resigned to the fact. But it didn't sit well with me. "Please believe I don't want her doing that," I told him. "I don't want to take anything that ought to be yours."

He shook his head and looked me straight in the eyes. "It's not up to you. It's all hers. And what Aunt Emma wants to will to whom, that's for her to decide. There's nobody has any right arguing with that. Not even me."

"I'm sorry," I told him. "I wasn't trying to influence her at all."

"Well, you're not insistent, I can tell that. You could've had the deed already. You think my aunt's pretty much a fool, thinking like this?"

"No. I think she's glad to be home. But I'd like you to tell me what I should do. It's not my intention to cause friction between you."

He glanced over at the house. "I guess you haven't. She asked me, you know, if I wanted the farm. But I've got my own life. I couldn't move down here now, even if it was mine. I'd have to sell it, that's what I told her. And if that's not what she wants, then she'll have to do whatever she will."

I swallowed hard at that news. "I'm not sure I want it. I'm not sure I can make this work."

"That's something you'll have to work out, I guess," he said. "I should've known better when Miss Hazel told me Aunt Emma was slipping from reality. She's sounder of mind than I am."

I could agree with that. "I owe her. I guess I always will."

Albert Graham nodded. "At least you've got the decency to be grateful. That was the best surprise coming down here. They told me you were cold as winter hills. I brought my father's shotgun, in case I had to scare you out of here."

Albert ended up staying overnight and part of Saturday. We went to Barrett Post's to see the heifer he'd promised us. Albert and Barrett laughed and joked like they'd known each other for years, which was more than likely the case.

Emma wanted Albert to stay and go to church with us on Sunday, but he had to get back. So Juli got busy and made him a batch of cookies for the trip. He promised to send Robert a fishing pole he had around but didn't have time to use. It sure was a relief to be parting on such friendly terms.

There seemed to be something different about Robert the next morning. He was up with the sunrise, slipping out of the house. I found him in the hayloft with the kittens and the Bible storybook he'd gotten from the library, reading out loud. That day, he went forward in his Sunday school class, even though no one else did and the other boys snickered just like he'd feared. He told me about it later and said he'd never been so glad to do anything.

Something was different about me too. I found that I was happy, even though I still didn't know what to do about the barn or about anything else around here. Maybe it was because my wife and children were happy. Maybe it was because I found I could belong a little bit, just like they did.

Nobody argued to our faces at church this time or came bustling up to set Emma straight. Not even Miss Hazel, who snubbed her nose and turned her attention to Selma Turrey's scandalous daughter who was caught wearing knickers the night before.

The next evening I sat down and wrote my mother a letter. It was the right thing to do. And it didn't even matter if she didn't write back. I had to tell her I loved her. I had to say that God can see much farther than any of us can, that he has a way of working out even the hopeless things if we just give him a chance. He planted us here because it was time. And here we'll stay, until he designs it otherwise. That's life. More of a marvel than I ever knew it could be. And not near so much in my own hands.

THIRTY-EIGHT

Julia

Chuckles the hen was sitting on four eggs now. And George Hammond came over, bringing two more hens to pay Emma for her help with the baby. I could almost taste the chicken we'd have come winter. He said he'd thought on bringing us another cow, but wasn't sure we'd be ready for that yet, since Posts were already giving us one.

Sam didn't get as much work with Barrett Post as he wanted in the next few weeks, and I knew it bothered him not to have the cash. But he did get Willard's tractor running for George, in exchange for the pledge of a decent share of the crop for Emma. A promise I prayed Mr. Hammond would keep. At least he sent over a chunk of salt pork and a casing of sausage, just because Emma loved them so well.

I found myself doing a lot of singing, picking strawberries, and managing to do a bit better with the milk gravy.

Corn and lettuce and all the rest came poking their little heads up, but days went by without any clouds, and I started praying for rain.

It was hard to wait for the blackberries and the hickory nuts and all the other things that come in their own good time. I kept on picking weed greens, even canned a few, hoping we'd have plenty of other things to can by the time the cold weather came. I felt a little scared, just thinking of the things we'd need by then. Coats and everything. Lord have mercy.

Emma gave her quilt to the Hammonds and started piecing a coat for Sarah out of scraps she had around. "I had me a crazy coat one time," she said. "Sure did love them colors." Seemed a little strange to be thinking of coats when summer was just starting. Sensible though. The way we ought to be.

Even though there was so much work to be done before winter, we still took the time to set Emma's precious little violas in a spot of their own beside the shed, and to move a batch of black-eyed Susan and trillium up to the yard.

Sarah named our new puppy Whiskers just as soon as we'd gotten him home. He kept us up half the first night, but finally settled down to sleep right outside the back door. Now I have to step out real easy to keep from colliding with the bouncy little thing. He chews sticks and barks at all the critters he should bark at, and the place seems complete, now that's he's here.

If Grandma Pearl could take a look around, she'd say, "Julia, you've got yourself a home. Don't worry about what you haven't got. Do your best, and God will make up the difference."

Leisha Kelly is a native of Illinois and grew up around gardens and hardworking families. She and her husband, K.J., have two children, eighteen peaceful acres, and several pets. This novel is her first book.